The marine broke emergency band. "G dummy!" But they alre The captain saw four men bending over the apparatus within the cave a microsecond before a crisscrossing grid of lasers chopped him down. He had time to notice that the four were grinning.

"I reckon it's time," one of the men said. Like the other three, he had lost his family to Earthie raids. They keyed the four switches. Had the captain had more leisure, and had he been expert in weapons history, he would have recognized the apparatus as a nuclear bomb-powered laser battery, Excalibur class, of late 20th century design. Long obsolete, crude but relatively cheap and simple to produce, it was just the thing for low-tech, guerilla warfare. It required no complex and expensive condensed energy tank. Each laser required the explosion of a nuclear bomb for its energy, and of course the entire apparatus was destroyed by the explosion, along with any operators. It could have been done by remote, but the four had volunteered for the suicide mission just to make extra sure.

The four beams lanced into the fleet, one for each cruiser, two for the battleship.

ERIC KOTANI AND
JOHN MADDOX ROBERTS

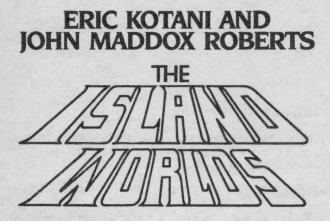

THE *ISLAND WORLDS*

BAEN BOOKS

THE ISLAND WORLDS

A Baen Books Original

Baen Publishing Enterprises
260 Fifth Avenue
New York, N.Y. 10001

First printing, June 1987

ISBN: 0-671-65648-1

Cover art by Alan Gutierrez

Printed in the United States of America

Distributed by
SIMON & SCHUSTER
1230 Avenue of the Americas
New York, N.Y. 10020

For Ulla and Beth

ONE

Just outside Denver there was a pinging under the
hood. Thor keyed the engine statistics and stuck his
finger into the computer contact. The car swerved as
the numbers flashed before his eyes and he bit off a
curse as he dragged it back on course manually. He
wished for an old-fashioned digital display. He had
bought the car when he was sixteen and gadget-happy.
In recent years he had tried to have a visual display
installed, only to be met with expressions of horrified
incredulity. "Alter a Porsche 2045 classic? You can't be
serious!" Now he no longer bothered, because he wasn't
going to be driving it or any other car for much longer.

He saw the plume of smoke even before the sprawl of
Greater Denver hove into view. It appeared to be
coming from the Ukrainian section, a rundown area
once inhabited principally by wealthy Arabs. Over the
years the Arabs had moved elsewhere and developers
had divided the estates into cheap housing projects.
The last wave of immigrants had been the result of the
People's Republic of the Ukraine breaking away from
the Soviet Union seven years before. Within four years,
the Ukraine had been bloodily forced to rejoin, but not
before more than seven million people had emigrated,
mostly to the United States. Now the suburb of Little

1

Burma was expanding into the Ukrainian sector and there were frequent riots.

He would avoid the inner-city area in any case. His destination was the mansion-studded mountainside community known locally as "Spaceville" because the fortunes of most of the mansion owners had been founded on the exploitation of extraterrestrial resources. The name had always struck him as funny, because he had grown up there and had hardly ever met anyone who had even been in space. It was like the old "Governor and Company of Adventurers of England Trading Into Hudson's Bay," most of whom had never governed, adventured or even traveled to Hudson's Bay, but instead had sat for generations in their London clubs while other, better men had reaped the wealth of Canada for them. The paper in his pocket was to be a break with that unworthy tradition.

As he climbed the road which hung magically off the mountainside, he looked down on the whole Denver complex. The smoke was coming from the Ukraine-Burma interface, all right. Once Denver had been proudly called "the mile-high city," but these days hardly anybody remembered what a mile was and somehow "the one-point-six-one-kilometer-high city" didn't have quite the same ring to it. For a long time it had boasted practically the only breathable urban air to be found on the North American continent, but the deindustrialization of the U.S. and the gradual disappearance of the internal combustion engine had restored clean air, although not without price.

The Porsche's engine cut out automatically as it neared a picturesque, chalet-type building situated next to the road. It was part of the ring of heavily-armored forts surrounding Spaceville. A man came out, dressed in Old West clothes and wearing a laser pistol molded to look like a Western six-shooter. His clothing was bulletproof and an ornament on the front of his Stetson hat holographed everything in his line of vision. "Howdy, Mr. Taggart."

"Good evening, Stuard." He punched the inspection control and hood, trunk lid and doors opened simultaneously. Stuard inspected each compartment while sensors embedded in the road scanned the undercarriage.

"You headed for the big party at the McNaughton estate?" the guard asked.

"That's right. I take it they've laid on heavy security for tonight?"

Stuard shook his head. "Heavy as I've ever seen. Senator Jameson came through about two hours ago. Since he may be running for President, he's got special protection paid for by his big money backers and you know what *that* means. Them Pinkerton guys always treat us like hick backwoods cops. There's a bunch of U.N. people here, too, and they all got their own security, and I have to reassure them all that we keep this place safer'n the Federal Reserve Bank. Twenty years without a snatch or bombing, though there's been plenty that tried."

"Nobody's ever had cause to complain, Stuard." The procedures were tedious, but Thor knew the value of good security. Spaceville's system had been set up by his paternal grandfather, Sam Taggart, who had been an intelligence agent of no mean repute back in his Earthbound days. "Were the U.N. people headed for the McNaughton party?"

"Yup. Okay, Mr. Taggart, you're clean. Be careful and don't drive that bomb off the road. We're no longer equipped for traffic accidents."

Thor buttoned up the car and sped off. The Porsche burned its precious gasoline so cleanly that it left not even a whiff of exhaust. It had better be efficient, he thought. His annual I-C engine tax was more than the price of a conventional, electric car. He wondered what the U.N. people were doing at the McNaughton party. Old Murdo McNaughton was not known as a supporter of that organization. It probably had something to do with Jameson's presence. He was heartily sick of the increasingly Byzantine political climate. He vowed not to let it bother him tonight. He would be shut of it all soon. Tonight he was going to have one last try at bringing Karen around.

Karen McNaughton's ski lodge was set amid tall aspens in a high valley with a breathtaking view of the lights of Denver. Like most large American cities, Denver was far more beautiful from a distance than from close range. The moon was setting in the west, a fingernail sliver. He killed the engine and then caught his breath when he saw the bright light shining from the dark eastern sector. Only heavy saturation illumination over hundreds of square kilometers could be so visible from Earth.

"Going to let me in on it?" Thor whirled to see Karen standing beside the Porsche. He was confused and embarrassed, as always when someone caught him unawares, daydreaming.

"Look at the moon!" he said. "The Mare Nubium settlement project must be under way. Have you ever seen such a sight?" He returned his gaze to the surrealistic view.

"I never paid much attention. I've spent the day looking in the other direction, down. Have you noticed that Denver is on fire?"

He swatted the dashboard impatiently. "What city in the world isn't burning most of the time? Earth is no longer where it's happening. Where it's happening is out there." He jabbed a finger in the general direction of Mare Nubium. "Climb in, we're late for the party already."

She looked at the new light doubtfully. "The moon? Who'd want to go there? You're not still serious about emigrating to the moon, are you?"

"Nope," he said. "Not the moon and not Mars, either. The asteroids!"

She sighed wearily. "I'd hoped you'd have outgrown that foolishness by now. Are you going to drive this thing manually again?"

"Of course. I like to drive my own car and pilot my own plane and sail my own yacht. I don't like to be the passive prisoner of a piece of machinery that I own."

"It's not safe. Do you know how many people used to *die* because they tried to control these machines?"

"I know," he said. He could not remember exactly when this change had come over Karen. Always before she had been enchanted by his predeliction for dangerous pursuits. Dangerous! Driving a car had been what people used to do just to get to work. Lately, she had grown impatient. She acted as if, by putting his life at a slight risk, he had been endangering some personal investment of hers. Had she really changed, or was it just that you never really saw someone you were raised with?

At some time, by a sort of tacit consent, it had been determined by both families that they would marry, to the greater good of both family portfolios. In childhood and in their young adult years, she had shared his enthusiasm for space. Somewhere, he was not really sure just where, they had grown apart.

"Asteroids?" she said. "You can't want to live there! You know what the Russians call the asteroids? 'Siberia without air.' "

"Not me," he said, "us. Karen, our future is out there. Do you want our children to live in a world where a thousand little ethnic and religious groups slaughter people who never heard of them just for the sake of media exposure?"

"You're still not over your parents' deaths, are you?"

"That was anarchists," he said, "not ethnics."

"And what do you mean by 'our children'? This is a pretty lame proposal, if it means what I think it does."

This wasn't turning out right. He'd had a wonderful, unanswerably persuasive speech all prepared for her, and somehow she had preempted him. Had he really neglected to propose to her? It had always been assumed and now he realized that he had never gone through the formalities. It also occurred to him that he might not want to.

He studied her, trying to look at her as if seeing her for the first time. She was petite, pretty and blonde. That much was common enough. Only a slight up-

ward tilt at the outer corners of her eyes bespoke the
tinge of Ameri-Indian blood passed down from her ma-
ternal grandmother, Frederike Schuster-Ciano, known
to one and all as Fred. If family legend were to be
believed, Old Lady Ciano had been a pistol-packing
agent as dangerous as her contemporary, Sam Taggart,
before becoming the mother of the incredibly numerous Schuster-Ciano family. He had loved Karen all his
life. Or had he? Had he just been infatuated with the
swashbuckling image of Fred Schuster-Ciano?

"Look, Thor, we'll discuss this later. There are important people at the party tonight that you'll have to
talk to."

He put the car into gear, backed around, and accelerated downhill. "You mean Jameson? Or the U.N.
people?"

"Good," she said with satisfaction. "You've been doing
your homework. These people will be very important to
you, I mean to us, of course, in the future. Especially
Senator Jameson. He's going to be President someday,
and probably Secretary-General before he's through.
He's a fraternity brother of Karl's, you remember?" Karl
was Karen's older brother. Thor detested Karl the way
the Popes had detested Martin Luther. If Jameson had
been a fraternity brother of Karl's, then it was a strike
against Jameson.

"Why are these people important to us?" he asked.

"Because you're a Taggart and I'm a McNaughton.
Between us, we're an important part of world economy."

Thor snorted derisively. "World economy! You mean
the world's economy depends on space exploitation."

"That's not how they see it," she said, coolly. "You'd
better start seeing it differently, too. Maybe the wild
men go out there to the frontier to mine in barren
rocks, but all the really important, powerful people live
here on Earth."

"They can stay here for all I care," Thor said. He
patted his breast pocket. "What I have here is official
permission to emigrate, and I'm taking advantage of it
as soon as I graduate."

To his utter astonishment, she turned furious. "Thor! You didn't! Why didn't you talk to me first? That was one of the reasons I was so anxious for you to come to this party, so you could talk to these people. I know they'd change your mind about emigrating. You're such a fool!" She turned away from him angrily. He could make nothing of it. He had worked for years to get permission to emigrate. Not that it was really so difficult; all you had to do was commit a crime, especially a political one. But, if you were rich and well-educated, there was a lot of red tape to go through before you could be permitted to leave. The Earth-to-space brain drain was much in the news lately.

She said nothing more until they pulled into the parkway-pad of the immense McNaughton estate. Then she caught sight of a shabby, ancient Harley-Davidson two-wheeler. "Oh, no! Uncle Bob is here."

"Hey, Bob's at the party?" It was the first cheering news he'd had this evening. Bob Ciano was one of his favorite people. More than sixty years old, he looked much younger in spite of his heroic efforts to drink himself to death. Bob was the youngest of Fred Schuster-Ciano's children. He rarely came out west, preferring to live in his father's ancestral domain of Brooklyn, where he ran a gang of septuagenarian motorcyclists like himself. In a world gone progressively more bizarre, he scarcely attracted attention.

Karen got out of the car and Thor turned the keys over to a Pinkerton man disguised as a parking attendant. She ignored him as they entered the front door and he surrendered his cape to the butler. "Don't announce Mr. Thor and me together," she told the robot. She turned to Thor. "It's not fitting yet, if ever." She said the last part through gritted teeth. "Let me go make some preparations." She swished off in a huff and he looked around for some inconspicuous place to hide temporarily.

Opening off the foyer was the family gallery, occupied only by a few peripheral types, lesser family members and the flunkies of the more important guests.

This was the only part of the McNaughton mansion that he liked anyway. The walls were lined with the portraits of family and historical associates and some of them were of his own ancestors.

First came a long line of sour-faced McNaughtons, clipper-ship entrepreneurs, opium smugglers and slavers who were far enough back in the family line to be respectable. His grandfather, Sam Taggart, was there, solemn in his Space Marine dress blues, replete with decorations and holding a calabash pipe. Next to Sam was his wife, Laine Tammsalu, even in old age a spectacularly beautiful woman. Fred Schuster was there, her German and Mexican-Indian heritage lightening the heavy north European tone of the ancestral gene pool. Ian McNaughton was there, co-founder of General Spacecraft, Spacecraft Underwriters, Space Technologies, Inc., and several other companies that had made U.S. space exploitation all but a McNaughton feudal fief.

Only one portrait was missing. It wasn't that the old bastard was larcenous, Thor thought, taking a glass of champagne from a robot waiter. It was the way the Western world had changed. After the freewheeling license of the latter Twentieth Century, the Twenty-First had lapsed into a veritable Victorian smugness and respectability. Great family fortunes, founded by piratical knaves, had to be made respectable. None had been more piratical than Ian McNaughton's partner, Ugo Ciano. Even in the popular press and in school textbooks, the McNaughton family fortune had managed to suppress any likeness of the fabulous Ugo.

"Well, the girl came by her looks legitimately," said a voice behind his shoulder. Thor turned to see Bob Ciano gesturing toward the portraits with a sloshing wineglass. In honor of the occasion Bob had worn a tuxedo to go with his buckled motorcycle boots. His gray hair and beard were uncombed.

"Bob!" Thor said, hugging the old man. "I haven't seen you in years. Where have you been hiding?"

"Don't disrupt my train of thought. Now that girl of yours has my mother's genes. No wonder she's pretty. But, is that enough?"

"What're you getting at, Bob?" Bob had a maddening habit of approaching any subject so obliquely that it could be months, if ever, before Thor could understand what he had been getting at.

"Thor, you're different from the rest of this Earth-bound family. You want to get off into space, like I never could." Robert Ciano had been born during one of his mother's infrequent trips to Earth. He suffered from a rare congenital heart condition, one which precluded his ever going into space. He had grown up waiting for the breakthrough which would allow him to enter space. The breakthrough had never come. He had studied to become a theoretical physicist, but he lacked the inspiration to be the kind of genius his father had been. He had taught for a while, then had retired from active teaching to ride his motorcycle and drink and generally be an embarrassment to his family. The only one he had taken any interest in had been Thor.

"Thor," Bob said with drunken intensity, "do it! Get the hell out of here and leave this degenerate bunch of hyenas behind." He linked an arm through Thor's and walked him along the row of portraits. Thor noticed that they were being watched by some of the flunkies.

"Now here's your grandpa, old Sam," Bob said. "I happen to know that he only wore those dress blues three times in his life. Two of those times was to get decorated by the President. The other time was for this portrait. And he never smoked a pipe. Over here's my dear old Mom. You know, if she'd just waited a couple of weeks I'd've been born in space and never left." The old man turned aside and honked into a handkerchief. The only thing about him that Thor didn't like was his tendency to turn drunkenly maudlin.

"But none of 'em would be more than a footnote In history if it hadn't been for my Dad. I never knew Dad, you know, except for TeleHolos."

"I know, Bob," Thor said.

"Yep, old Dad was a great man. Probably the greatest genius who ever lived. Used to tell me so himself, frequently. I'll tell you something else that not many people know: Old Ugo was a dwarf, or damned near. That's another reason these McNaughtons don't want to allow his portrait in here. They have the best looks money can buy and it'd hurt their image."

"I know, Bob," Thor said. He had heard all this before.

"I'm not referring to Karen, of course. Her looks didn't come from a surgeon. At least I don't think so. But back to your plans to emigrate. What's it to be? Mars, the Jovian moons?"

"The asteroids."

"Good choice! Have you picked a destination?"

"I've applied to several of the scientific stations and it looks as if I can have my pick. I finish my final year of graduate work at Yale next spring and I can leave any time after that. My permit to emigrate came through today." He patted his pocket once more.

"What was it you were studying? Space-habitation engineering?"

"That's right."

Bob stood with his hands behind his back, studying a model of the *Donald McKay*, flagship of the McNaughton fleet in the mid-'twenties. He rocked back and forth on his feet, seemingly about to topple. His voice, when it came, was quiet and utterly sober. "Thor, if I were you I wouldn't wait. In fact, I'd walk right out of this house, convert all my assets into liquid or transferable form and get on the first ship out, even if I had to travel in steerage with the laborers and dissidents."

"What the hell's going on, Bob?" He had never figured out Bob's web of personal contacts and information sources, but he knew that the man wouldn't speak this way idly.

"There's something in the air. I live, by choice, in one of the most depressed working-class neighborhoods east of Calcutta. The Earth First party is gaining strength.

In the past six months, street-level propaganda has gotten really fierce. They're blaming just about everything on the Offworld colonies, especially the independents in the asteroids and on the Jovian satellites."

"That's ridiculous!" Thor protested.

"Of course it's ridiculous!" Bob snapped, causing some heads to swivel. Then, more calmly: "So what? Truth and probability are of no importance in propaganda. What counts is loudness, volume and frequency of repetition. It's all over the place these days and people are getting stirred up. There's agitation to get all emigration offworld stopped."

"That kind of talk's been going on all my life," Thor said. "They've never amounted to anything and the world economy is too dependent on offworld resources to allow them any access to power."

Bob snorted through his beard. "I wish you'd taken some time from your science and engineering classes to study some history. Being the source and controller of an irreplaceable resource has been the death of more peoples than I can readily name. Also, no political opportunist was ever blind to the fact that there's no unifying force like an external enemy. If one isn't there already, they'll create one. If you're dumb enough to stick around for the next few months, keep an eye on the news. We'll be seeing big, organized demonstrations shortly. The Earth Firsters have gotten real backing lately. They're going to make the offworld colonists a credible and much-hated enemy of Earthbound mankind. An enemy that's free and rich is the best kind. There's nothing like envy to give a little spice to everyday hate."

Thor wondered if Bob had finally pickled his brain beyond repair. "I'll grant you the free part, but rich? Most of the people out there are doing pretty well just to stay alive. It's the toughest kind of frontier, espoially in the Belt. All the riches come down here." He waved around, indicating the spectacular mansion.

Bob shook his head and grabbed another glass of

wine from a passing robot. "You're not listening, Thor. We're talking here about propaganda. Reality is nothing. Only perception counts. Look, if the news is too depressing for you, watch the pop entertainment programs. Plug your head into a Holoset for a day or two and see how the programming differs from what it was ten years ago. You were plugging into holo ten years ago, weren't you?"

Thor nodded. "That was about when I got away from it, in my mid-teens. Once you start taking up serious study, it's hard to go back to something as stupid as the pop holos."

"When you're a professional bum like me, you get to be an avid observer of popular culture. Often as not, you'll spot new social trends months before the learned researchers start commenting on them over the public information programs. I spend a good part of every day scanning the holos and talking to the street people. I see something really ugly coming along soon."

"You're not a bum," Thor said, smiling.

"Yes I am. I've been a bum all my life, and proud of it. But I'm a rich bum, and that makes a difference. I've been in contact with old friends in the university labs, in the courts, the military, business, everywhere. What I'm getting from all of them is the same: funding cuts, cancelled contracts, standby alerts, all of it aimed at offworld development."

"Even so," Thor said, uneasily, "what's it got to do with me? I'm not out there yet, and when I am I'll be away from them."

"They may not let you go, Thor, unless you move fast."

"It can't be that bad!"

"Thor," Bob said with mock patience, "where did you learn to think like that? Yale? It can *always* be that bad, except when it's much worse. Earth First has come out of the lunatic fringe. Old-line Republicans, Democrats and Constitutionalists are switching allegiance in droves. And it's not just confined to the U.S. It bids fair to become the first really popular international party since the early days of communism."

"Wait a minute, Bob," Thor held out a restraining hand. "You're going too fast. Last I heard, Earth First was a little group of nutcase xenophobes and antitechs, loud but harmless. Now you're telling me they're the wave of the future?"

"Exactly. You've been in school all your life, Thor, you've turned inward too much. Get down in the streets and look around, only don't drive that car of yours or you'll be dead in no time. The world doesn't consist of colleges and mansions, and you're not engaging in real life by driving antique sports cars or sailing yachts. If you're going to stick around Earthside for a while, I'd advise you to get a look at what's going on with the rest of humanity."

Thor studied a portrait for a few moments to cover his confusion. It was unlike Bob to be so serious and urgent.

"Aha!" Bob said, sounding drunk again. "Here comes my esteemed kinsman and co-director, Murdo McNaughton himself."

Murdo was elegant in tux and red-heeled boots. He had the spuriously aristocratic look common to tall, whip-thin men with narrow facial features. "Good evening, Robert," he said frostily. "I must take young Thor away from you, I fear. We have things to discuss."

"You go right ahead, Murdo," Bob said, jovially. "I'll just avail myself of your excellent eats and liquid refreshments."

"As you always do. Robert, when are you going to grace our Directors' meetings once more? I really do need your vote on a number of important matters and it's so tedious to send men to scour all your haunts to get you to sign a proxy."

"Matter of fact, I figure to attend religiously from now on. I have a sneaky suspicion that you and the rest intend to sell McNaughton-Ciano Enterprises down the river very soon. You'll have a fight on your hands."

"Just be there," Murdo said.

"Thor, look me up before you leave here tonight. There's some things I want to put you onto." He turned and walked away toward a buffet, listing to one side.

"Every family has its resident eccentric," Murdo said. "Robert is our cross to bear. What were the two of you talking about?"

"Cars, motorcycles, planes, the usual." He was delighted that the glib lie came to him so easily. He had a feeling that he was going to need every bit of obfuscatory advantage he could summon at this party.

"Come along, Thor. Senator Jameson's in the main salon, and I know you'll want to meet him. Anthony Carstairs is with him, and so are a number of important U.N. people. You'll need these contacts in the future."

They walked past the portrait of Sam Taggart. God, I wish the old warrior was with me tonight, Thor thought. Carstairs, now who was that? The name sounded familiar, it had been in the news somewhere lately. Bob was right, Thor thought, he'd had his head in the clouds too much in recent years. He had fallen into the common elitist mindset of thinking that the concerns and interests of the proles were too trivial for his attention. People had walked up the steps to the guillotine thinking that way.

Murdo nodded to the glittering guests as they passed. "Karen is in a towering snit tonight. Is it this emigration business again?"

'I'm afraid so," Thor admitted. "I'm ready to go and she's balking."

Murdo grinned. "Ah, the simple enthusiasms of the young. Thor, space travel is a fine idea, everybody should try it once. But, if you stay out there too long you can't come back. The body just won't readjust. When you and Karen are married, I've arranged for a honeymoon on one of the lunar resorts. After that, we have several openings for people with your qualifications in the Belt, the outer satellites, the ell-fives, just take your pick. That way you can spend plenty of time in space, with frequent returns to Earth and have the best of both worlds. Emigration is one-way."

Thor disliked the man's patronizing tone and he disliked the easy, casual way he was mapping out Thor's future. Now that he thought of it, Murdo had always done that. In fact, it was the practice of the whole McNaughton-Taggart-Ciano family. Now was no time to be openly rebellious, though. He was about to take an irrevocable step in his life, and it suddenly looked as if it wasn't going to be as simple as he had thought. He had to know more. "I'll think about it."

"Good," Murdo said. "I think these people will help you see things in a clearer light." They entered the main salon, a throwback to the opulence of nineteenth-century robber barons. A facade of old-fashioned elegance was laid atop a complex of the latest technology, providing comfort, security and luxury. It was like the McNaughtons, Thor reflected, to pretend to ancestral eminence by aping the manners of earlier tycoons. They had even married some of the family members to the impecunious heirs of ancient European titles, as if anybody cared any more.

"Thor, have you met Senator Jameson?" Murdo asked.

"No, I haven't had that pleasure." Thor extended his hand. He knew of Jameson, of course. The young Constitutionalist senator from Colorado was in all the news reports, lately. He was a likely contender for the presidency of the U.S. within the next decade, once a few old Party warhorses had had their shot at the title.

"Mr. Taggart, it's a great pleasure to meet you." Just in shaking his hand and exchanging greetings, Thor could see why the man had risen so fast and why everyone raved about his great future in politics. He had the instant likability of the born politician. He inspired confidence just by standing there. He made the commonplace greeting sound like one of the all-time great pronouncements from Olympus. Whatever charisma really was, David Jameson had it.

He was precisely six feet tall and had mature but boyishly handsome features. His gaze was steady and his teeth were perfect. He was groomed within an inch of his life. No breath of scandal had ever touched him and he was happily married, a true rarity in the modern world. His speaking voice was deep and well-modulated. He never forgot a face or a name. Like Kennedy and Burdick, he would be the kind of president who seemed to have been born in the Oval Office.

"And this is Mr. Anthony Carstairs, National Chairman of the Earth First Party." Oho, Thor thought, I seem to be tripping all over that outfit tonight. Carstairs was a short, powerful fireplug of a man, neckless and bullet-headed. He had a handshake like a machine tool. He put Thor in mind of an old-time labor union leader. He would have made a very passable Prohibition gangster. This man was not the kind who could be a credible candidate for office, but he would keep the party in line and turn out the vote on election day.

"Pleased to meet you," Carstairs said. "I'll confess I wasn't expecting to feel very welcome here tonight, in the middle of the founding families of space enterprise, but Mr. McNaughton here has been most hospitable." Carstairs had a touch of Liverpool in his accent. "I was surprised to find that we really have a great deal in common."

"I'll be interested to hear about that," Thor said.

"And so you shall," Murdo said. He gestured with a wineglass in the direction of a group of exotically-dressed people who were chattering excitedly among themselves. "We're having a sort of mini-U.N. meeting here tonight. After the main festivities are over and most of the guests have gone on to other parties, some important business is to be discussed. I'd like for you to sit in on the meeting, Thor. This is going to be of utmost importance to the future of the family interests."

"I'd be glad to," Thor said. "I notice that there are no Soviets among the U.N. people."

"They wouldn't show had they been invited," Jameson said. "You see the tall fellow over there in the robe and turban? He's a representative of the People's Islamic Republic of Iran-Kazakhstan. The Soviets still claim Kazakhstan and won't recognize any of its representatives."

"The Soviets are headed for the trashbin of history, Thor," Murdo assured him. "All these people here tonight are Third Worlders, and they haven't voted with the Soviets for decades. They are, however, the most powerful single bloc in the U.N. and as such they must be courted."

"What's the nature of this meeting?" Thor asked.

"That will have to wait," Murdo said. "Our security is the best, but we can't very well go searching our guests for bugs, snoops and pickups. The meeting will be in the theater and our precautions will be very thorough."

"Excellent," Carstairs said. "Wouldn't do to let this leak to the media prematurely."

"This is beginning to sound like a conspiracy," Thor said.

Carstairs laughed unaffectedly. "Every political maneuver in history started with a conspiracy. Nothing gets done, otherwise."

"Now tell me," Murdo said, changing the subject, "while we're on the subject of media leaks, what's this I hear about Senator Jameson renouncing his Constitutionalist affiliation?"

"It's true," Jameson said. "I've finally and sadly come to a break with the Party. Over the years, Constitutionalist policy has become as antiquated and irrelevant as Republican and Democrat. They all had their day, but that day is over."

"Senator Jameson has come over to us," Carstairs said. "And I'm going to see to it that he gets our nomination to run for President in the next election."

"Good choice," Murdo said. "Let me be among the first to congratulate you on acquiring the Senator, Mr. Carstairs. He'll make the future of your party."

"The people will make the future of the Party, Mr. McNaughton," Carstairs said, seriously, "but they have to have a spokesman, and I'm certainly not qualified for that task."

"Quite so," McNaughton said. "And let me congratulate you, Senator. You'll have a chance at the office while you're still young and vigorous instead of having to wait for seniority to take its course."

"Far more important," Jameson said, "I'll be in the forefront of the movement that will determine the future of mankind on this planet. To serve that cause, even in a small way, is a privilege for which I'm grateful."

Was this really how things got done? Thor wondered. Carstairs obviously meant every word he said. Jameson sounded like he was talking for reporters. It struck him that several people were standing near enough to eavesdrop, and Jameson might expect every word he said tonight to appear on every screen in the country along with the rest of the morning news.

Thor spent the rest of the party in small talk with relatives and acquaintances. He did not see Karen. She was probably still angry with him, and he found that this didn't bother him nearly as much as it should. He looked around for Bob, but couldn't locate him. It had been a long time since Thor had attended a family bash. If the political element, especially the foreign one, was a new factor, there were also some notable omissions. There was not a single Kuroda present.

The two families had been close allies in the early days of commercial space exploration. In recent decades they had been fierce competitors, but they usually observed all the polite conventions on formal occasions. Few of the Kuroda clan had stayed on Earth. On a hunch, Thor made his way into the den. Several of the Islamic fundamentalists were there, getting away from the contamination of alcohol. As he had suspected, the portrait of Goro Kuroda was gone from its place above the mantel. The old samurai had been a close friend of Sam Taggart. Somehow, the whole family was shifting gears. He was glad that he had decided to leave. He didn't like the look of this.

When he returned to the main salon, the party was breaking up. Murdo signaled to him and Thor followed the group of political guests to the theater. It was a small auditorium with a sloping floor and rows of seats. At the bottom of the slope was a small stage surmounted by a multimedia screen.

Murdo mounted the little stage. "Please be seated, ladies and gentlemen. For those desiring them, each seat has a headset for simultaneous translation. This discussion shall be conducted in English, so just key the language of your choice. Are there any questions at this point?"

One of the Islamics stood up and made the usual *pro forma* protest against being seated with women. No attention was paid the protest, nor was any expected. The house lights dimmed and stage lights came on. "Please forgive the dramatic lighting," Murdo said, "but later we shall have some screen figures for you to examine. Our first speaker is Mr. Boniface, of Haiti. Please give him your closest attention."

Boniface was a plump, professional-looking black man with graying hair and artificial corneas. His clothes were several years out of date. He cleared his throat. "What we discuss here, my colleagues, will be common knowledge in the United Nations within a few days. The purpose of this meeting is to give the nonaligned nations of the world a chance to discuss and prepare themselves for a monumental piece of legislation which is about to be proposed." He had an oddly high-pitched voice.

"The international Earth First Party, of which I have been a member for many years, and of which the distinguished Senator Jameson has recently become a member, have drafted a proposal which they wish to have adopted as law by the United Nations as a whole and, severally and with alterations, by the individual nations as well. I think that you will agree with me that this legislation is not only fair and just, but long overdue.

"The proposal will now be explained to you by Mr. Anthony Carstairs, United States National Chairman of the Earth First Party. Each of you will be given a printout of the complete text of the proposal and the proceedings of this meeting. We ask that you do not communicate any of this to the media until it has been made public in the United Nations General Assembly."

Carstairs took the stand. He had taken off his coat and pushed his sleeves back to the elbows. His forearms, as heavy-muscled as an athlete's leg, were covered with coarse, black hair. The bristly hair of his head was cropped so short that his scalp shone through beneath the overhead lights. The crude vulgarity in these elegant surroundings did not seem to be a calculated pose. Thor had never before seen a man of such forceful presence. He revised the union leader-gangster image. Who was that Italian dictator of the last century? Bob was right, I'm deficient in history, he thought. Mussolini, that was it! But Mussolini had been a strutting buffoon. This man was the real thing. He made men like Murdo and even Jameson fade into the woodwork.

"All right," he began, "I'm no orator, so I'll just speak my mind. Not to mince words, this planet's been heading down the toilet for some time now." Thor felt a touch of amusement. This was what he'd been saying to Karen a few hours ago. "Now is neither the time nor place to thrash out the hundreds of problems that the peoples of the various nations are suffering from. We're here to address the root problem that has lain behind most of the others for more than a century: the drain of manpower and capital into the colonizing of space!"

There was a subdued murmur in the room and Thor looked around for signs of protest at this radical statement. There were none. "Most of you are aware of the policies and beliefs of Earth First. Briefly, when the infamous arms race of the last century wound down, it was replaced by the all-out space race. The prospect of immediate nuclear annihilation was eliminated, but the long-term effects of the space race were as bad and we're feeling those effects right now. The arms race drained wealth and resources from much-needed social programs and funneled it into useless military hardware. Stupid as it was, at least the treasure and the scientists stayed right here on Earth.

"At first, people all over the world sighed with relief. The danger is over, they said. This exploitation of space resources is going to make us all rich, they said. At first, it really did look safe. Sure, people died up there, but it was in small numbers, not like a real war. Even the Djakarta disaster, which was as destructive as a nuclear attack, didn't cause people to wake up to the dangers inherent in the irresponsible way that the commercial exploitation of space was carried out, and still is."

Thor winced. That was striking close to home. The Djakarta Incident had been the blackest mark on man's exploration of space. It had been in 2015. On a routine mission, a chunk of ore-rich asteroidal rock was being steered into Earth orbit when a maneuvering rocket attached to the rock had misfired. Instead of achieving a stable orbit, the rock had struck squarely in the Sunda Strait, inundating Djakarta and the southern tip of Sumatra. The death toll had been over a million and Borneo had tried to take advantage of the disaster by annexing Indonesia. A bloody war had followed, with millions more dead. The International Space Council had forbidden any large chunks of extraterrestrial matter to be brought into Earth orbit again. Mining and refining operations were to take place in deep space from that time forward.

"We've had no such disasters as that in the years since, thank God," Carstairs went on, "but space operations are still carried out in the same antiquated, irresponsible fashion. For a century, now, a very significant portion of the Earth's wealth and time have been spent on building space colonies, wealth and time that might better have been spent solving the problems of this planet. What's more, all too many people have taken advantage of the education provided by the great universities of this planet and then, as soon as they have their degrees and are ready to begin returning to the world economy something of what has been invested in them, they emigrate and go into cushy jobs in the offworld colonies! This Earth-to-space brain drain may prove to be the worst effect of the whole disastrous space program."

Carstairs paused and drank from a water glass on the podium before him. "Well, we can't undo what's been done, but we can correct *how* it's done in the future. For better or worse, and I happen to think it's for worse, we've become dependent on materials from the offworld colonies and on technologies developed in offworld labs. They have a choke hold on us as deadly as that wielded by the energy cartels of the last century.

"All of which brings us to the proposal which the Earth First Party is putting before the U.N. It's the opening campaign in our program to seize back from the offworld elitists we have created the future destiny of the people on Earth. This bill will be submitted simultaneously to the International Space Council and to the U.S. Senate for ratification. The protocols are as follows:" The lights dimmed further and a facsimile of the printout before Carstairs rolled up on the screen behind him.

"Item One: All technical professions essential to space exploration, settlement and exploitation, shall henceforth be under the licensing board of Space Council member states. A licensed professional must be under contract to the government of a member state.

"Item Two: All professionals in the critical categories may be placed under control of a licensing board even without their applications.

"Item Three: No licensed professional may break contract while on an extraterrestrial assignment. Any contract jumping without first returning to Earth is a felony punishable by imprisonment of up to seven years.

"Item Four: Any individual leaving the environment of the Earth-Moon twin planet system must leave his/her assets, to include currency, stock holdings, bank holdings, real property and any other possession defined by law of the licensing nation as 'asset,' save for such currency, property, etc. as shall be necessary for maintenance of life during the said extraterrestrial assignment, at the pleasure of the licensing government. He/she may reclaim all such assets by returning to the Earth-Moon system within a period of five years except when that individual is absent from the said system under a specific order of the government for a longer period. If he/she fails to return within five years, the said assets are forfeit to the government. The outerworlders with holdings on the Earth-Moon system may continue to enjoy their property ownership if they return within five years of the passage and ratification of this bill. Until their return, all such assets shall be in custody of the ratifying state or the International Space Council.

"Item Five: All of the above to be in effect immediately. However, those in the critical professional categories who are already off the Earth shall be licensed within six months or be returned to the Earth for retraining."

The screen winked out and Carstairs put his paper down. "Well, there you have it. That's essentially the form in which our proposal will be put before the General Assembly and the Space Council. However, the Earth First Party is truly international, and there might be changes desired by signing member nations, to be binding only upon citizens of those nations. For instance, under some legal systems, the definition of the word 'asset' alone could run for paragraphs or pages."

Murdo rose from his seat and stood beside Carstairs. "Thank you, Mr. Carstairs. Are there any questions or comments at this time?"

"Crap," said a voice from the back of the theater. Thor looked around and grinned. He knew that voice.

"Robert, how did you get in here?" McNaughton was raging beneath his unflappable exterior.

"I walked. You didn't really think you could keep me out, did you, Murdo? Who installed all your security gear?"

"National Fortressystems," Murdo said.

"And who owns thirty percent of National Fortressystems?" Bob asked.

"Hmm, I see what you mean. Well, since you insist, you might as well have your say."

"Yes, I'd be glad to hear what you have to say, Mr—Ciano, is it?" Carstairs seemed genuinely interested, not belligerent. Bob rose from his seat and walked down the aisle, lurching slightly. In one hand he held a huge brandy snifter.

As he passed Thor, Bob winked and whispered: "Just keep your mouth shut, kid."

He mounted the platform. "Mr. Carstairs, you've implied that the current deplorable state of the planet is the result of the expansion of humanity into space, much of that expansion pioneered by the direct ancestors of people in this very room."

"I don't blame our space efforts alone," Carstairs said. "I do say that it has been an important aggravation of other problems and a truly significant drain on our resources. Very limited resources, I might add."

"We'll let that stand. I'm here to tell you that, not only have our space colonies, settlements and exploratory expeditions not been a drain on this planet, they have repaid many times their initial investment. I say further that not only have those enterprises not contributed to the collapse of world order, they're all that have kept this planet from going straight to hell decades ago!" There was a lot of chatter from the audience.

"Robert," Murdo said, "why don't you sit down?"

"No, Mr. McNaughton," Carstairs said, "let him continue."

"Let's have a metaphor," Bob said. "I used to be a slick man with a metaphor, back in my teaching days." He put his brandy snifter on the podium, freeing his hands for gesticulation. "Our situation here on this planet is like that of a ship sinking, only it's sinking very slowly. As the food and water run low, the ship keeps getting low in the water." His hands made settling motions.

"Now, way off in the distance, but just visible, is an island. But, there's only one boat and getting to the island is a dangerous journey, with lots of rocks and tricky currents. However, a few brave souls man the boat and make it to the island. They report back that the island has water and you can grow food there, but it's going to take a lot of work. Go to it, say the people on the ship. A few of the bravest and most enterprising make trips out to the island. Sometimes the boat over-turns and people are drowned, but there's always a few volunteers for each trip. Now there's no way that you can get everyone off the ship and to the island in that one little boat. But the fact is that most of those who could go don't want to. They prefer their luxury cabins. Even a sinking ship is more comfortable than an island, until the water comes in under the door.

"As the food and water stocks keep getting lower, the people on the boat keep demanding more from the island. They keep raising quotas on the people on the island even as the ship passengers are falling out and fighting among themselves. And that ship is sinking all the time."

One of the Third Worlders stood up in the audience. "Are you saying that the people of Earth are practicing imperialist exploitation against the space colonists?"

Bob thought for a moment. "Well, I wouldn't have put it that way, but I guess you're right."

"A very pretty metaphor, Mr. Ciano," said Carstairs, "but I've noticed that metaphors are seldom accurate."

"This one isn't really accurate," Bob admitted, "be-cause unlike a real ship the one we're on is getting more crowded all the time and the people on it are starting to blame the folks on the island for the hole in the bottom of the goddamned hull!"

"Go home and sleep it off, Robert," Murdo said. "You're just embarrassing everybody. McNaughton En-terprises will be supporting the Earth First proposal."

"That's McNaughton-*Ciano* Enterprises, in case you've forgotton, Murdo. And if you think *our* company is going to support this hysterical garbage, then you and I are going head-to-head." He stormed down from the podium and crooked a finger at Thor as he passed. In the hubbub of the assembly breaking up, Thor left. He retrieved his cape and found Bob standing by his Harley.

"You see why I said you have to get offworld quick?" Bob asked. "Wait six months and you might not be able to go. Or if you do, it'll be as a hireling with more strings on you than a marionette." He waved his printout of the protocols. "Item One makes you a civil servant. Item Four makes you a *broke* civil servant."

"You're talking as if you expect that nonsense to pass!" Thor said.

"It'll pass, count on it."

"But, if I leave before I finish school and get my degree, I won't have any position waiting for me when I get there. The scientific stations aren't interested in anybody without an advanced degree."

"Then you may have to ship out as a laborer. There are worse things to do at your age. It really is a place where you can work your way up on guts and ability. I'd go right now if I could get a new ticker. But even if you can't go up with your degree, you might be able to protect some of your goods." He handed Thor a small card. "Look this guy up. He's an old friend of mine, name of Richard Swenson. He's a Norwegian, crazy as hell, but he can give you a way to protect some of your money. I'll talk to him tomorrow."

Thor put the card in his pocket, along with his emigration permit. "Thanks, Bob. If you think it's that urgent, I'll talk to him. Tell me something, if you think this thing is inevitable, why did you put on that scene back in there?"

Bob grinned. "Because now they have a villain. They can focus on me and maybe they'll leave you alone while you're making your arrangements. You're going to be under enough pressure, Thor. You're the future of the corporation and it's important to them to get your cooperation in this business." He straddled the bike and kicked it into life. It purred quietly, unlike the old hogs. Even with an I.C. engine license, noisy vehicles were strictly forbidden. Thor shook Bob's gauntleted hand. "See you, kid." Thor watched the taillight careening down the perilous mountain road. Bob was handling the curves with the ease and skill of a sober man one third his age.

Thor made diplomatic farewells. Karen didn't deign to show up to see the guests off. He had been planning to drive back to New Haven after spending a few days in Denver, but he had changed plans. He'd follow Bob's suggestion and spend a while getting a feel of the real world. It had not occurred to him that he had been living in an artificial environment until tonight. As soon as he was on the Interstate highway, he set the car's autopilot for Los Angeles. He cranked the seat back to horizontal and went to sleep.

TWO

He woke up on the outskirts of L.A. His eyes were gummy and he had a bad taste in his mouth. He was slightly hung over from the modest amount he had drunk at the party. He'd never had a strong tolerance for alcohol. He stopped at a charging station and found a restroom where he could wash his face and brush his teeth. The attendant behind his bulletproof barrier looked askance at his classic car and formal clothes. He pulled the razor out of the dashboard, then put it away. If he was going to be moving among the *hoi polloi,* an unshaven face might be good protective coloration.

There was a lot of L.A. to choose from. The Greater Los Angeles area stretched from Chula Vista to San Luis Obispo. Huge stretches of the megalopolis were Hispanic, and large areas were Ukrainian or Asiatic. In this immense, polyglot community was to be found everything that was happening in America.

He drove to Eagle Rock, an area that was still predominantly Old Establishment middle-class and found a motor inn that looked acceptable. In the lobby he punched the attention plate and the screen lit up. The clerk looked like a college girl working part-time out of her student apartment. "May I help you, sir?" She looked Hispanic and had a nice smile.

"I need a single room for a few days. Do your rooms have holo service and infonet screens?"

"Yes, sir, all our units are fully equipped. Please place your card in the slot and I'll key it for your room." Thor put his card in the slot and the girl's eyes widened when she read the credit rating.

"Is there a car rental nearby?" Thor asked.

"That information should be on the infonet, sir. All the nearby restaurants and entertainment centers will be listed, too. Just key in the name of your hotel: Omega Inns, Eagle Rock location number two."

"Thank you," Thor said. The girl's image winked out and the number of his unit appeared on the screen along with a disembodied voice for the visually impaired or the illiterate: "Your unit is five six six. Your unit is five six six. Enjoy your stay."

He parked the Porsche and took his bag up to the room. He chose some anonymous sports clothes from his small selection and found a nearby coffee shop for breakfast. Today he would institute his casual study of changes in holographic programming. He stopped in a convenience store and picked up several self-heating meals and appropriate beverages. This was going to call for a few inert days as a cushion veg, so he reminded himself to find a nearby dojo and make reservations for a daily workout.

With his bag of supplies in one arm, he stuck his card into the slot beside the door. The door slid open and he set the bag on a table. The room wasn't what he was used to these days, but it was at least as good as his first-year college digs had been. It was a small cubicle about five paces on a side, with a fungusbed large enough for two, a small table with two chairs, and a tiny bathroom. One wall was a picture window looking toward the old downtown section of L.A., where several small smoke plumes probably denoted modest riots. Best of all, another wall was covered by a holoscreen. He studied its controls and found a fairly complete listing of channels and services. It had a mask for retinal projection, but he disliked the gadgets. They gave him headaches and made it difficult to focus his eyes for an hour after he removed them.

He dragged a floor cushion before the screen, stuck his card in the screen slot, and keyed into the infonet. He punched the keyboard for Media; Visual; History: –10 years; Daily program guide. An instant later the Greater Los Angeles guide for that date ten years previously began rolling slowly up the screen. He modified his request to the programming of the five major networks. He was instantly transported into a major nostalgia-wallow. There were all the programs he had grown up with. Many of them had been long-running series even at that date. At least one show in five had featured spacers in some way or other. By the beginning of the twenty-first century, space opera had become the premier format for action-adventure programming, and had stayed in that place for the next several decades. Only police and war series were even in competition.

There was *Pioneers*, set in the asteroid belt at the time of the earliest mining operations; *Tarkovskygrad*, about the terrible first years of Martian settlement; *L-5*, a semi-comedy in which the builders of the wholly artificial orbiting environments found themselves in a new, insane predicament every week. There was *Space Marine!*, which had been his favorite program while growing up, because Sam Taggart occasionally showed up as the senior commandant of the Corps. Makeup and computer enhancement had transformed the actor into a virtual duplicate of his grandfather.

Besides these historical and contemporary programs, there were many set in the fictional future of exploration. The science in those series had usually been so bad that even the fifteen-year-old Thor Taggart had winced, but they had abounded with energy, excitement and optimism. The series *Aliens* had featured a new first-contact story every week, many of them based on classic tales.

Documentaries about the progress of exploration and

exploitation had been common as well, although they had never been nearly as popular as the pure entertainment programs. Thor keyed in a few minutes of each program to refresh his memory. He remembered many of the episodes. The dialogue and plotting were hopelessly simple-minded and naive to his adult sensibilities, but he could still feel a faint tingle of the excitement that had so stirred his adolescent imagination.

He spent the first half of the day going over the old shows, sometimes going back as far as forty years, long before he had been born. Always, a significant part of the programming had been space-oriented, expanding or shrinking as fads had made or dropped other genres. Virtually all of it had been sympathetic toward the adventure of space exploration. There was the occasional exception. *Space Pirates,* for instance, or the utterly bizarre *Star Tarts,* which had run for two seasons before the Islamic bloc had forced a worldwide crackdown on media porn. In all, it was much as he had remembered.

He opened one of the trays he had bought and poured water over it from the bathroom tap. The meal began to heat and reconstitute and he ate it with the plastic fork provided. He washed it down with genuine milk and felt fortified to face the next part. It was time to look in on contemporary programming.

After four excruciating hours he sat back in his cushion, appalled. His first selection had been titled *Asteroid.* It had sounded something like the old *Pioneers.* What he had watched instead had been the "family saga" of an incredibly rich and corrupt clan of psychopathic degenerates who mined gold (gold?!) from space rock, working slave-gangs of transported convicts. When they weren't chuckling over the death-agonies of the miners, they were usually indulging in a lot of kinky (off-screen) sex or crooked political wrangling, all of it amid surroundings of free-fall opulence fit to set any Earth slumdweller frothing with rage and envy.

Then there had been *Space Cop,* an actioner about a team of handsome, incorruptible customs agents dedicated to keeping Earth free of goods smuggled in from space. In the space of a single hour they had dealt with a gang smuggling drugs made in secret, free-fall labs, another smuggling low-priced high-tech equipment, sure to put millions of Earthmen out of jobs, a third gang bringing back dangerous criminals exiled to Lunar colonies and a fourth bringing in a sinister political rabble-rouser. All four gangs were bloodily annihilated by the end of the hour. In this epic, "space scum" was one of the milder references to offworlders. Thor had a suspicion that, had media blue laws not been so strict, the references would have been considerably more graphic.

Frantically, he had switched around looking for something more hopeful. Every time he found any appearance by space settlers or explorers, they were invariably depicted as sociopaths, criminals, exploiters, sinister political schemers or, at best, deluded fools. How had he missed all this? The answer, of course, was that Bob was right: he had been hopelessly out of touch. He had spent too much of his life in colleges and with his rich friends and relatives. College establishments and the rich were always the last to accept change, or even notice it.

He needed to find out when this change had taken place. Had it been sudden or gradual? Had all networks changed at once or had one instituted it and the others followed? What was behind it? The sponsors? The Writer's Guild? It was a complex problem and he had no time to tackle it himself. All right, then, if he had spent too much time in the college network, at least he knew how to use it to get things done.

He keyed in the Greater L.A. University complex. When it appeared he keyed the Media Studies department and examined the sub-department headings. He selected Popular Holovision first and eliminated all the technical fields. He cross-referenced History of Programming and Media Propaganda. A list of courses and professors and assistant professors appeared. He eliminated them and keyed Independent Study Assistants

For Hire. A long list of names appeared. All of them were grad students needing food, rent and beer money. His less fortunate friends in grad school had all worked the independent study network.

There were hundreds of names, but one attracted his notice instantly: Chih' Chin Fu. It used the old transliteration, before the adoption of Pinyin. The modern equivalent would probably be something like Jeijing Vung. It suggested a California family of more than a century's residence. There was no creature on Earth the equal of an old-time Californio for feeling out popular trends. It was imprinted on the nervous system.

He keyed the address code. The screen showed a blond young man with squarish features. "May I help you?" he asked in a heavy Ukrainian accent.

"I'm trying to find Chih' Chin Fu. I have a study to commission," Thor said.

"I'm Panas Chubar. Fu is my roommate. Just a moment." The screen panned to another part of the same room, where a thin young man sat amid a clutter of computer and infonet equipment. He wore a sleeveless coverall of silver fabric and his hair hung in a shoulder-length tangle. He looked sixteen but had to be older.

"Fu here," he said with a toothy smile.

"I'm Thor Taggart. I see in the U. infonet listing that you're qualified for independent study in trends and propaganda uses of holovision."

"Not only am I qualified," Fu said, "but I'm probably the best in the net."

"I'll give you a chance to prove it," Thor said. He outlined his problem. Throughout the recitation, the young grad student kept in continual motion. At first, Thor suspected some drug at work, but the boy moved very precisely, picking things up and putting them down, tapping out rhythms on the console before him, sipping periodically from a teacup. Thor decided that it was just an abundance of nervous energy. The kid spent too much of his time in front of a console.

"Let's see if I have it straight," Fu said. "You need to know the when, where, why, how and, most of all, who of the switchover from pro- to anti-spaceploitation in the pop holo medium?"

"That's it."

"Well, a study like that could take a while, and I have a heavy class load to cope with, plus a teaching assistantship."

"I don't have much time. How much would a rush job cost me?"

Fu scratched his bushy scalp. "Well, taking all the time and inconvenience into account, say, forty gee?"

Forty thousand dollars was a bit steep for a hungry grad student. Undoubtedly he could bargain the price down, but he didn't want to waste time and the money meant little to him, anyway. "Agreed. How soon can I have it? I'm only going to be in L.A. for a few days."

"Well, you're not too far from here. Will an hour from now do?"

"I said a rush job," Thor said, "but even the best in the net can't be that fast!"

"No, I got it right here." Fu rummaged through a file drawer and came up with a messy stack of printout sheets. "I did this a couple of months ago for a holoprop class. I was thinking of doing my thesis on it. You want me to transfer it to micro? That'll take a couple of hours, but I'll throw it in for free."

He had been neatly snookered. You had to admire that kind of gall. There was something in the way Fu moved—"Tomiki System?" he said on a hunch.

Fu gave him the toothy grin again. "Among others. You're *aikidoka*?"

"Among others," said Thor, smiling back, this time. "I'm looking for a good dojo. Could you recommend one?"

"I use the Ronin Hall. It's about thirty minutes from where you are. I'll be heading over there this evening for a late workout. You want to meet me there? It's jodo tonight, but you can probably find an instructor for some aikido."

"What time?"

"I go there at twenty-thirty. I'll flash you the address." He punched the location, then looked back up. "If you don't mind my asking, your name's Taggart, and your facial features resemble a certain gentleman of that name prominent in the early days of spaceploitation. Any connection?"

"If you're talking about Sam Taggart, I'm his grandson." This kid was quick.

"No kidding," said Fu, grinning. "And I only took you for forty gee! I'm going to be looking forward to meeting you in the flesh."

"Just bring the study. And yes, reduce it to micro. See you in a few hours." Fu broke the connection and Thor stretched. It was late afternoon and he'd accomplished a lot already. There was still a lot to get done today.

Leaving the Porsche in the subterranean parking garage of the hotel, he walked a few blocks to a rental agency and rented a battered electrical runabout. When he put in his deposit, his card got the raised-eyebrows treatment once again. That was another thing he had to change. His first stop was a bank, where he arranged for a more unobtrusive card, one which showed a modest credit balance. The teller showed no surprise at the request. Apparently, it was common for slumming rich types to adopt such protective coloration.

At a second-hand store he bought a workingman's outfit of trousers, tunic, vest and boots. He studied the array of cheap jewelry in the case at the purchase counter, but decided to pass it up. He knew vaguely that body decorations served as insignia of sorts, and he didn't want to send out the wrong signal through ignorance. He returned to the hotel to don his new apparel and by then it was time to make his way to the dojo.

Ronin Hall was located in the shabby, rundown Beverly Hills section, an area of thronged streets, shops selling cheap goods and old mansions cut up into slum housing for immigrants. Signs glared and flashed in multilingual profusion, projecting holographic images of goods or entertainments to be had. The dojo was located in a wing of a building which had once been the palatial home of a series of briefly famous flat-screen stars.

He saw no sign of Fu outside, so he went in. The place was arranged on several levels and from somewhere he could hear the clatter of a kendo class. In a side room, he caught the glitter of real swords, wielded by iaido practioners. A short Japanese with a slightly pockmarked face walked to Thor and bowed slightly. He wore a lightweight *gi* of the karate practitioner. "May I help you, sir?"

"I was to meet Chih' Chin Fu here," Thor said.

"He should be here in a few minutes for the jodo class. Are you a jodoka?"

"Aikido. I'm here from out of town and Fu said I might find an instructor for an aikido workout here."

"We might be able to accommodate you," the man said. "Dr. Kobayashi will be finishing his iaido class in five minutes. He's always looking for someone new to practice Tomiki system with. If you'll let me have your card, I'll put you down for an hour and get you an outfit." The man walked away with his card just as Fu walked in the door.

Fu was a bit taller than he had appeared on the screen. He still wore the silver coverall, with the addition of a beefeater hat and a brass-tipped walking stick. He grinned toothily as they shook hands. "You find somebody to practice with?"

"A Dr. Kobayashi," Thor affirmed.

"That old guy will work you to death. He just loves it. Look, I have to go change. We'll get together when the class breaks up and we'll go someplace where we can talk, okay?"

"Fine," Thor said. The manager came back with Thor's card and sparring clothes. In a dressing room, he changed into the long, black hakama trousers and white jacket. An elderly man with a white goatee introduced himself as Kobayashi and conducted him to a side room floored with straw mats. On the way, they passed the jodo class, which Fu was teaching. The students were sparring vigorously with fifty-one inch sticks and, by ancient custom, they wore no protective gear. Many of them already sported red marks and swellings where they had not defended quickly enough.

Kobayashi proved to be far stronger and fitter than he looked and was every bit as fierce as Fu had predicted. It was a long, hot, sweaty hour and Thor finished it sore and bruised, but he was feeling much better. He showered and resumed his street clothes.

Fu met him at the entrance. "You had dinner yet?"

"No. I'm starved." He realized that he was truly ravenous.

"I know a good place a few blocks from here. We can walk if you like."

"That sounds good. I need to work out some of these bruises. I'll leave my car here."

On the street, Fu studied him. "First thing, though, we have to find something for your head."

"My head?" Thor said, mystified.

"No question about it. You're trying to pass as a prole, aren't you? The clothes are okay, but the haircut's all wrong. Come on." A few doors down, Fu led him into a clothing shop where he selected a black silk bandanna and tied it around Thor's head buccaneer-fashion. "That's better." He turned to the girl at the sales counter. "You got any lipstick, my sweet?" he asked.

"What color?" she said, flashing irridescent eyelids.

"Yellow?"

She reached into her beltbag and came up with a stick of the requisite color. He drew a horizontal stripe beneath Thor's eyes and across his nose. "This is an Apache stripe. Face paint is very subdued this year."

"You aren't wearing any at all," Thor said.

"California students aren't wearing it this semester. Come on, let's go get something to eat."

On the way, they stopped in front of a bank and put their cards into the row of slots set into the facade. Thor

keyed the instrument to transfer the forty thousand
dollars from his account to Fu's. Fu handed over a
plastic carrier with a tiny crystal imbedded in its face.
Thor stuck the carrier into his pocket.

"That's the cheapest piece of first-rate scholarship
you'll ever buy," Fu assured him.

Thor noted a glowing graffito on a stained brick wall,
painted over the faded graffiti of years past. "What's
that?" he asked. "I've been seeing that symbol everyplace since I got to L.A." The symbol consisted of two
figures: $\oplus 1$.

"You haven't run across that one before? It's been the
top graffito for months!"

"I've been out of touch," Thor said, defensively.

"You must've been on the bottom of the Marianas
Trench. The cross in the circle is one of the old astro-
nomical symbols for Earth. The other figure, as you've
no doubt already figured out, is a one. What's that
make?"

"Earth First," Thor said.

"There you go," Fu said. "And here we are." They
went into a small restaurant where robot carts wheeled
among the tables, bearing trays of dimsum. The place
was crowded and noisy. Most L.A. establishments were
open twenty-four hours. They found an unoccupied
table. A cart came by and Fu reached for his card but
Thor made restraining motions. Fu wasted no time in
returning his card to his pocket. Thor thrust his card
into the cart's slot. "Help yourself," he said. They took
bottles of beer from the refrigerated basket on the
cart's bottom level and loaded their table with plates of
pork buns, shu-mai, spring rolls and stuffed duck's feet.

"It's none of my business," Fu said, "but this study
you've commissioned and got with such commendable
speed is not what I'd expect from a scion of the illustri-
ous founding families of our expansion into space. It's
what I'd expect from a media consulting firm, or a
programming survey analyst."

"You're right," Thor said. "It's none of your business." He dunked a pork bun into a sweet dipping sauce. "But, what the hell. I'll tell you anyway." He took the folded Earth First manifesto from his pocket and handed it to Fu. "This is what the Earth Firsters are going to put before the U.N. and the Space Council in a few days. They asked that we refrain from showing this around before they go public, but screw 'em. I don't owe them any favors." He found himself telling Fu the whole story; about his plans, the party, his talk with Bob and his revelatory viewing of holo programs that day. There was no real reason for saying all this, except that he had to talk to somebody, and he sensed a kindred spirit in Fu.

Fu handed the paper back. "I've been wondering when it'd come to this. It's been in the air a long time. It's only the first move, you know."

"I got that impression. Carstairs referred to it as an 'opening campaign.' What I can't figure is why the McNaughtons are backing it."

"I can't help you there. Big-business practice isn't my field. My field is media history and trend, and I know that the fastest way for a government to bring any medium to heel is to threaten to yank its broadcast license. That's the history of control, my friend. Once you control licensing, everything else falls right into your hands." He surveyed the litter of empty plates and bottles atop the table. "I think we've done all the damage we're going to do here. Do you feel up to some slumming or are you too tired?"

"I'm up to it," Thor said. "Are you offering to be my guide?"

"I can save you a lot of time. I'll steer you to just the kind of place your friend Robert Ciano would consider to be most educational. And all of it free, gratis."

"Then lead on." They walked back to his rented vehicle and Fu twirled his walking stick like a baton. The streets were as crowded as ever. Thor looked up and could not see a single star. The air of Los Angeles was clean these days, but it was so ablaze with light

around the clock that on the clearest night it was difficult to see a full moon.

Fu examined the battered little electrocar with a
critical eye, poking it here and there with his stick.
"Good choice," he pronounced at last. "Very inconspicuous. What do you usually drive?"

"A 2045 Porsche."

"I might've known. Manual drive?"

"The works. I even brake it manually. Or should I
say pedally?"

Fu climbed into the vehicle and propped his stick
between his knees. He leaned forward and keyed a
destination into the dash control. "Our first stop will be
the Watts development. Ever been there?" Thor shook
his head. "Well, it can be a rough place. If we should
run into trouble, just remember: take no prisoners, call
no cops and just walk away from it if you're in any
condition to walk. That is, unless you feel like spending
the next few months in the never-never-land of the
L.A. court system."

"It's that bad?" Thor asked.

"My, my," Fu shook his head in wonderment, "you
have been out of touch!"

Thor leaned back in his seat and watched the city-
scape go by. All of the most splendid buildings were old
ones. With their nighttime illumination, they gave the
skyline a fairyland look. But Thor knew that, close up,
most of them would be shabby and dilapidated.

"How about you?" Thor asked. "How did you come
to do a study on changing attitudes toward the push
into space?"

"Changing *popular* attitudes," Fu corrected. "The
attitudes of people who think seriously about it have
changed little if at all, for or against. People who take
the trouble to study, to read and keep track of developments, usually form their own opinions. Popular opinion, mass culture, that's something completely different
and that's where holovision comes in. The vast majority
of people in the First World and much of the Third get

virtually all of their information about the world around them from the holos. It's the most effective propaganda tool ever invented." He was gesticulating enthusiastically, clearly onto his pet subject.

"It's replaced virtually all other media. Radio is gone except for intervehicular communication. Television is obsolete because holo is so much more effective. Less than twenty percent of the population is literate because it's too difficult a skill to acquire and who'd read anyway, with their heads plugged into the holo every non-working hour? Those that have work to do, anyway."

He took a deep breath. "Well, you'll get most of this when you go over my study. I chose that subject first of all because it's the most notable trend in holo programming these days, but also because I've wanted for years to emigrate and I keep an eye on developments like that." He began tapping out a snare-drum rhythm on the dashboard.

"Where were you planning to head out to?"

"The Moon. I have relatives in Armstrong and some other places. My clan's a big one."

"You may have to move sooner than you thought, if you don't want to go out as a licensed contract employee. Of course, your field may not be one of the ones they put under government control."

"Don't you believe it, man. Anything having to do with media handling is going to be under their thumb. That's why I plan to get out as soon as I can."

"And what would you do out there? I know there's always a demand for people with technical skills. Is there a lot of media work to be had?"

"Sure. Miners and settlers and convicts need entertainment and information, too. They have their own networks and info services and there are always teaching positions to be had in the schools. But that's not what I expect to be doing."

"What, then?"

"Politics." He seemed reluctant to expand on it, perhaps thinking he had already said too much. Thor knew it wouldn't take much to get him talking again.

"I wasn't aware that there were any politics to practice offworld."

"There will be. Agitation for some degree of independence is already starting. Where there's political agitation, parties are going to form. And what's the first thing a political party needs?"

Thor thought a moment. "Publicity, media exposure."

"In a word," Fu said triumphantly, "propaganda. That's where I come in." He glanced sideways at Thor. "Look, you don't impress me as a professor or a business exec. The way I read it, you're a grad student like me. Am I right?"

"That's right. Space-habitation engineering."

"So you've spent, what, six or seven straight years in university?"

"Closer to eight," Thor admitted.

"Then how come you're so far out of touch with what's going on? Universities are medieval institutions, I grant you, but students are the trendiest people on Earth. Undergrads, especially."

"I got my degree at Yale," Thor said, self-consciously. "I've been doing thesis work at Cambridge and Bern."

"That explains a lot. Where were you hoping to work? But, hell, you're a Taggart. I guess you can just take your pick."

"It's not that easy," said Thor, shaking his head. "I'm headed for the Belt. They won't take any deadwood out there, and family connections don't count for much if you don't have the needed skills. Besides, there isn't much love lost between the Earthbound and offworld branches of my family. There are more Taggarts and Cianos out there than they know what to do with anyway."

"You figure on going to Luna first?"

"That's the way it's looking," Thor said. "This is in strictest confidence, but I may just be going out unofficially and incognito. I want to finish my grad work. By that time, I won't be able to emigrate except as a licensed public servant under contract. But I'll have no trouble getting a temporary visa to go to the Moon for study or tourism. From there, maybe I'll be able to buy a passage out to the Belt. Business is conducted on a pretty freewheeling basis out there."

Fu was silent for a moment. "I may be able to put you onto something. Let me think about it for a while."

The Watts complex was coming into view. It blocked out an unbelievable section of sky. Parts of it blazed with light but large sections were dark. Inaugurated on January 1, 2001, the Watts development was to have been the showpiece answer to the ugliness of urban sprawl and the decay of the inner cities. Touted as "the housing of the Twenty-First Century," the Watts development had called for the razing of an immense slum and replacing it with a forty-story structure of near self-sufficiency. The upper levels were mostly for housing, the lower levels being devoted to shopping malls, entertainment arcades, schools, public services, even light manufacturing. It was to lead the way in solving the urban problems of a century.

Now it was a run-down, outdated slum area. It had been outdated before its completion. Such structures were too laborious to construct and could not keep up with the tide of immigration. In its early years, there had been fierce competition for housing in the Watts development. Now even the L.A. Police were reluctant to enter it.

As they slid from the freeway into the web of streets surrounding the development, Thor took manual control of the little vehicle. Fu pointed to a flashing sign which shifted to several languages in turn. The English part read: "Safe Parking." There was also an image of a car inside a stylized cage: the universal illit symbol for a guarded parking facility. They drove into the small lot and were stopped by a boy who stood in the center of the drive approach, holding a fire ax at port arms. As they climbed from the car, another boy, perhaps fourteen years old, emerged from a shack next to the drive. Inside the shack, they could see a group of younger boys and girls, most of them with holo masks on their faces.

"You going into the Big W?" the boy asked. He wore a coverall of red imitation leather and had a chromed ball-pean hammer thonged to his chain-belt. His shaven scalp was covered by a tattooed spider and contact film transformed his eyes to scarlet orbs.

"For a couple of hours," Fu said. "How much?"

"Two C," the boy said, rubbing the thumb and fingers of his raised right hand in the gesture which had appeared coincidentally with the invention of paper money.

"Capitalist pig!" Fu protested. "Quarter-C, tops."

The boy grinned, displaying teeth enamelled the color of blood. "One C, exploiter of the masses. Less buys less protection."

"Three-quarter C, enemy of the people," Fu said.

"Done," the boy said. "Three-quarter C for two hours. For every hour or partial hour after that, one half C. After ten hours, we declare you dead and ransom the car back to the rental company."

"Agreed," Fu said.

"Three-quarter C in advance." The boy took a slotted credit box from his belt and Thor thrust his card into it, transfering seventy-five dollars. The boy in red turned and said something to the ax-bearer, speaking fast in a dialect Thor couldn't follow, although it seemed to have some English words in it. The other boy tossed his ax into the back of the car, climbed in and drove the little vehicle into a caged area. There were several other conveyances there, some of them expensive models. Thor and Fu began to walk the two blocks to the Watts development.

"What was that language that little bandit was speaking?" Thor asked.

"Yankrainian. It's a youthspeak like Burmex, used by the twelve-to-sixteen crowd. There's two L.A. holo stations that use nothing else. On your toes, now. We're in Injun country."

A sour smell hung over the whole district, as if the sanitation systems had been failing for years. There were few people on the streets at this hour, and they displayed little curiosity toward Thor and his companion. The general attitude was one of dejected apathy.

"Stop looking around like you were expecting these poor losers to jump us," Fu said. "Relax. Nobody's going to bother us except groups of three or more. The gangs mostly hang out inside the complex."

"And that's where we're going," Thor said uneasily.

"You want to see what's happening, you have to take the risks." The hulking building was getting closer, looking more like a cliff than an artifact.

"Do you come down here often?" Thor asked.

"Maybe once a month. Down here is where the politics of despair are generated. To get the other end of the spectrum, I hire out part-time to a catering firm that supplies waiters for rich people's parties in the silicon-and-wine territory. They like the feeling of having humans act as servants for them. I can pick up a lot by listening to them talk."

"I'm surprised the McNaughtons haven't picked that up yet. They're still high-tech, only robot servants."

Now they were at the base of the structure. The walls were covered with luminescent graffiti to a height of twenty feet. Splintered glass crunched under their feet as they walked through a wide entranceway from which the doors had long since disappeared. The entrance opened onto a huge atrium twenty stories in height. Lining the atrium were twenty elevator tubes. Four or five of the elevators seemed to be in working order. The other tubes were filled with several stories of trash cast in by upper-level dwellers.

On the lowest levels, lurid neon and holographic signs enticed passersby into establishments catering to every possible taste. Bizarrely-costumed groups wandered about aimlessly. In the center of the atrium, a group of perhaps fifty persons in all-enveloping sackcloth robes and masked hoods constantly blew the same two notes on battered trumpets.

"Slaves of the New Apocalypse," Fu said, nodding toward the horn-blowers. "They've been blowing those two notes in shifts for more than a year now. They figure if they keep it up long enough, God will notice and destroy the world and take them up to heaven."

They mounted a stair to the second level, where entertainment was the order of the day or night. Everywhere, huddled against the walls or sprawled in the walkways, were the inert forms of drunks and druggies. Colored smokes emerged from dim doorways and the sound of music was raucous and unending. Holographic shills appeared outside entranceways and clamored for attention, promising untold delights to be had within.

Most of the dense crowds wore the shabby clothing of the proles or the idiosyncratic uniforms of youth gangs. Some were in the native dress of whatever part of the world they had fled to come to this place. Dozens of languages were to be heard. Here and there were individuals or small groups in expensive, fashionable clothes; the bored rich out for low amusements among their inferiors. They were invariably accompanied by hulking bodyguards.

Thor found it a disturbingly stimulating place. It was far livelier than the dismal streets outside, but its grotesque combination of gaiety and misery was disorienting. He leaned on a railing overlooking the atrium floor and nodded to a crowd of Francophone Asians filing into a restaurant. "What do they come here for?" he asked. "I mean, not just here, but L.A. Hell, all of the U.S. is headed down the tubes. That's no surprise, of course, what with the insane redistribution of productive middle-class income to dole-hungry lower classes, while upper classes are immune to serious taxation. Not to mention the socially self-destructive educational policies and the legislations catering only to the special interest groups. What draws all these immigrants here?"

"Because, compared to whatever Third World hellhole they come from, this is still heaven."

"It's appalling," Thor said. "What is there for them to do when they get here?"

"Very little," Fu said, pushing back his hat, his eyes following a richly-dressed woman trailed by a security robot. "This country was always the immigrant's dream, but it was built by taking land away from Indians and giving it to the immigrants. When most of the Indian land was gone, there was industry opening up and needing lots of labor. Now that's gone, too.

"The frontier's in space now, and space unfortunately isn't a frontier for the masses. If all the resources of the planet were devoted to building ships and sending out as many people as possible, it wouldn't put a dent in the annual birth rate." He shifted his grip on his stick slightly as four youths in leather masks walked by, studying the two truculently through slanted goggles. The four wore metal-plated gloves. They passed on and Fu relaxed slightly.

"What's left," Fu went on, "is despair and envy."

"Despair I can understand," Thor commented, "but why envy?"

"That brings us back to holo programming. You saw some of this in your sampling today, but it pervades all of popular programming, not just the space-oriented series like *Asteroids*. Everywhere, the emphasis is on the doings and possessions of the absurdly rich. These people we see all around us here spend most of their day, vicariously, amid the surroundings of the filthy rich and they know that they'll never have access to a life like that. Worse, they can't even have the illusion that the rich and powerful are somehow superior to themselves. They see that those people are just jerks like everybody else."

"So what can they do?" Thor asked.

"They can vote," Fu said. "With any degree of solidarity, the unemployed or semi-employed underclass forms the most powerful voting bloc in any nation that has a popular vote at all. That's too much potential political power to just leave lying around unexploited. Earth First has figured a way to make use of them." He nodded to a group of men who had just entered the complex. They looked like factory workers just coming off shift from some light industry facility nearby. They wore coveralls with a company logo on the breast that

Thor couldn't make out, but each wore another device on his back that was large enough to read from the second level; it was the symbol $\oplus 1$.

"Now they're being told that it's the offworlders that're bleeding them," Fu said. "Precious tax money is going into expensive projects in space from which they derive no benefit. It's a stroke of genius, really."

"Why do you say that?" Opposite them on the same level, he saw a sign advertising a drug service which tailored its product to the body chemistry of the buyer.

"Well, because you can have great big demonstrations and mass rallies without ugly pogroms. After all, the people they're learning to hate are millions of klicks away."

Suddenly, Thor was profoundly depressed. The sheer immensity of the problem paralyzed the mind. "Come on," he said, "let's go."

"But there's lots more to see," Fu protested. "You haven't even gone inside one of the pain palaces yet."

"Not tonight," Thor said. "I'll come back later. I've had enough for now."

"It's a little too much to take in all at once," Fu agreed, leading the way back down to the entrance. "Rest up tomorrow and I'll take you to some other places. There's a religious revival over on Cahuenga that's been going on for three months. You have to see it to understand what despair is all about."

They walked back out through the littered entrance and found the four leather-masked men waiting outside. "You belong to the Baron," intoned one in a hieratic voice.

Fu smiled. "We're just sightseers, friends. We don't even have anything valuable on us." He held his stick lightly by the middle, balanced casually over one shoulder.

"We don't steal," said one. "We've vowed two goats to Baron Samedi. You're it." With no more warning than that, they attacked.

If Thor had had to think about it, he would have died

in the next second. The attack was so sudden, so unprovoked, so *unbelievable*, that the conscious part of his mind still had no idea what was happening. The unconscious part, though, had been conditioned by thousands of hours in the *dojo*, so that thought was unnecessary. He sidestepped the knife before his senses even registered its presence and his right hand shot out into the bump in the center of the mask, between the slanting eyepieces of the goggles. The deadly *shomen-ate* crushed the man's nose to a pulp, jerking his head backward. A second man was already swinging a chain overhand toward his head and Thor stepped inside its arc, blocking overhead with his left forearm as the stiffened fingers of his right hand lanced upward beneath the man's sternum. The attacker doubled up, gasping. The vicious blow to the solar plexus could easily render a man unconscious, and this one did.

Thor looked about wildly and saw the other two masked men lying peacefully on the sidewalk. Fu leaned with both hands on the top of his cane, his hat at a jaunty angle, looking fresh and elegant and absurdly resembling a soft-shoe dancer. Thor hadn't heard the impacts of the stick, but they had been effective. A number of people went into or out of the building, sparing no more than a glance for the aftermath of the little battle.

"It worked," Thor said, wonderingly. "It really worked!" He began to notice a burning pain across his back, where the chain had connected after his block.

"Worked just fine," Fu said. "You've never done it for real?"

Thor shook his head and knelt by his first attacker. "I might have killed this one," he said, tugging at the mask. The mask came off, revealing a blotchy, pale face. The man was around thirty and had a scraggly red beard. He was breathing stertorously and was bleeding from the nose, but seemed otherwise undamaged.

"He's fine," Fu said. "A skull that thick would be hard to damage. They'll all live. As I advised earlier, we won't bother the police. These vacuum-heads would just sue us. Come on."

Thor got up and walked with Fu back toward the parking lot. He began to tremble slightly with delayed reaction and thrust his hands into his pockets to hide it. "Would they have killed us?"

"Deader'n hell," Fu assured him. "The courts won't touch them, but don't despair. Baron Samedi is going to be very pissed off at them. Probably turn them into zombies." He thought for a moment. "Not that it'd be much of a change."

Something struck Thor. "That one I unmasked was white. I thought *voudon* followers were all black. Haitians, mostly."

"Not any more," Fu said.

They retrieved the car and set out for Fu's apartment. For once, Thor was glad to have an autopilot. The sudden, shocking outburst of violence had shaken him badly. When they were out on the freeway, Fu broke the silence.

"Thor, there's someone you need to contact when you get to Luna. Man by the name of Martin Shaw. He's a cousin, sort of. The name Shaw is Chinese, by the way, not English, like George Bernard Shaw. He doesn't look very Chinese, though. He's a Eurasian from Singapore. Kind of like Lenin, he looks slightly Asiatic to Westerners and slightly European to Asians. Anyway, he's a smuggler these days, strictly respectable, though. And he's a revolutionary, which is what got him kicked off Earth in the first place. He was sent out from Singapore after some indiscretions involving explosives and government buildings. Of course they would've shot him for that, so he let them pick him up for publishing his unlicensed newspaper before the other things could be pinned on him.

"They sent him up to the Tranquillitatis relocation Center and he was running the place in a month. He busted or bribed his way out, I don't know which, and now he's big in the underground economy. The important thing is, he has his own ship and he can probably get you out to the Belt."

"He sounds like a man of many talents," Thor said. "How would I get in contact with him?"

"He's sometimes to be found in the Earthview Room of the Armstrong Hilton. Ask around and use my name. If he doesn't remember me, remind him that I belong to the L.A. laundry-restaurant-and-computer Fus."

At his apartment building, Fu got out of the car, then leaned in the driver's window. "You handled yourself really well tonight, for a Yale man. Keep in touch." He sauntered toward the building, twirling the cane and then breaking into a quick Maurice Chevalier dance step. Thor smiled and set the car for his inn. He hadn't looked forward to a good night's sleep like this in a long time.

THREE

Thor peeled the top from a self-heating plastic can of coffee. He pressed the colored patches on the side of the can and artificial milk and sweetener were injected into the steaming liquid. He sipped for a while, planning out his day. He had considered using this time to catch up on contemporary news broadcasting. For the last few years, he had subscribed to a prestigious print-out service in lieu of watching the holos.

Fu had intrigued him, though. He decided to look into the study he had bought. He fed the crystal in its holder into the slot of the holo set and sat back. After a brief title sequence, Fu appeared, considerably changed from the way Thor had seen him the day before.

Fu's hair was tied neatly back and he wore the long, formal robe of a Confucian scholar. His face was lightly made up to resemble that of a much older man and he wore artificial, three-inch fingernails. His skullcap was crowned with a coral button and a red tassel and as he appeared he was writing on a paper scroll with a brush dipped in vermilion ink. The table and chair were massive, garish, tasteless Manchu Dynasty pieces, heavily lacquered and deliberately chosen to offset the studied elegance of his dress and bearing. He was sitting in a courtyard and behind him was a spectacular view of the fantastic mountains of the Li river valley, stripped of their ugly twenty-first-century accretions.

Except for Fu and his costume, of course, it was all a computer generation. Actually, everything in the picture, down to the artificial lines in Fu's face, could have been produced by com-gen, but Thor doubted that the student could afford the complete process. In reality, he was sitting in an empty, all-blue studio and even his shadow on the tabletop was faked. The illusion, though, was flawless. It was decades since computer imaging had been in any way distinguishable from reality.

Fu glanced up from his scroll. "The time to begin is not now but at the beginning. Popular attitudes towards manned space exploration and settlement are inseparable from the actual developments." The voice was deeper and more resonant than Fu's actual speaking voice. "Therefore, let us return to the beginning of this century, when the first, faltering steps into space gave way to the rapid emigration and settlement which persists to this day."

The view moved past Fu, off the terrace, and towards the mountains. The point of view angled upward and moved towards the clouds, as if the holocamera were mounted in the nose of a rocket. The clouds flashed past and the sky darkened. Stars appeared. The point of view swiveled and now the viewer was looking back toward Earth. "More than a half-century ago," Fu's voice narrated, "the continuous-boost ion drive space vessel made its first appearance in the still mysterious and controversial joint U.S.-Soviet manned mission to a comet. U.S. records of that incident are still under seal and shall remain so until the next century. Whatever the actual circumstances of that mission, it ushered in the era of practical exploitation of interplanetary resources.

"Even with the initially available continuous acceleration rate of some point oh-one gee, or one-hundredth of the gravitational acceleration at the surface of the Earth, one could reach Mars and return within a few months. The size of the Solar System all the way to Saturn became comparable, in travel time, to that of the globe to European mariners of the sixteenth century." From the Earth, spectral figures of wooden ships, sails billowing as in a Holbein painting, began to spiral outward.

"This early stage was adequate for exploration. Carefully-chosen crews were picked for emotional stability to endure the long, dull stretches of voyage time. Although the time frames were similar, these explorers could make their crossings in far greater comfort and far less danger than those early mariners."

The ghostlike sailing ships were transformed to solid images of early exploration vessels with their chaotic shapes made up of boxes, spheres and tubes, bristling with spikes and knobs. "Within a few years, the compact nuclear fission engine was perfected. At last, real exploitation and settlement of the solar system was a paying proposition." The perspective changed to a compressed solar system, with lights blossoming on Luna and Mars, then bright, circling dots as artificial colonies were built in orbit, then random lights among the asteroids. Last of all, small lights sprung up on the Jovian and Saturnian satellites.

"Early expeditions were all sponsored by the governments of the technologically-advanced nations, led by the U.S.A. and the U.S.S.R. and closely followed by the Western European Consortium and Japan. As soon as the cost of space ships became low enough through mass production, giant private industries in the capitalist world began their ventures. When discarded spaceships, abandoned on the Moon or in orbit for economical or other reasons, became available for bargain prices, private entrepreneurs and special interest groups pooled their resources, bought ships and joined in the high adventure." Thousands of bright dots burst from Earth and sped to various destinations within the solar system.

"And adventure it was, since the second-hand ships, many of them decades old by that time, were not nearly as reliable or as safe as they had been in government

service. Many of the early second-stage expeditions
simply were never heard from after leaving Earth or
Lunar orbit. That grim fact didn't slow the tide. Religious and political splinter groups left Earth by hundreds, fleeing political repression or moral contamination,
or just looking for a good place to practice their way of
life without interference or distraction. Many of these
early ventures based themselves on the various satellites, but these remained dependent upon Earth for
many essentials. When it was established that some
asteroids were rich in hydrocarbons, quasi-self-supporting
island colonies became a practical proposition." Now
lights were leaving the Moon, Mars and many satellites, headed for the Belt between Mars and Jupiter.

"Concurrent with these developments was the per-
fection of the long-anticipated medium of holographic
reproduction. With its unprecedented apparent realism, it was a quantum jump in communication technology, as superior to television as television had been to
rock-painting. I say *apparent* realism because the holographic medium, coupled with the concurrently-
developed technology of computer imaging, is able to
present images of such detail and such apparent solidity
that an effect of incredible realism is achieved, even
though the subject may be entirely imaginary. For instance, the image of the solar system you see now looks
quite realistic, whereas in reality it is as stylized as an
Egyptian hieroglyphic.

"Because of this spurious impression of realism, there
is a tendency among the mass audience to accept anything they see in the holos as fact. This was not lost
upon the propagandists of the time. In democratic nations, there was a rush of legislation to prevent seekers
of public office from using computer-enhanced holos to
present a deceitful image, but these measures were
almost universally struck down on grounds of interfering with rights of free speech. Ancient political hacks
began appearing on holovision with young, handsome
faces, perfect physiques and resonant, confidence-

inspiring voices, just as your humble presentor has used the same technology to present an older and more dignified appearance than he is entitled to by nature, along with a similarly melifluous voice." The image returned to Fu in his mandarin getup and fairytale surroundings. He gestured with his long-nailed hands toward his environment. "All of this is illusion. I am illusion. And thus, holovision has become the most potent tool for controlling the mass perception of reality ever to fall into the hands of propagandists.

"By the nineteenth century the importance of the popular media in gaining mass support for government policies had been recognized. By the twentieth, every totalitarian regime made total state control of all means of information dissemination a priority, second only to control of the military. The systematic use of popular media for purposes of opinion control was first codified by Dr. Joseph Goebbels of the notorious Third Reich, who said—" abruptly and repulsively, Fu's image was transformed into that of a ferret-faced little man in a brown, outdated uniform. In a heavy, Teutonic accent, Goebbels said: "The mass mind is far more primitive than most of us can imagine." Goebbels melted and coalesced into Fu once more.

"This contempt for the mass audience has infused every aspect of media manipulation from Goebbels's day to this. Early surveys conducted by marketers for purposes of advertising indicated that the most effective approach to advertising on television was to aim at the reasoning power and attention span of the mind of an eight-year-old child. The result indicated, more than anything else, an exceedingly low opinion of the eight-year-old mind.

"To the vast majority of world inhabitants, however, holovision was not a propaganda tool, but entertainment. With the profusion of satellite communications systems and low-cost holovision sets manufactured in Third world sweatshops, this mass medium became truly worldwide. Only in nations like the U.S.S.R. and many of the Islamic states, which had jamming facilities, were the effects of worldwide holo programming diminished.

"The inhabitants of Zimbabwe became samurai-adventure addicts while those of Lima thrilled to American westerns. Above all, the populace of the poorer sections of the world found in these three-dimensional fantasies escape from the drudgery of their lives. The propaganda value of even these unreal, popular fantasies had long been known, but it had been manipulated mainly for commercial purposes. In the democratic societies, it was all but impossible to gain control of these popular media save through subversion. There were limited sanctions imposed worldwide, as when the Islamic bloc pressured the U.N. Media Affairs Committee to pass a ban on internationally-broadcast pornography, since there was a possibility that pirate booster stations might be set up in their countries and their people contaminated by access to such entertainment. The suppression of pornography was successful since there was already much agitation in the West against it. Other Islamic demands were ignored, such as a ban on images of pigs or unveiled women.

"However, the precedent made it possible to enforce other sanctions on holographic broadcasting as various pressure groups sought to force their standards into law. By tacking a rider onto the anti-pornography rule, for instance, religious fundamentalists managed to ban a great deal of formerly common language which they deemed indecent. Other groups followed suit, with varying degrees of success.

"It is, however, the use of popular entertainment programming to influence public attitudes toward manned space settlement and exploration that concerns us here. With this background in mind, let's look at the early years of holographic programming as it parallelled the expansion of man into space."

Thor switched the set off. All *that* just as a prologue? Fu hadn't been kidding when he said he'd put a lot of work into it. He got another coffee, resumed his seat and switched the set back on. The next few hours were somewhat reminiscent of his informal survey of the day before, but with far more depth and scholarship. Fu's study involved not only the programs themselves, but also their sponsors, the political connections of their owners, the guild affiliations of the writers.

About halfway through, Thor began making connections. As the spacer-hostile programming of the last few years proliferated, the same connection appeared again and again. It was something Fu had missed, because he wasn't a student of corporate systems and practices. Neither was Thor, for that matter, but this struck close to him. At first he couldn't believe it. It had to be a coincidence. By the end of Fu's presentation, he had to accept the truth of his first hunch.

The minute the recording ended, Thor keyed Fu's code, hoping he would catch him at home. Fu's apartment appeared and the screen panned to a console where Fu sat, his fingers dancing across a keyboard. He looked up and grinned. "Wasn't expecting to see you again so soon. What's up?"

"We have to talk. Do you have a few minutes?"

"Sure," Fu said, puzzlement in his voice. He picked up a cushion and dropped it to the floor, then sat on it crosslegged. The two young men sat almost knee-to-knee. Except for being unable to touch, they might as well have been sitting in the same room.

"I just finished with your presentation," Thor said.

"All of it today? Figure you got your money's worth?"

"Great work. But I spotted something you didn't."

Fu frowned. "Didn't think I could've missed much."

"It's not something you'd have been likely to spot. I've found a thread tying all of this stuff together, going right back to the beginnings of the hostile programming, five years ago."

Fu grinned again. "Hot damn! I love conspiracies. What is it? Closet Earth Firsters among the producers? I checked into that, but it didn't seem to pan out."

"This is something so weird I couldn't believe it at first. The first of the hostile shows was *Defenders of Earth*. Do you remember who the sponsor was?"

Fu's brows knit in thought. "Some dogfood company. Purina?"

"No, it was Petcuisine, a brand marketed by Mid-America Feed and Grain, Inc."

"No connection yet," Fu said. "Elucidate."

"M-A Feed & Grain is a wholly-owned subsidiary of Space Technologies, Inc, which is a McNaughton enterprise."

"How does the McNaughton cartel happen to own a grain firm?"

"They did it back when the first hydrocarbon-rich asteroids were discovered. McNaughton wanted to have a lock on developing new high-grade fertilizers and developing new strains of grain to adapt to Ell-Five, lunar and Martian conditions. They figured the easiest way was to have their own grain company and the quickest way was to buy one that was already there. They picked up a faltering firm at a bargain price, pumped new capital into it, and made it pay for itself while they built their labs and did their research. Like most feed and grain firms, M-A ran a sideline in live-stock and pet food."

"Not all of those shows are sponsored by dogfoods," Fu said.

"No, but the story's still the same. *Asteroid* is sponsored by Domestic Robots, Inc., which is owned by Space Technologies, Inc., which is a McNaughton firm. *Space Cop* is sponsored by Atlas Cleaning Products, a subsidiary of Eurochemical, which is owned by guess who. It goes all the way through this. Every last show in the first three years of hostile programming was sponsored by a McNaughton subsidiary. Now that's no longer true, because the trend has been set and every-body's leaping on the bandwagon."

Fu smiled like a saint who has just been granted beatific vision. "Boy, I can see I'm going to have to make some real changes in this study before I use it in my thesis! There's one real flaw in all this, though."

"I know," Thor said. "Why the hell would the world's biggest space exploitation company want to torpedo the whole idea of manned settlement of space? They're cutting their own throats."

"Obviously," Fu said, "we're working from incomplete data. There's a factor or factors that're not in our calculations. It could well be that the answers are not to be had here. It might involve the politico-economic situation in the offworld settlements."

"That could well be," Thor admitted. "In any case, I'm going to put a few people onto this and see what I can turn up. Do you have pretty good connections in the professional holo community?"

"I know some people," Fu said. "What do you need?"

"I'm wondering about the Media Writers' Guild. The producers only worry about money and schedules, the studios are interested only in audience share and profit margin but somebody has to write this stuff. If I was looking to get control of what people see in the holos, the writers' guild is the first place I'd try to control. Maybe the directors' guild, too."

"I'll get on it," Fu said. "I won't even charge you for the service."

"If you need money to buy information, let me know," Thor said. Fu signed off and Thor keyed a limited-access number he had never used before. He hoped Bob was at home and not out terrorizing New Jersey or something.

Bob was standing behind a rough wooden table with a motorcycle engine in pieces before him. He looked up irritably, then smiled. "Thor! Wasn't expecting to hear from you. Where are you?"

"L.A. Bob, I'm sending you a study on holoprogramming and I want to tell you about what I've been up to. Sorry to be so abrupt, but I think this is important."

"Send it over," Bob said. He disappeared from range while he fed a crystal-carrier into his set, then he returned. "Now, let's hear it."

Briefly, Thor told his story. Bob looked uncharacteristically somber during the recitation. "I must say," he said, when Thor was finished, "when you decide to rejoin the world, you don't waste time. This looks even worse than I'd feared. The change in attitude in pop holos I already knew about. I didn't think that it was some kind of plot, for Chrissake. I sure as *hell* didn't think that McNaughton was behind it. Damn!" He fumed for a while. "I told you you'd been out of touch. I've been worse. All this has been going on under my nose and I should've known about it. I'm going to have to do some digging."

"Bob," Thor said, "don't go in blustering and shooting your mouth off. I have a bad feeling about this."

Bob smiled frostily. "I didn't get to be this old by being careless. I'm sorry now that I made such a scene at the party. They'll be watching me. Believe me, Thor, where sex, money or politics are involved, people won't hesitate to kill you. The only thing missing here is sex and it may turn up yet. I'll be busy, but I'll keep a low profile. I have a controlling interest in one or two security agencies, you know. I'll put some people to work. Send me the code for your friend Fu. He sounds like somebody I should get to know. Us pro-spacers may have to go underground soon, and it's not too early to start setting up an organizational apparatus."

"You think it's coming that quick?" Thor asked.

"These people have been at work on this for a long time," Bob said grimly. "You've seen for yourself how far back it goes. They'll make their moves very quickly now that they're in the open. I think it's time for you to see my buddy Swenson. Catch a flight for Montana later today. I'll tell him you're coming."

"Montana?" Thor said. That was cowboys-and-Indians country, never developed beyond the agricultural stage even in this century.

"Yep. He runs a field station there. Protects endangered species of birds."

"Birds?" Thor was flabbergasted. "Tell me more."

The station was tucked into a cleft in the high mountains where the winter's snow still lingered. As the hired rotocraft settled onto the little meadow before the

station, the door swung open and a man emerged. Thor
had expected someone of Bob's generation and was
surprised to see that Swenson was little older than
himself. He was a vision from another century, dressed
in jeans and plaid lumberjack shirt, with logger's boots
and a stetson hat. He waved and Thor climbed from the
rented vehicle. They shook hands and Thor took a deep
breath of the thin, mountain air. It was a change from
L.A.'s sea-level air and smelled much cleaner.

"Come on inside, Mr. Taggart," Swenson said. "From
what Bob said to me, we have a lot to talk about."

As they walked toward the station, an unpretentious
prefab building, Thor spotted a small bird perched in a
nearby pine. It had a striking blue head and red beak.
"I never saw one like that around Denver," he said,
indicating the bird.

"Not likely you would have," Swenson said. He had a
trace of Norwegian accent. "That one's from the Peruvian
Andes. It likes the altitude here. The wildlife up there
has been dying off fast, since the Amazon basin industrialized. I'm not sure how long the air up here will stay
clean, though."

"I thought North American air had been clean for
years," Thor said.

"That's a popular misconception," the young man
answered. "What got cleaned up was low-level urban
air. And only in the first world countries. It's destruc-
tively polluted in South and Central America, and in
much of Africa and Asia. And pollution isn't the worst
of it. The deforestation of the Amazon basin has cut into
the oxygen supply."

"I've been hearing about that for years," Thor admitted as he passed through the door. "I thought it was
mostly alarmist talk."

"Not any more. Oxygen levels are dropping danger-
ously worldwide. Even here in the U.S. agriculture is
no longer profitable at some higher elevations. The air's
getting too thin to breathe. Can I get you some coffee?"

"Thanks." Thor looked around the little building. It
was as plain and Spartan as a Ranger station, and he got

the impression that Swenson spent little time indoors. There was a bunk, a table with two chairs, cooking equipment, a holoset and little else. Swenson set a pot of water on a heater. It seemed that he actually brewed his own coffee. They took seats at opposite sides of the table.

"Bob Ciano tells me," Swenson began, "that you're having some problems with the government that I may be able to help you with."

"That's the case. Did he tell you anything about the nature of my difficulties?"

"Just that you want to emigrate and that it now looks as if all your earthside assets could be seized."

"Right. He tells me that your foundation is in serious financial trouble. It seems we have a community of interest. Over the next few weeks, I'd like to funnel several hundred million into your foundation. Your share of the total sum is fifteen percent."

"You're being awfully trusting. How do you know I wouldn't just take all of it?"

"Bob trusts you, and I trust his judgement. And, to be truthful, I don't have many options. My financial skills aren't the best and I have very little time."

Swenson got up and checked on the coffee. He returned to the table with two thick, old-fashioned china mugs. "What about the interest?"

"I'm not sure when I'll be calling that money back in. Any interest it earns in the meantime we split fifty-fifty."

Swenson thought for a moment. "You're talking about an awfully large contribution to my little foundation here. I can spread it out among some others. That way it'll do a lot more good here and look less suspicious."

"Fine," Thor said. "The more holes it's hidden in, the harder it'll be to trace. Once I'm established offworld, I intend to set up another charitable foundation. When I send you word, you're to transfer the funds, minus your percentage, to the new fund. That should keep you in the clear should the feds come nosing around."

"As long as my foundation and I are in the clear, it sounds good," Swenson said.

"There should be no problem. I'm under no suspicion at the moment. By the time the Council suspects that I've emigrated for good, the money should be safely out of your hands and you're clean. You just transferred a donation from one charitable account to another. Maybe this way I can salvage some of my inheritance and we can save a few birds in the meantime." The two men shook hands.

FOUR

It wasn't the first time he'd been to the Moon, but he had been in his teens on the last visit. He had to reaccustom himself to the one-sixth gravity, relearning the gliding moonwalk. Out on the surface, in the pressure suits, people had to use the bouncy, from-the-ankles hop made famous by the early lunar explorers. Indoors, the Lunaires had developed the glide as a more esthetically pleasing alternative.

The shuttle had set down on the pad in the middle of Armstrong Crater and the elevator had lowered the ship into the sublunar cavern housing all of the settlement's legal vessels. The armored door had slid shut overhead and a passenger umbilicus had snaked out from the nearest wall. It would have been wasteful to pressurize the entire dock.

Customs check was more thorough than he had remembered. The baggage scan was perfunctory. Between the instruments on the Earth end and those aboard the ship, it was almost impossible to sneak anything larger than a microcrystal through conventional transportation. The questioning required for visa validation was far more searching than he remembered it.

"Purpose for visit?" asked the uniformed agent. The man was ignoring Thor and staring into the screen which gave his face a phosphorescent green tinge.

"I'm going to do some caving," Thor said.

"Is this recreational, professional or scholastic?"

"Scholastic. It's part of my grad work in space-habitation engineering."

The customs man punched a code and Thor knew he was keying a list of the occupations which now required licensing. "You are aware," the man said, "that members of your profession are no longer permitted to travel off Luna except aboard earthbound vessels, aren't you?"

"Very aware," Thor said, still burning over his last interview with the Director of Graduate Studies at Yale. "It's just a formality," the self-important little boob had insisted. "We only wish to cooperate with the government on this. Before we can grant your Ph.D. in your field, you have to sign an agreement to be licensed under the new laws. Licensing would be automatic in any case, but refusal to sign would mean that we could not issue your degree."

"Not to mention that it always looks better when the victim acts content to be shafted," Thor muttered.

"I beg your pardon?" the Director said.

Thor told himself to simmer down. He had nothing to gain by disputing with this nonentity. He had no intention of honoring this atrocity, signed or unsigned. "Show me where to sign." The voice of the customs man brought him back to the here and now.

"How long do you intend to stay on Luna?"

"The full length of the visa, sixty days." He wanted to have as long a grace period as possible before people came looking for him. He saw the man's hand straying toward a pressure plate and had a sinking feeling that he was about to key a truth verifier. Thor had never had clandestine conditioning to defeat truthsnoops. He decided it was time to play his hole card. "I also plan to visit my grandparent's gravesite."

The hand hesitated. "Your grandparents were pioneers out here?"

"Yes. Samuel and Laine Taggart."

The hand withdrew from the truthsnoop. "You're one

of *those* Taggarts?" The man was enormously impressed. "Don't hide the fact. That's a respected name in these parts. Drop it from time to time and you'll get the best service in all the hotels. Here's your passport and I hope you enjoy your stay, Mr. Taggart." Thor took the carrier with its tiny crystal and sealed it into his coverall.

At the baggage-claim area Thor hired a hovercar to take him to his hotel. He stuck his card in the dashboard slot and said, "Hilton." The car's fans hissed faintly and it rose on a cushion of air. At one-sixth gee, little power was necessary to raise the little craft, and the controlled environment prevented dust from gathering in most places, so that the hovercar's passing was marked only by a slight displacement of air.

The long sublunar tunnels were brightly lit, dotted at intervals with emergency air and pressure stations, against the unlikely event of a failure of the artificial atmosphere or a breaching of the sublunar system. It was believed that only an act of sabotage or a really large meteoroid strike could cause such a failure.

"Hilton," announced the car. They were pulling into an immense undermoon complex, somewhat reminiscent of the interior of the Watts development, but in much better shape. A vast cave had been hollowed out of the lunar interior to form the settlement of Armstrong. Inside was a multitiered structure facing inward upon an open atrium. It was still the most efficient use of large indoor spaces. In the center of the atrium a fountain played, sending thin streams of water to a seemingly impossible height, from which they fell back to the pool below with stately grace, humidifying the air along the way. The sound made by the falling fluid was something Thor would never have associated with water.

Near the Hilton elevator was an entry to one of the Moon's famous birth clinics. Wealthy women frequently moved to the Moon early in pregnancy in order to endure their condition in low-gravity comfort. The low gravity bestowed a multitude of health benefits. Lower back pain, fallen arches, hernias and varicose veins were all but unknown unless one arrived with them. The Lunar settlements did a lively resort trade for Earthies seeking relief from these and other afflictions, but it was only for the wealthy.

The elevator deposited him in a lobby of modest size. No Lunar hotel had to cope with large crowds of guests. He looked for a check-in screen, but found instead an actual human clerk behind a desk. She was young, pretty, Chinese and breathtakingly slender. Native-born Lunaires had no need of the redundant muscle mass of Earthies. "May I help you?" she asked, smiling brilliantly.

"I'm Thor Taggart. I have a reservation."

"Oh, yes, Mr. Taggart. Here, let me key your card." He passed her the card and she crossed to a slot in a console and thrust it in. She moved with a grace that made him feel gross and clumsy. The finest Earth ballet dancer was a lumbering ox compared to an average Lunaire.

"Here, your room is Blue Six." She handed back the card. "I have something else for you here." She opened a drawer marked with a blue stripe and a numeral six and took out a crystal carrier. "This came for you from Chih' Chin Fu."

Thor took the carrier. "How did he—" then a suspicion struck him. "What's your name?"

"Ambrosia Fu."

"I thought as much. Why didn't he send this to me before I left?"

"He couldn't get it to you in time so he sent it along on the same ship that you took."

"And it got here before I did?"

She smiled again and performed a wonderfully expressive shrug. "It didn't go through all those tedious customs formalities. Why bother?"

"Why, indeed? I can see that Fu is going to be a valuable contact. How do I find the Earthlight Room?"

"Just take the elevator up until it doesn't go any higher. The Earthlight Room is the lounge. There's also a restaurant. They have the best view in Armstrong. Is there anything special you'd like for dinner? Irving Fu runs the kitchen."

"I might have known. No, I'm still a little queasy from the zero-gee."

"Ask the bartender for his Welcome To Luna Special. It works just about every time."

"Is he a Fu, too?"

"No, his name's Miklos, but he's a cousin. I hope you enjoy your stay."

Thor crossed the lobby to an elevator and stepped aside as a group of Hindustanis emerged and exited through the front door of the hotel, which opened onto a broad terrace overlooking the atrium. Beyond the terrace, Thor could see the lazily-arching columns of water from the fountain far below. He got into the elevator and touched the blue plate. Silently, the elevator ascended several levels and opened for him. Because of the step-back of the tiers, the elevator opened directly onto the "outside" terrace.

As he stepped from the elevator, Thor misjudged his stride and went stumbling over to the waist-high balustrade. He caught the railing and was greeted by a dizzying view of the atrium, three hundred feet below. It was frightening, but the worst consequence of a fall from this spot would have been to land atop the scantily-clad lady on the terrace twelve feet below, not at all an unattractive prospect. He reminded himself that a sheer drop of three hundred feet, at one-sixth gee, would kill him as dead as a fall of fifty feet on Earth.

He managed to make his way to his room without further mishap and let himself in. The room was spacious, its walls and ceiling heavily padded to protect careless Earthies like himself. The bed had a thin mattress, all that was necessary in the light gravity. In its center was an odd, orange cushion. Thor got his second fright of the day when the cushion got up and stretched. It was the biggest, most grossly obese tabby cat he had ever seen.

"How'd you get here?" he asked. He tickled it beneath the chin and the cat purred and kneaded the bedspread. He crossed to the screen and keyed the desk. The face of Ambrosia Fu appeared. "Yes, Mr. Taggart?"

"Who's this?" Thor asked, jerking a thumb over his shoulder toward the massive cat, who was now sitting on the bed, licking its left shoulder blade.

"Oh, that's Athos. If you see a lean, stripey gray, that's Porthos and the fluffy, all-white Persian is Aramis."

"How do they get in?"

"We use robot chambermaids, and they never notice the cats. They'll warn us of any human intruders, though. Don't let them con you into feeding them. They scavenge plenty from the kitchens and they ought to be out catching mice anyway."

"You have mice?" Thor asked.

"Oh, not the hotel! We're absolutely vermin-free. But the city has them. Don't worry, they don't carry disease. They're descendants of white lab rats that escaped into the vents and hydroponics fields fifty years ago. They're very smart little beasties."

"I should imagine. Thank you, Miss Fu."

"Just toss Athos out onto the terrace when you want him out. Are you satisfied with the room?"

"Oh. Yes, it's very pleasant. Thank you, Miss Fu." The screen winked out. He turned back in time to see the cat sail off the bed. Sail was the only word for it. It came trotting up to him, bouncing off one tiny foot at a time, its rolls of fat and fluff swaying majestically as it came up to his leg and commenced rubbing and purring. Thor stroked its back. "Haven't been here an hour and I've already made a friend."

The cat's ears perked up, it tensed, its tail twitched, and it launched itself into a fantastic leap, springing twenty feet across the room and clearing the bed by two or three feet. An instant before its front feet struck, Thor saw something white dart from beneath the paws and scurry along the wall. The door was still partly open and the little rat turned and glared at him with feral red eyes before darting out. Athos tried a fast change of direction, but his fat was still obeying Newton's laws of motion and he made a soft splat against the wall before he could work up enough traction to make a dart toward the door. He poked his broad head outside but could see nothing.

"You need to lose some weight, sport," Thor told him. "It was a good try, though. I'll have to tell Miss Fu that this place isn't quite vermin-free after all." Athos looked at him with an expression that said that this was war to the death, and charged off in pursuit of the rat. Thor didn't think much of the fat cat's chances. That had been one smart-looking rat.

He unpacked the few items he had brought and took a shower. He had forgotten how odd water felt here. As if it had the consistency of honey it oozed its way down his body and made its slow way to the drain. Dried, shaved and changed into clean clothes, he felt ready to try the city. He chose an anonymous black jumpsuit of the type worn by at least half the Lunar population and space-dwellers in general. His slick-soled shoes weren't practical here and he reminded himself to buy a pair of the locally-favored soft boots.

Armstrong worked on a round-the-clock schedule, with no attempt at a regulated "day" or "night." With ships coming in at all hours and transports to and from other lunar settlements in constant flux, households and businesses set their own hours for work, sleep and recreation. For convenience, each twenty-four-hour "day" was divided into three eight-hour shifts, observed by all government functions and by almost all manufacturing enterprises using human employees. Which shift was employed for what was largely a matter of individual choice.

Thor decided to explore the city before giving the Earthlight Room a try. He found that it was about the middle of the second shift and he knew that it would be toward the end of the shift that customers began filling up the bars and restaurants. His previous visit to Luna had been years before, and Armstrong had not been one of his stops.

He found the settlement well-populated but not

crowded. Unlike the cities of the U.S. and Europe, there were no crowds of idlers, although there were a few ship's crews raucously celebrating the end of lengthy voyages. Clothes were for the most part colorful but functional, without the determinedly eccentric touches so common on Earth. Most people seemed to be intent on some business. There were many visitors and recent emigrants like himself, and he saw quite a few of them entering or leaving the offices of agencies hiring for lunar projects or for projects farther out, on Mars, in the Belt or the even more remote Jovian and Saturnian satellites. The awkward gait of the newcomers was unmistakable.

On impulse, he decided to test the vacuum and try a few of the hiring offices. The first he walked into was a tiny, hole-in-the-wall room with a single, small desk in its center. On the door was a plain sign reading: "Rockbusters, Inc. Work Available." Behind the desk was a man sprawled uncomfortably in a lounge chair. Unlike the vigorously-bouncing Earthies and the gliding Lunaires, this man was plainly used to no gravity at all. He wore a black coverall and vest, both garments sporting a great many pockets along with snap-hooks and tie-straps for fastening things to the person. His coverall had integral stockings instead of the usual boots.

"Looking for work?" the man asked.

"Depends. What do you have to offer?"

The man ran a hand over his slick-shaven scalp. Zero-gee people usually favored little or no hair. "Name of the company kind of says it all, don't it? Rockbusters. That's what we do, we bust rock. We're a hardrock mining outfit. Highgrading, mostly. No smelting or refining, we leave that to others. Company operates out of Avalon. We have sixteen ships now and we're buying four more. Twenty per ship's crew and we work on shares. Pay depends on how much ore you bring back and how high-grade it is."

"What kind of ore do you look for?"

"U-235, mostly. We've found and exploited some of

the best rocks in the last ten years. You had any military experience?"

"No. Why, is that desirable?"

The bald man looked at him as if he were simpleminded. "I said we were high-graders, didn't I? No bulk cargoes for Rockbusters. Everybody knows it, too. We get claimjumper raids all the time. There's plenty of boosters and hijackers out there. That's one reason we work on shares. All of us have a stake in defending the cargo. Get a few successful voyages under your belt, you might have enough socked away to buy into a ship of your own. It's hard work and it's dangerous, but it pays. You interested?"

"Maybe. Let me check around. By the way, do you know of a man named Martin Shaw?"

The man stared at him, utterly without expression. "Never heard of him."

Two more hiring offices turned out to be another mining outfit and a freighting company, neither of them as hard-bitten as Rockbusters, Inc., but both looking for people more robust than the standard, First World Earthie. None of them had ever heard of Martin Shaw, either. Pointedly.

The next office came as a surprise. Lettered on the door was, simply: "Sálamis." The man behind the desk rose to shake his hand. He was tall and spare and he wore a silver-gray coverall with high, black boots and shoulderboards striped red and gold. Oddest of all, he wore a holstered pistol at his belt. "Good day, young man. I'm Captain Moore, the enlistment officer."

"Enlistment officer?" Thor said. "I'm Thor Taggart."

The tangled gray eyebrows raised fractionally. "Taggart. I might have known. Those genes stand out. Was General Taggart your grandfather?"

"Yes. I never knew him, though."

"I saw him a few times when I was an enlisted man. I served under two of your uncles and one of your aunts as well. Are you considering carrying on the family tradition and taking up the military profession?"

"To tell you the truth," Thor said, "I just got to Luna

a few hours ago. I've been looking into the possibilities of extra-terrestrial employment and happened to notice your office. Just what *is* Sálamis?"

"Sálamis is an asteroid, approximately twenty kilometers by five kilometers by two, which has become a military establishment. A man your age could do worse than enroll in our academy. After a four-year course you would enter the outerworld armed forces as a commissioned officer."

"Actually, I've spent all the years I want to in universities. Ah, I was wondering, just what do you *do*? Last I heard, there was no employment for a military force out there. The Space Force and Marines, such as they are, seem to have a monopoly."

"That will change, in time," Moore said, calmly. "Someday, there will be a call for an organized military arm among the space settlements. Until that time, we keep the military tradition alive."

"But, how is all this financed? Are you mercenaries?"

Moore regarded him frostily. "If you mean are we hired guns for anyone with a private war to fight, the answer is decidedly 'No.' We take an occasional security mission, just to keep in practice, but we would never undertake aggressive operations. We have an endowment and find our funding to be adequate." He smiled ruefully. "You'll have noticed that I'm pretty old for a company-grade officer. When I retired from the Spacer Marines, I was a lieutenant colonel. As always, promotion is slow in peacetime. That, too, is a situation I expect to change before long. Until then, there are always a few who prefer the military life."

"If you don't mind my asking, why did you resign a field-grade commission to start at the bottom out here?"

"Actually, I do mind. But I'll make an exception since you're a relative of some of my favorite C.O.'s. I spent my career watching a proud service become a petty police force putting down brushfire insurgencies on Earth and harrassing honest settlers out here. Pretty soon, we were going to be down to rounding up political dissidents and guarding them in detention camps. I didn't want to stick around to see that, so I resigned and emigrated. I'd rather spend a career toting a rifle as a private than see my profession prostituted. So that's my story. Now I'll give you some advice. On Sálamis, we go by the old Foreign Legion rules: Never ask a man about his past."

"I'll remember that. And I appreciate your candor. By the way, do they really let you carry a sidearm around here?"

Moore smiled and sat back in his chair. "Only after they've confiscated the power pack. But it's part of an officer's uniform so I wear it anyway. Keep us in mind, Mr. Taggart. You may decide that a military career is what you need after all."

"I'll think about it." As he reached the door, Thor turned back. "By the way, have you ever heard of—oh, forget it."

"You mean Martin Shaw?" Moore asked.

"Yes," Thor said, surprised.

"I never heard of him either," said Moore, solemnly.

By the time Thor had located a clothier's and purchased a pair of soft boots, it was near the end of shift. He decided to give the Earthlight Room a try. The lobby of the Hilton was empty and the same impossibly thin Chinese girl was behind the desk.

"Any messages for me, Miss Fu?" he asked.

She looked up blankly, then smiled. "'Oh, you must be Mr. Taggart."

"Don't you remember?"

"I'm not Ambrosia. I'm her sister. We're twins," she added, unnecessarily.

"Don't tell me, let me guess. Would your name be Nectar?"

"You win no prize for that. No, no messages. Is your room satisfactory?"

"Fine. But there was a rat in it, and Athos was too slow to catch it."

She rolled her eyes upward theatrically. "They're everyplace. And they get smarter every year. There's some kind of weird accelerated evolution going on here.

They know all about doors and traps and poisons. I think they'll take over some day."

"Well, should anybody be looking for me while the rats are plotting, I'll be in the Earthlight Room for the next two or three hours." He stepped into the elevator and keyed it for the top level. Above the residential levels, the elevator tube emerged from the step-back of the hotel and for a minute he had a breathtaking view of the entire atrium. Then the tube disappeared into an overhead structure of spidery struts and buttresses. As he passed through the supports, he caught a glimpse of furry, white forms darting among them. Then the elevator was inside the overhead structure, rising through several meters of solid moon rock before entering the bar-restaurant complex. He had gone over the charts provided by his room screen, and he knew that the Earthlight Room was actually part of the spaceport complex, and there were other entrances besides the Hilton tube. On reflection, it only made sense. Modern though it looked, the Earthlight Room was built in one of the oldest structures on the Moon, and a man as shady as Martin Shaw would never frequent a hangout without plenty of bolt-holes.

The elevator let him out on a broad terrace from which steps led down in two directions. To his left was the restaurant, to his right the bar. At his back was a wall of lunar rock, part of a natural cliff. He decided to try the bar first. The view from the top of the steps was fabulous, and he paused for a moment to admire it.

The bar was on a slight rise of ground with a cliff at its back, overlooking the landing pads. Beyond the pads stretched miles of lunar plain, ending abruptly in another towering cliff. Above the far cliff was the impossibly blue sphere of Earth, wreathed in bands of white cloud. He could just make out the eastern coast of Asia, the Malay archipelago and the bulk of Australia. Most of what was visible was blue Pacific.

The bartender was young, with Mediterranean features and curly, black hair. He was polishing a vacuum-blown glass, about two molecules thick and nearly unbreakable. It was made of the same material as the vast window that slanted overhead from the face of the cliff to the lunar surface.

Thor seated himself on one of the spindly stools at the bar. "Are you Miklos?" he asked.

The bartender nodded. "What can I serve you?"

"Ambrosia Fu says your Welcome To Luna Special is good for an upset stomach."

"Just arrived, eh? I'll fix you right up." The bartender turned his back to preserve the mysteries of his craft as he arched liquids for spectacular distances into the goblet he had been polishing. He presented the completed product with a flourish. Thor sampled it and found that it did, indeed, have a settling effect on his stomach.

"That's just what I needed," Thor said. "By the way, I've heard that a certain Martin Shaw frequents this place. I need to meet with him."

"I've never head of any such person," Miklos said, in a low voice. "However, when he doesn't come in, the place where he won't be sitting is that table over there near the base of the window, under the rubber plant." He nodded toward the plant in question.

"When won't he be coming in?" Thor asked in an equally conspiratorial tone.

"He shouldn't be arriving in about an hour and a half," Miklos assured him.

"Good. That gives me plenty of time for dinner. What do you recommend?"

"Since it's your first day, stick with something light. The tempura plate is great. Our tanks raise shrimp better than anything on Earth." He nodded toward the blue ball in the distance.

"I'll be back," Thor said.

An hour and fifteen minutes later, he sat at the table beneath the rubber plant. The tempura had been as advertised and he was beginning to feel acclimatized. That was good, because he had a feeling that he was going to need to be in top form to deal with the mysterious Mr. Shaw.

Idly, he studied the rubber plant. It was a gene-manipulated species which looked identical to the common Earth ornamental plant, but had been engineered to double its oxygen output. Everywhere one looked in the lunar settlements, there were plants springing from pots and planters. They softened the sterile environment, recycled the atmosphere and gradually built up the supply of arable soil.

"Excuse me, sir." Thor looked up and saw a young woman who facially resembled Nectar and Ambrosia. Apparently yet another of the innumerable Fus. "I'm afraid this table is reserved at this hour. If you don't mind, I'll find you another place and bring you a drink on the house."

"I have an appointment with the gentleman in question," he lied.

"Oh, that's different," she said, doubtfully. "Please excuse me." Thor smiled and admired her as she walked gracefully away. This was getting to be better than an old holothriller. But this place was the last where he would have expected to find a classical man of mystery like Shaw.

The Earthlight Room was full at this hour, and most of the patrons were business people, pilots and other officers from the nearby port, and a large gaggle of tourists, instantly recognizable by their clothing and awkward gait. In short, the place was almost absurdly respectable. Even the stripper pirouetting on the little stage didn't detract from the middle-class atmosphere. The old art form was enjoying a revival on the Moon, and dancers from Earth were coming up to practice it, taking advantage of the kinder effect of lunar gravity on Earth dancers past their prime. Thor judged the lovely, dark-haired woman on the stage to be in her mid-forties, but nothing sagged in one-sixth gee. As he could very plainly see, she showed no signs of surgery.

"You're Taggart."

Thor whirled in his chair. Where had the man come from? Just his luck to be staring at a naked woman at the crucial first moment of his meeting with Shaw. To cover his confusion, he gave Shaw what he hoped was an arrogantly evaluating once-over.

Shaw was a man of medium height and sturdy build, dressed in a spacer's coverall absolutely devoid of insignia or ornament. His face was broad, with a dark beard framing his jaw. His cheekbones were wide and his green eyes had the slightest hint of epicanthic fold in their inner corners. His most prominent feature was his broad, bulging forehead, further emphasized by a high hairline. In classical Greek sculpture, such a brow had been the trademark of the higher gods, and it lent tremendous force to his countenance. The head was a bit large for his body, making Shaw appear shorter than he was. Martin Shaw looked like a formidable man.

"That's who I am," Thor said. "Please have a seat. We have business to discuss."

"I think I will, since this is my table. Whether we have business to discuss is another matter. What line of work do you think I'm in, Mr. Taggart?" The waitress brought Shaw a drink and left discreetly.

"It's difficult to say, since nobody's ever heard of you. Chih' Chin Fu told me you might be able to help me. I need to disappear."

"Did he tell you I was a magician?"

"Of sorts. Just hear me out, then tell me if you're interested." Briefly, Thor gave him the story of his doings since the McNaughton party. He omitted most of his financial arrangements, figuring Shaw had no real reason to know those. "Will you help me?" he asked when he was finished.

"I can. The price is two million gold."

Thor nodded. That was about ten times the pre-crisis price for a passage to a typical asteroid world, but he would have been suspicious had Shaw asked much less. Thor was running a fairly high risk of imprisonment, although he had family connections to call on in a worst-case scenario. Shaw was running a far higher risk, and consequently played for higher stakes. An easy, low fee probably would have meant a quick, unceremonious exit from an airlock somewhere outside lunar orbit. "No problem with that. Half now, half on arrival at Avalon."

"Avalon," Shaw said. "So you want to head straight for the action?"

"Being stuck on some remote rock would be a poor start for a new life."

"You're a cautious man. Payment is to this account in Panama." He took out a pad of self-destruct paper, good for twenty-four hours, and wrote out a long number with a stylus. "Make the transfer as soon as you get back to your quarters. This number becomes nonfunctional at the end of the next shift." The intricately-coded numbers used for international gold transfers were untraceable even by the most sophisticated government computers. If Shaw should disappear with the advance, Thor could absorb the loss. Instinct told him that Shaw could be trusted, though. With matters of price settled, they ordered another round and sat back. Thor noticed two men who were not drinking sitting at a nearby table. One was a thin, saturnine man with close-cropped hair and beard. The other was a villainous-looking redhead with a scarred face. Watchdogs.

"For the next few days," Shaw said, "I'll be setting up the operation. Keep up your spelunking. It's good training for the island worlds and that's how we'll engineer your disappearance. We lose a few every year, out caving."

"That's about how I figured it," Thor said. "I'll leave the details up to you."

"You know, Taggart, you have a famous name, but it won't cut any ice out in the Belt. I know more Taggarts, Cianos, Kurodas, Tarkovskys and such than you do. It takes more than a name, out there."

"Not to mention that you don't have much use for rich kids who decide to skin out for cushy jobs in the Belt because they're bored on Earth."

Shaw smiled very slightly. "That, too. They do come in handy as paying customers, though. And in any case, you'll find that cushy jobs are hard to come by out there."

"That suits me. I intend to make my own way. I'm good at what I do and I'm not going to waste my life as a jumped-up bureaucrat for some Earth agency."

"That's good," Shaw said, approval in his manner for the first time. "Maybe young Chih' Chin wasn't wrong about you, after all. He says you spotted some things in your media scan that he'd missed."

"There are still a lot of holes in it," Thor admitted, "but I think we can crack the problem."

"I hadn't been keeping up with the Earth media lately. That's an oversight in an old radical publisher, I admit. I've been more action oriented lately. I think I can clear up one or two things, though, especially about McNaughton." The way he pronounced the name bespoke little affection for the clan.

"That's been the major mystery," Thor said. "Why are they torpedoing their own operation?"

"We'll have plenty of time to talk about it," Shaw said. "We have a long trip ahead of us. Right now, I have other matters to attend to." He glanced at his watch. "Just do your caving, be visible, do all the usual tourist stuff. I'll be in contact in a few days."

As Shaw was leaving Thor called, "Mr. Shaw."

He turned. "Yes?"

"Tell me something: Is it possible to pick a direction and throw a rock around here without hitting a Fu?"

"There isn't a bookmaker on Luna who'd give you odds," Shaw said. As he left, the two watchdogs got up and followed. No employee of the Earthlight Room paid the slightest attention. Shaw might as well have been invisible.

FIVE

"He's a dangerous man," Moore said. Now that Thor had actually met Shaw, people were a little freer in talking about him, but not much. Like any other small, tight community, Armstrong thrived on gossip, and within twenty-four hours of his interview with Shaw, everyone in the nonofficial culture seemed to know about it. The Sálamid officer had left his recruiting duties for the afternoon and they toured the little museum next to the casino.

"What other kind of man would take up his occupation?" Thor asked. He stopped before a holograph of Sam and Laine Taggart's tombsite. The recorded narration droned on about the freak meteoroid strike of '36, in which they had died.

"Don't get me wrong," Moore said. "Smuggling and immigrant-running are respectable occupations out in the Belt. But Shaw is more than that. He's a revolutionary, and when an independence movement really gets going out here, I expect him to be in the middle of it."

"Chih' Chin said that he'd been involved in revolutionary activities back on Earth, underground publishing, bomb-planting, that sort of thing. I'd think that's just the kind of man who'll be needed when the colonies finally decide to make the break."

"He's the wrong kind," Moore said. "Nothing wrong with his spirit, and I don't know what his ideals are, but I've dealt with him a few times and I know what his tactics will be. Terrorism. He'd never spend years in tedious organizing and building up a viable economic-military base when setting off a few bombs might do the trick. It's the kind of thing that brings about massive retaliation."

"It sounds as if you Sálamids have been studying the problem," Thor observed.

"Scenario construction is a large part of military staff work in peacetime," Moore said. "If you don't work out contingencies and continually update them with new data, you foster stagnant thinking and you're caught flatfooted when the action starts. Mr. Shaw figures prominently in our projections." He paused, carefully considering his words. "You might, too."

Thor looked up from the holo, surprised. "What do you mean?"

"It's coming fast, Thor. The independence movement, I mean. They're dreadfully disorganized out there. You'll have to see it to believe it. Someone has to pull those people together and it shouldn't be left to the likes of Martin Shaw. A young man like you, from one of the first families of space settlement, could make a real difference."

Thor shook his head. "I'm going out there to work, not to play politics. But what about you Sálamids? I'd think if there's going to be action you'd be in on it."

This time it was Moore's turn to shake his head. "We're pledged to wait for a constitutional government to represent the bulk of the settlers, then we'll put ourselves under its orders. Anything else leads to military government, which is bad for the governed and ruins the military."

"Well, I'm afraid you'll have to look elsewhere for your Washington or Lenin or whatever." Moore nodded sorrowfully, but when Thor's back was turned he smiled.

*   *   *

Caving helped keep Thor in top condition. Moving around on the Moon only *looked* easy to Earthies. Each day he chose a more distant, remote cave to explore. He wanted that on the record. When he wasn't caving, he spent a lot of time in the one-gee gym, where Earthies could keep their bodies in shape for a return to full gravity. Thor had no intention of returning, but he knew that, at the best of times, life in the island worlds involved hard work and great physical hardship.

He was rapidly getting bored. He had been here almost a month, and even lunar caving and exploring could lose its charms. If he had been involved in one of the new development projects it might have been different, but he was just a glorified tourist. He returned from his latest caving expedition to find Porthos and Aramis tussling on his bed and a message light on the holoscreen. He tossed the cats out onto the terrace and keyed the message. He was rewarded with an intricate series of numbers, belonging to no code he had seen used locally. Excitedly, he keyed it in. After a few moments, Martin Shaw appeared. "It's about time you got back," he said, irritably.

"It's about time you got in contact," Thor answered. After all, it was his two million in gold.

"Be ready for departure tomorrow afternoon."

"Tomorrow!" Thor said, both excited and outraged. "That doesn't give me much time."

"Tough," Shaw said unsympathetically. "Things are getting tight around here and we have to move fast. Tomorrow morning you'll go caving. Here's your grid coordinates." The screen flashed an eight-digit number and Thor copied it down. "The cave you're going to explore is designated A-7 in that grid square. It's been visited a few times, so the dust is disturbed enough to confuse things. Bring along as much as you can carry in your kit bag. Anything else just leave in your room. We'll get it to you later."

"What do I do when I get to the cave?"

"You'll be met there. Just follow instructions and it'll look like you went in and never came out."

This was it. This was the final break. After he took this step, he would be a criminal, by Earth anti-space emigration laws. "I'll be there," Thor said.

"Going out again today, Mr. Taggart?" The attendant was polishing a helmet which didn't need it. "You're the most enthusiastic explorer we've had through here in a long time." He gestured at the near-empty airlock facility. Over in a corner, a small geology class was suiting up under the supervision of their professor.

"If I'd wanted to stick to indoor activities I'd have stayed on earth." Thor was already suited up except for his helmet, his bulging kit bag slung across his back.

"You planning a longer trip than usual?" the attendant asked, eying the bag.

"I may stay out for a few days this time. I've been building up my endurance, you know. I'm tired of getting out to my site then having to turn around and head back after just a couple of hours underground."

The attendant looked doubtful. "I wouldn't advise it, not alone. Fatigue can catch you from behind and you can lose track of time easy."

"I can handle it," Thor said, confidently.

The man shrugged. "It's your neck. Okay, if you'll come over here, we'll get you checked out." They crossed to the parking area and the attendant slapped the dust shield of a moonbuggy. "I'm giving you the same one you had yesterday, D-17. She's fully fueled and you have oxy tanks, rations and water for a week. Your distress signal's been checked out and everything's in working order. Sign here, please." While Thor signed the sheet on the clipboard, the attendant made entries in the logbook that stayed with the buggy.

Thor climbed in and disengaged the brake. Slowly, he rolled the spindly vehicle into the airlock and waved at the attendant as the hatch closed behind him. He dogged down his helmet and his respirator engaged automatically. When he was satisfied that everything was in order, he got out of the buggy and pressed the wall switch, holding it down as the air was pumped from the lock. He felt his suit inflate slightly as the exterior pressure dropped. Slowly, the door opened. He continued to press the wall-switch. Had his hand dropped from the switch, the door would have shut immediately and the chamber would have repressurized. It was an old safety precaution.

The hatch was fully opened and he remounted. On its oversized, metal-mesh tires, the buggy rolled out onto the lunar surface. No matter how many times he did this, it was always a thrill. He wondered if deep space would have anything to match it. Here near the settlement, decades of traffic had cleared away most of the dust, but it began to fly as soon as he was a half-kilometer away, the plumes thrown up by his mesh tires falling back almost vertically with no supporting air. He always had an urge to floor it as he had with his old Porsche, but he restrained himself. Now was no time for a real accident, when he was engineering a fake one.

The flatscreen map in front of him gave his current position as well as his destination, laid out neatly in map grid form. He rotated the flat image ninety degrees and was given a three-dimensional schematic of the terrain ahead. His path wound between the abrupt, uneroded cliffs and rock formations which characterised so much of the lunar surface. The eerie silence gave the journey a deceptive monotony, and Thor knew that he had to keep alert every moment. As the attendant had said, there were a lot of ways to die out here. The airless environment was utterly unforgiving.

From time to time, he crossed over lines of footprints or the tracks of surface vehicles. Here and there, the radiating lines of a spacecraft takeoff or landing scarred the terrain. The marks might have been left days, years or decades before. The dust of Luna could lie undisturbed for centuries.

Four hours of travel brought him to the cave designated A-7. He checked the holographic image against the cave before him to make sure. He'd feel awfully silly if he ended up going into A-6 by mistake. Nope, this was the one. He drove up to the entrance and saw that there was a scattering of tracks and footprints, attesting to the few mapping expeditions that had come to this remote spot.

Carefully, he went through the normal routine he would have followed had this been an ordinary outing. He dismounted from the buggy and removed the air tank he had been using. He replaced it in its rack and took a fresh tank and clipped it on. He took three packs of semi-liquid rations, as if he intended to spend a full shift inside. Each tank was good for that much air. He made sure that the buggy was parked well in the open, so that it could be easily spotted from above, then he picked up his kit bag and walked to the cave entrance.

When he was about twenty meters away from the entrance, he noticed the rope dangling down the cliff face and hanging into the entrance, just clear of the floor. He looked up and saw a suited figure at the top of the cliff. A voice, not Shaw's, came over his helmet speaker.

"Just walk on in, just like you would for a regular trip. As you pass, grab hold of the rope and go inside with it, past the dust. Clip the rope to one of your shoulder D-rings and tug on it twice. I'll haul you up. Don't try to climb, just use your hands and feet to stay clear of the cliff face. Got it?"

"Check," Thor said. He strode into the cave, catching the rope in one hand. The dust ended abruptly a few meters past the entrance. He walked a few steps more, so that he left faint, dusty footprints on the bare stone, then he stopped. The rope terminated in a snap-hook and this he fastened to the D-ring atop his right shoulder. He gave the rope two sharp tugs and gave a little bound to clear the floor as the man above began hauling.

He sailed backward through the entrance, his feet now several meters above the floor. As he came up to the cliff face, Thor pushed away from the rock. If the man above was alone, he had to be very powerful. Even in one-sixth gee, a suited man with a full kit bag was no small weight to haul hand-over-hand. At the top of the cliff, the man grasped him beneath the arm and helped him scramble over the lip of the cliff, which had been covered with a polymer sheet to keep them from leaving marks.

"All okay?" the man asked.

"Right," Thor answered. He did a quick check of his suit and gear and found all well.

"Careful, now. We're going along that ridge of rock." The man pointed to a long hump of rock behind them. Thor could make out nothing of the man's face through the opaqued visor. He stepped onto the ridge while his companion gathered up the polymer sheet behind them. The ridge was steep on both sides, leaving only a narrow, sharp edge in the center. It made for precarious balance, but little dust could settle on the edge and they left no tracks.

The ridge ended two kilometers from the cave, and Thor saw a moon buggy, much like the one he had left at the cave, parked beneath a camouflage net. Behind the rear wheels was rigged a contraption Thor failed to recognize.

"Climb into the rear seat," said his guide.

Thor stowed his kit bag while the other man took down the camouflage net. "What's your name?" he asked.

"Mike," the other grunted, plainly not interested in exchanging pleasantries.

Thor climbed into the rear seat and Mike took the controls. The buggy started up and headed north at moderate speed. Curious, Thor turned to look at the apparatus hanging behind the mesh wheels. The dust raised by the wheels was caught in a metal trough and sifted back onto the lunar surface. There were no tire tracks left in the dust behind them.

"How far are we going?" Thor asked.

"You'll know when we get there."

Thor settled back and ran a routine systems check. Everything was in order. "How long will they look for me?" Thor said. "Those caves can be pretty dangerous. I'd hate for—"

"Nobody's going to waste a lot of time on you," Mike

interrupted. "They won't start looking for days. They'll see your prints going in, they'll see you only used two tanks, and they'll know they're looking for a dead man. Hard enough staying alive out here without running extra risks for a stiff. They'll write you off and head back for Armstrong. Relax."

In a way, it was a relief. He hated to think of an elaborate rescue operation being mounted for him, with people risking their lives because of his ruse. On the other hand, it was a bit humbling. Back on Earth, the disappearance of a scion of a family like his would mean turning out the fleet and searching for weeks. If they were this tough on Luna, what would the Belt be like?

Thor nodded off, but was jerked awake abruptly when the buggy halted at a nondescript outcropping of rock. "Get out and give me a hand," Mike said. Puzzled, Thor dismounted as Mike crossed to the rock and pried a section away. It swung open on hidden hinges and inside Thor saw a clutter of gear, most of which he could not identify. In one corner was a rack of laser rifles and handguns. All such weapons were highly illegal for civilians to possess. Thor helped Mike stow the camouflage net, then they unbolted the track-hider gadget from the back of the buggy. Apparently, this was a clandestine warehouse for smugglers to store the equipment they could not afford to be caught with. As they drove away Thor noticed that the area they had entered was heavily-trafficked, with crisscrossing tire tracks everywhere he looked. That seemed odd. He had assumed that they were headed for some clandestine smuggler's port. This looked like the area near Armstrong.

They passed through a gap in a low ridge and then were looking out onto a broad plain flooring an ancient crater. One high wall of cliffs on the edge of the crater was studded with lights. "That's Armstrong!" Thor said.

"Of course it's Armstrong, you dummy," Mike said disgustedly. "You want to get off Luna, don't you? Well you need a spaceport for that." He drove the buggy onto a crushed-gravel road slanting down the low crater wall. "Amateurs," Mike groused. "I hate dealing with amateurs!" Thor decided to keep his mouth shut from then on. As they crossed the crater floor, a spidery landing craft descended to the floor on a plume of white-hot gas. It settled onto a pad and was lowered beneath the lunar surface.

Instead of heading for the airlocks of the main facility, to which Thor had always returned from his outings, Mike steered for a long row of utility locks near the landing pads. This area was a warren of old warehousing caves, tunnels, abandoned military facilities and other derelict structures. Even the short history of lunar settlement had been sufficient to produce this tangle of semi-abandoned facilities, and Thor suspected that some of the confusion was deliberate. He had studied several maps of this region, and all of them were mutually contradictory.

They passed through an airlock hatch with a number code painted on its face, over several earlier generations of numbers. The machinery was antiquated but well-maintained. Good machinery would last nearly forever on Luna, free from the corrosive effects of an atmosphere and its attendant moisture and microorganisms. Mike left the buggy in the lock and Thor unshipped his kit bag as the inner hatch cycled open. He followed Mike into a long, featureless corridor carved roughly out of the lunar rock and both men pulled off their helmets. Mike was the scar-faced redhead who had sat at the table near Thor and Shaw in the Earthlight room.

They passed into a room where silent men were working busily, packing things into crates and bundles. Thor and Mike climbed out of their suits and Mike called one of the men aside. "Get all the ID numbers off this suit," he held up the suit Thor had been wearing, "and sell it over in Armstrong or someplace." He flashed Thor a very brief, gap-toothed grin. "Moonsuit won't do you no good where we're going. You'll need a rockjumper suit out there."

They passed through a maze of tunnels and rooms. Mike seemed to navigate by cryptic marks painted on the walls in a multitude of colors. Then they were in Warehouse 17. Thor knew that this was a private facility rented by one of the outerworld transportation concerns. "Put your bag there," Mike said, pointing to a wheeled cart stacked with personal kit bags. Thor tossed his on the top of the heap and followed Mike into a small room opening off the main warehouse area. To his surprise, it was a small bar. The tables were thinly occupied by spacers and dock workers, and a few people were playing electronic games at the bar, with the loser paying for the drinks. Mike strode to the rear of the room.

"Here he is, Boss," Mike said.

Martin Shaw looked up from the table where he sat with the other man Thor had seen in the Earthlight Room, the dark one with the stubble of hair and beard. "Have a seat, Taggart," he invited. Thor and Mike both sat.

"You disappoint me, Mr. Shaw," Thor said.

"How so?"

"Well, first the Earthlight Room, now this." He waved at the busy warehouse facility beyond the barroom door. "It's all kind of mundane. The holos back home all have people like you operating out of freewheeling buccaneer ports and clandestine landing sites, not using legitimate facilities."

Shaw showed the very faintest of smiles. "What do they know of people like me? Besides, hidden ports may sound romantic, but the idea is impracticable. There are damn near a century's worth of spy satellites orbiting around this rock. A kid couldn't launch a toy rocket out away from the settlements without something picking it up. No, smugglers have always known that even better than clandestine ports are ports with a large volume of legitimate traffic, so large that official inspection is perfunctory at best. And best of all is official cooperation."

"People are packing up here to leave," Thor said. "Is that why the short notice I got?" A little, wheeled robot waiter came by the table and Thor punched an order.

The drink was duly delivered up from the robot's innards, in an inelegant but unbreakable plastic tube.

"You keep your eyes open," Shaw admitted. "Yes, I'm closing down lunar operations. It's been good here, but the new laws are cracking down hard. Mike will stay back to close down our facilities and sell off everything we're not taking with us. I've decided to clear out now, before they shut off all our exits. Some of my competitors are staying around. People are getting desperate to get out and are paying high prices. That's acting greedy and they're going to regret it. They'll be caught when the net goes out." Shaw seemed to be much more relaxed than the last time Thor had seen him, almost friendly. Perhaps the decision to pack up and go had relieved him of a lot of tension.

"So you think the isolationists and Earth Firsters are going to win?" Thor asked.

"They've won," Shaw said. "They won years ago, but most people are just waking up to it. I saw it coming long before I left Earth. The signs were all there."

Thor nodded, thinking of his casual, popular-media survey. "I know, but they were pretty subtle signs."

Shaw shook his head gently. "Only if you weren't paying attention. Most people weren't. But I was a political activist. Unfortunately, most of my fellow radicals were unable to see beyond their short-term goals. They wanted things better for Singapore, or Zanzibar, or wherever, and to hell with the rest of the world. They picked easy targets like old, bankrupt colonial powers, and big, exploitative corporations. All they wanted to do was drain wealth from some other part of the world to support their own. They talked about saving humanity, but their goals were always limited and local."

"So you headed out," Thor said.

"I was transported," Shaw corrected him, "as I'd planned. Out here, a revolutionary can do some real liberating. We have a long trip coming up. I'll give you some of my work to read along the way. It's not the kind of education you get at Yale."

The man was such a classic pirate chief that it seemed

odd to think of him writing political tracts. Yet, how much did he know of Shaw? It was plain that he was a many-faceted man. It would not do to take him at face value. "Do we leave soon?"

"In about an hour. Lazlo here is going with us. Here's your documents." He slid a crystal carrier across the table. "You're going up as a trained vacuum-welder on a three-year contract, along with about a hundred other workers and immigrants. Around half of them really are what they claim."

"Half!" Thor said. "You mean the other half are all illegal?"

"Right around that," Shaw affirmed.

"Is that because of the new laws?"

"No. For the last six decades, at least one third to one half of all outerworld immigrants have been illegal political refugees, escaped convicts, absconding embezzlers, crooks not wanting to face investigations, cashiered military personnel, disgraced younger sons, and just plain cantankerous sons of bitches who don't care to be registered and tracked by various governments. You name it, and chances are good that it's taken the low road to the outerworlds."

"Then the population out there—" visions leaped into Thor's dazzled mind.

"That's right," Shaw nodded. "It's more than twice what the official figures say, a fact that's going to cause Earth authority some real problems one of these days."

A loud bong reverberated through the facility, followed by an artificial female voice. "Passenger freighter L-96 boarding in five minutes." The message was repeated twice more.

"That's your shuttle," Shaw said. "But you won't be going up the regular passenger tube. Mike will take you in a supply van through another check point where one of the guards works for us. That ID won't get you past the passenger check. Our service rocket will take you off the Moon and transfer you to the shuttle in orbit before it reaches the space station. From there, you will be able to board my ship without problem. See you up there."

They shook hands and Mike led him to an obscure corner of the warehouse, where he climbed into the enclosed van amid a pile of unidentifiable gear. Locked inside, he thought of the risk he was taking. What was to keep Shaw from cycling him into space without a suit? Nothing, obviously. But then, Shaw impressed him as something far more than a mere profit-oriented bandit. Besides, had he intended treachery, Mike could simply have killed him and left him out on the lunar surface. So little of the Moon was actually used that a body could lie in the open for centuries without being discovered. He felt vibrations and bumps as the van's module was dismounted and put into the hold of the freighter.

Thor leaned back against a wall of the module, feeling cramped and claustrophobic. Something dug into his back and he switched on his portable light and turned to see what it was. A small, dogged hatch was fitted into the wall. It had no handle on this side and it had been one of the metal dogs that had bothered him. He wondered what a hatch was doing in such an odd location and he had no doubt that it was for some nefarious purpose. After all, he had to get out of this box somehow, and he certainly couldn't walk out through the broad front door into an unpressurized hold.

Sitting tensely in the dark, he felt the vibration and the mild acceleration of takeoff, then freefall. He closed his eyes and managed to doze for a while. A sound jerked him awake and he scrambled to the little hatch. As he had suspected, the dogs were turning. Involuntarily, he held his breath as the hatch began to open. He had a moment of panic as the pressure dropped and his ears popped, but the lowering of pressure was slight. A man wearing a respirator stuck his head through the hatch and waved urgently for Thor to come with him. Thor wormed his way through the hatch and found himself in a short, plastic umbilical tube, apparently part of some escape system leading from the hold to the ship proper.

At the end of the tube, he was pulled into a chamber about the size of the average shower stall. "Fast, into here." The man's voice was muffled by the respirator. He hustled Thor from the little room and into a much larger chamber, crowded with couches in which dozens of men, women and children were strapped. Nobody paid any attention as the man strapped Thor into an unoccupied couch. From the look of their pale, queasy faces, Thor figured that they had woes of their own to worry about. This bunch hadn't been out from Earth long, and they were still suffering from space sickness.

After a few minutes, the same man returned and strapped a man and a woman into other empty couches. Apparently, Thor was not the only passenger enjoying the Shaw cargo express on this flight. A boy of about ten turned and looked at Thor mournfully from a higher tier to his right. "They said free-fall was gonna be fun! First I spend all my time throwing up, and now I'm over that, they keep me strapped in this chair! This ain't fun!" The boy's indignation was truly massive.

"There's plenty of time for that," Thor assured him. "They'll turn you loose in the passenger ship."

"They better," the boy vowed. Sometime later, attendants unstrapped the passengers from their couches and conducted them into a space station that was crowded with emigrants from all nations. This was just a staging area, little more than a warehouse for human cargo, and little had been wasted on comfort or conveniences for those passing through. Thor spent four miserable hours, feeling grubby and unshaven. It had been a long time since he had left his room at the Hilton.

A wizened little black man in the space station's uniform floated up to him. "You Taggart?" he asked.

"That's right," Thor said.

"They'll be calling for people to board the *Spartacus* in less'n an hour. That's your ship."

"Thanks," Thor said, but the man was already floating away. From a nearby machine he took a freefall bulb of hot coffee. At least his stomach was making the transition from weak gravity to no gravity without mishap. The call for boarding the *Spartacus* came, and attendants efficiently herded the emigrants into the umbilicus connecting ship to station. As each entered, a crewman checked a name off his list. They were then conducted into the passenger compartment.

"Hold" would be a better word for it, Thor thought. He surveyed the cavernous chamber, crudely partitioned into cubicles with struts and thin plastic sheeting. Each cubicle held four emigrants, although, if desired, sheets could be removed to make room for larger families. The facilities were Spartan in the extreme, but that had been the tradition of emigrant vessels throughout history. A ship's officer was delivering a safety and emergency procedures lecture when Thor felt a touch at his elbow. It was Shaw, now wearing a freefaller's coverall, studded with rings, snap hooks and friction fasteners.

"Come on, Taggart," he said. "I'll show you my ship."

"I could use a bath and a shave first," Thor said.

"Get used to it. You think this is a luxury liner? This is a thirty-year-old freighter sold off by McNaughton when they laid in a new fleet ten years back. Strictly no-frills. We have a chemical bath you can use later on. It's not very satisfactory but your fellow passengers won't be in any better condition." The walls were covered with spongy material and Shaw pulled himself along from the hold into a long tunnel by a series of soft handholds.

"Which way are we going?" Thor asked. "I'm disoriented."

"Aft. I'm going to check the engines now. The control room is the other direction, forward. We're on auto now, just one crewman on watch to keep track of the computers."

"Are we going to get any gravity?" Thor asked.

Shaw laughed derisively. "This ship was made for cargo, not for comfort. No spin. You'll adapt. Once you're used to zero-gee, even a slight artificial gravity is uncomfortable. By the time we reach Avalon, you'll have a spaceman's stomach."

"When do we arrive?" They had reached a hatch blazing with warning signs and Shaw began to key a code onto its lock-plate.

"About two months. Our acceleration is about one-hundredth-gee, not even enough to feel."

"Sounds slow," Thor said doubtfully, "but my specialty is environment engineering, not flight dynamics."

"It is slow," Shaw said, "but in about three days, we'll be doing around thirty kilometers per second, which is about the speed at which the Earth orbits the Sun. In a month, when we start deceleration phase, we'll have hit a heliocentric velocity well in excess of what's needed to escape the solar system. If we were to just keep on going, we'd clear Neptune and Pluto eventually and disappear into interstellar space, just like all the probes." There was a wistful note in his voice. Thor figured Shaw would really like to try it. The hatch opened and Shaw went through, closely followed by Thor.

A shaven-headed woman whose scalp was painted with a spiral galaxy looked up from a bank of readout screens. "Everything's in order, Boss. Good reaction mass this trip."

"Ought to be," Shaw said. "I told Mboya I'd have his skin made into a coverall if he sent up a batch of gravel like last time."

"This ship is a duster?" Thor said.

"That's right. Old-fashioned, but it works." He pointed to a humped form covered by a molded metal housing. "That's the vaporizer. It turns angstrom-sized dust into ionized atoms. That's where that crook Mboya screwed me last time. Some of that dust he sent up was so coarse you could see individual grains with a microscope. Gave us hell on the trip out to the Belt."

"Wouldn't a hydrogen ion drive engine be more efficient?" Thor asked. "The charge-to-mass ratio of hydrogen ions is much higher than rock dust ions."

"Sure it'd be better," Shaw said, "if you can pay for it. Our cargoes aren't in that big a rush. You don't see hydrogen drive ships much except for military craft or luxury passenger liners. They carry along a tank of liquid hydrogen." He chuckled ruefully. "Hell of a thing, isn't it?"

"How so?" Thor asked.

"Hydrogen is the most abundant element in interplanetary space, but it's pretty diffuse. The only concentrated source is water, which is too precious to use for fuel. There's plenty of rock, though. We pick up dust at each end of a voyage."

"When do we leave lunar orbit?" Thor asked. There was still a slight chance of being picked up by Emigration agents. He was anxious to get away.

The woman with the tattooed head looked at him in pitying disgust. "We started fifteen minutes ago."

"A continuous-boost ship doesn't work quite like the skyrockets that take off from Earth," Shaw said. "When we left the station, we moved out at a slow walk. We're up to a steady run, and accelerating all the time. We'll get there."

Thor reddened slightly. He knew all this, but it was another thing to be actually experiencing it. In spite of himself, he still expected violent acceleration, noise, flashing lights and broadcast warnings to strap in.

The ship had several "holds," actually just enormous, detachable cylinders adapted to carry cargo or passengers. Some of these were sealed and Shaw was reluctant to reveal what was in them. For an unabashed smuggler, that suggested to Thor that some things were unacceptable, even in the freewheeling society of the space settlers. Drive, holds and control were all in separate modules, connected by struts and passage tunnels. It was a common system for ships never intended to make planetfall, allowing great flexibility of size and function. "Also," Shaw told Thor with a sharklike grin, "it makes it very difficult to keep up with how many and what type of ships are out here. If the authorities were looking for *Spartacus*, I'd break her up and rearrange her modules with other ships. You can have as many ships as you have command and drive modules."

"It must be a nightmare for customs authorities," Thor observed.

"We do our humble best. Hijacked ships are never found again because they're broken up and utilized or sold off as modules. You'll have to go to a ship sale some time. There's no pirate hangout like in the holos. Word just gets passed that there's going to be ship hardware for sale and everybody just sort of congregates at a certain set of coordinates that all the bartenders seem to know about. I've seen whole government military vessels broken up and sold, weaponry and all."

"Military!" Thor said, aghast. "I thought that was supposed to be impossible. Are there hijackers powerful enough to attack a Space Service ship?"

"Who attacks?" Shaw said. "Usually, it's just a matter of paying someone to look the other way. The degree of corruption in the higher echelons of the military is immense and has increased tremendously in the last fifteen years. It was historically inevitable. I'll let you read my monograph on the subject. There are other ways that service vessels make it onto the black market. Sometimes, a whole crew will decide to take early retirement from the service and bring their ship along with them."

"I think that society out there will be quite different from what I anticipated," Thor mused.

"I can guarantee it," Shaw said.

"In the meantime, what's there to do to pass the next two months?" Thor glanced through the small viewport set in a wall of the control module. Earth and the Moon were there, but soon they would be gone and there would be nothing to look at but a starscape that would soon become monotonous.

"You're looking at the best of the sightseeing now," Shaw said. "Otherwise, you can read. This ship has an extensive library, which is true of few of them. There are holos if that's to your taste. There are limited exercise facilities, which I suggest you use daily or your muscles will start deteriorating soon. And you're going to need them if you go into any of the mining trades. People make the mistake of thinking that zero-g means that no effort is required for anything. Otherwise, there's always the spacer's religion."

"What's that?" Thor asked.

"Poker."

The poker table was riveted to the "floor" of the small recreation room. No stools were required, but the players could stay in place by means of the snap hooks on short cords set at intervals around the circumference of the table. These could be fastened to metal rings on the travelers' coveralls. Thor had already had several such rings sewn to his own outfit.

Around them, a few passengers were boredly working out with spring-loaded exercise apparatus. There were five around the table. Besides Thor and Shaw, there was a baldheaded, muscular man named Jake, a fat man called Slim, and a nondescript man named, appropriately, Joe. All three were heavy construction workers, or claimed to be.

The cards were slightly magnetized, as were the chips, which were bought with uranium-backed Avalonian currency. Thor recognized the other three from the dining facility. They seemed to hang around together much of the time. Thor had acquired the reputation of being a shrewd poker player at college, but he realized that these men played the game far more seriously than any bunch of students. From habit, Thor played a cautious game, keeping close track of the mathematical odds, remembering every card shown. After four hours of play, he noticed that the odds stayed with Jake with unmathematical consistency, especially as the pots got larger.

They had begun with petty stakes, and there had been other players at first, and they had played five-card stud. When the number dropped to six, they had switched to five-card draw. The sixth player had dropped out when the stakes had risen above her limit.

Thor began to feel distinctly uneasy about Jake's game.

He was winning consistently when Thor's hand was a good one. From the way Shaw had been betting, his hands had been good ones, too. Slim and Joe had kept in, raising the bets, then folding or losing to Jake. They seemed oddly unperturbed about the substantial sums they were losing. Thor was sure of the collusion but he didn't know how to prove it, or what to do about it if he could prove it.

Jake was dealing. Shaw, at Jake's right, cut the cards and the big man picked up the deck, his thick, working-man's hands flicking out the cards with incongrous delicacy. Thor had three kings in his first hand, discarded a six and a ten and drew a pair of jacks. Jake had discarded one and drawn another, but left his hand on the table, not bothering to look at it. Joe and Slim made heavy bets and Jake looked at Thor. "You in, friend?"

Ordinarily, he would have bet heavily on a full house, but pat hands seemed jinxed in this game. Still, there was something different in this hand. It was like ozone in the air and he decided it had something to do with Shaw's attitude. He pushed two hundred dollars worth of chips forward. The uranium-backed Avalonian currency was worth more than fifty times the equivalent in degraded U.S. currency. "I'm in."

Shaw was already shoving his chips forward. "So am I." Jake picked up his cards. "And I'll raise you—" he fanned the cards and his perpetual grin faltered as he looked at them. "No, guess I'll fold." He had made a quick recovery, but Thor had caught the surprise. As Jake tried to toss his hand among the discards, Shaw's hand clamped around his wrist.

"The reason you didn't fill your hand," Shaw said conversationally, "is that I slipped a card on the bottom of the deck when I cut."

Jake looked at him levelly. "You calling me a bottom dealer?"

"If there's a nine of diamonds in that hand, you sure as hell are." He twisted the imprisoned wrist and the offending cards lay face-up on the table: a four, five, six and seven of spades, and a nine of diamonds. Shaw turned the remainder of the deck bottom-up. The bottom card was an eight of spades. "That sure would have beaten my king-high straight. Would've beaten Thor's no doubt high hand, too. What is it, Thor? Flush?"

"Full house," Thor answered, wondering where this was going to lead. He didn't have to wonder long.

"If you and these two flunkies are going to cheat," Shaw said, "you'd better stick to amateurs. I caught your system by the third hand."

Jake lashed out with a powerful punch that caught Shaw high on the cheekbone, but Shaw had released Jake's left wrist and the punch had little effect in zero-g, merely pushing both men apart. In a well-practiced move, Shaw released the hook that tethered him to the table, grabbed Jake's still outstretched right forearm with his left hand, and delivered a vicious blow to Jake's left temple, using only the first two knuckles of his right fist. With the two men thus firmly anchored together, the blow was as effective as in a one-g environment. Jake's body went limp, then the minuscule acceleration caused it to begin settling almost imperceptibly toward the floor. The brief, brutal fight had lasted perhaps two seconds.

Joe and Slim released their tethers as Shaw pushed himself back from the table. He hit the wall feet-first, with knees bent, and launched himself at Joe, aiming for his face. In midair, Shaw dextrously somersaulted and kicked Joe in the solar plexus. Shaw had no weight, but mass remains constant and the kick landed with something near the force it would have had at one-g. Joe, braced for a high attack, folded double around Shaw's foot and slammed against the padded wall to his rear.

Thor had no time to admire Shaw's virtuosity. With no warning, Slim wrapped his hands around Thor's throat and commenced to squeeze. Thor couldn't figure out why the fat man was attacking him, but decided to speculate later. He applied a flat-palmed *shomen-ate* against Slim's chin while sweeping Slim's left leg with his own right. Slim's throat-grip broke, but instead of falling back on his head, as he would have on Earth, he merely floated away. Neither of their ensuing punches and kicks had any effect, either. Thor tried a few throws with no effect besides tossing himself in confusing directions. He had never appreciated how important gravity was to classical grappling and striking.

Slim threw a punch and Thor grabbed the wrist and tried to apply a joint-locking technique. Leverage, at least, should work in zero-g. Not so. As he floated across the room to bump into an exercizing passenger, Thor had leisure to reflect upon the words of Archimedes upon discovering the mechanical advantage of the lever: "Give me a place to stand, and I will move the Earth!" Thor had the leverage, but he had no place to stand. All those years in the *dojo*, he thought. Wasted.

Anchorage was the key, he thought as he went back in. Shaw's first punch had been effective because he had locked his body and his opponent's together while delivering the blow. This time, when he caught Slim's wrist, he pulled himself in, behind Slim's back. Like a wrestler, he wrapped his legs around the fat midsection and applied a *hadaka-jime*, or "naked choke" with his arms. After a few seconds of futile struggling, Slim was unconscious, the blood supply to his brain cut off. Thor released him before any permanent damage could be done.

"Not bad, for a beginner," Shaw said. He was idly chatting with a crewman, pointing out the subtleties of the combat.

"Where were you?" Thor said indignantly. "You started this."

"Me?" Shaw's eyes went wide with hurt innocence. "They were cheating. I couldn't let them get away with it."

"Then why didn't you give me a hand?" Thor said.

"There was only one after you," Shaw pointed out reasonably. "You have to learn to take care of yourself. Count your blessings, it could have been somebody far more dangerous than that clown."

The three men were coming around. "I'm fining

you three for cheating at cards and losing a fight despite a three-to-two advantage. The usual penalty for gross incompetence out here is death, but I'll let you off easy and fine you—" he counted all the chips on the table "—thirty-two hundred Avdollars. Now get out of here."

Sullenly the three made their way out. As Slim was leaving, Thor said, "Hey, wait a minute. Why did you attack me? I wasn't doing anything."

"Hell," Slim said with an upside-down shrug, "you was there, wasn't you?"

"Good enough reason," Shaw observed.

"Some of those chips are mine," Thor protested.

"That's your fee for the freefall combat lesson. I'll work out with you daily from now on, no charge."

"Thanks," Thor said, "it looks like I'll need to know how it's done. But, why are you taking me under your wing? I'm just another paying passenger."

"You're a man with a future, Taggart, if you live. Once you drop your silly Earthie notions and gain a little experience, you could become a real power out in the outerworlds."

Moore had said much the same thing, back in Armstrong. What did others see in him that he himself didn't? It was time for a change of subject. "Why did you let those thugs off so easy? They attacked the captain of the ship, didn't they? Aren't you going to clap them in irons or make them walk the plank or something?"

Shaw clapped him on the shoulder, an odd gesture in their contorted bodily juxtaposition. "You have a lot to learn, Thor. That which happens at the card table occupies a frame outside most law and custom. Put briefly, if you can't handle the situation, don't sit down to play. If they'd attacked me under any other circumstances, or acted insubordinate or rebellious to my position as captain, I'd have put them on the vacuum diet. When I took a place at the table, I became simply another gambler."

"But they were cheating!" Thor said.

"Out here, cardsharping is damn near a respectable

occupation. The disgrace isn't in cheating, it's in getting caught. Those three were so obvious it was laughable. Even you caught on after a while."

"I have my moments," Thor said, stiffly.

"Come on, let's play something less demanding. Can you play *Go*?"

That "evening," after having been soundly and expensively beaten at *Go*, Thor retired to his plastic-screened cubicle with a stack of Shaw's political and economic monographs. They had been written in a mixture of Chinese characters and phonetics, the standard written language of Singapore, but Thor's translator handled them readily. Within minutes he was engrossed. The mystery of Martin Shaw was beginning to unravel. He was a largely self-educated man, as his writing showed plainly, but he was also a brilliant and decidedly revolutionary political thinker, and he systematically exposed the bankruptcy of all the current Earth economic systems along with the corruption and obsolescence of their space settlement policies.

McNaughton came in for particular dissection. Like the British East India Company, McNaughton's Earth ownership had become a mere corps of directors who had no direct connection with their activities in space. More and more, they had left the actual work of the company in the hands of space-based subcontractors and contributed nothing to the running of the company while demanding ever-higher quotas from those who did the work. From being a developmental power in space settlement, McNaughton had become purely extractive and exploitative, a mere leech on the organism of space colonization. The space subcontractors were rebelling against McNaughton control. Thor began to understand why the corporation was backing a government crackdown on space activities. They were going to use government power to protect their profits and bring the rebellious colonists to heel.

For two months, Thor studied hard. Yes, indeed, Martin Shaw was a very, very dangerous man.

SIX

The average Earthie, confronted with the expression "Asteroid Belt," conjures up a picture of a densely-crowded ring of planetoidal rock. Thor had actually seen it pictured that way in many holos. In reality the Belt is mostly empty space, the asteroids widely separated, and only a few tens of thousands of them larger than a couple of kilometers in diameter. Spread over a volume of space with a mean heliocentric radius of about four hundred million kilometers and a width of tens of millions of kilometers, the mean distance among such asteroids is greater than the separation of the Moon and the Earth. Given the small size of the asteroids, it is rare for one even to be visible from another without instruments. Of course, for purposes of exploitation, some of the smaller asteroids had been moved closer to one another.

Avalon was not the largest of asteroids, but it was certainly among the larger ones, with a roughly spherical shape and a diameter of a little more than 100 kilometers. It had once been known by the name of an obscure Greek goddess, but it had become customary to give the permanently-settled worldlets the names of real or mythical islands, and no resident would call it anything but Avalon, legendary resting-place of King Arthur.

106

As Thor studied Avalon through the viewport, it had little of legendary glamor about it. In fact, it looked decidedly unpromising. It was a hunk of black rock hung against a bleak starscape, as austere and forbidding as an armored fortress. Bits of it were illuminated, and from time to time he saw brilliant flashes from its surface, as if the little world were under attack, but he knew that these were the flares of lasers and arc torches. Mining, tunneling and surface-altering operations went on around the clock on Avalon, most populous of the island worlds.

Avalon had been one of the first-settled asteroids, by virtue of its size and its location in a relatively crowded sector of the Belt. In recent decades, a number of smaller asteroids had been moved closer to Avalon, to have their mineral resources stripped more conveniently. It was a slow but cheap process, and Avalon was now the Belt's major center of economic activities. The nearest asteroids were rich in minerals and hydrocarbons, including unusually rich concentrations of uranium isotope 235.

Several years previously, a periodic comet with a large perihelion distance had been snagged from its old orbit and enticed to settle near Avalon, providing the all-important water. There had once been a plan to snatch Halley's Comet at the time of its perihelion approach in 2062 but the proposal had met with violent protest as an act of space vandalism and historical sacrilege. No matter, there were plenty of other comets.

Just now, that comet and its water meant one thing to Thor: a bath. The chemical bathing facilities aboard *Spartacus* had proven every bit as unsatisfactory as advertised. He was bearded and felt utterly filthy. His coverall was shabby and stained. It had been disinfected every few days by spending a few minutes of vacuum-time in the airlock, but that did nothing to improve its appearance. He had pictured himself stepping triumphantly from a luxury liner into one of the island worlds, immaculate and loaded with the prestige of his wealth and professional qualifications. Instead, he was sneaking anonymously from a smuggler's ship, a filthy tramp with no prestige and few friends.

The trip had been uneventful after the fight. Oddly, Jake and his cronies had been perfectly friendly after the altercation, and had even continued to play poker with Thor and Shaw, but with no cheating. The odd morality of space customs allowed such compartmental-ization, just as mercenary soldiers could fight a vicious battle on opposite sides of a conflict, then sit and drink together afterwards with no hard feelings.

Shaw joined Thor at the viewport. "Here's where you get off," he said.

"What will you be doing?" Thor asked.

"Organizing. Rebuilding my business after the move from the Moon. I have cargo to deliver and I'll have to arrange for more. I'll be back to Avalon pretty fre-quently from now on. Keep thinking about what you've read on this trip, Thor. The time for action is coming soon and it's going to catch most people unaware."

"I'll be thinking about it." He stuck out his hand and Shaw grasped it. Actual hand-shaking was not practiced in freefall, as it could result in injury.

Spartacus settled slowly to the surface of Avalon, the one-hundredth-g gravitation of the little planet provid-ing a scarcely perceptible landing shock. Many years before, Avalon had been provided with a spin to give it artificial gravity in the interior, so ships landed at the poles where the centrifugal effect of rotation was negli-gible. An umbilical tube extruded from the surface and latched onto the passenger lock and the passengers prepared to debark.

From the viewport, Thor could see other ships. Most of them, like *Spartacus*, could never land in any kind of real gravity, but "landing" on a planetoid like Avalon was more a matter of making physical contact, then anchoring down to keep from flying away. Enviously, he saw a luxury passenger liner moored nearby. Its hydrogen-ion engines had allowed a passage from Earth in a fraction of the time *Spartacus* had required, and the wealthy passengers had made the trip in comfort.

Through the envy, though, he felt a prideful contempt. What kind of *real* spacer needed such amenities?

Spartacus was docked at the north pole. The passengers pulled themselves along the umbilicus and through two airtight doors to a large room labeled "health check." A woman in a nondescript coverall directed each passenger to thrust an arm into a diagnostic instrument while she watched its display screen. Thor stuck his arm in and felt a slight stinging sensation.

"Okay, you're clean," the woman said. "Next."

"Don't you want to see any ID?" Thor asked.

"What for? What you call yourself is your business. We just want to know if you're carrying anything that's contagious. Your blood's just been checked and cleared. You also have a UV tattoo on the inside of your wrist. It'll show up on a health check."

"Which way is Customs and Immigration?" he asked.

"No such thing. There's a reception hall past that hatch." She pointed to a large door in a far wall. Bemused, Thor passed through it. In the large room beyond, people milled about in the negligible gravity like bubbles in champagne. Elated at having a large space to play in for the first time in weeks, a group of children had improvised a frantic game of tag, darting from wall to wall with blinding speed. In the immemorial fashion of children, they had fully adapted to low-to-no-g and performed their acrobatics without jostling their elders, most of whom were still uncomfortable in zero-g. Some of them would never adjust.

Near the equator of Avalon, the artificial gravity was near Earth-normal. It was there that most of the travelers who expected to return to Earth would be staying. The nearest thing to "up" in Avalon was the direction of the axis of rotation. The closer one got to the axis, the lighter the gravity was. The same occurred when approaching the poles. After the last of the passengers from *Spartacus* had passed health check, a man entered wearing a plain coverall with some kind of shoulder patch.

"Welcome to Avalon," he said. "I'm with the Avalon

North Pole Port Company. This isn't customs, this is
orientation of a sort. How many here have jobs waiting for them?" About half the adults raised their hands.
"You people go in there," he pointed to a hatch in one
wall. "There's a vacuum tube station through there.
Take the train marked 'Fingal's Cave.' When you get to
the end of the line, you'll be met by representatives of
your employers. They're picking up the tab for your
transportation." Those who had jobs left through the
designated door. The man turned to the rest.

"How many want to work?" All the other adult hands
went up, including Thor's. "Good. Not much of a life
out here for those who won't work. You people head for
the tube station, too. Catch the train marked 'HMK.'
That'll take you where you can find work. I'd advise you
not to be too picky about that first job. The air here is
free, but that's about it. Everything else, water, food,
lodging, entertainment, education for the kids, it all
costs."

"What does HMK mean?" somebody asked.

"Hall of the Mountain King. Don't ask me why. It's
the main commercial center of Avalon. All the hiring
offices are there, along with entertainment and other
facilities. You'll be needing some of those, after coming
out here in steerage."

"Baths?" somebody said hopefully.

"With real water. The train should be arriving in a
few minutes. Good luck. I hope you all make it. Work
hard and you will."

No Statue of Liberty, Thor thought, but no Ellis
Island either. He could do without the first if it meant
being spared the second. The train station was a cavernous, rough-walled chamber with a metal-mesh tube
through its center. A rush of displaced air announced
the arrival of the latest train, which turned out to be a
string of cylindrical gondolas connected by mechanical
links. A door in the mesh tube opened flush with the
sliding door of each gondola. Thor filed into one of the
gondolas and saw that one surface was flat and marked
"floor" in giant letters. There were rows of footprint-

shaped depressions in the floor, and several passengers from previous stops were standing in some of them. Thor placed his feet in a pair and felt them gripped gently by some sort of hydraulic tubing. There were spaces for ten passengers in each car.

The car started up slowly but swiftly gained speed. It was powered by magnetic repulsion and operated in perfect silence. Idly, Thor studied the interior. Holographic advertisements covered the walls, but he could understand little of their content. Most seemed to be concerned with mining equipment, ship hardware, electronic supplies and other such pragmatic goods. There were a few ads for entertainment facilities and a listing of Avalonian churches. Mercifully, there was no canned music being broadcast over the PA system. Avalon was a no-frills society.

The car drew to a stop at a station where a sign flashed "HMK" repeatedly. Thor stepped out and passed through a low, arched hallway. The gravity here was about one-sixth-g, roughly lunar. It wasn't a great deal, but for the first time in two months Thor could feel his weight. It felt good. Extended zero-g wasn't as pleasant as it looked in holographs.

The Hall of the Mountain King was an immense, domed chamber, much like the sublunar cities, but with even less sense of up and down. The tiers of balconies were draped with plant growth. The majority of the architecture seemed to be devoted to commercial enterprises. Just before the tube-station entrance was a directory and Thor found a hotel listing. Not wanting to show a high profile, he chose one in the mid-price range called the Hotel Trier.

The attendant behind the desk was a young, hairless man who wore only a pair of briefs. His arms and chest were lavishly ornamented with gold chains and he pushed himself back slightly as Thor entered the minuscule lobby. "Just off the boat?" he asked as Thor keyed in his name.

"That's right," Thor mumbled, feeling like a wino in a soup kitchen.

"Well, you're welcome to a room, but we don't have private bath facilities. No offense, friend, but I have to ask you to pay a call at the public bath across the square before you claim your room."

"Just point me in the right direction."

Two hours later, feeling infinitely better, Thor stood in his cubicle. "Room" seemed too grand a word. It was tiny and cramped, little more than a closet with a cot. Well, he didn't plan to be here long. One wall had a holoscreen featuring a seascape to combat the inevitable claustrophobia of the surroundings. He keyed the holoscreen to mirror mode and studied himself. He was clean-shaven once again. He was not yet ready to shave his head, but he had had his hair cropped to about a centimeter, little more than a stubble. He had been in good physical condition when he left Earth, but the combination of *Spartacus'* gymnasium and iron-ration diet had pared away the last traces of body fat. He felt he was beginning to look like a spacer.

He drew on his new coverall, one with integral boots and replete with rings and snap-hooks. At his waist hung another spacer's standby: a sort of super boyscout knife which contained dozens of miniature tools. It was time to look for a job. He had come out here to work and it was time to get at it.

He drew a fat zero on his first round of potential employers. The scientific stations were those with most demand for his skills, but they worked closely with Earth authorities and were unwilling to take on anyone with Thor's alleged qualifications and shady circumstances. So much for starting at the top.

Pondering his next move, Thor had lunch at an open food stand. The Chinese owner served up shrimp grown in Avalon's tanks along with a tofu concoction made from gene-altered soybeans. There was no seating and none was needed in an environment where feet and backs seldom got tired.

As Thor raised his plastic chopsticks, a sign across from him caught his eye. It bore no lettering but in its center was a design that looked familiar. It was circular, with three stylized plum blossoms arranged in a triangle in the center. It was a Japanese family *mon* and he tried to remember where he had seen it before. Then he had it. It had been on the ceremonial kimono worn by old Goro Kuroda in the portrait that had once hung above the fireplace in the McNaughton mansion.

As he considered giving the mysterious sign a try, he studied the scene around him. A high proportion of the people here were Chinese or other East Asians. The majority looked to be of European descent, and there were many who appeared to be a mixture of every Earth racial type. He saw nothing that looked like police, but nobody was obviously armed except an occasional person in the uniform of Sálamis. He suspected that their holstered pistols had not been deactivated here. Everything seemed quiet and extremely busy. There was none of the idleness and rowdy activity he was used to in any Earthly urban environment. No desperation, either.

The sign was set above a door in a wall that was utterly shapeless. It was in a side-tunnel fifty meters high that branched off the main chamber. The wall was a sort of hillside made of an extruded foam hydrocarbon. It looked as if a machine making the stuff had been started and somebody had forgotten to turn it off. The hardened foam was translucent and chambers and doorways of every conceivable size and shape had been hollowed out of it. Thor brushed aside a hanging-bead curtain and walked inside.

The woman behind the desk spared him a flickering glance. "Just off the boat?" she said.

"I thought I looked saltier than that," Thor said.

"The hair's right," she told him, "but the coverall's too new. Your complexion isn't quite right either."

"There's nothing wrong with yours," he said. In fact, her complexion was a perfect gold and looked as delicate as peach skin. Her features were vaguely oriental, with eyes of a startling, brilliant green. To his relief, she had hair, a fair amount of it, a rich chestnut in color, its complex waves held in place by some static process that was new to him.

"Are you looking for work?" she asked coolly.

"That's right. I'm a space-habitation engineer."

"We can't use one. Check with Atterjee Construction."

"I already did. I left Earth in what you might call a hurried and informal fashion. They weren't interested. What company is this and what kind of work do you do?"

"We're Kuroda-Sousa Freight. We haul highgrade ore."

"And you're one of the Kurodas? I thought you looked like one."

She looked at him sharply. "I'm Caterina Sousa-Kuroda, related to both sides, and how do you know what a Kuroda looks like?"

"I'm Thor Taggart."

She was supremely unimpressed. "Another Taggart. I hope you're not expecting to trade on the name. Did you just arrive on the *Galileo*?" It was a famous luxury liner, probably the one he had seen at the North Pole port.

"Just arrived, but on the *Spartacus*."

Her eyes widened a bit and her manner relaxed a bit less. "One of Martin Shaw's ships. Have a seat, Mr. Taggart."

As he floated back into the unnecessary chair, Thor felt a pang of annoyance. He didn't impress her, but Shaw did. He found himself wanting to impress this woman, but he knew better than to try. "It makes a difference, what ship I came in on?"

"Shaw brings in some rough specimens," she said, "but he never brings in bums or deadbeats. It's a point of honor with him. He's a remarkable man."

"That he is," Thor said, and he was surprised at how hard it was to admit it.

"How did you meet him?"

"He was a name given to me by a friend on Earth. I contacted him in Armstrong and we arranged a passage. Had to fake my death, though." Who the hell was she interested in, anyway, himself or Shaw? Well, that one was easy to figure out.

"He smuggled you off Luna? On short notice? He must see something in you."

This was getting to be too much. "He was well paid."

"So what?" she said. "Shaw doesn't give a damn about money. He has a cause to finance, but he's brought plenty of people out here for nothing when he thought they'd be an asset to the outerworlds. I hear he soaks the rich ones to cover the ones who can't pay."

He was about to bite out something about how Robin Hood legends often gathered around enigmatic crooks, then thought better of it. "What kind of work do you have available? I can learn." He remembered what he had heard about highgrading on Luna. "And I'm not afraid of a little risk."

"What about a lot of risk? What do you know about it?"

"Just a little that I heard from a hirer in Armstrong. He worked for an outfit called Rockbusters. He said that hijacking was a problem."

"They're a good outfit," she said. "Rough as they come, but honest. We don't handle any of the mining like they do, just the freighting. Our clients are small mining concerns, mostly shoestring operations that can't afford their own barges. We've never lost a ship yet, but people keep trying."

Something about it troubled Thor. "I don't get it. This place seems to be a lot more law-abiding than any Earth city, but I keep hearing about hijacking, piracy, organized violence on a big scale. Why is that?"

"On Avalon, you're seeing the best of it. Some settlements are wide open, and not every skipper who brings in immigrants is as conscientious as Shaw. The outerworlds have been used as a dumping grounds for felons, as well. Most of them are pretty good settler material, but some are scum. And there are the times, as well. In the last few years, it's become almost impossible for new independent operators to get trading permits. It's like the Earth authorities *want* to strangle the economy that's keeping them all afloat. It's driven a lot of otherwise good spacemen into the pirate camp. They'd rather steal than starve." She seemed to realize that she was being garrulous with a mere Earthie and broke off abruptly. "We don't have many specialists in our ships except pilot and engineer. The rest do whatever job is handed out; quartermaster, cargo handler, purser, et cetera. Think you could lay in rations for a voyage?"

It seemed simple enough. It would involve the kind of calculations he was used to from his environment engineering studies. "I don't see why not. Size of crew?"

"Six. Say it's for a four-week voyage."

"Food only, or are there other consumables?"

"Everything. Food, water, air, plant nutrients, the works. As a matter of fact, follow me. I have to buy rations for my ship, so I might as well see how you handle it."

Thor was bemused by this unconventional job interview, but he couldn't think of anyone he'd rather follow just now. She hung a closed sign over the doorway as they left. There was nothing to lock and nothing inside but a desk and two chairs anyway.

"That's the ugliest architecture I've ever seen," Thor commented as they left.

"Isn't it ghastly?" For the first time she sounded almost friendly. "About thirty years ago a bunch of architectural students came out here and proclaimed that they were going to free mankind from the tyranny of rectilinear housing. They were going to make use of asteroidal hydrocarbons to make 'organic, womb-like environments of psychic value.' " She grimaced. "They perpetrated this complex before they were run off. I think they went straight back home and designed concentration camps. It's like being in the digestive system of some unthinkable monster. Father O'Herlihey has a little church way up there at top. He says he now appreciates the torments of Jonah in the belly of the whale."

"Why do you have your office there?" Thor asked.

"It's cheap. In fact, anybody who wants to move in

can do so. Nobody will claim to own it, so all you pay is utilities." They were now out in the main chamber and she led him to a descending ramp. The lower level was an immense warehouse and market, with no internal partitions. Instead, factors stood by heaps of various goods stacked in areas marked off on the floor with red tapes. Some had signs on poles and there were rough districts for everything: foodstuffs, electronics, water, gases, engine hardware, *ad infinitum*.

Thor admired the way Caterina walked. The Avalonian walk was somewhat different from the Lunarian glide. The people here were used to a fluctuating gravity, or zero-g. She was slender, but not as breathtakingly so as the Fu sisters. Space work involved a good deal of hard manual labor, and the usual build was hard and sinewy. She stopped at a sign reading "Chow, Inc."

"Here's where you pick up rations," she said.

"Do you have a recycler?"

She shook her head. "For a four-week voyage, we only recycle air and water. We have a collector for solid wastes and we sell that to Agrispace, Inc. to defray costs."

Avalon, Thor knew, was large enough to have its own agricultural system. Specially-tailored plants were grown in artificial soil or nutrient baths, high-yield grains on short stems so that planting trays could be stacked as high as interior space allowed. Spacers thought in terms of cubic acreage instead of flat fields. Thus, if the trays could be stacked fifty deep, an acre of floor space could yield as much as fifty acres of Earth land. The gene-tailored grains yielded at least ten times the mass of edible matter that the best of Earthly grains had provided a century before. Other vegetables were grown as well, but the staples were grains and soybeans. As the great Ugo Ciano had said when he started the first orbiting agricultural station, "Vegetables is fine, but ya can't make beer outa celery!"

Animal protein was provided mainly by immense salt and fresh water tanks swarming with fish and, especially, shrimp. The tanks also provided seaweed and algae. Quadrupeds had been experimented with in the past, but few could adjust to low gravity and they were inefficient converters at best. Thor realized, sadly, that he had probably eaten his last steak.

An extremely tall, thin Nilotic with ebony skin and an electric-blue coverall came to greet them. "Good to see you, Cat. You buying for *Sisyphus*?"

"He is," she said, jerking her head toward Thor.

"Breaking in a new one, eh?" The towering Nilotic looked down at Thor and grinned. His teeth were filed to points and laquered in rainbow colors. "What will it be, sir?"

Thor calculated furiously. Shrimp paste, processed soy, and what about dietary customs? He should have asked if there were any Orthodox Jews who couldn't eat shrimp. Oh, what the hell. "Crew of six, four weeks. The usual."

The Nilotic guffawed and Caterina looked at him furiously. "That's cheating!"

"Dealing from the bottom is cheating. This is using my head. He knows you, he knows the ship. He's provisioned her before, so why knock myself out calculating rations?"

"Got a new product, Cat," the Nilotic said. "Shrimp paste and soy, processed and textured to look and taste just like pork. Want some?"

"What's pork?" she said.

"Pig meat," Thor told her. "Don't you ever watch holos?"

"Don't have the time," she said. "But I know how you Earthies eat animal flesh." She made a face. "Disgusting."

"Shrimp is God's creatures too, Cat," the Nilotic said, with a tic of his cheek to Thor. Thor decided the tic was equivalent to a wink.

"Shrimp are too ugly to qualify," she insisted. "No, thanks in any case." They agreed upon a price and went off to find more provisions.

After an oxygen-buying operation, they stopped at a sign atop a huge plastic bladder full of amber liquid.

The sign proclaimed: "Trés Estrellas Cerveza." The merchant handed them tall, frosted tubes of beer. Thor still had trouble coping with low-gravity fluids. The way they moved always made them look thick and gluey. The beer was the best he had ever tasted and he said so.

"It is the water, *señor*," the merchant said. "The best beer can only be made with comet water. Think of it, sir; for untold billions of years, since fifteen minutes after the birth of the solar system, this cometary ice has roamed the farthest reaches of our system, keeping itself pure and pristine until space travel could be developed so that brewers might have it at their disposal. This water, sir, has never formed on ocean, which is an unsanitary environment. It has never flowed across dirty ground. It has never passed through the digestive system of any animal. At Trés Estrellas we use only ice fresh-cut from comets, never mere recycled H_2O. This beer sir," he waved at the tube Thor was holding, "has never, and will never, form any urine except your own. This beer—" further rhapsodies were cut short by a commercial transaction transferring a two-keg bladder of the product in question to the *Sisyphus*.

"So you take beer on a voyage?" Thor said.

"Beer or wine, nothing stronger. We make beer and *saké* here in Avalon because we're the biggest grain producer in the Belt. The best wine comes from Canary, which grows nothing but grapes. We'll be picking up some of that over at the vintner's market. Except for some of the ships run by religious communities, running out of wine or beer is considered grounds for mutiny. The outerworlds don't produce the variety of foodstuffs you have on Earth, but Canary alone produces more than four hundred types of wine. It's fighting words out here if you suggest somebody can't tell a good Tokay from a bad one."

"I'll remember that," Thor assured her. He saw a familiar form across the cavernous room, near a fuel dealer's booth. "I think that's Martin Shaw over there," he said.

"Where?" Caterina said. He began to point but she pushed his hand down. "Not with the hand. It's an insult."

He faced Shaw and jerked his chin in the general direction. "By the fuel booth, in the gray coverall. His hair's kind of long in back."

"Introduce me."

"Do I get the job?" he needled.

"Sure. Now quit wasting time." He wondered what she found so fascinating. Shaw was impressive, but so were other men. Thor was sure he was at least as good-looking.

Shaw grinned as they approached. "Thor! Hadn't expected to see you again so soon." He turned to Caterina and raised a hand before his chin, palm down. It was the equivalent of a bow, developed for freefall, where bowing was meaningless. "And I believe your companion is one of the Sousa-Kurodas. Are you Joana?"

She smiled like a Catholic who has just been singled out of a multitude for the personal attention of the Pope. Thor wanted to belt her. "I'm Caterina. Joana is my cousin."

"I've done business with your family," he said. He turned to Thor. "Both the Kurodas and the Sousas are among the oldest families of space settlement."

"So are the Taggarts and Cianos," Thor said.

"Uncle Minoru," she said, ignoring Thor, "has hinted that it was you who went down into the Hong Kong riots five years ago and snatched Tomás Sousa out of the People's Detention Center where he was being tortured. He hints that you got him out here without passing through a single emigration checkpoint."

"I'm just a businessman," Shaw said, modestly. Thor wanted to floor him and jump up and down on him for a while, at full gravity. "People just talk a lot. How is Tomás, by the way?"

"Almost fully recovered. His hands will never be good for much, though."

"It's his mind that counts." Now Shaw was being

dead serious. "It won't be long now. Tell him I'll be in contact."

"So soon?" she said. "I wasn't expecting anything for years."

"Is anybody going to let me in on all this?" Thor asked. Caterina glared at him with barely concealed hostility, as if he were some kind of spy eavesdropping on a conspiracy.

"You've read a lot of my writing, Thor, you know what to expect." He turned back to Caterina. "I've just been arranging for publication of my writings throughout the outerworlds. It will be done simultaneously, so the authorities can't get wind of it and clamp a ban on it. Not for several months, though. It's a delicate operation, especially getting around the computer censors on Luna and Mars."

"Thor here can fill me in on what he's read during my next voyage. He's coming along on the *Sisyphus*." Oh, I can, can I? Thor thought. Presumptuous, arrogant bitch.

Shaw smiled slightly. "Good name for a rock-hauler. Give Thor a thorough grounding in Belt business. I have real hopes for him."

"Oh?" she said, looking Thor over again, as if trying to figure out what Shaw could possibly see in him. "I'll keep an eye on him."

"And now, I must go," Shaw said. "I'm late for a duel, a severe breach of good manners. I'll see you both in the next few months sometime."

They made their goodbyes and went on to arrange for delivery of their purchases to the *Sisyphus*. Thor found himself fantasizing about things like humiliating Shaw and leading the crew of the *Sisyphus* against Caterina. Could this be love?

SEVEN

From the writings of Martin Shaw:

It was the tragedy of the earliest phases of the space programs of the Earthly nations that the immensely valuable rewards of exploration were not immediately tangible. Most were scientific, abstract. From the beginning, the actual payback was tremendous in almost every field, but this was not easily perceived by the public. Sovereigns had always known that the commons and the nobility would grumble at the special taxes levied to outfit an expedition, but that all that would be forgotten in the general rejoicing when the ships returned, laden with gold, rare spices and slaves.

Well into the third decade of space exploration, when the rewards of the program were all-pervasive, the average citizen of America, Europe or Japan had little knowledge of the fact. The typical American, whose heart pacemaker, portable calculator, and innumerable other indispensable possessions, could never have existed without the space program, was almost always blissfully unaware of this fact. To this citizen, the space program was a waste of his taxpayer's money. The tons of hardware shot out into space seemed to bring back nothing tangible. Thus, from the earliest days, the average citizen of the democratic nations of Earth was con-

ditioned to consider all *space operations as futile, wasteful
and parasitic*.

The Soviet space program, needless to say, did not
suffer from this problem of poor public image. The
Soviet program, planned rationally and proceeding stead-
ily while the West moved by fits and starts, suffered
from other problems. The Soviets were always techno-
logically backward compared to the West and suffered
from shortages of all resources. Some of the backward-
ness could be remedied by pirating Western technology,
but never enough. Most fatally, the huge bulk of the
Soviet economy was enslaved to their military machine,
and Soviet scientists had a continually more difficult
struggle in wresting even a minimal budget away from
the military. The result was to concentrate on those
aspects of space exploitation that were of military significance. (see the author's "Nekrasov's Tunguska Bomb—
The True Story")

The same fatal link between space scientists and the
military took place in the West. As the heady exhilaration
of the early space flights wore off and the populace
demanded to see results they could understand, space
authorities fell back on the oldest of pleas—national
security. If funding could not be had for mere science,
perhaps people would vote the money if it made them
feel safer. The military, always looking for a new area
in which to extend its influence, was glad to oblige. The
early U.S. space shuttle program almost certainly would
not have existed had the military establishment not
supported it, insisting that it was essential to the national defense. Appalled, many serious space scientists
watched as more and more of the space program passed
into the hands of the military. And the military had no
interest in space beyond the orbital phase. The military
was interested in looking in only one direction - down.
When the Moon became militarily important, it, too,
came under military observation.

In the democratic countries the fighting for government money became more and more brutal as resources
dwindled and immigration from the Third World strained

available social services. In many countries, the space establishment was lumped together with the military as the enemy in the battle for government handouts. (from the foreword to "The Great Schism—Motherworld vs. the Outerworlds")

The earliest entrepreneurs of free enterprise in space were not, to be sure, the most reputable of specimens. But then, in the history of Earthly exploration, it was seldom the comfortable, successful middle class who pioneered in the new frontiers. The trails were broken by desperate men and adventurers—the ruined sons of the nobility, turned-out soldiers from recent wars and men one step ahead of a hangman's noose. The first European presence in the New World was not that of courtiers or merchants or professors from Oxford or the Sorbonne. It was conquistadores and buccaneers. China was opened to the West by opium smugglers and Africa by slavers. India was subdued by a mercenary army owned by the British East India Company.

The early free enterprisers in space were of much the same mold. Luckily for all our souls and consciences, there were no natives in the solar system to be brutalized, enslaved or murdered en masse as so often in the past. If the free traders and explorers of space were not as brutal and murderous as conquistadores and buccaneers, they very much resembled the hard-driving Yankee clipper-ship captains and crews of the nineteenth century, undertaking insanely perilous voyages in tiny, fragile ships for the sake of high profits and the sheer, exhilarating adventure of breaking new ground.

Many of those who pooled their resources to buy cast-off government spacecraft and go exploring were persons that the authorities were not sorry to see the last of. Beset with constant crises, Earth had little room for adventurers. As always when adventure beckoned, young men out to prove their manhood contrived to find a way onto a ship. In the age of liberation, young women took the same course for the first time in history. Many an independent skipper, after carefully looking the other way on leaving Luna, found that there was a "stowaway" on board; a boy or girl from some high-school expedition. Coincidentally, rations were always available for such a newcomer, and very little else except a great deal of hard labor. Great were the protests from parents', teachers' and humanitarian groups, but to no avail. Many of the most famous skippers and settlers got their starts as runaways.

Perhaps the most famous of the early entrepreneurs was the legendary Ugo Ciano, who got the jump on everybody by being fabulously wealthy before he began his independent operations in trans-lunar space. Unlike most such businessmen, who are far more interested in protecting their wealth than in high-risk capital venture, Ciano spent his capital like water, seemingly uncaring whether any profit was realized or not, as long as the cause of Man in space was advanced. He was a constant trial to his partner Ian McNaughton, a cautious, canny businessman if ever there was one. Luckily, Ciano had a Midas touch and most of his ventures paid off handsomely.

He was also a trial to his closest friend, Samuel Taggart, commandant of the Space Marine Corps. Along with his inordinate genius, Ciano had a corresponding lack of any respect for the laws of Man or God. A true Nietzschean Übermann, Ciano blithely waved all such considerations aside as irrelevant. In his seeming amorality, Ciano probably did mankind more good than all the "humanitarians" in history. Anecdotes abound.

When Ciano needed some geologists and other scientists for his first voyage to the asteroids, he simply went to the nearest source of supply—the Soviet Lunar scientific station at Khruschevgrad. He spirited away the entire staff without the boring formality of consulting with the Soviet government. He was the only man ever condemned to death in absentia by the U.N., with all the non-capital-punishment nations voting. He considered a lengthy criminal record to be an asset when hiring skippers and crews, but he financed the first cathedral on the Moon entirely out of his private funds.

When he learned that Europharmaceuticals Inc. were keeping the supply of their carcinogen-suppressant drug artificially low in order to maximize profit, he put his orbiting laboratories on a crash program to develop a far more effective drug. The cost was enormous, as the drug could only be manufactured in freefall under the most stringent conditions. Ciano then flooded the Earth market with it, at a price so low that even the poorest cancer victims could afford it. It did not bother him at all that the World Medical Cooperative saw to it that he got no credit for the revolutionary treatment. He had set out to destroy Europharmaceuticals and he had succeeded.

Ciano could be a fearsome enemy, but he never acted out of petty motivations or spite. When he took aim at a person or organization, rest assured that they had richly earned disaster. He had a reputation as a ruthless competitor, but he believed in competition so strongly that he often bailed out bankrupt competitors just to let them have another shot at him. Fanatically loyal to his friends, he would give anyone a break, once. He could not stand to be praised or even thanked for his generosity, but any who betrayed his trust were never heard from again.

Ciano was one of the most mercurial, contradictory personalities in all of history. Generous and ruthless, ferocious and kindly, crude and chivalrous, he had three qualities which remained constant throughout his long life: he was loyal, he was courageous, and he would not tolerate injustice. He was, perhaps, the prototype of the ideal spacer. Legends grow up around such men, and he was no exception. The circumstances of his death are as mysterious as his origin. As always, there are those who say he never died. (from "Saints and Rogues: The Free Spacers" by Martin Shaw)

One rule of politics is as rigid as any law of physics: Those who protest most vehemently at government money being used for a space venture will always be the first

to demand "their fair share" of the profits when it is
successful. (from "The Loony Bin: A History of Space
Funding" by Martin Shaw)

"Hey, Thor!"

Thor looked up from the holographic game he was
playing with Ortega. Two years in *Sisyphus* had left
their marks on his face. The Mexican took advantage of
his momentary distraction to wipe out all his warships.
"Pay me!" Ortega exulted. Automatically, Thor handed
over the credits while he sought the source of the hail
in the crowded room. Then he saw a bulky form sailing
across the chamber, brushing aside dozens of floating
miners and freighters. Thor grinned as he recognized
the ugly face with a large scar across the left cheek. The
man looked like a cross between a fighting Pict and a
marauding Viking. His red hair and beard were braided
and his bare arms were ringed with the rare precious
metals and gems sometimes found in the asteroids.

"Sean Roalstad!" Thor called. "When did the *Odin*
get in?"

"Got me a new ship," Roalstad said. "Named her the
Longship. I turned the *Odin* over to my boy, Loki. It's
time he had his own command. Here, have one." He
had been trailing a string of balloon-like spheres and
Thor and Ortega took one each. They punctured the
balloons with straws and began to suck out the beer.
"Jesus, Thor, where'd you get that?" Roalstad pointed
his chin at the red new scar that slanted from Thor's
right ear almost to the corner of his mouth.

"We got hit by boosters just after we finished taking
on highgrade at L-505. Some son of a bitch got me
alongside the face with a knife before we drove them
out of the ship. They didn't shut the door before they
left, either. Good thing Josue here, and Patrice were
suited up. They got us into rescue bubbles before we
croaked. Had bends for a week as it was."

"Any idea who they were?"

"No, they were all in pressure suits. We know who

gave them the time and coordinates, though. Two miners on L-505 named Chang and Youssoupov disappeared with the boosters when they cut out. Those two are dead men if I ever find them. We put their likenesses and specs on the KOS net."

"I'll scan it first chance I get," Roalstad said. The Kill On Sight net was universally respected in the lawless, courtless far reaches of the outerworlds. "Won't do much good, though. They'll be back in circulation in a month with new looks and new names." Plastic surgery clinics asked few questions. "You still with the *Sisyphus*?"

Thor nodded as he scanned the chamber. Delos was a small asteroid with a convenient location, where freighters auctioned their cargoes to refiners. Most of all, it was a way station, providing R&R for spacers on lengthy voyages. Here they could relieve the long, tedious hours in space with conviviality and gossip and do a little business on the side. His expression didn't change, but his heart beat a little faster when he saw Cat crossing the chamber.

"I got a good price for the highgrade," she said without preamble. "Almost double the usual shares for everybody. There was also a summons for me at the message center. We're heading back for Avalon."

"I thought we had to pick up a load at Z-221," Ortega said.

"It'll have to wait. We'll go out later with an extra hold. This is from the family. The whole Clan's gathering for an emergency session. Don't ask me what." She handed a broad envelope to Thor. "This came here a couple of months ago from Luna. It's been chasing you around for a while."

Puzzled, Thor took the envelope and broke the seal. Inside were several printout sheets clipped together. On top was a news printout.

WASHINGTON—President Jameson, in an unprecedented move, declared outlaw the so-called Humanity for a Future information network. In a statement to the press, Attorney General Percival Meeks called the underground information net "traitors to our President personally, and traitors to the United States of America and all of the human race." Blanket arrests were ordered for the network's financier, Robert Ciano, and all local operators. "This fifth column trafficking with our enemies must be nipped in the bud," said the President. "Better that freedom of information be slightly abridged, than that the offworld powers should have the aid of this nest of traitors in our midst."

Scrawled at the bottom of the clipping, in vermilion ink, was a short message. "Needless to say, I split. Living in Armstrong now. Sorry about the next part. Luck, Chih' Chin Fu."

Thor passed the clipping around. "So we're the enemy now," said Sean. "It's official. That's all right. I never had any use for Earthies anyway."

"What in hell are the 'offworld powers'?" Caterina said. "Us? We may be offworld, but a power we ain't. We're the most disorganized mass of humanity in existence."

Thor was reading the next page, a handwritten note in beautiful, feminine calligraphy:

Dear Mr. Taggart:

A few days ago, Mr. Robert Ciano showed up at the Hilton. He told us who he was, but not to use his real name because the police were after him. Cousin Chih-Chin confirmed this. He threw wild parties for everybody and was always dodging police raids. They had orders to shoot him, if you can believe that, but we kept him hidden. In the middle of one party, he quite cheerfully informed us that the g-forces of his clandestine flight from Earth had fatally strained his heart and he had only two or three more days to live. The next day, he bought a surface suit and a buggy with four days worth of air and he drove out through the number five lock.

When we realized he was gone, we sent a search

*party out for him. On the crater rim, they found all his
emergency signalling gear. There are nearly a century's
worth of tire tracks up there, so there was no way to
find which were his and he obviously didn't want to be
found, anyway. After three days we held a wonderful
wake for him. He would have loved it. Please accept
our deepest condolences, we know how much you loved
him. We did, too. The rest of these papers he left for
you.*

It was signed by Nectar and Ambrosia Fu. Thor's
eyes stung as he passed the paper to the others. Tears
are a terrible thing in freefall. They just stay there on
the eyeballs and have to be brushed away. The others
let him get control of himself before commenting.

"I'm sorry, Thor," Caterina said. "You've told me so
much about him I feel like I've lost a kinsman, too."
She was sincere and it was quite different from her
usual tone with him.

"One thing's for sure," said Roalstad. "When they
arrest billionaires like him, things are getting serious.
In normal times, wealth like his buys immunity from
almost anything."

"What did he send you, *amigo*?" Ortega asked.

Thor scanned the sheets, which were all covered
with incomprehensible symbols. "It's in code," he said,
puzzled.

"Then it's important," Caterina said. "Turn it over to
a data service when we get to Avalon. And we'll be
there soon. Drink up, we're pulling out. Sean, I'd
suggest you go too. Something big is up."

"I'll beat you there," said Roalstad

"Five hundred says you won't."

"You're on." They left the teeming, noisy chamber,
and around them word spread that the times were
changing.

The scene in HMK was chaos. There were groups
gathered around signs, others in uniforms of a sort.
There was shouting and fist-waving and slogan-bearing
banners had been hung prominently. "I think I detect

the fine hand of my friend Shaw in all this," Thor said. Beside him, Caterina nodded. At one end of the cavern, a tall, spindly speaking platform had been erected, and he saw Martin Shaw pulling himself up a rope hand-over-hand to its apex. Apparently, Shaw had no use for magnified holographic images. He waved his arms and the hubbub subsided.

"If you don't know me by now," Shaw said, "I'm Martin Shaw." There was cheering and waving from the crowd. Apparently, Shaw was a popular man. The PA system made his voice boom throughout the cavern. "I represent the Outerworlds Survival Party. Because that's exactly what we're facing, people: survival. What we decide and do in the next few months will determine whether offworld humanity is to be a continuing part of human history or just a footnote; a failed experiment in the course of Earth's self-destruction. If we fail, what the history books will say won't concern us greatly, because we'll all be dead!" There was restrained pandemonium from the crowd below him.

"You notice something?" Thor said. "Most of the noise and fist-waving is coming from immigrants. The Spaceborn have no feel for mob action."

"Shh!" Cat hissed. "He's talking."

"By now, most of you have heard of the latest decrees and actions of the United Nations of Earth." Thor instantly caught the "of Earth" qualifier. It was the first time he had heard such an expression. "The resolution passed by the General Assembly and the Security Council amounts to a declaration of war in all but formal, legalistic terminology."

A professoral-looking man leaped to a height of five or six meters and shouted: "The U.N. has no power to declare war on behalf of the member nations!"

"Nothing is being done on behalf of the member nations," Shaw answered. "This is being done by and for the Earth First Party. And forget about declarations of war, nobody's used one in over a century. You can make war without declaring it just as easily as you can commit murder without declaring it. Supposedly, the

U.N. can only vote for military action to enforce peace
where war has already broken out, but nations have
always known that you can wage war as effectively with
political and economic action as with guns and bombs.
Lock a man up in a cell and starve him to death and
you've killed him just as dead as if you'd shot him.

"For years, Earth First has tried to portray the
outerworlds as an evil parasite exploiting humanity.
While we've gone our merry way concentrating on how
to out-compete each other, they've reaped most of the
profits while turning us into the enemy in most peoples'
perceptions. And we've nobody to blame but ourselves!"

"How come we're at fault?" yelled a man leaping
upward and drifting slowly downward. "We've done
nothing to the Earthies except support 'em!" Lots of
murmuring in support of that one. The timing was good
and Thor wondered whether Shaw had coached the
questioners beforehand.

"I'll tell you why! It's because we've come out here
and turned our backs on the mother world. We've
cultivated the mystique of our own superiority for years
and we've come to despise the homeworlders as con-
temptible Earthies. When you're contemptuous of somebody, it's easy to forget how resentful and dangerous
they can be. We've pretended we were some kind of
aristocracy and we've committed the aristocrats' historical sin of blindness and self-absorption. Even now, with
annihilation staring us in the face, most of us would
rather cherish our vaunted 'independence' than unite
against a common threat. All our 'independence' is
good for now is ensuring that we'll hang alone instead of
together. The kind of independence we need now is
national independence. The individual kind does us
little good in a war."

Another man jumped up. He wore the brown coverall of the Brethren of Patmos. "I'll fight the heathen
Earthies if need be, but," he flung a pointing finger
about him in a dramatic gesture, "I'll not ally with these
godless money-grubbers."

Next was a man with fluffy side-whiskers. "The Soci-

ety of Friends cannot countenance war. Independence
with peace would be a good thing for us all, but if thee
preach violence, we are not with thee."

"It's just this kind of divisiveness we're going to have
to overcome," Shaw shouted. He pointed across the
chamber to a ledge near the one where Thor and Caterina
were standing. Thor could just make out Sean Roalstad's
extravagant, feathered cape in the midst of a knot of
crewpeople from *Odin* and the *Longship*. "Sean Roalstad!
How do you stand on this?" Shaw pointed a directional
mike at the skipper.

Roalstad looked uncomfortable and embarrassed. "You
all know me. I'm not afraid to fight and never have
been. But war isn't fighting. It's murder on a big scale.
Besides, it's bad for business. Maybe not for Earth, the
Earthie industries get fat on wartime manufacturing
and service contracts. But we're prospectors and miners
and shippers. If we can't move about freely, we're
ruined." His words were sobering and the crowd grew
less agitated.

"Exactly!" Shaw pounced triumphantly. "We are heading into a time of trial that is going to cost us all dearly.
Anyone who paints a rosy picture for you is a fraud! To
survive and prevail, we will all have to sacrifice. We
must sacrifice our precious exclusivity. You can't accomplish anything if you can't work with people you
don't much like. A lot of us may have to sacrifice our
lives. Let the Earthies call it what they like, what's
coming is war and people get killed in war. A lot of us
are going to lose everything material: savings, businesses, ships, the works. That's tough. We'll just have
to start over when it's done.

"Some three centuries ago, another group of colonists
sat down to hammer out the terms of their independence. A number of them were the richest men in the
colonies, those with the most to lose, and those surest
of the traitor's noose should they fail. They pledged
their lives, their fortunes and their sacred honor, to the
effort and signed their names so that there could be no
doubt of who they were. Whatever happens, you can

keep honor, but sometimes at the cost of the first two items. If we aren't prepared to go as far as they did, we might as well capitulate and accept slow death now." The scene on the floor turned to chaos as everyone cheered, booed or demanded to be heard.

"Let's go," Caterina said. "This will go on for days. We can catch the highlights on the holos."

"Where are we going?" Thor asked. "I was looking forward to a bath and a beer."

"Sidon," she said. "That's where the family is meeting."

"You want me to come along?" Thor was suspicious. He had never attended one of the inner-family conferences. Even the Taggarts and Cianos out here treated him like a poor relation, a steerage Earthie with a mere two years in the outerworlds. He had expected to be welcomed with open arms and was somewhat embittered by his near-rejection.

"The family may have work for you," she said, leading the way into the nearest tube station.

"The family already has work for me," he said. "I've been crewing on one of their ships for a couple of years now, remember?"

"I mean *important* work. Not just family business." She climbed into a four-passenger tube cab and strapped herself into one of its seats. It could make the trip to Sidon in twenty minutes instead of a train's hour or more.

"What's so important?" he asked, taking a facing seat.

"You'll find out. Maybe it'll be nothing." She seemed distracted and refused to respond to Thor's proddings. He was used to these moods of hers. From the day he had arrived in Avalon, she had been maddeningly inconsistent in her attitude toward him, alternating between a warm friendliness and impersonal disdain. On at least a dozen occasions, he had sworn to give up trying. Not that he had remained celibate while pursuing his abortive courtship. There was Gallina Federova, who bossed the operation on L-591. There had also been Titania Carrara, who had crewed in the *Sisyphus*. Affairs within the closed little world of a ship were always touchy and potentially volatile. His with Titania had not lasted long, but he had taken comfort in the way Caterina had treated him like a leper for months afterward.

The car pulled into the small station at Sidon. They were a few degrees north of the equator, but well into the interior, near the axis, so that the perceived gravity was about one-third Earth normal, roughly Martian level. Thor felt a little wobbly on his legs in the unaccustomed gravity. He had found that he was most comfortable when he had just enough gravity to feel his weight and have a definite sense of up and down. HMK was near-ideal. Few except the Spaceborn ever felt truly comfortable in freefall but he had decided that only an idiot would ever want to return to full gravity.

The main Sidon chamber was an old, worked-out mine site, which had been worked into the near-universal system of stepped-back tiers. It was largely residential, with a small commercial and convenience area serving mainly the local residents. Near the center of the public plaza, Thor saw a group of schoolchildren playing a complicated game involving a great deal of high jumping and somehow involving the capture of various colored kerchiefs, all under or above the eye of a stern-looking supervisor. With a shock, Thor recalled Shaw's inflammatory speeches. If the man wasn't exaggerating, these children might have to be evacuated to obscure mining rocks, perhaps to spend the bulk of their childhood amid the grim, bleak surroundings of the little mining operations. It was a depressing thought.

They ascended to the highest tier, a level where the encircling terrace was broader and the doorways fewer. If there could be said to be an exclusive housing district in Avalon, this was it. They stopped before a door bearing the plum-blossom motif and Caterina placed a palm against its lock plate. The door hissed open and Thor saw that it was a massive, vault-like construction, suitable for withstanding a major disaster or a siege. They went in and it hissed shut behind them. Beyond was a short hall and another, similar door. Thor spotted sensors everywhere, along with the snouts of gas projectors and shortbeam lasers.

"No wonder there's no welcome mat out front," Thor said.

"Our ancestors believed in castles," Caterina told him, "and so do we. This isn't the only one, though it's the biggest and best-known. Other Taggarts and Cianos and McNaughtons and Kurodas and Sousas have come up here from Earth in the past. Not all of them have made it past these doors. Come to think of it, you haven't yet."

"If they don't laser me down," Thor said caustically, "I'll consider it an honor." Just then the inner door slid open and they entered the inner sanctum. The foyer was the largest living area Thor had seen since leaving the Moon. It was sparsely furnished but the walls were beautifully polished and there were many beautiful art works and tapestries to relieve the austerity. In the center, a small fountain sent up a multicolored, slow-motion spray. A woman came into the room and for a second Thor's heart paused. She was Fred Schuster come to life. Then he saw that this woman looked no older than her mid-fifties.

"You must be Thor," she said, extending her hand graciously. "Robert spoke of you often in his messages. I'm his sister, Brunhilde."

Thor took the hand. He had to cant his head slightly to look her in the eye. She was well over six feet tall. "Bob was a good friend and a brave man," Thor told her. "You've heard about his death?"

"Yes. Let's not mourn. Few of us get to choose the manner of our death, and Robert picked the one he wanted. We should all be so fortunate." She turned to Caterina. "Tomás and Saburo are in the great hall. Most of the inner family are here, and the collateral branches are gathering. The meeting begins at 1900. You'd better report to Saburo and pay your respects. I'll take charge of Thor." To Thor's utter astonishment, the younger woman bowed deeply.

"It's good to see you again, Elder Aunt," Caterina said. Then she turned and left the room.

"Come along to my place, Thor. We must get better acquainted." Thor followed her. Brunhilde walked with the snakelike grace of the Spaceborn. She was wearing a black, diaphanous gown, the first such garment Thor had seen here. They passed through a narrow tunnel and into another foyer, this one cluttered with all manner of objects, souvenirs and memorabilia. There were pieces of scientific apparatus, a few weapons, two spacesuits of antiquated design, holographs and oil paintings. The eccentricity and indiscipline had Ciano written all over it.

"This is my home," Brunhilde said. "It's a separate complex from the Kuroda mansion next door. This whole level and several below it are occupied by the founding families. They're interconnected into a single warren, but that's mainly for defensive purposes. The corridor between my place and the Kurodas' is open now mainly because of the meeting, so we can all get back and forth without attracting attention." She waved at a pair of low couches. "Get comfortable. What do you drink?"

"Would you have any beer?" he asked.

"I hope so. I own a brewery." A little robot came in and delivered their drinks. Brunhilde took a glass of ruby wine. It looked like a genuine Earth wineglass.

"If you don't mind my asking," Thor said, "why am I suddenly part of the family?"

"You've passed. We've been keeping an eye on you since you reached Armstrong. We don't accept just anybody, no matter what the name."

"I've done pretty well on my own," Thor said, nettled. "I don't really need the family."

"If you'd *needed* us, we'd have had no use for you. Bearing the name doesn't cut it. Let me tell you what Father used to lecture us about. He had only a limited faith in genetic inheritance of his own qualities, which were superlative by his own admission. 'You want the Cianos to stay a family of superior people,' he used to say, 'then find people with the qualities you want, then marry 'em and *make* 'em Cianos! Support no dead-wood.' That was Ugo. The asteroid-based families have largely followed his advice. The Taggarts mostly went into the military, of course, a profession that has its own weeding-out process. They're mainly Luna-based any-way, and there haven't been as many Taggarts as there have Cianos and Kurodas. We've maintained close ties, though.

"Anyway, you've survived two years on Caterina's ship. She's a difficult young woman, but a good skipper. You seem to have come through with mind and body intact," she eyed the still-fresh scar, "well, mostly in-tact anyway. I can't say about your heart, though. You have the look of a young man who finds it easy to fall in love with women of strong character."

Thor was taken aback at this unflinching assessment of his character. "Nothing easy about it," he said. "You're right, but don't tell her. She already has enough lever-age on me."

Brunhilde laughed unaffectedly. "You think she doesn't know? I said she was difficult. One of the difficulties is that she'll settle for nothing but the best in men. That means she has to put them through a very rigorous ordeal first. To the best of my knowledge, nobody has passed yet."

"It doesn't surprise me," Thor said ruefully. He was amazed at how easy it was to relax with this woman. It was a relief to let down the guard that always had to be maintained in the tight, hard world of the ships and mines. "You're right about my taste for women of char-acter. I grew up with a portrait of your mother in the house. I think Fred Schuster was always my ideal woman."

"An ideal few women could live up to," Brunhilde acknowledged. "Caterina just might. Don't let her be the only one doing the testing." She put her glass aside. "I'll have a room fixed up for you here. The meeting will probably run on late into the night. I know you'd like a bath and a change of clothes, but I think it's time you met Ugo."

"I guess I didn't hear you right," Thor said. "I could have sworn I heard you say that it was time I met Ugo."

"That's exactly what I said. Come along." He followed in a bemused daze. Things were just happening too fast. She led him to a door upon which was hung a pirate's black skull-and-bones flag. "This is Father's office. Go on in."

Mystified, Thor complied. It was dim inside and Thor started when the door shut behind him. The lights came up slightly and Thor felt a prickly sensation on the back of his neck when he saw the man seated on a chair in the center of the room. The man's hair and beard formed a white, swirling cloud and he stared at the chair opposite him with a sort of barely-suppressed ferocity. It was Ugo Ciano. What had Shaw's book said about the rumors that Ciano had never died?

Ciano pointed to the chair he faced. "Siddown!" he ordered. Thor complied with a great sense of relief. Some indefinable quality of the voice told him that this was a holographic image. "The fact you're here," Ciano said, "means two things: One, you're one of me and Fred's descendents, or one of Sam and Laine's. Two, I'm dead. That's a depressing thought, so don't expect no happy greetings, understand?" The Brooklynese dialect was so grossly abrasive that it was almost a burlesque.

"You got this far, which is good," Ugo continued. "Don't let it go to your head." Abruptly, Ugo got up and began to pace. Even sitting, Thor was taller. "By the way, don't mess with my stuff or handle my papers." He waved around the room, which was indescribably cluttered and messy. Thor couldn't imagine how his worst efforts could possibly do any damage. "Now, pay attention, I'm telling you the important stuff here."

The tiny man fretted and waved his arms wildly, as if his diminutive body simply could not cope with all the energy it contained. "As a Ciano or a Taggart, you got a duty to humanity. Granted, most of humanity ain't much to feel a duty for, but maybe it'll get better. Most of the clowns who come out here wanna get rich quick. Mostly they get dead quick and serves 'em right. They're doing their bit as pioneers, but you gotta have more important things on your mind. Primarily, you gotta see to it that humanity has a future in space. You ought to be able to hold up your end of the job. After all, you got a good genetic inheritance. If you feel you ain't up to the task, marry somebody smarter than you and try to breed somebody who can. With enough generations, somebody like me has to come along sooner or later."

Ugo had his back to Thor, but now whirled around to face him. Although Ugo must have been in space for several decades when the holo was made, he had nothing like the grace of the Spaceborn. All his movements were excessively forceful and he was always having to check his follow-through. "In order to guarantee that future in space, I've set several projects in motion. For one, me'n Sam, God rest his soul, have bankrolled a bunch of cashiered officers to set up a military academy in a rock called Sálamis. I never had much use for a military myself, but Sam convinced me how important it was for the colonies. Give them your help and support. They'll save your butt some day.

"Second, I'm working on a new kind of engine. You see, it ain't enough to run around pulverizing rocks here in the solar system. That's as dead a dead end as Earth is. We gotta go out there!" He waved a stubby arm at a picture-hung rock wall. "Interstellar space! New stars! We get out and settle around a bunch of them, then maybe we got a future. That brings me to this engine. I'll be testing it soon. It may not work quite like I planned. Come to think of it, maybe that's why I'm dead. What the hell, life ain't been much fun since Fred died. Anyway, by way of precaution, I've left some of the specs with my boy Bob down on Earth. He'll never be as brilliant as me, but he's a good kid and takes after me and Fred. Knocks back Wild Turkey like a champ, too. Anyways, what it may come down to is, someday there may be nothing for the colonies to do but escape. By then, you gotta have that engine perfected, because it's the only way you're going to get away. Work on it."

Ugo returned to his chair. "That's about it. Do your best, help make us a star-spanning species. If you don't, what the hell, somebody else probly will. Don't disgrace me. Now get outta here and send the next one in." The image froze.

Thor rose from his chair. So that was Ugo Ciano. It was quite an experience, and he felt a new respect for Sam Taggart and Ian McNaughton. Brunhilde was waiting outside for him. "Was he always like that?" Thor asked.

"In his milder moods, which were few and far between. Mother kept him in line most of the time, but after she died he reverted to type. Come on, I've had dinner laid out." She led the way back into the foyer.

"What was that business about an engine?" He remembered the coded pages Bob had sent him but decided not to mention them just yet.

"That was how he died, if he died." She reclined at a small table and Thor took the opposite couch. The food was mostly extravagant concoctions of textured vegetable proteins, along with the usual fish and shrimp dishes.

"What do you mean, 'if'? I keep hearing hints of some mystery surrounding his death."

"One day," she speared a shrimp in lemon sauce on her fork, "Ugo left his lab—that's a deserted rock now—and got into a ship named *ad astra*. She was a little military shuttle he'd equipped with his mysterious engine. The only one with him that day was his lab assistant, a half-crazy old coot named Roseberry. Roseberry stayed in the lab while Ugo ran the engine through its tests. Then he tried the final testing stage—ignition."

She refilled her glass. "I'd like to say that his final words were something noble, poetic and inspiring, but that wouldn't have been like him. First he said, 'You ready, Fred?'—he'd taken to talking to Mother a lot in those last years. Then he said, 'Let's fire this bitch up and see what happens.'

"There was a tremendous flash that burned out half the sensors in this part of the Belt and was recorded as far away as Mars. That was the last of him. It was Roseberry who insisted that he wasn't dead, and still will, if you buy him a drink. But, after all, there was no evidence whatever left behind, so maybe he really *is* still out there somewhere, heading for the stars."

Thor raised his glass. "To Ugo Ciano, wherever he is." She clinked her glass against his.

EIGHT

The great hall of the Kuroda stronghold was a long gallery left over from an early mining operation. The floor was polished smooth but the walls had been left rough, with the marks of the miners' tools still visible. Aside from the straw mats upon which the assembled family spokesmen were seated, the only furnishing in the room was a rack of swords, ancestral treasures of the Kurodas.

Perhaps a hundred men and women sat in a double line facing one another. At one end of the double row was Saburo Kuroda, patriarch of the clan. Near him was Brunhilde and several others Thor recognized. Some he had met, others he knew by reputation. Caterina signalled for him to sit next to her, far down the line. A few late arrivals took their seats and Saburo nodded to the doorkeeper. The young man ceremoniously shut and bolted the door.

"By now," Saburo began, "you are all aware that we face a crisis. It is one we should have seen coming long ago, but did not. For this I blame myself. I am entrusted with the security of the family, and I paid too little attention to the trends on Earth and to warnings sent me by colleagues there, including our late cousin, Robert Ciano. The damage is done. It remains for us now to assess our situation and take steps to protect ourselves. As always, we shall formulate our policy as a unit and pursue our goals in the same fashion. Representatives of all the founding families are now here. Tomás Sousa will now bring us up to date on the most recent developments."

Sousa had a gray beard and a strong, ugly face of perfect serenity. His mutilated hands were encased in delicate servos to give him some limited power of manipulation. "I will not waste your time by detailing the various actions taken against the outerworlds over the last few years. By now, you've all studied that. The important things are these: Over the last six months, the President of the United States and the heads of state of a number of nations have taken to referring to the Outerworlds as "the enemy," something unheard of in peacetime. These are not slips of the tongue. This trend represents policy. Literary and holographic references to the outerworlds have become uniformly negative. In nearly all nations, any expression sympathetic to the outerworlds is a punishable offense. The United States has virtually suspended freedom of speech and the press in this matter, another measure never before taken in peacetime.

"Yesterday, the U.N. passed a resolution condemning the outerworlds for practicing what they call 'economic warfare' against the Earth. A unanimous vote in the Security Council empowered the U.N. to levy a virtually unlimited military budget from the member nations. It is also empowered it to draft young men and women from the member nations into the U.N. military forces for the first time in history. They are preparing for war."

A babble broke out as dozens tried to be heard. Henryk Van Doorn's voice boomed above the others. "They speak of 'the outerworlds' as if there were such an entity, and there is not! There are only multitudes of independent and semi-independent colonies. The nearest thing to a city-state we have is Avalon, which is little more than a functioning anarchy."

"Quite true," Sousa said. "In order to have a war you need an enemy, and they have created one."

"But why?" shouted a woman Thor did not recognize. "Granted that they depend on us for vital resources. Nobody likes that. But it's a wide leap from resentment to war. What can they gain? We have to sell our products to them at ruinously low prices as it is, ever since the U.N. Economic Council has started controlling the market, entirely ignoring the forces of the free market. Even if they could take over all our operations, it would be many years, if ever, before they could run our operations as efficiently as we do."

"It's greed!" said Hjalmar Taggart. "Everybody knows that McNaughton is behind all this. Murdo McNaughton wants a monopoly on space commerce. They've been losing business out here for years." He glared at Reiko McNaughton, who sat across from him. Reiko was the head of the Spaceborn McNaughtons.

"We broke with Murdo and the Earth family decades ago!" Reiko said, furiously. She gripped a folded fan in a white-knuckled fist. "Murdo is just a catspaw for the Earth Firsters and the national leaders are going along because their ruinous social policies have bankrupted the whole planet! A war will take peoples' minds off their misery."

"There are elements of truth in all these things," Sousa said. "But what we are seeing is the result of a plan many years old and of very great scope."

Things he had experienced and things he had found in Shaw's writing came together in Thor's mind. The chaotic situation on Earth began to have sense and shape. He leaned forward and spoke. "They're trying to forge a world-state."

His quiet voice cut through the babble and Sousa turned to look at him. "That is a most perceptive comment, young man. I do not believe we have met."

"I'm Thor Taggart, grandson of Sam and Laine. I immigrated a little over two years ago and I've been crewing aboard the *Sisyphus*. This is my first time here."

"Welcome among us," Saburo said. "Robert Ciano spoke well of you in his messages."

"He said you were a callow young punk but capable of learning," Brunhilde amended.

"Ahm," Saburo murmured, "Robert and his sister have always shared their father's bluntness."

"He sent us a copy of the study you and young Chih' Chin Fu put together, the one about the change in attitude of the popular holographic entertainments," Sousa said. "Its scholarship was sloppy and casual, but it was full of important material and gave me much matter for thought. He mentioned that you have met both President Jameson and Anthony Carstairs, head of the Earth First Party." Thor was dumbfounded. He had never dreamed that these people were even aware of him.

"You mean," said Hjalmar Taggart, "that you had them both in one place and you didn't shoot them?"

"It was at one of Murdo's parties," Thor said, "and—"

"All *three* of them?" Hjalmar said.

"Let him speak, Hjalmar," Saburo chided.

"Murdo we know all too well," Sousa said. "Please give us your impressions of the other two."

"Jameson is a smooth political hack," Thor said. "I doubt if he has a firmly-held principle in his head. He wanted to be President and he made it. He also wants to be Secretary General and I'm sure he'll get that, too. It looks as if he's going to make sure that the Secretary-General is virtual planetary dictator by the time he steps into the office. But he's a front, a media-created image for others to manipulate."

"That tallies with all I have been able to find out about the man," Sousa said. "What of Carstairs?"

"A different proposition entirely. He's a convinced ideologue and he means every word he says. He's an enormously impressive man in person but he doesn't have the kind of slick style you need to run for elective office these days. And I got the distinct impression that he'd never met Murdo before. I don't think he was faking it. He's smart and tough and I think he'd be a dangerous opponent. Let me put it this way: If he were a philosopher, he'd be Nietzsche. If he were a political theorist, he'd be Marx. If he were a general, he'd be Napoleon. He has that kind of personal force. But it wouldn't come across on holovision and he can't run for office."

"But if he had not met with Murdo before," Sousa said, "then he was not the original architect of this trend."

"I don't bleieve so," Thor said. "I think Murdo, but more likely a consortium of business and political people, hatched this plan years ago. Murdo was able to exert his influence through his sponsorship of a great deal of programming. At about the same time, they began cultivating Earth First, which had been an obscure, lunatic-fringe party up to that time. When they saw that Jameson was the man to watch in U.S. politics, they scduced him away from the Constitutionalists to Earth First. It may just be chance that Carstairs was running Earth First. If they think they're going to manipulate *him*, they're wrong."

"Thank you," Sousa said. "Many things fall into place now. We face a triumvirate, but more likely a cabal, fronted by Jameson. But Carstairs is the one to watch. The others may be motivated by profit and power, but he sounds like a classic visionary. I don't doubt that he acts from the noblest motives, by his own lights. History is full of such men: Cromwell, Robespierre, Lenin, they are the most dangerous specimens of humanity. He probably sees a worldwide dictatorship as the only way to save Earth. He could well be right. But the only sufficient unifying force is an external enemy. We have been elected to fill that role."

"They have the enemy," Brunhilde said, "now they need a face and a name. You can't focus hate on a faceless population. They'll want a bogeyman to scare the children with."

"They have one," Van Doorn said. "Martin Shaw. That rabble-rouser is already stirring people up to who knows what kind of violence."

"Martin's not a rabble-rouser!" Caterina said hotly. "He's our first and maybe only patriot. He's out there urging unity while we sit here like an inner circle of the chosen. He knows there's a fight coming and he wants to be ready for it. He's for action, not talk!"

"Calm yourself, granddaughter," Saburo said with steely gentleness. "We, too, shall take action. We formulate family policy here."

"You all know," Sousa said, "that I owe my life, and more importantly my freedom, to Martin Shaw. But I cannot allow my personal affection and gratitude to cloud my judgment. He is a brilliant political thinker and a great leader of men, but he could ruin us all. He wants to use force and he wants to use it unrestrainedly. He will call for us to strike at Earth first and hit hard. He is a terrorist at heart. I know that he has looked into the possibility of reviving Nekrasov's Tunguska bombs."

There was shocked silence.

"Barbaric!" Reiko said. "The man should be arrested."

. "It's worse than barbaric, it's dumb." Hjalmar said contemptuously. "It's the first thing they'll think of. Ever since the Djakarta incident they've built a whole battery of weapons to destroy rocks or ice headed for Earth."

"Never properly tested and never intended to seek rock or ice bombs equipped with screening devices," Saburo said. "He could just pull it off. We have to keep an eye on him."

"In the meantime," Brunhilde said, "he serves a valuable purpose. While the Earth holos are putting horns and a tail on Martin, maybe we can operate without attracting the wrong kind of attention. It's time to decide on our course of action."

"Martin Shaw is correct in one thing," Saburo said. "We must become a unified nation. Our carefree anarchy must end. To that purpose, I appoint Tomás to draw up a constitution for us that will be agreeable to the greatest number of the island worlds. This we must publicize as widely and as soon as possible. Then we'll have to set up a constitutional convention to ratify it.

Distasteful as it is to us all, this will call for a political party and an administrative bureaucracy. To handle these positions we shall appoint temporary heads from among those present here. As soon as feasible, most of these positions will have to be handed over to non-family members. Otherwise, we'll be accused, justly, of running a nation as a family operation."

"Do we have a name for this party?" Brunhilde asked.

"If it is agreeable," Sousa said, "I have chosen Eos. It means 'dawn' in Attic Greek, and we are at the dawn of a new age for mankind. Best of all, it is short, easy to remember and difficult to misspell."

"Sounds catchy," Brunhilde said. "I nominate Tomás Sousa as boss or chairman or whatever of the Eos party." The vote was unanimous.

"Hjalmar," Saburo said, "you've had extensive military experience. Put together a security force. It will be the nucleus of our own military force, should the Sálamids not join us."

"They'll come in with us," Hjalmar assured him. "For one thing, Sálamis is full of Taggarts. Just what kind of security will we be needing?"

"First of all," Saburo said, "there will be spies to catch. I know this because a man came to me a few days ago saying that he had been sent by the European Intelligence Agency to spy and report on Kuroda activities. He wanted to know if I would pay him to act as a double agent. We can be sure that many more have been sent disguised as emigrants, and that some of them will be more conscientious than this one. We can expect sabotage as well. Cooperate with Shaw in this, Hjalmar."

"We'll catch them," he promised.

"We need a diplomatic branch," Sousa said. "And it must begin work immediately. The task will be a daunting one. Our spokesmen must persuade the most cantankerously individualistic people in history to join a nation. Young Thor, that sounds like a natural position for you. You're comfortable with people in all walks or perhaps floats of life. You have an engaging manner and an impressive sincerity. Will you become our first diplomat?"

"I've never had any experience in diplomacy," Thor said, "but if you trust me I'll give it a try."

"Don't be dismayed by your lack of experience," Saburo said. "Nobody else out here has ever had any experience, either. You'll start with Sálamis. As soon as we appoint a treasurer, you'll be given a budget to work on and a ship will be detached from the family fleet for your use."

"What do I tell them we want them to join?" Thor asked. "A nation needs a name."

"Tell them that our new nation is the Confederacy of Island Worlds," Saburo said.

General Maas pushed back from his desk. At near Earth-normal gravity, some effort was involved. Sálamis was given a high rate of spin and all personnel had to spend a minimum number of days under heavy gravity to keep them in top physical condition. Thor found it exhausting. How had he ever lived like this?

"Get your constitution ratified," Maas said, "and you've got a military arm. We've prepared for this for years, ever since General Taggart and Ciano set us up. Of course, this setup looks weighted in favor of the founding families, but if, as you promise, wider representation is forthcoming, then we'll have no objection to placing ourselves under the command of the Confederacy. I've talked it over with my staff and we have one proviso: We want it spelled out in the Constitution that Sálamis, under the direction of a civilian Secretary of Defense, runs the *sole* military establishment of the Confederacy. Politicians are forever trying to set up independent paramilitary organizations and it's deadly. No uniformed thugs, no privateers, no mercenaries. And no political commissars to ensure our loyalty. If you don't trust our honor there can be no morale."

"I think that will be agreeable and I'll urge Dr. Sousa to include the single-military force clause immediately. After all, the last thing we need is a Wermacht-SS split in our forces. I'll recommend that Hjalmar's new force be disbanded as soon as you're ready to take over our defense." Thor made a note on his recorder.

"Don't disband them," Maas advised. "Form them into a civilian internal-security force. We shouldn't handle that and you'll need such a force for the duration. Just make sure that their charter is for police duties, not military action or external security. I'll appoint a liaison so that we can cooperate."

Thor was relieved that his first assignment involved people who not only were sympathetic to his cause, but who had thought out all the details years before. The next ones would be much harder nuts to crack.

"Now that we have that settled," Maas said, "let's have a drink." He touched a sensor plate and an antiquated robot rolled in with glasses of whiskey. Maas raised his. "To the Confedcracy."

They drank and Maas refilled both glasses. "My sources on Earth inform me that the Earth forces are weeding out soldiers who have relatives out here. I'm afraid that they've arrested all of your relatives in the officer corps. We've been urging them to get out and come over to us, but some of them took too long to make up their minds."

An aide came in and saluted. "Sir, the men in Assault Force Five have uncovered a spy. New recruit named Albrecht. We got him away from them before they killed him, but he's in damaged condition."

"I want a full report. Keep me informed on the interrogation." The aide saluted again and left.

"Has this happened before?" Thor asked.

"This makes three. I hate it, it's bad for morale when every soldier is suspicious of his mates. It's hardest on the new recruits because they're the most likely suspects. We should have the last of them weeded out soon, then there won't be any more since emigration has been halted."

"Recent arrival isn't conclusive," Thor pointed out. "There's always the chance of sleepers."

"We're taking that into account. Now, speaking of

divisive elements, I want to go on record about Martin
Shaw. I recommend, the minute you've formed a legitimate government, that you have him arrested. He'll get
us all killed."

"He's forming his own political party," Thor said.
"That's perfectly legal by any democratic standards. If
we start cracking down on opposition for being opposition, all the communities will turn against us. It's just
the kind of thing we all came out here to escape."

"Opposition, hell!" Maas said. "He's a terrorist. Don't
get me wrong, I admire Shaw a great deal. I wish he
was one of our officers. With his brains and nerve he
could be a top commander. But he's a political ideologue and he sees nothing wrong with terror attacks
against Earth. There are always a few idiots who'll go
along with that kind of thinking, especially the young
idealists. It seems to promise quick results, it guarantees a lot of danger and excitement, and it doesn't
burden them with too much thinking. We have a long,
complicated war ahead of us and there'll be no quick
fix."

"Not too long, I hope," Thor said, apprehensively.

Maas massaged his long nose. He had long, bony
features with a high forehead emphasized by a receding
hairline. "I'm afraid it's got to be long. You can only
win a war quick by using overwhelming force, and we
just don't have it. Unless, of course, you want to use
Shaw's tactics. That'd be quick, all right."

"Hold it," Thor said. "Are you telling me that you
can't win a war and Shaw can?"

"Sure you can win with his methods, if you don't
mind hundreds of millions of deaths on your conscience
and a name that'll stink for ten thousand years. We just
can't win a *short* war on any other terms and we really
can't win a long one. But, we can make them lose it."

Thor found himself wishing he'd paid more attention
to history in school. "You mean you can win without
victory?"

"Without any *big* victories. In fact, without winning
any battles at all. It's how guerillas and small powers

have always had to fight to prevail against major military powers. You don't think the United States won its independence by beating the whole British Empire, do you? They won in Parliament, not on the battlefield. The same in Southeast Asia and Africa and a hundred other places. You make the big powers quit in disgust without any decisive battles. If you can manage one big face-losing, propaganda defeat like Dienbienphu, all the better, but it's not essential. But you have to have the will to endure enormous suffering and loss."

"And what if there's a limit to how much you can bear?" Thor asked.

"Then you deserve to be a slave and you had no business rebelling in the first place," Maas said, pitilessly.

"The Earthies can't get along without our resources," the fat man said. "For decades, they've depended on us for rare minerals. This xenophobia is mere hysteria. It will pass and things will go back to normal before long, you'll see. They'll come around as soon as their stockpiles are exhausted and they start feeling the pinch." He leaned back and smiled complacently. He was Gunther Armanjac, Director of Delos.

Thor was bone-tired. This was his twentieth stop. All too many of them had been like this; self-deluding optimists unable to face their situation.

"You're wrong, Director," Thor insisted. "This is a policy that has very little to do with our value to Earth. We're a distraction, the object of a hate campaign. From now on, everything that goes wrong on Earth will be blamed on us. The hate won't stop. If you try to stick it out alone, they'll come and take over here and you'll be stuck with nothing if you're alive at all."

"And what will happen if we join your republic?" Armanjac said, eyebrows fluttering quizzically. "I'll tell you what: There will be taxes to pay for your war. If we acknowledge your government, we'll recognize their right to regulate our business. No, thank you, Mr. Taggart. We're doing nicely as it is."

"But, damn it, can't you see that the alternative is to

lose everything! The Earthies aren't going to let you go on with business as usual."

Armanjac continued to smile. "It won't come to that. You and your Eos Party are just alarmists. Everything will be fine. Good day, Mr. Taggart."

"There is really no point in uniting for a common defense," the monk said. He wore a coverall of brown sack cloth with a hood. "What we need is more prayer and good works. Look around you." Patiently, Thor did so. Iona was a small rock, perhaps two kilometers along its longest side. It had been almost completely hollowed out fifty years before and the remaining rock wall was riddled into a honeycomb of tiny cells. In most cells, a monk drifted crosslegged, tethered by a cord and reciting prayers. In the center of the hollow space, a monk with a loudspeaker announced the beginning of each new prayer.

"After all," the monk continued, "the cosmos would have come to an end twenty-seven years ago had it not been for our prayers. We try to intercede with God to delay the end of the cosmos so that more souls may be saved by the time the end comes."

"But," Thor said craftily, "if the Earthies lob a nuke into your laps, your prayers will be ended and the cosmos with them."

"That," the monk said imperturbably, "shall be God's way of telling us to shut up and let him get on with his work. His will be done."

This was the fifty-seventh stop. Thor was sure he would be cracking up soon. "Between business and religion," he said, "I think I've taken on a hopeless task."

The monk laid a comforting hand on his shoulder. "If you think we're difficult, Brother," he said, "wait 'til you deal with the ladies over on Lesbos."

"I wish you hadn't said that," he groaned.

"Yes! We will join you!" It was good to hear someone so enthusiastic for a change. Of course, there was some-

thing in the burning eyes of the turbaned man, something in the way he waved his sword, that said this
community would be a problem. "Yes!," he continued,
"we shall smite the unbelievers! We shall hew them
asunder and bring them to godly ways! We shall show
them the paths of righteousness and truth! Shall we
not, my children?"

Throughout the immense temple, turbaned men
shouted and whirled their swords and went into low-g
spins, their robes fluttering and turning the temple into
a field of white flowers. Behind screens of stone trac-
ery, veiled women ululated like demented banshees.

"I am afraid," Thor said quietly, "that it may not be
quite that kind of war."

"Ever since Guru Mahatma George Rajagopalachari
led us here fifty years ago, we have prepared and
purified ourselves for the holy war against decadent and
impure Earth. We shall aid Lord Shiva in obliterating
that sink of iniquity and establishing the rule of purity
and truth!"

"Actually," Thor said, "what we'd like for you to do is
join in our Confederacy. The war itself will be conducted by Sálamis under the direction of our Congress."

"Complete religious freedom?" said the guru, now all
business. "And equal representation in your congress or
parliament or whatever?"

"Absolutely. If we were a more homogenous people, the population of each state might be the deter-
mining factor. Since we are made up of such disparate
and cantankerous people, representation has to be by
republic. One island world with a few hundred colonists gets the same vote as a community of several
asteroids with thousands of inhabitants."

"Taxation proportional to population, of course?" the
guru prodded.

Thor shook his head. "It's a percentage based on each
world's or community's income and reserves. The pre-
liminary levy for the Confederacy's war chest will be a
heavy one."

"That is unacceptable!" the guru said.

"Come off it," Thor insisted. "Everybody knows that the Golden Isle of Shiva is one of the richest of the island worlds and that you've been socking away a precious-minerals reserve for decades. The Earthies know it, too. They may try to nuke some of us and they may pass by some of the more insignificant colonies, but they'll come here in force. Make up your mind—give up a percentage of what you have to keep what's left or end up with a hundred percent of nothing." It was good to have some leverage for a change.

The guru thought for a while. "Our young men to serve in ships only with others of our own faith and under our own officers?"

"No deal," Thor said. "Once under military command, all service personnel will go where they're told and do what they're told. We already have assurances from Sálamis that nobody will have to participate in anybody else's religious services and that religious practices will be respected as long as they don't interfere with duties."

The guru pondered some more, then stuck out his hand. "Done." Thor took it. Then the guru turned back to his flock. "To the Holy war!" There was much more shouting and waving of swords.

Thor was looking drawn and haggard as he tendered his report. Everybody looked tired. It had been a grueling seven months and few of them had anticipated how difficult the founding of a state could be.

"Sálamis was a dream," Thor said. "They had all my work done before I got there. The high-tech scientific, research and manufacturing stations were fairly easy. They grasped the advantages of a Confederacy, both defensive and commercial, almost immediately. The merchant settlements were difficult. I convinced a few, but most of them can't see past their ledger books. A state means one thing to them: taxes. They won't face up to the danger from Earth and when they think about it at all, they're sure they can buy their way out."

"Most will come around," Saburo said. "There's nothing like an ocean of red ink to make a merchant see the light. What about the others?"

"The miners, freighters, refiners and such are not such a problem. They're cantankerous and hard to organize, but they know how to face danger and they're willing to unite, at least for the duration of the crisis. As for the religious communities," Thor raised his hands in despair, "I had no idea there were so many loonies out here. Some won't countenance violence at all, not even in self-defense. Others want to kill all unbelievers, including most of us. Many follow Earth-based religions and are decidedly cool to any movement that breaks their ties with Earth." He buried his face in his hands. "I'm sorry. I'm afraid my mission wasn't much of a success."

"You did fine," Sousa said.

"Are you joking?" Thor said.

"Not at all. I wasn't expecting more than about twenty-five percent positive response this early and you've turned in almost thirty percent positive. There are about twenty percent who will never join us, mostly for religious reasons. The rest will come around, eventually, out of pure self-interest. Many just don't believe that Earth will attack. They are in for a rude awakening. If we can just hold steadfastly in the early days of conflict, most of the others will be attracted to our cause."

The other diplomatic missions reported as well. Their stories were much the same as Thor's. Reception had ranged from enthusiastic to lukewarm to hostile, with the latter two heavily weighted. Still, most of them had kept well within Sousa's twenty-five percent acceptance range. They had the nucleus of a republic.

"It bothers me," Thor said, "that many of those who have opted for us are those with the smallest populations. Some of the scientific stations are virtually automated."

"There is a great deal of hidden population out here," Sousa reminded him. "Some of the scientific stations and a great many mining colonies have substantial populations out on small rocks or on ships. Taken all together, the actual population is far greater than the apparent figure."

"Just what is our population?" Hjalmar asked.

"The Space Authority census gives a total off-Earth figure of some ten million, including Luna, Mars, the orbiting stations, the outer moons, everything. Their figures are probably accurate for everything but the Belt. People have been emigrating to the island worlds for over half a century now, a great bulk of that emigration has been clandestine, and we run to large families, most of which go unreported. Earth census estimates around two million in the Belt. The accurate figure is closer to ten million."

"Impossible!" somebody said.

"We certainly hope the Earthies think so," Saburo commented. "But I've double-checked our figures. There's no way to get an accurate count, of course, but it must be somewhere near that figure. It's only that we are so widely scattered that makes our population seem so slight."

"What has Shaw been up to while we were out looking for support?" Thor asked.

"He's kept very busy. All manner of young fools have been joining his movement." Saburo looked glum. "Along with others old enough to know better." Thor hoped that didn't mean what it sounded like. He hadn't yet had time to ask about Caterina. When he had left for his mission, she had been sent out to shut down family operations until the situation was clarified. He hadn't seen *Sisyphus* when he'd landed, but it might have been at the other pole or moored out of sight somewhere.

The meeting broke up with a spirit of tightly guarded optimism. The situation was far from ideal, but it didn't seem as hopeless as many had assumed. Sousa's reassurances were comforting, and the stunning news of the huge invisible population put things in a different light. Most of them had been oppressed by their smallness and weakness compared to huge, populous Earth. True, ten million only made a small-sized nation by Earth standards, but the island worlds had no bulk of idle, welfare-supported do-nothings to act as a drag on its economy or, if need be, its military capability. Nearly every adult was a vital, functioning part of society, although Thor held his doubts about the ever-praying monks.

Saburo stopped Thor as he was about to leave the room. "Thor, I'm afraid I have some bad news for you. It looks as if Caterina has thrown in with Shaw." Thor's heart sank. He didn't need this, not now. "She's here in Avalon someplace," Saburo went on. "Try to find her and talk to her. You might be able to make her see sense. She regards you highly, and you two are near the same age. She thinks that Tomás and I, and most of the family elders, are timid and ineffectual plodders. Shaw's call to action is seductive."

"If she regards me highly," Thor said, "she's hidden it from me pretty thoroughly. I'll do what I can, but I don't think I'll make much progress. Maybe it isn't Shaw's personal magnetism that attracts her and the others. It may be because Shaw's way, brutal as it is, is the only one that has a chance of working."

"Not you, too," Saburo said, wearily.

Thor took a deep breath and let it out in a long sigh. "No, but my experiences these last few months have been enough to strain my belief in our chances of living through this."

"We'll have to convince people otherwise," Saburo said. "The mass rally starts in ten days. We have to declare independence and form a government, one that people will have confidence in. Shaw may promise action, but there is a great deal more to running a nation than killing foreigners. And we have Sálamis."

He found her in a spacer's R&R center called *The Rockhounder*. It was situated near the south polar dock and in recent months had become a well-known center for Shaw's followers. One of the rooms, formerly a hiring office for transient spacers, had been converted to a nerve center for Shaw's movement. That was where he found her, sitting at a console and issuing orders to a small band of young people, mostly teenagers. There was nothing that could be called a uniform, but all wore Shaw's black-and-red armband.

"Hello Cat." She looked up and her expression changed slightly. He couldn't interpret it. The youngsters drew slightly together and he could feel the tension in the air. He wasn't wearing an armband. He was an outsider, possibly hostile.

"Good to see you, Thor. I hear you've been busy, drumming up support for Eos."

"Eos?" said one of the youngsters with infinite adolescent contempt. "This one's an Earthie-lover? You want us to chuck him out, Cat?"

"I doubt if you could. He's pretty good in a rough-and-tumble. I've seen him at work myself. Martin trained him." She smiled slightly. So far, so good.

"Oh, you're a friend of Cat and the Chief?" the boy said. "Sorry, Earthie-lover."

"We need to talk," Thor said.

"I think we should." She turned to her loyal little band. "You all know your jobs. Get to it and report back at 2200." The youths drifted away in the slight gravity.

"What is this?" Thor asked when they were gone. "The Children's Crusade?"

"They have enthusiasm," she said, "and they have guts and they don't know what defeat means."

"Those are the virtues of ignorance," Thor said.

"In case you hadn't noticed," she said, unsnapping herself from her chair, "that's who fight wars, not old businessmen who can't do anything but negotiate."

"Negotiation is a part of war, too," Thor said. "If you do it right, sometimes you don't have to fight at all."

She shook her head as they passed into a huge lounge that was crowded with spacers talking excitedly. With the shutdown of most operations, there were many spacers at loose ends. "Ever the optimist," she said. "It'll be war. Martin expects the first overtly hostile acts within the week. They'll certainly try something during the big rally. Maybe sabotage. Their spies must have informed them in plenty of time to mount an Earth-based attack, if they want something spectacular."

"Then we'd better hope that the Sálamids have their defenses in place by then," Thor said. He accepted a beer from a robot server and Caterina took a bulb of tea. They stood close together because of the noise. There were no sitting facilities in the lounge because of the low gravity.

"And the first thing you'll do if Eos comes out in control of the new government," she said hotly, "will be to order us disbanded and have Martin arrested!"

"Disbanding, yes," Thor said. "We can't have two fighting forces in competition and we can't have another party making military and foreign policy in opposition to the government. As for Martin, if he avoids doing anything foolish, such as pulling off an attack on his own, there'll be no reason to arrest him."

He shrugged, an Earth habit he still had. The Spaceborn didn't have the gesture. "It won't be up to me anyway. I'll probably be out of a job. I'll still be a Party member, but my position is purely temporary. As soon as a new government is formed I'll most likely be dismissed. I won't be sorry to go, either."

"What will you do?" she said. "You're pretty good in a tight place, why not come over to us? Even you can't believe that Eos is going to lead us into anything but disaster."

He shook his head. "I won't be a party to mass murder. I'm considering accepting a direct commission in a Sálamid ship. In a non-command capacity, of course."

"You'd serve in a warship?" she said with reluctant respect. "If Sálamis tries to take on the Earth fleet, your life expectancy won't be long."

"Colonel Moore tells me he's putting together a reconnaissance squadron. Small crews, like in *Sisyphus*. I can serve as executive officer while I'm learning the trade."

"You won't have time to learn anything," she insisted. "You'll be dead. We can't be fighting space battles with

Earth! And we can't sit here waiting for them to attack, either. We'll have to take the war to them."

"And wipe out huge noncombatant populations!" The remark was overheard and drew hostile looks. He reminded himself where he was and lowered his voice. Red-and-black armbands were everywhere. "No population in the history of war has ever been bombed into submission," he added. He had been studying. "It just stiffens resistance and makes them more determined to win."

"Nobody's ever had anything as devastating as our ice and rock bombs," she pointed out. "They'll come from nowhere and the Earthies will see no enemy to strike back at. Their morale will crack. After all, it's not as if we've been invading and occupying their planet. They'll see they've been duped, throw out Earth First and sue for peace."

"You're working hard to convince yourself," he said. "But it's easy for you because you've never been to Earth. To you they're not actual people down there. I was born there. To me, those are real cities we'd be wiping out. Do you want us to found our republic on the biggest bloodbath in history?"

"Nobody wants that," she said, "but they're forcing us to it, can't you see that?"

"Everybody tries to shift responsibility to the other side," he pointed out. "You attack and say 'They made me do it!' It doesn't work that way. If they come out here and we fight them here, there's no doubt who the aggressor is."

"What are you worried about, the history books? Those are written by the winning side. That's sure to be the case in this war, since there'll be none of us left to set down our own version when it's over. The Earthies will create their own version of events, just as they're doing right now!"

"Didn't I hear Shaw say something like that just recently? Besides, there's more to it than the opinion of posterity. I agree that the verdict of history shouldn't concern us just now. What should concern us is keeping opinion split on Earth. Earth First grabbed power by some slick political maneuvering and very clever propagandizing. It's not the kind of thing that makes for a solid and stable power base. There must be plenty of opposition wanting to grab power back.

"If we drop rock bombs on Earth, the opposition won't dare open their mouths for fear of being considered traitors to Earth. But if the Earth government draws them into a long and costly war with no end in sight, that support will fade away. Public hysteria just doesn't have the lasting power to sustain that kind of effort."

"That could take years, even if we can survive the attacks, which I doubt. You think Earth is disunited? There isn't a chance that we could hold together through years of fighting. A quick offensive against Earth is the only possible answer."

He wasn't making much headway. "Look, Cat, everybody who ever went to war, especially amateurs who'd never seen war before, started out with a foolproof, elegant plan that was going to win a quick victory and everybody goes home by Christmas. It never works out that way. For one thing, they always depend on the enemy to go along and act according to plan. That never happens, either. If you think Earth will roll over and play dead because of a few rock attacks, you're underestimating them. If you think we don't have the stomach for a long war when our lives and our independence are at stake, you're underestimating us, too."

"What makes you an expert on our spirit?" she said. "You're just a transplanted Earthie yourself."

"I was wondering when you were going to get around to that," he barked. "Like the rest of the Spaceborn, you think you belong to some kind of natural aristocracy!"

"Hey," said a scar-faced man standing nearby, "your well-reasoned political discussion is degenerating into a lover's quarrel. What do you say you carry it outside?" Mortified, Thor saw that nearly everyone in the room was looking at them with great interest. Fortunately, the armband-wearers didn't seem inclined to lecture him with violence. As yet, few of the Spaceborn had the instinct for mob action.

Sheepishly, the two made their inglorious exit. In the closed and crowded world of shipborne and asteroid-dwelling life, engaging in a private argument in public was a serious breach of etiquette.

"I have to get back to my post," she said when they were in the outer hall. "We're not accomplishing anything with all this talk."

"You'd be surprised at what you can accomplish with talk. Martin knows that. He was a theoretician, a journalist, a publisher and propagandist, all before he took up smuggling and a life of derring-do."

"Do you think I'd follow a man who wasn't good at both?" she said. "But there are words with a purpose and there's meaningless babble, which is what you and Eos are dealing in. And you've put too much faith in Sálamis. What do you really expect from a bunch of cashiered officers who couldn't cut it in the Earth forces and came out here to play soldier?"

"More than you'll get from half-educated kids with guns and explosives. Have you got them planting bombs yet?"

"This is getting us nowhere," she said. "We're just going to have to see how people decide in ten days. Goodbye, Thor." She turned and glided away in a low-g stalk. Thor tried to think of something to say but he was uncomfortable with addressing a back. The first to turn had an unfair advantage.

Thor caught a tube train and returned to HMK.

NINE

"We couldn't crack it, Thor." The head of Avalon DataSystems handed the pile of sheets back. "We ran it through our computers a dozen times, applied every program and key we have, and turned up nothing. This code uses some kind of personal key and we have no way of figuring out what it is. About all we can make out is that it probably isn't a message. The groupings of figures and symbols make it look more like a formula of some kind. It has the look of a mathematical calculation. Sorry we couldn't help."

"You did your best." He was thankful that they hadn't been able to break the code, now that he had some suspicion of what it might be. He sealed it into a plastic envelope and left the office.

HMK was packed with people, more than he had ever seen in one place since leaving Earth. Most were here for the convention that would thrash out a government for the previously ungoverned island worlds. Banners were hung everywhere and dozens of minor political parties had been formed. The colonists were taking to this new form of entertainment like spacers reaching a resort rock after a long voyage. Most of the parties were small and represented narrow interests and limited constituencies. Only Eos and Shaw's Defiance party had broad-based appeal.

There were representatives from many of the asteroid colonies, especially those near Avalon. Others would be voting by remote. There was an air of excitement compounded of a consciousness of being present at one of history's turning points and a welcome break from the hard routine of spacer life. Thor wondered how long the holiday atmosphere would last. No longer than the first attack by Earth forces, most likely.

He descended to the warehouse level, which was quiet and sparsely populated. In the uncertain times, few enterprises were outfitting and merchants stood forlornly by their stacks of wares, commiserating on the poor business prospects. There were several small bars and restaurants opening off the main cavern and he entered one with the name "Bat Cave" carved into the stone above its ragged entrance.

The light inside was dim, revealing a small gallery from an old mining operation. The walls still showed the clean but uneven cuts of shortbeam laser cutters. There were a few occupants and a holo screen on one wall displayed the scene in HMK above. As Thor's eyes adjusted to the dimness, he spotted a wild-bearded old man standing at one of the small, spindly tables. As he walked over, the old man fixed glaring, crazy eyes on him.

"Are you Roseberry?" Thor asked.

"That I am. You Taggart?"

"Yes." They clasped hands. Roseberry was the oldest specimen Thor had seen since leaving Earth. Between good medical treatment and the beneficial effects of low gravity, a spacer lucky enough to survive accident and violence could reasonably expect to be healthy and active past the age of a century. Thor estimated Roseberry to be one hundred twenty, at least. His ancient, stained coverall bore on its breast the sigil of the South Polar Port Authority. Hjalmar's men had located him working at the facility as a maintenance specialist—a polite title for janitor.

"Thank you for letting me run up a tab at your expense, Mr. Taggart," Roseberry said, "but I'm a little

curious as to what kind of business you have in mind."
He snatched up the concoction delivered by the little
rolling robot and drained it. He exhaled loudly and an
expression of contentment crossed his withered face.

"I need information first of all. If the information
turns out to be what I'm looking for, I may have a
longer-term job to offer you, at generous pay."

A comically crafty expression took over Roseberry's
face. "Nothing too illegal, I hope? And I don't rat on
my friends." The crafty look was replaced by one of
extreme nobility.

"Nothing illegal," Thor said. "Yet," he amended. "I
need to know some things about Ugo Ciano. I understand you worked for him in his last years."

"Ugo was a great man. Great man. Greatest man that
ever spaced, by God! I helped him in tho lab. He never
let nobody else go into the place, not even the family."
He swelled his chest with pride and took another drink
from the robot.

Thor sipped at his beer. "Just what was this drive he
was working on when he died?"

"Why you asking?"

"I have reason to believe that Ugo wanted one of us—
one of his descendants or Sam Taggart's, to have the
secret of that engine."

"That so? What proof have you got?"

Thor let the packet of coded sheets fall slowly to the
table. "Ugo gave these to his son Robert and Robert
sent them on to me before he died. I can't crack the
code, but I think it has something to do with that drive.
Whatever the secret is, we may need it desperately
before this war is over."

Roseberry canted his skinny neck a bit and squinted
down his long nose to study the top sheet. "That's
Ugo's code, all right. Don't prove nothing by itself, but
that does." He placed a dirty, yellow-nailed finger on
an especially complicated symbol that looked like a
Mayan glyph.

"What does it mean?" Thor asked.

"It's a personal message to me. Says I'm to cooperate

with you. I remember when old Ugo put these sheets together. He always hoped it'd be his boy Bob who'd come out with them, but they never licked that heart condition. Most folks don't know it, but Ugo sunk billions into heart research. Probly a hunnerd million people walking or floating around today that'd be dead if it wasn't for Ugo's heart research. Didn't do young Bob no good, though." A tear rolled slowly to the end of his nose and he brushed it off. "Anyways, this sign means I can take you to his lab."

"Lab?" Thor said. "Brunhilde said it was a deserted rock."

"That deserted rock never was anything else. He kept the real location of the lab secret from everybody, even Hildy. Before he tried out his drive, he gave me the ephemeris and said not to give them to anybody else until somebody showed up with them sheets."

"He was taking a big chance," Thor said. "You might have died in the meantime, or these sheets might have fallen into the wrong hands."

"He always had backups. I 'spect the ephemeris are in there somewhere, but you'd have to be as smart as Ugo to figure it out. I think that was what he really wanted, to pass it on to someone that was like him."

"Do you have any idea what it was?" Thor asked.

Roseberry leaned close and whispered conspiratorially: "It was the antimatter drive!"

A wave of disappointment washed over Thor. The antimatter drive was one of the great chimeras of pseudoscience. Reputable scientists had discarded the notion for nearly a century. There was nothing wrong with the basic premise: The most efficient way to produce energy, for a given mass of fuel, is to convert it totally to energy. This can be accomplished by combining equal quantities of matter and antimatter. By comparison, the fusion of hydrogen atoms to helium, the process responsible for the H-bomb and harnessing the energy of the Sun, converts less than 1 percent of the mass of hydrogen into energy and is relatively inefficient.

Antimatter was created in laboratories but the quan-

tity thus produced was minuscule. Toward the end of
the twentieth century, antiprotons were produced primarily through the use of gigantic particle accelerators.
The production capacity was severely limited and the
storage of antiprotons in significant quantity presented
a serious engineering problem, one analogous to the
ancient conundrum about inventing the universal sol-
vent: if it will dissolve anything, what do you store it
in? Reputable scientists had tended to consign the matter-
antimatter energy process to the same oblivion as the
perpetual motion machine

"It can't exist, Roseberry," Thor said, sadly. "It's
been proven."

"Proven!" Roseberry sputtered. "You think that'd stop
Ugo? You know what he used to say? 'History consists
principally of an unbroken chain of experts who have
been proven dead wrong.' That's what he used to say."
The old man nodded furiously. "Besides, just what do
you think he blew hisself up with, if he blew hisself up
at all? That flash was recorded all the way to Mars! You
think he did that with gunpowder?"

The old man had a point. Thor had looked up records
of the incident. Whatever had caused the flash had
been a process unknown to science of the time. It had
all been disregarded as another of Ciano's mad experiments, this one fatal. He had had many narrow escapes
and had taken insane risks after the death of his wife.
"Whatever it is, I want to find out about it. Don't talk
about this to anybody. I'll arrange for a ship. How long
a voyage is it?"

" 'bout a two-day haul from here. He wanted to keep
it close to Avalon because the family set up here. No
particular efforts to hide it. It's just a dinky little chunk
of rock nobody'd pay any attention to. People've landed
there from time to time and took core samples and
never found the lab. I know where the entrance is and I
got the code."

"I know of a two-man prospector ship we can use. I'll
call your boss and tell him I need your services for a
few days. Stay where I can get in contact with you and

be ready to leave at any time in the next few days. Here," he passed across several slips of Avalon's gold-backed currency, "this is a down-payment. If we find something really important, there's a big bonus in it for you."

"Well, I'm really doing this for Ugo," he took the money, "but a man's got to provide for his old age. 'Course," he said reflectively, "I probly ain't got much old age left to provide for." He walked away just as three men entered the bar. One of them was Shaw and the three walked to Thor's little table.

"Good to see you, Thor," Shaw said, extending his hand.

Thor took it. "Same here." He was surprized to realize that he meant it. Despite the politics, despite Caterina's clear rejection of him for Shaw, Thor was truly glad to see him. Mike was with him and another man Thor didn't recognize; an elegant, dark-skinned man with shiny black hair and a look that made him vaguely uncomfortable.

"Thor, you know Mike. This is Thierry Ruiz." They clasped hands. Shaw hadn't said what Ruiz was and Thor decided not to ask. "What were you and old Crazy Roseberry talking about?"

It wasn't like Shaw to ask such a question, but things had changed. Had Caterina told him about the coded sheets Bob had sent? "He used to work for Ugo Ciano. I wanted to hear about it."

"He's one of the real pioneers," Shaw said. "Helped build Armstrong and the first L5 colony. He must be one of the last of that generation. Has some interesting stories, for an old lush."

"What brings you down here?" Thor asked. "The warehouse level is enduring a depression. I'd expect you to be up politicking in HMK."

"I wanted to talk to you. Some of my people reported seeing you down here."

"We're getting to be like Earthies, aren't we?" Thor said. "Living in each other's pockets, keeping tabs on each other, establishing domestic spy systems—"

Shaw favored him with a thin-lipped smile. "It's the times. You know damn well if you wanted to find me you'd go to your cousin Hjalmar and his watchdogs would tell you where I was and what I had for breakfast."

"Here's to the times," Thor said, raising his glass.

"Happy as I am to see you again," Shaw said, "this isn't an entirely social visit."

"I presumed as much," Thor said. "What's on your mind?"

"Thierry, here, is the media specialist for Defiance," Shaw began. Thor translated it as Minister of Propaganda. "He's been keeping track of our image in the Earth news services. Tell Thor how things stand, Thierry."

"Needless to say, we are all portrayed in a bad light," Thierry said. "Defiance is the primary target. Mr. Shaw is routinely depicted as a mad-dog fanatic who would annihilate Earth if he could only get his hands on the weaponry."

"How ever did they get that idea?" Thor said. "Mere mass murder doesn't constitute annihilation." Shaw looked annoyed but said only: "Wait'll you hear the next part."

"Eos comes in for almost the same amount of vilification, and you are now a fiend of only slightly less notoriety than Mr. Shaw."

"Me?" Thor was stunned. "What have I done and why am I so important?"

"You've been out recruiting for the cause, that's what," Shaw said.

"There is, of course, far more to it than that," Ruiz went on. "Your early activities among the colonies made you the most visible of Eos members. You were the first that Earth intelligence people could put a name to. Also, it's a well-known name, and a single, recognizable villain has far more emotional appeal than a faceless consortium. Since you lack, shall we say, Mr. Shaw's flair for violent rhetoric, you are instead depicted as a lurking, Machiavellian schemer, slyly drawing your evil designs against the people of Earth."

"That means that you and I are both targets, Thor," Shaw said.

"Come off it, Martin," Thor said. "They won't try to assassinate me after they've gone to so much trouble to make me a symbol of evil. If you think you're going to scare me into some kind of alliance with this, you're wrong."

Ruiz inclined his head, slightly but respectfully. "You are getting good at this game, Mr. Taggart. But the conclusion you should be drawing from all this is that your party's soft line toward Earth is gaining you no friends there. They can't afford to allow *any* separatist movement to have any prestige or favor at all. If we lose, we'll all be executed indiscriminately."

"If we lose," Thor said, "there won't be many of us left to execute. Eos is just as determined to fight this out as Defiance. We differ on *how* to fight."

"I think you'll change your mind once hostilities start," Shaw said. "It's always a new game when that happens. Presumed assumptions and untried theories kind of go into the mass converter then. By the way," he placed a fingertip on the pile of coded sheets on the table, "I heard you got some encoded data a while back. Maybe my crypto people can help you crack it."

Thor's spine tigthened. So that was it. "Just some private correspondence. Your spooks have more important work to do."

"Don't try to sit on something that might be crucial to us all, Thor," Shaw said. His tone was dead serious and Thor wondered if he could handle all three of them. Not a chance.

"Thor!" It was a bellow from the doorway. Hjalmar Taggart swaggered in. He was a huge, bullet-headed man and he towered over the rest of them. Outside, behind him, Thor could make out at least six of Hjalmar's men. He let out a relieved breath. "I was wondering where you were. We need you for a family conference. Hello, Martin. How's the criminal activities going? Now I know Mike, but who's this? Why, this must be Thierry Ruiz, who was in Military Intelligence back when I was a frigate captain. What was it they cashiered you for, Thierry? Blackmailing your superiors, wasn't it?"

Thierry's face turned crimson but Hjalmar just stood confidently. He didn't appear to be armed but Thor was sure he was. Hjalmar turned to Shaw. "I know, Martin. Good help's hard to find, isn't it? I guess every political boss needs an assassin. That was another of his specialties, you know. Take good care of him and keep his nose clean. If I ever find half an excuse, he's a dead man. Don't turn your back when he's around, either."

"You talk like some kind of official," Shaw said. "In a few days, you could just be an ordinary citizen and I could be President of the Confederacy."

Hjalmar grinned. "These people may be ornery," he said, "but they aren't likely to pick a butcher for their first president. Come on, Thor, we're late."

"Good to talk to you, Martin," Thor said, picking up the coded sheets. "Come see me again. Alone."

The two walked out into the warehouse cavern and Hjalmar's men closed discreetly around them. "Thanks, Hjalmar. That almost turned really bad."

"When my people said Shaw was heading for the place where you were meeting Roseberry, I came on the double. When are you going to let me assign you a bodyguard?"

"Never. But get to Roseberry right away. Don't let Shaw's people find him."

"I'll hide him in Saburo's *saké* works. He'll be happy as a mouse on a grain ship." He nodded to one of his men, who trotted off to do his bidding.

"Shaw knew about this coded message," Thor said, holding out the sheets, "and he knows it's something important. I didn't know myself until a little while ago."

"How he found out about it is no question," Hjalmar said. "Cat would sell out her family for that man."

"You don't know that," Thor said stubbornly, knowing in his heart that Hjalmar was right.

"Be that as it may, he might not really know anything. Maybe he's guessing. When people don't have much confidence in their capabilities, they start casting about for secret weapons. Old Bob wouldn't have sent it coded unless it was something he wanted to keep from Earth authority. Maybe Shaw figures it's some kind of weapon design."

"It isn't Bob's," Thor told him. "It's Ugo's. And I think it's something so crazy I can't even speculate about it. You'll think I'm crazy too."

"I think we're all crazy," Hjalmar said. "But if it's one of Ugo's inventions, it may be worth looking into. Probably a damn time machine, if half of what I've heard about him is true."

TEN

"There she is." Roseberry withdrew his head from the prospector's little observation bubble. Thor thrust his inside and looked around until he saw an irregular chunk of rock, one side of it brightly washed by sunlight. It was no more than one half kilometer on its longest axis. As Roseberry had said, it was just a dinky little chunk of rock. But it was quite large enough to hold the biggest laboratory on Earth with plenty of rock to spare.

Expertly, Thor guided the tiny, cramped vessel toward the rock. The prospector was equipped with proximity detectors to prevent a collision, but Thor knew better than to trust them completely. He followed Roseberry's directions until they drifted over a shallow depression with a streak of silver-flecked black rock running across its bottom. Roseberry ran their broadcaster through a series of frequencies and the entire depression swung inward, exposing a small landing dock.

"I'll take over now," Roseberry said. In spite of his reservations about the man's competence, Thor was willing to let him take the helm. It was a decidedly odd-looking landing dock. Gently, the old man eased the ship inside until they were floating within the dock, and the disguised hatch slid shut. Lights came on and Thor could see that the dock was smoothly finished

175

inside, a far more elaborate setup than the usual aster-oid dock. Roseberry rotated the ship and brought it to rest against the "outer" wall—the one nearest the out-side of the rock. He placed anchors to secure the ship firmly.

"Why are we anchored here?" Thor asked.

"So's we'll be oriented right when I start the spin on this old sucker. We'll get about one-sixth gee when she's spun up to speed. Takes about half an hour."

"Artificial gravity in this little place? Old Ugo went first class, didn't he?"

"You would too, if you could afford it. No exterior-mounted rockets, either. You could search out there for a month without finding where the exhausts are hid. He rigged a specially designed reaction wheel for the spin." He glanced at the screens on the console before him. "Good. Pressure's coming right up outside. Won't need no pressure suit in the dock. Ugo always hated to suit up just to get out of his ship, and he thought an umbilical tube was undignified, for some reason. 'I like to get outta my car and walk to the front door,' he used to say. Feel that? Gravity's taking hold now."

There had been no trace of vibration as the rock had begun to spin. First class all the way. They ran through a routine checkout sequence until the dock was fully pressurized and maximum rotation had been achieved. Then they dropped through the hatch in the belly of the ship and Thor followed Roseberry to a large hatch at one end. Thor figured that Ciano must have had some fairly large objects to move between the lab and the dock.

"This place brings back some memories," Roseberry said.

"Is the combination to the door among them?"

"Lessee, did it start with nine or a hundred thirty-seven?" He scratched his head and grinned at Thor's look of dismay. He poked a small, green plate with a finger and the door swung open. "There's a combina-tion, all right, but this is quicker. It's keyed to my fingerprint." Thor wondered why he never seemed to link up with anyone normal.

Lights came up as they entered the lab. There was no hesitancy or flickering, despite the decades since the switches had last been tripped. There was nothing in the place that wasn't the best. The room was cavernous, parts of it devoted to computer space, parts to chemical apparatus, and some areas that Thor was sure a medieval sorceror would have felt at home in. Here and there small, old-fashioned robots waited patiently for their orders.

"So, somebody showed up at last." Thor was obscurely proud that he hadn't jumped. The voice came from a catwalk above them.

"It's him!" Roseberry said, superstitious awe in his voice. "It's Ciano! Them stories was true, about how he never died!"

"They were your stories to begin with," Thor said. "This is just a holo. There's one like it back at Brunhilde's place."

Fifty meters from where they stood, Ciano descended from the catwalk. The illusion was perfect except that his feet made no sound on the metal stairs. "Never fooled me," Roseberry muttered.

"I made a bunch of these for when somebody showed up," Ciano said when he or his ghost was closer. "Most of 'em is pretty short on account of the intruders get laser-fried out in the lock. This one's for when it's Roseberry brings someone in. Good to know you're still alive, Roseberry, which is more than I can say for me. Don't take it personal, but I wish it was Bob that showed up instead of whoever you are. However, the scan must've cleared you as part of the extended Ciano-Taggart clan, or it'd be a different holo playing right now.

"Anyway, welcome to Castle Ciano and I'll bet you're desperate to know what the hell it was I was working on here, right? Well, come along and follow Uncle Ugo and he'll show you." The little image whirled and stalked away. They followed after and Thor was amazed to see tears glittering in the corners of Roseberry's eyes. The recitation had come out in a rapid staccatto, almost in a single breath, with much arm-waving. It was an astonishing performance for a man who had been ranting for no audience but a holographic recorder. It must have been one of dozens of recordings he had made against different eventualities. Ciano was the kind of man who threw himself whole-heartedly into everything he did.

Somewhere along the way to the rear of the lab, Thor saw the figure make a minute twitch. The greeting sequence had been blended with the standard lab lecture, Thor presumed, so he only had to make the latter once. Ciano halted before a glass wall and flung his arms wide. "There it is! Ta-daaaa! The secret of the antimatter drive!"

Thor looked inside. There was nothing but an empty room. Maybe Ciano had just gone crazy in his old age. That figured. He had been crazy when he was young, too. But what had made the flash?

"I know what you're thinking," Ciano said. "Old Ugo's nuts. There ain't no antimatter drive. Of course, maybe somebody else's discovered it by now, but I doubt it. Brains like mine don't come along very often. So listen up, and all shall be made plain."

Ciano stuck a finger in the air, as if testing the direction of the wind. "What's the big question that stumped all the geniuses of the twentieth century? Except me, I mean."

Thor could think of several. "The existence of God?" he hazarded.

"Why you can't tickle yourself?" Roseberry chimed in.

"Right!" Ciano said, triumphantly. "The Unified Field Theory. The problem was, there wasn't enough fields, or maybe too many, if you look at it another way. We had all the known four-dimensional fields; gravitational, electromagnetic, nuclear and so forth. But I knew, in my brilliantly intuitive way, that all these fields had to be mere manifestations of an underlying, all-pervasive field that exists in indeterminate n-space. Assuming such a field, all the problems afflicting the Unified Field Theory become as snowflakes in hell, as farts in the whirlwind, as the dew which flees before the rising of the sun." He clasped his hands behind his back and began to pace frantically up and down before the blank window. "I thought long and hard about what to call this field. It was, after all, the most momentous discovery in the history of humanity. At last, I came up with the perfect name: the Ciano Field. Having figured out how everything works and named it, I set about proving its existence."

"Kind of did things backwards, didn't he?" Thor said.

Roseberry shrugged. "Always worked for him."

Ciano was going on obliviously, as might be expected. "What, you may ask, has all this to do with the antimatter drive? Well, it was a byproduct of my experiments to prove the Ciano Field. See, using the Ciano Field, which exists in indeterminate n-space, I could safely store antimatter atoms. Nothing new about making them, just storing them. But I did figure out how to make anti-matter, using the field, without some godawful particle accelerator taking up a hundred miles of desert. Reversing pair annihilation was my first discovery. I developed a method for reversing the process of particle-antiparticle pair annihilation, which produced a gamma-ray photon. My process converts a gamma-ray photon into a particle (e.g., proton) and antiparticle (e.g., antiproton) pair!" Thor had never heard anyone use e.g. and parentheses in conversation.

"Are you following all this?" Thor asked.

"Hell, I don't even understand ordinary electricity," Roseberry answered.

"Given a suitable supply of energy," Ciano bulled on, gesticulating wildly, "the Ciano Field can be used to energize visible light photons or even radio wavelength photons and turn them into gamma-ray photons. I worked this up utilizing the old inverse-Compton effect. If the energy of the gamma ray is appropriate, you can produce proton and antiproton pairs. How do you like that? Pretty good, huh?"

He whirled around and stared at where he thought they should be, which was a few degrees off true. Unconsciously, Thor and Roseberry edged over to be standing in the right place. "And that ain't all! I even figured out a way to combine antielectrons, antiprotons, antineutrons and a bunch of other anti-elementary particles to create antimatter atoms! Man, sometimes I dazzle myself!"

He spread his hands expressively. "The antimatter is isolated and stored using the Ciano Field. Of course, it takes a tremendous amount of energy to create the antimatter. The most abundant supply of energy in the solar system is from the sun. I knew my work was gonna take lots and lots of energy, so that's why I built all those big power stations when me'n Ian first set up shop in space. Everybody said I was crazy because it'd be a century before the space colonists would need that much energy, but old Ugo was thinking all the time. It about drove Ian's auditors nuts trying to figure out where all that power was going, but I never gave 'em a clue. Heh, heh." Ciano chuckled at the discomfiture of his plodding contemporaries. "Now, I know what you're thinking: Why, you're asking, does anyone want to convert solar energy, or nuclear energy, for that matter, into antimatter? Especially since you're just gonna get it back in energy form again?" In fact, Thor was wondering exactly that.

"Ain't it amazing how he could read minds?" Roseberry said.

"Well, I'll tell you!" Ciano shouted, bringing both fists down and springing several feet from the floor. When he came down, he went on more calmly. "Despite the inevitable loss of energy in the conversion process, antimatter as an energy source provides a means of packing tremendous energy into an extremely small mass." He demonstrated his point by holding his forefinger and thumb a minute distance apart. "I mean, them little suckers is *small*!"

"Atoms usually are," Thor muttered.

"Shh," Roseberry chided.

"Think how efficient this stuff is for rocket fuel," Ciano said. The thought had already occurred to Thor. "Now, there is one little effect of this stuff that I maybe would've preferred it didn't have," Ciano muttered into his beard. My God, Thor thought, he's embarrassed! The great Ugo Ciano is capable of embarrassment! "See, inevitably, something this compact, that releases so much energy, is just the greatest stuff ever devised for making bombs."

Thor felt a prickling at the back of his neck and he remembered Shaw's fingernail poking the top sheet of the stack Bob had sent him. "I mean," Ciano went on, "not just bombs, but *BOMBS!*" He flung his arms wide to demonstrate the magnitude of the concept. "In fact, it's my considered opinion that, using this stuff, you could probably blow up the whole damned galaxy, which is predominantly made of matter. It'd be a little redundant, though. Wouldn't take all that much to wipe out everyplace people live."

A look of aggrieved hurt took over his gnomish countenance. "Hey, don't blame me! Is it my fault my fellow men are so uncivilized? Hell, somebody just like me discovered how to make fire. Was it his fault that the rest of the cavemen devised burning at the stake before they thought up cooking? Hell, no. Just remember: When I give you the code key to decipher my process, you got a hell of a responsibility. Use it wisely, okay?"

Thanks, Thor thought, for delivering into my hands the secret of how to destroy the galaxy. It's just what I needed. But he knew he had to accept it. To hell with bombs, if this antimatter drive was for real the Confederacy had to have it. He could foresee a time when escape would be far more crucial than destruction.

"What can I do with this?" Thor fretted on the way back. He had been thinking the question since they left the lab and now said it aloud for the first time.

Roseberry thought about it for a while. "Set up in business? He give you the patent rights, after all."

"Sure," Thor said disgustedly. "Just trot these over to the U.N. patent office and register them in my name."

"Guess that wouldn't be such a good idea after all, now that you mention it."

Who could be trusted? The Sálamids? Somehow he had an aversion to handing a potential super-weapon to people who spent all their time planning for war. None of the new political parties were yet coherent enough to weigh their trustworthiness, not even his own. Besides, he had a conviction that, in time, the outerworld politicians would prove to be no more savory than their Earth counterparts. Not knowing why, he voiced some of his predicament to Roseberry. He had to talk to somebody.

"Don't make much difference, I reckon," Roseberry said. "Might as well hand it over to one of the high-tech outfits to develop for you. You ain't gonna get that genie back into the bottle whatever you try."

After a few minutes of thought, he decided the old man was right. For all of human history, people had tried to disinvent one new development or another. He was aware of no instance of success at the attempt. Science and technology were as inexorable as any other historical trend—they grabbed people by the nose and dragged them to whatever destination was waiting for them. No, he couldn't expect to eliminate this threat, but he could try to guide its course.

"Let's forget Avalon for a few days," Thor said. "I'm setting course for Aeaea."

The tech station with the unlikely name was not, for a change, a hollowed-out asteroid. It was a glittering construction of metal, ultraglass and glaring-white mooncrete. Built in Lunar orbit thirty years before and moved to its present location later on, it had been at that time the largest man-made object in space, and larger than all but a few Earthly structures. It could not compare for sheer mass with the Great Wall of China, but it easily surpassed all the pyramids, with the Pentagon thrown in for good measure.

Aeaea had been built by a consortium of high-tech companies wanting a number of things available only in space: Pristine, zero-gee conditions, secrecy and security from the competition, tax advantages and freedom from government interference. Huge as it was, Aeaea manufactured few products. Almost all of its output was pure, abstract technology. The founders had given the ship-colony-scientific station the name of Circe's island both because of their intent to work sorcerous miracles in their labs and as a subtle reminder to the competition and interfering governments of what happened to people who messed with Circe. Just in case anyone missed the point, their corporate logo was a pig wearing a Greek helmet.

Aeaea had not been one of Thor's stops on his whirlwind diplomatic tour. Someone else had been there, and had reported on the Aeaeans' reluctance to take sides in a conflict when they viewed all parties as customers. They also proclaimed to have no fear of Earth aggression. Thor was pretty sure that they were bluffing, but he was equally sure that it would be a long time before anyone felt confident enough to call the bluff. In the meantime, if there was such a thing as a safe, neutral spot in all of human-occupied space, it would have to be Aeaea.

The woman across from Thor wore a white sari modified for zero-gee. Her left eye was some kind of weird instrument that showed only a curved surface of faceted glass and it gave her a daunting stare. She looked about fifty but could be easily twice that. A lot of medical research was done in Aeaea. She was in some kind of contact with other scientists within the facility, through a communication system Thor had never heard of. He suspected that it had something to do with the eye and with the slight bulge implanted in her skull behind the left ear. Most of the people he'd seen here had ungodly-looking biomechanical implants. They looked creepy and caused him to question the wisdom of what he was doing.

Too late to do anything about it, though. The woman had stuffed his sheets and crystals into a console and was now going through them at incredible speed. She appeared to be in a deep trance-state. He turned to Roseberry, who floated beside him. The Aeaeans favored zero-gee. "Have you ever seen anything like this?"

"People gets peculiar when they been isolated for a long time," Roseberry said. "I been to rocks where you'd swear the people wasn't human any more at all. This ain't bad."

Thor was sure that everything they were saying was being recorded, but he had better things to worry about than sparing the Aeaean's feelings. If they wanted to be complimented for their looks, they could damn well hide their electronic excrescences. The room they were in was the main office. At least, it seemed to be the location from which business was transacted. The walls were of some translucent material that shaded from transparency to white at an indefinite depth. They had entered through a door but it was invisible now. It was like being inside a cloud.

Abruptly, the room was full of people. They were holographic projections, but might as well have been real. They jabbered away at one another in some kind of scientific shorthand language from which Thor could snatch only scattered words. A man in bug-eye goggles turned to Thor with a maniacal grin. "This is it! With this, there's no limit to what we can do!" Thor wasn't sure he liked the sound of that.

An enormously fat, Buddha-like man dressed in a loincloth smiled serenely. "I had thought that Ciano died with more secrets locked in his skull than Nikola Tesla. This is like a gift from the gods." Except for his obesity, the man seemed normal. Then Thor noticed that there was an electronic gizmo in his belly button.

"God help us," he whispered to Roseberry, "they're all nuttier than Ciano."

"That'd be going some," Roseberry said cautiously.

The jabber died down and the woman in the sari spoke. "You have our attention, Mr. Taggart. What is the nature of your proposal?"

"In return for the rest of Ciano's research, I want you to develop something exclusively for the Confederacy."

The woman held up a hand. "Before you go any further, I must tell you that, until the present unpleasantness is settled, we will not develop anything that can be used as war materiel."

"The farthest thing from my mind," Thor said. "Quite the contrary, in fact. I want you to develop fully the engine Ciano was at work on when he died. I want big engines, lots of them. I want engines that will take a whole asteroid, whatever its size, on an interstellar voyage."

There was a span of silence, then another woman spoke. Her entire head was encased in a delicate lattice of crystal and metal. Such features as were visible were Asiatic. "This would be a worthy commission. We've not had such a challenge in too long. We are all tired of petty, profit-oriented commissions. It would be good to stretch ourselves."

"We are not set up for heavy industry," said the voice of a man who had chosen to remain invisible. "Such engines would be massive and thousands of them would be necessary."

"We can build the facilities and have automated labor robots manufactured to our design," said the sari-clad woman.

"Testing could be a problem," said the fat man. "We know from Ciano's mishap that the process could produce a spectacular display."

"During the testing phase we'll stay on the move and conduct the tests at widely-separated locations. Nobody will know what the displays signify in any case," said the sari-clad woman. There was more of the incomprehensible jabber, then she said: "Are we agreed, then?" She turned to Thor. "You have a deal. The contract will be recorded and registered under strictest seal."

"You'll have the rest of the data as soon as I have confirmation of the contract from Dula, Wong and Metuschaskayasky." D, W&M was Avalon's most reputable legal firm. "And now, I must be off. I have a convention to attend and I've already missed the first day."

Two days later, when he got back to Avalon, he found that not only was the convention under way, but the opening moves of the war had begun.

ELEVEN

Hjalmar spotted Thor from clear across the floor of HMK. Thor stood on the balcony outside the train station overlooking the cavernous chamber. Red-faced, Hjalmar stormed across the packed floor, his ploughing bulk sending shock waves through the crowd. He leaped thirty feet to grab the guardrail of the balcony and hauled himself over it. "Where the hell have you been, Thor?" he shouted. "We've been trying to find you for days! Figured some Earthie spies had snatched you or set you out to breathe vacuum."

"I had business to take care of and I don't care to talk about it here," Thor said. "Fine security chief you are, anyway. Didn't you figure out that I took that little prospector ship out for a short voyage?" The agitation below was unbelievable. There were big holo screens set up and some of them played the expected political speeches but others displayed scenes of devastation. Thor began to have a bad feeling about this.

"Of course I found out about the prospector," Hjalmar fumed. "And about you and Roseberry taking it out, but it wasn't anything that couldn't have been faked. I happen to know that snatch teams are out looking for you and Shaw. Shaw can take care of himself, but the family doesn't want me to lose you."

"Disinformation," Thor said, shrugging. "I've told

187

you before, there are no snatch teams and no assassins. I'm too valuable as a symbol. If they killed me, they'd have to create another villain. Hjalmar, what the hell's going on?" He pointed at one of the screens. It displayed an asteroid and the rock was spraying sparks and molten rock from numerous fissures.

"You mean you haven't heard? The war's under way. Yesterday about this time, the Earthies landed a nuke on M-255. It was in a rock driller. Just bored its way to the center and triggered. An ore freighter waiting to load got these pictures."

There was a sinking feeling in Thor's chest. So it had begun. He had hoped that, somehow, it might be averted. "How many?"

"There were four hundred miners there at the time. There can't be any survivors. We don't know how many ships were docked there yet."

"Why a remote mining rock?" Thor asked. "Why not Avalon or one of the other key settlements?"

"Because it was easy," Hjalmar said, bitterly. "They got a quick 'victory,'" his mouth twisted wryly at the word, "an impressive body count, at least it'll be impressive when they announce it for the folks back home. They had a spy satellite sitting a few hundred kilometers from the rock to get pictures of the destruction. It's a damned impressive sight, to see a nuke go off in an asteroid, in case you've never seen it."

"So what will we do now?" Thor said wearily. "We'll have to retaliate." They began to walk toward the cave that had been set aside as Eos party headquarters.

"We already have by now," Hjalmar said. He smiled grimly at Thor's look of surprise. "The Sálamids sent out an expeditionary force months ago. They've been in position for a long time, waiting for the Earthies to make the first move. They plan to strike as soon as the attack on us is announced. There's nothing like immediate reprisal for an object lesson."

"What's the target?"

"Something military, I'm told, either in Earth orbit

or on Luna. They've picked a facility where most of the personnel are from the First-World countries."

Thor stopped in his tracks. "Why be so selective?" He knew it was illogical, but it hurt to know that the victims would be his former countrymen.

"Because the families of the servicemen will likely be notified. That way, there's no way they can hide the casualty count. Plus, their media will be flooded with our pictures of the raid."

"But they've been jamming all our transmissions for months," Thor said.

"Some genius on Luna has set up a station that can bull through any jamming the Earthies can set up. If he keeps it moving and keeps the broadcasts short, there's no way they can keep his transmissions out."

Thor thought of Chih' Chin Fu. That boy was playing a dangerous game.

Party headquarters was full of people shouting at each other or into communicators. It was also full of people talking in very low voices. It looked to Thor as if there were a lot of deals being made. A good many of those present were members of other parties. He saw none of Shaw's people. He decided that this kind of political collusion was the inevitable accompaniment of a parliamentary democracy.

"Thor!" someone said. "When did you get back?" Heads swiveled his way.

"If spacers smoked," Thor said, "this would be the proverbial smoke-filled room."

"Huh?" Nobody understood the reference.

"Never mind," he said. "What's been happening at the convention? I've already heard the war news."

Sean Roalstad pushed through the crowd and took Thor's hand. "We're winning by a landslide," he said, and Thor was struck by the inappropriateness of the image in space. "Eos has pulled in a big majority of seats. That's why all the other parties are here. They want to talk coalition. The new parliament's to be called the *Althing*, after the ancient Icelandic assembly. That was my suggestion," he added, proudly. "The constitution is based on the old Confederate States of America's, with additions from the Iroquois League and a half-dozen other systems. Tomas Sousa's to be President, as head of the majority party. Saburo and some of the others have stepped down so's it won't look so much like a family operation. He calls it the House of Saud syndrome."

"I don't see any of Martin's people here," Thor said. "I take it they aren't interested in making deals."

"We haven't heard anything from them since yesterday," Hjalmar said. "I suspect we'll be hearing about them pretty soon, though."

"Your attention, please," said someone. "The holos of our counterattack against Earth have just come through." Silence descended as all eyes turned to the display covering one wall.

A million tiny, colored specks converged to form a robed man. It was Chih' Chin Fu in his Confucian scholar persona. "Greetings, brothers of Earth and space. This is the voice and image of the Free Holographic Network, bringing you the true story of the terrible war which is about to engulf us all. Yesterday we showed you the authentic pictures of the unprovoked attack on the peaceful mining asteroid M-255, in the first deliberate use of atomic weaponry against human beings since 1945. Today, you shall see how the Confederacy of Island Worlds has retaliated."

The scholar's image disappeared and a massive, orbiting fortress of metal and mooncrete took its place. A broad arc of Earth could be seen in the background. "This is Orbital Base Thunderbird. It is a staging area for proposed offensives against the Confederacy." Abruptly, blue-white flares erupted all over the base. "What you have just witnessed was the destruction of all the station's defensive and sensory apparatus by precision laser fire. The Confederate warships approached without difficulty, since Earth forces really don't believe in those powerful outerworld battle fleets they have been frightening you with for several years. The next stage of the operation was a commando raid into the base. The following sequence was holographed by a camera mounted on a raider's armored spacesuit. The action has been smoothed out, but it is still somewhat jerky."

The point of view was now the red-lit interior of a small craft. Hulking, armored forms could be seen bristling with enigmatic weapons. The forms were facing a round hatch broad enough for two or three raiders to pass through at the same time. There was a jerk as the vessel's motion ceased and the hatch slid aside, revealing the outside of an airlock hatch. Lasers flared and metal sparked as two of the raiders cut through the hatch with heavy-duty miner's shortbeam cutters. As the hatch was cut free, a raider slapped a charge in its center and detonated it, sending the hatch flying into the interior of the lock. At the blast, the raiders rocked back on their tethers.

Some kind of temporary emergency seal kept the air within the ship and the base. The raiders loosed their tethers and flew into the airlock on tiny, compressed-gas jets. Inside, the inner hatch was cycled open and the commandos flew into the base proper. The raider was recording sound as well as sight, and the base was a deafening pandemonium of alarms, bells, sirens and shouting personnel. Startled, unbelieving faces turned to stare at the armored commandos as beams, taking their energy from backpack power plants, began to sizzle out from forearm-mounted lasers, destroying every piece of equipment the raiders came upon, as well as personnel foolish enough to try to protect the facilities. A man in a sergeant's uniform came through a hatch with a beam rifle cradled in his arms. Before he could aim it, he was met by a stream of gas-driven ceramic pellets, no more than one millimeter in diameter, but traveling in great numbers at a velocity of four thousand meters per second. The effect was instantaneous and gruesome.

The raiding party worked its way through its assigned area of the base, remorselessly destroying anything of value but attacking only persons who showed resistance. After perhaps thirty minutes, they worked their way back to the airlock and reboarded their vessel. Near the hatch, one raider was carving something on the mooncrete wall near the lock. The raider carrying the camera paused and faced the inscription. In blackened letters carved deeply by an arc-torch, it read: "We could have dropped this station on Earth."

Fu reappeared. "Six such parties landed on Base Thunderbird. Later today, I shall broadcast all their holographs. Another part of the expeditionary force struck at a shipbuilding station near Thunderbird, destroying two cruisers and a frigate under construction. You shall see views of that as well. At this moment, an official U.N. broadcast is being shown depicting large numbers of casualties from a ruthlessly assaulted hospital ward. This is a holographic fabrication, as the most cursory analysis will demonstrate. The most rigorous analysis will prove the authenticity of the Free Holographic Network's holos. I will be back in two hours, with the next installment of our continuing report on the action at Base Thunderbird. This is FHN, where truth is the best propaganda." The holo faded to a starscape.

There was little cheering at the end of the broadcast. Faces were pale and voices were subdued. "It's good," Roalstad grunted, "that we have had a chance to see real fighting close up. Maybe now we won't have so many long-range fire-eaters anxious to send other people out to win glory for them."

"How long can Fu get away with it?" Thor wondered.

"If he can last more than a few days," Hjalmar said, "then he will have to be incredibly clever. He—" Hjalmar's head tilted slightly to one side, as if someone were whispering in his ear. "Your attention, please," he called out. "I have just received word that the ships *Spartacus, Simon Bolivar, Garibaldi* and *Jeanne D'Arc* have left simultaneously and without filing a spacing plan or personnel roster with port authority."

"All of Shaw's ships!" said someone. Thor looked

around and saw that it was Reiko McNaughton. "We should declare him an outlaw at once!"

"He's done nothing treasonable yet," Thor said.

"He will, and soon," Hjalmar said. "I'll have the bastard put under death sentence when he does."

"Hold it," Thor said. "We've just become a nation and we're already splitting up. This is not a good start. Solidarity should be everything now."

"Thor," said Brunhilde, who had been operating one of the vote-counting computers, "we have to denounce him. He's going to take unilateral action and we can't recognize him or Earth will blame his atrocities on us. What's more, they'll be right to do so." He couldn't argue with her. It was true. The events of the last few days bore down upon him with crushing weight. They were a nation and they were at war.

TWELVE

Natalie Tomalis sat facing herself, making up her eyes. The other Natalie was a holo projection, and she was sitting because Manhattan had been given a high-speed spin, yielding almost a full gee. It was more gravity than she had ever felt in her life. Just walking and breathing were a struggle, but making love with the two-hundred-pound Cornelius de Kamp was a nightmare. But Cornelius was special aide to the Fleet Admiral and being his mistress gave her privileges and special access to important ears. Just now she had some special information to deliver and she was taking particular care with her makeup.

The beautiful silk dressing gown Cornelius had given her was pooled around her hips and she had arranged herself as seductively as possible. There was no way she could move gracefully in the awful gravity, so she had learned to exploit Cornelius's visual and olfactory preferences.

De Kamp paused to appreciate the scene as he came in the door. After a hard day's work, the sight of Natalie nude from the waist up was refreshing. Two of them, at artistically-chosen angles, almost recharged his tired batteries. Almost. The Earth Navy had made the island world of Manhattan their home port. It had been one of the first asteroids occupied in the war. It was close enough to the main centers of resistance for convenient forays, but far enough to be fairly safe from attack by the jerrybuilt Sálamid Navy.

The problem was the Manhattanites. The original plan had been to transport them to concentration camps on Luna, although it was generally believed that the transportation vessels would be somehow "lost." The need for cheap labor had been too great, though, and using virtual slaves was far cheaper than bringing out Earth personnel or robots. Every laborer or construction specialist brought out was one less serviceman to man the ships. But the chance of sabotage was great and the Earthmen could never relax. It had its compensations, however. Natalie was one of them. In every occupied territory, there were women who saw that cooperation with the conquerors was far preferable to the life of the conquered.

"What would your neighbors do if they saw you now?" he said.

She turned, acutely aware of the heavy sway of her large breasts. The motion seemed grotesque to her, but she knew that he liked it. The fixation of his eyes confirmed it. "They'd shove me out the nearest lock. That's what they do to traitors and collaborationists here."

"You aren't a traitor, my dear, just a patriotic woman doing her best for Mother Earth." Guiltily, he realized that the thought of this exquisite woman being killed excited him in some obscure fashion. He steered his thoughts away from that. Natalie was the only woman he had found out here who had the kind of fully-fleshed body he liked. Most outerworld women were rail-thin. Natalie was *Spaceborn*, but she was a throwback to her more voluptuous ancestors.

She got up and went to the side table, walking carefully to avoid stumbling, having to tighten her abdominals against the unaccustomed weight of her viscera. She poured him a whiskey over ice. It had taken her days just to learn to hit the glass. She carried the drink over to him, rippling her stomach to let the gown slip an inch lower. "I've heard something. It may be important."

"What might that be?" Her perfume made it difficult to concentrate. He was tired and didn't want to think about duty. Not so tired that he wasn't growing excited, though. The holo was still on and he could watch her from the side as well as from the front.

"How would you like to catch Martin Shaw?"

The sexual excitement dropped away and was replaced by another kind. He took a sip of the whiskey, not tasting it. "Tell me more."

"You know my contact has always been reliable." It was not a question and he nodded confirmation. Natalie's tips had been few and relatively unimportant, but they had always been reliable. The items he had been able to pass on had earned him his commendations and the trust of the Admiral.

"There's a rock called Galveston. It was named by a Texan back before they ran out of island names. There were some mining operations there, but they played out years ago. In two weeks, Shaw and several of his top aides are to be meeting there."

"Why would they pick an asteroid to meet?" he asked. "They have ships, why not rendezvous in space?"

"My source says they may be using Galveston as a staging area for attacks against this sector. I didn't want to press him too hard."

"You did the right thing." He sipped at his drink distractedly. Martin Shaw! If only he and his top men could be captured, taken back to Earth for a show-trial. Then they would be hanged and the terrorist movement would lose so much face that only the Sálamids would be left to deal with. Then Earth could win this frustrating war, because the Sálamids fought by the rules. That meant that Earth would win, because the weaker power couldn't prevail, fighting by the rules. The terrorists, on the other hand, fought by no rules at all. Several rock bombs had already been intercepted on collision course with Earth. The Sálamids intercepted them, too, but that information was kept from Earth.

De Kamp got on the security phone and asked for an emergency meeting with Fleet Admiral Marat. There had to be a rear-admiralcy for him in this, at the very least. As he turned from the phone, Natalie wrapped her arms around his neck and pressed herself against him. "And don't I deserve any reward for this?" She smiled up at him.

Gently, he disengaged her arms. "I'll take care of you, my dear. You know I always do. But right now, I have urgent business." He used the holo to straighten his uniform and rushed out the door. When he was gone, Natalie pulled up her gown and switched off the holo. So, there would be no sweaty, suffocating coupling in his bed tonight. Thank God.

Battleship *Kiev* was one of the most powerful fighting machines ever built. Along with her sister ships, they constituted the *Imperator* class. The battleships carried four long-range laser guns energized by the ship's extremely costly Condensed Energy Tank. The CET was an elaborate name for a super-battery, charged up by the ship's nuclear power plant. Only a battleship carried a power plant and CET powerful enough to supply four laser guns. Once discharged, the CET took hours to recharge. Depending upon conditions, the big guns had a range of twenty to sixty thousand kilometers. By interplanetary standards, that was still close range. The battleships also carried nuclear and non-nuclear missiles as well as defensive missiles and rail-guns used primarily for destroying attacking missiles.

Battleships were few. They were huge and incredibly expensive to build, as well as being limited in their tactical applications. More than anything else, they were an expression of Earth's might, a form of spacegoing propaganda in metal and plastics and ultraglass.

More numerous and versatile were the cruisers. Cruisers were scaled-down battleships equipped with only

one laser gun. Smallest of the warships, and in many
ways the most useful, were the frigates. Lacking the
capacity for a laser gun, they depended on fast acceleration. Conventionally, a frigate would stay out of range
of a battleship's or a cruiser's laser guns. In a pinch, it
could deploy decoys to distract the bigger vessel's
imaging-sensor-computer system guiding the laser gun.
The battleship would be reluctant to waste its slow-
recharging laser power against decoys. In the fraction of
a second required for a laser beam to reach its target,
the target could move several times its own dimension.
The laser was perfect for destroying ballistic missiles
that did not change course or speed, but it was not
satisfactory against ships that were programmed to change
course and speed at random. They did discourage smaller
vessels from getting too close. Only if the enemy were
coming in a straight collision course were the lasers
used ship-to-ship at long range. They were also useful
for taking out the defensive batteries of an enemy port.

In practice, the Confederacy had no large warships.
Thus, much of the action fell to the frigates. Most of the
Confederacy ships were classed as frigates of some sort,
along with the personnel-carrying raiders.

No, Admiral Marat thought, as *Kiev* sped toward its
rendezvous with Shaw, the problem was not firepower.
In every aspect of firepower, Earth was immensely
superior to the Confederacy. The problem was in bringing them to battle. Space was so vast that random
ship-to-ship encounters were all but unthinkable. Advance intelligence had to reveal an enemy fleet's course
or location to allow an intercept. On Earth, sea battles
had almost never taken place on the high seas, but in
straits, river estuaries of ports. Space was the same.

The favored Sálamid tactic had been to wait until an
Earth fleet left its base and then hit the base. Marat's
own subordinates had been surprised when he had
ordered out not only his six frigates but the two cruisers and the battleship as well. All to pick up Martin
Shaw and his ragtag little squadron. Marat was sure

that Manhattan was safe. The Sálamids never cooperated with the terrorists.

The reason he wanted to take *Kiev* along was that, without the whole fleet, there was no excuse for the Admiral to be along on the operation. Damned if he was going to send out a flotilla and let a commodore garner all the glory. It looked as if there were going to be damned few naval actions in this war, so the public would only hear about the officers who turned in those victories. Why, because of the numerous landing actions on crucial asteroids, the people back home were thinking of this as a *Marine* war. Most civilians could rattle off the names of a half-dozen decorated Marine officers, but only Grand Admiral Fitzsimmons was familiar to most earthmen.

Kiev took up position at a discreet distance of one hundred thousand kilometers from Galveston, matching its heliocentric motion. This was close enough for a high-resolution imaging sensor, but far enough to escape detection by an ordinary ship's field scanner. Almost immediately, a small ship showed up on the kilometer-sized rock. Analysis confirmed it to be *Spartacus*, the ship most often used by Shaw.

"Frigates to siege positions," Marat ordered. Strapped into his commander's chair, he smiled. His chair was on a dais above and behind that of Ali Almansur, *Kiev's* commander. The frigates would assume a roughly circular formation around the asteroid on the ecliptic and be ready to fire on warning.

"All frigates in position, Admiral," said Almansur some time later.

"Very good, Captain. Cruisers in, marines to commence assault immediately upon reaching position."

"Aye, aye, sir." The order was relayed and the two cruisers, *Drake* and *Togo*, headed toward Galveston. *Drake* halted at a range of one hundred kilometers. The other cruiser worked its way in toward the entrance structure built over the old mining operation. When they were within one kilometer, the marines left the ship in space jeeps—short distance personnel carriers propelled by a slow-impulse rocket motor.

The marine captain couldn't believe their luck. They had achieved complete surprise. The terrorists were so sure of their secrecy that they weren't even posting lookouts. The marines maintained radio silence as they entered the double airlock. Two men had been preassigned to guard the entrance.

Shortly after the last of his mates disappeared inside, the senior of the two guards saw his partner giving him frantic hand-signals—"*something wrong.*" He pointed toward the hulk of the terrorist ship, a hundred meters away. The senior man studied it. There *did* seem to be something odd about it. He flipped down his magnifier and slowly raised its light and image enhancement. Details became plain—a spindly, metal-strut frame showed below the sheet-metal body, its ports painted on. Only the upper surface, the part the fleet's enhancers would see, had been lovingly detailed.

The marine broke radio silence on the emergency band. "Get out! The ship's a dummy! It's a trap!" But the thickness of rock kept his signal from reaching them and, in any case, they already knew it was a trap. The captain saw the four men bending over the apparatus within the cave a microsecond before a crisscrossing grid of lasers chopped them down. He had just time to notice that the four were grinning.

"I reckon it's time," one of the men said. Like the other three, he had lost his family to Earthie raids. They keyed the four switches. Had the captain had more leisure, and had he been expert in weapons history, he would have recognized the apparatus as a nuclear bomb-powered laser battery, Excalibur class, of late 20th century design. Long obsolete, crude but relatively cheap and simple to produce, it was just the thing for low-tech, guerrilla warfare. It required no complex and expensive condensed energy tank. Each laser required the explosion of a nuclear bomb for its energy, and of course the entire apparatus was destroyed by the explosion, along with any operators. It could have been

done by remote, but the four had volunteered for the
suicide mission just to make extra sure.

The four beams lanced into the fleet, one for each
cruiser, two for the battleship. The two cruisers were
destroyed instantly. The battleship, at the extreme edge
of the lasers' effective range, fared better. One beam
punched through the ship's armor, killing a handful of
the crew. Immediately, hermetically-sealing doors closed
off the damaged section. The unfortunates who were
not killed instantly and could not get to rescue bubbles
died painfully, of explosive decompression. It was one
of the grim advantages of space warfare that it left few
wounded or crippled. Most either survived whole or
died.

Marat was pale and raging. "Give that rock two pene-
tration bombs!"

Ali Almansur did not argue, but relayed the order.
Any fool could see that it was unnecessary. The rock
was spouting lava from a hundred fissures. But the
Admiral was not just any fool. He was a great fool.
"Damage report," Almansur said.

His XO studied the screens. "Damage confined to
landcraft maintenance and topographical analysis sections. Thirty-two killed, none wounded." Implanted instruments fed the computers a continual report of
personnel health.

Praise Allah, Almansur thought. Not the weapons,
not the engines, not life support. It could have been far
worse. He was filled with rage at Marat for allowing his
ship to be hurt. Unlike Marat, he kept his head.

"Frigate *Valiant* reports no survivors from the cruisers," said a communications officer.

It began to sink into Marat's consciousness that his
career was probably in ruins. Somewhere out here, he
knew, that damned Free Holographic Network was getting detailed images of this action. His friends in the
government wouldn't be able to protect him. They'd be
the first to call for his head. He looked at de Kamp,
who sat, pale and sweating, at an information console.

"When we get back to Manhattan," Marat said, "I shall watch while you strangle that slut of yours. If you perform that task to satisfaction, I just might allow you to live."

"Yes, sir," de Kamp said.

"Sir!" said the imaging officer. "We've picked up four vessels, closing fast with the fleet. Dead collision course!"

Marat felt a surge of exultant rage. He would have revenge! He just might salvage something from this disaster after all. "They must think they've hurt us badly," he said, almost laughing. "They want a quick kill, before we can begin repairs." That was why they were coming on a straight course. It was the fastest, but it was also the *only* approach that gave his lasers a faultless shot at an approaching ship.

"Master Gunner," Marat said, "I want those four ships obliterated as soon as they are well within range."

"Aye, aye, sir!" grinned the fire control officer. "We'll show these rock lice the power of Earth guns."

Marat smiled. These colonial pirates were tricky and clever, but they were unaware of the capabilities of modern weapons. He clenched his fist as all four guns fired at the same instant. A fraction of a second later, the *Kiev* was annihilated by four converging laser beams.

The skipper of frigate *Dauntless* was intent on his weapons status screen when he heard someone gasp. He looked and saw that everyone on the bridge was staring at the screen trained on *Kiev*. "Holy shit!" someone cried. The gigantic ship had become an eruption of flaming, molten metal. Horrified, he saw the tiny forms of humans silhouetted against the glare of exploding engines and weapons.

"Enemy still on course," said the imaging sensor officer.

"What happened to the flagship?" said the second officer. "She fired, then she was gone!"

"I can make a guess," said a young ensign. He looked as if he had begun to shave last week.

"I'd be glad to hear it," the skipper said. "Meanwhile, we set course for Manhattan." Those were standing orders in the event of such a setback. All the other frigate captains would be giving the identical command.

"Those pirates are mounted with phase conjugate mirrors. I learned about them at the academy. It's an old theory, a mirror that'll bounce back a laser beam to its point of origin in its *original* undispersed concentration. Its use as a defensive weapon has been largely theoretical up till now."

"Of course," said the skipper. "Why bother? After all, our propaganda keeps telling us we're only dealing with low-tech criminals." He was aware that his words were being recorded and would be held against him as evidence of disloyalty. He just didn't give a good goddamn any more.

"Enemy still closing at top speed," reported the imaging sensor officer. "They're launching smart missiles."

"Take evasive action," said the skipper. "It'll be rail guns next. They have the speed on us. Today we run and be glad to get home with a tail to hold between our legs. Tomorrow, we'll be back to fight; pray to God that our bonehead superiors stop sending battleships and cruisers to fight a frigate war."

Dauntless made it back to Manhattan. So did three others, although two of those were limping. One of Shaw's ships had suffered some damage.

Martin Shaw raised his glass. "Rubinoff, Matsunaga, Chavez, Gilbert. We won't forget them."

"We won't forget them," echoed the assembled officers. They were gathered in the tiny asteroid Shaw was using as a headquarters this month. He had ordered a spin so that they would be able to drink a toast to the four volunteers in proper fashion.

"By the Prophet's beard!" said a scar-faced Nubian. "A battleship, two cruisers, two frigates and two more hurt! What have the damned Sálamids done to match that?" The others growled and cheered.

"Hey, Chief," Mike said, "this just came in from Chih' Chin Fu. He thought you'd get a kick out of it."

The big redhead punched the holo control and an image formed. It was Shaw. Or rather, it was a parody of Shaw. He was making a speech. It had been dubbed in Urdu with perfect lip-synch. All of his features had been subtly altered. The eyebrows had an exaggerated arch, the slant of the eyes was more oblique, the corners of the lips were turned down. He might have been Ming the Merciless in an old film.

Shaw laughed aloud, a rarity for him. "When I was a freshman, we did a production of *Doctor Faustus*. I played Mephistopheles and I was made up just like that." The image changed to one of Thor Taggart. He, too was making a speech. His hawklike features were rendered even more aristrocratic—the hair lightened, the nose lengthened, the lips thinned, the chin sharpened. His eyes were bluer than blue. The holographic manipulators had dressed him in a bizarre black uniform. All that was missing was a swastika armband.

Mike shook his head and clucked. "It's a shame how that boy turned out. I had real hopes for him, thought he was smart and gutsy. I thought sure he'd come in with us. It's hard to believe he's old Sam Taggart's grandson."

"Thor's done fine," Shaw said. "He's chosen his path and he's done damn well in it. He's the best man Eos has and probably the best man out here, period. We're always going to need men like him, even on opposite sides." He sipped at his drink and an uncomfortable silence fell. Sometimes the things Shaw said disturbed his followers, although they would never admit it.

Caterina switched off the holo. "I'm still not satisfied about that Ciano business. I wish I'd brought those sheets to you instead of giving them to him."

Shaw turned his unnerving glare on her. "Nobody's asked you to be satisfied, Cat."

She looked away. Inwardly, she quailed. Why was he like this? And why did she continue to worship him, as they all did? She had all but thrown herself at his feet, and he had never laid a hand on her. At least she knew that it was not another woman. Shaw would never touch a subordinate. A noted hell-raiser, roisterer and womanizer before the war, in combat he was like some ascetic saint. Party discipline came before everything and he relegated his physical needs to the dustbin of irrelevancy for the duration.

She was grateful when a distraction came. The inner lock door opened and a spacesuited figure entered. She knew who it was, the instant she saw the way the bulky suit bulged here and there. Mike wrestled off the helmet and a cloud of black hair burst out, framing the face of Natalie Tomalis.

"Natalie!" Shaw said, embracing her. "Welcome back. You are now an official heroine."

"Great," she said, returning the hug. "Now, Martin, I've delivered the goods. Give me back my ship and find some other big-boobed woman to do your undercover work."

Shaw smiled. "Don't worry, I've already found out that his replacement likes them thin. Now have a drink and socialize. *Juarez* comes in tomorrow and you'll be a skipper again. Then it's back to war for us all."

She sat at a small, packing-crate table with Caterina. The two had been half-friendly and wholly futile rivals for Shaw almost since the founding of the party. Caterina liked Natalie and admired her nerve and her skill as a skipper, but she felt like breaking the woman's neck when she saw her making a play for Martin. The feeling was reciprocated.

"God!" Natalie said. "My spine has a permanent curvature and my breasts are three inches closer to my navel. No wonder Earthies are so awful. Imagine having to live in that gravity all your life."

"I'm glad I didn't have to do it," Caterina said. "I don't know what I'd have done if Martin had called on me for that duty." She wasn't referring to the gravity.

"You'd have done just what I did," Natalie said. "In war, we can't be delicate about our sensibilities. When we know the enemy has a weakness, we exploit it, and we use whatever weapon is best for the job. In this case—" She waved a hand gracefully, sweeping down her spectacular figure.

"When do we do it again, Chief?" called a skipper with flat, Mongolian features.

"This?" Shaw said. "Never, most likely. The worst thing we can do is establish a predictable pattern."

"Sure," said a young gunnery officer, "but the Earthies are dumb! You can keep suckering them like this forever!"

"Not so!" Shaw said, and his serious tone had their undivided attention. "The Earthies aren't dumb, and never think that your enemies are all alike just because they wear the same uniform. Here we had a unique set of circumstances; the Fleet Admiral was an inexperienced incompetent and his men's morale was low because they knew it and because they were being badly used. His aide, we found from a theft of their psych files, had a weakness for women of a certain physique, one very rare in these parts. By an amazing coincidence, we had a brave and loyal officer who just fitted the description without surgery." He raised his glass to Natalie and she raised her own in ironic salute. "This time, everything worked perfectly. Never expect the same thing to happen again." They listened respectfully, because Martin never let an opportunity slip to improve their education in military or political matters.

"For instance, do you think I'd have tried this with Admiral Yi over in their VI Sector? That man's as good as Nelson or Halsey or Yamamoto and his people are keen and well-trained. But we're never going to let him prove it because neither we nor the Sálamids will come out and fight him. Given time, with no victories to his credit, internal politics will remove him from the scene and some flunky with connections at the U.N., some fair-haired boy of Secretary General Jameson's, will take over. Morale in that sector will plummet like a rock bomb, because everybody loves Yi and will hate his successor. *That's* when we'll strike in VI Sector, but only after we've analyzed the new Admiral and staff to find where they're weakest. That's what it's all about, my friends: not individual heroics, although they have their place, but a careful, detailed study of the weaknesses and foibles of our *individual* enemies—the ones in positions of power. The weaknesses of their political and economic systems we know well and have been exploiting for a long time. Never mistake the system for the man. They are people just like ourselves, and if we can't get inside their heads and think like them, they'll beat us, because they have more of everything than we have."

THIRTEEN

The interior of the raider was red-lit, to spare the night-vision of the men about to go into combat. There was always a chance of night-vision equipment malfunctioning. The raiders were tethered in a double row behind Thor, helmets off, talking quietly among themselves. The Sálamid forces did not have the soldier-navy-marine distinctions of the Earth military. All forces were shipborne and most pilots and bridge officers doubled as landing-force raiders from time to time.

Thor studied them, musing on the changes four years of war had made. Most of the raiders were young, but there were middle-aged men and women among them. They were from a great variety of island worlds, united now to preserve their freedom.

The pilot followed the direction of Thor's gaze. "Strange sight, isn't it? Not long ago, most of 'em wouldn't have given each other the coordinates to the john. Now they're like brothers and sisters."

"It'll be a strong bond," Thor said, "after the war. Even when they go back to their own worlds and take up their lives again, they'll remember how they fought together." He shook his head. He was thinking like a statesman again. There would be time for that later. Right now he had to concentrate on the job at hand. He wore the armored suit of a raider and he was commander of this force.

The target was A-261; a featureless rock like many others in this sector, except that they had found out that it was a holding station for Confederate POWs. There weren't many in this war. Most had been taken off disabled ships. Saboteurs in the occupied habitats were summarily executed after rigorous interrogation. Shaw's people were given the same treatment. Repeatedly, the Earth government had urged the same treatment for all captured belligerents, since the Confederacy was not recognized as a legitimate government. Earth military leaders had so far refused, on the simple grounds that the Confederacy had far more Earth prisoners. Both military and government were stymied. Their propaganda had been telling Earth that all Earth prisoners were executed by the Confederates after torture. What to do with repatriated POWs after the war was a problem. Nobody had to expend too much imagination on the likely solution, one reached by Josef Stalin many years before.

In the meantime, POWs were being held in A-261. The location had been determined in a simple but drastic fashion. A gutsy volunteer had allowed himself to be captured after allowing himself to be wounded so severely that no plot was suspected. Sent immediately to an Earth frigate's surgery, he bypassed the routine electronic scan. As he was being transferred from the ship's infirmary to the asteroid, he fired a microsecond, narrow-beam transmission to the waiting Confederate squadron. The rest was planning and timing. A defunct mining company's records turned up the original plan of the mining galleries within the rock and the military plotted probable improvements undertaken since occupation. The rest of the operation would be guesswork and playing by ear.

Thor checked the imaging screen and saw that the fireworks ship was almost in position. That craft would be attacking the main, heavily-protected entrance while Thor's team pulled the actual attack and snatch on the other side of the rock. The old mining firm's diagrams had revealed a gallery dug to within one meter of the surface of the rock on that side, and that was where they were going in.

As they headed for their destination, the space around the rock came alive with chaff: dummy rockets, aluminum balloons, hurtling magnesium flares, all manner of meaningless garbage to jam and confuse image sensors, radars, heat detectors and sensory apparatus of all kinds. Lasers and rockets began to come from the rock, but the chances of their hitting a vital target in the midst of all the chaff were scarcely above zero.

The raider's belly was equipped with a "remora"—a circular, rubbery dam that would leech onto the rock, sealing hermetically and forming a secure, temporary airlock between the ship and the asteroid. The remora gripped the rocky surface, its soft edges flowing into the pores and irregularities of the asteroidal surface. When a green light signalled a complete seal, the interior was pressurized and Thor's team went to work.

The rest of the raiders, all experienced hardrock miners, pulled themselves into the lock and began working on the face with shortbeam laser cutters. Another team with a vacuum hose sucked up the rock and dust as it was cut away. Their visors opaqued against the blinding glare of the cutters, the rest of the team waited within the ship, cradling their weapons and explosive charges. Within five minutes they were through the rock. The pressure within the remora was deliberately lower than that within the asteroid, so that the final rock debris was blown outward and into the vacuum hose.

The assault team, led by Thor, piled through the opening and into the gallery. It seemed to be undeveloped, a mere rough-walled tunnel. That was all to the good. He led them toward where the nerve center was calculated to be. They moved warily. A prison wouldn't be swarming with heavily-armed marines, but it was likely that it was rigged with remote weapons systems in case of an outbreak of resourceful prisoners.

At the end of the gallery a wall had been erected and

an emergency door had been shut across it. All the emergency doors in the prison had been shut by now. A breaching team dashed forward with their charges, pre-shaped and faster than cutters. The raiders only had to stand a few meters back as the preset shaped charges efficiently cut a large, rectangular hole in the wall.

First through the breach was a glittering little robot, covered with angled mirrors and small lasers. True to prediction, automated laser batteries began firing at the intruder. The beams bounced harmlessly from the passive mirror "armor" and the robot's own lasers took out all the batteries within two seconds. The raiders came in after the robot and bullets and darts rattled off their own armor. While Thor and the main body forged ahead, others followed more slowly to take out the remote guns. They were no threat to the raiders, but might harm the prisoners they would be evacuating.

Floating along with them was a recording robot. As soon as the action was successfully concluded, the data would be beamed to one of Chih' Chin Fu's pirate holo satellites, thence to be beamed all over Earth to counter enemy propaganda. Never before in the history of warfare had such fierce fighting been carried on over the lines of communication. Sometimes Thor felt that it was more a fight between rival holographic systems than a real war.

They emerged into the main gallery to a fine display of flashing lights and blaring sirens, but no sign of defenders. That was to be expected. Prisons always functioned with minimum personnel and maximum use of automated systems. Between the robot and their own weapons, they made short work of the defensive systems. They progressed down the main gallery, blowing side doors as they went. There were no individual cells in the prison. Side galleries were used by simply installing doors across them to deny exit. Within the galleries, faces looked up at the forcible opening of their cages. Some were incredulous, some wildly excited, some merely pathetic.

"Sálamis Raiders!" Thor shouted. "We're taking you out of here. Everybody keep calm and follow instructions. Escort teams will take you back to our ship. They'll give each of you respirators just in case the Earthies use gas. Come on, let's get going."

Other galleries were being opened and addressed in the same way. Thor felt a tug at his armored sleeve. A man in the rags of a Sálamid uniform wanted his attention. He turned down his radio communicator to hear.

"Captain, they brung in a new batch of prisoners yestiddy. May still have 'em under questioning."

"Show me," Thor ordered. He signalled and two men in marauder suits accompanied him. Marauders had twice the armor and armament of ordinary raiders. Thor took the man under one arm and followed his pointing finger as gas jets bore the four along a corridor. Ahead of them, the robot took out defenses at far more than human speed.

The prisoner directed them to a heavy door near the center of the rock. The marauders cut through it in seconds while Thor held the prisoner behind him, shielding him from the sparks and molten metal that filled the air. Then they were through.

The men inside made no move to attack or defend. There were three of them, tethered by a bank of instruments. In its holo screen was a detailed image and readout of the woman who was strapped to a framework at one end of the room. Just now, the image showed her heat distribution in a rainbow of colors. Her every mood and emotion would be laid bare to a skilled interpreter. Few could lie convincingly to a truth machine. They could only try to keep quiet, and even then much could be learned, if the interrogator were very skillful and experienced.

One of the marauders leveled a wrist-gun at the hatchet face of the center man, the one who wore the rank of colonel on his collar. Thor said, simply, "Torture?"

The man's life depended on what happened next. His expression remained impassive and he shook his head. "No. Drugs, fatigue, rigorous questioning. All permitted by the rules. Ask him." He nodded toward the prisoner who had led them there.

"It's true," the man said reluctantly. "Never heard of no real torture. 'Bout all I can say in the bastard's favor, though."

"We don't execute them just for being bastards," Thor said. "Only when they commit atrocities." He turned to one of the marauders. "Take these three back as prisoners and give them the usual scan." To the other: "Help me with this woman."

The freed prisoner, not wearing gloves, unfastened the straps binding the woman to the frame. As they pulled her free, the cloud of hair obscuring her face drifted back. For a moment, Thor's heart jumped, a reaction all the adrenaline of combat had not accomplished. "Cat!"

Caterina Sousa's dulled eyes focussed on his visor. "Thor? Is that you?" Tears began to form globes in the corners of her eyes. "You have to do something, Thor! They've captured Martin!"

Althing was already in session when Thor arrived. He had beamed ahead, requesting an audience before the entire assembly. He had expected a wait of weeks while the representatives were gathered, only to find that they had been gathering for some time and were now in full session. He was sure that this portended something bad.

From the North Pole Port, he took the tube to Althing Gallery, a mining operation turned government nerve center. With him was Caterina. He was still in his grubby uniform, redolent of the Spartan accommodations aboard the raider. The presence of the freed prisoners had strained the already limited resources, but he did not bother to change and wash up as he went to address the government. It was not a matter of time, but of propaganda. He was aware that a battered, filthy soldier, straight from the battle zone, was far more impressive than a sleek scion of one of the founding families.

The representatives in the tiers stood and cheered as the two entered the hall. The Speaker, Karl Eberhard, rapped on his podium with an antique gavel scrounged up from somewhere. When there was quiet, he said, "It is our privilege to welcome Captain Thor Taggart, who has just returned with one hundred thirty freed prisoners of war and eighty enemy POWs." There was more cheering. "Although," he went on, "his companion may soon be a prisoner again. There's a blanket arrest warrant for Martin Shaw's followers, Caterina."

"You think I don't know it?" Caterina demanded. "I wouldn't have come within a parsec of this place if I didn't have crucial news to bring you."

"An understandable exaggeration of distance," Eberhard said. "Could this news have something to do with Martin Shaw's capture?"

She was taken aback. "You know about it," she said, unnecessarily.

"Indeed we do," said Tomás Sousa. "We were informed by none other than Secretary General Jameson himself."

"I think," Eberhard said, "that further discussion of this matter should take place within the security council."

"No," Thor said. "I have something to say to the Althing and all the members should hear it."

Eberhard peered at him ironically. "Do you have some official capacity, Thor? I wasn't aware that you were more than a respected member of our armed forces these days."

"I'm a citizen with a petition. Have we been a nation so long that our governmental procedures have become fossilized?"

"Good point," Eberhard conceded. "Let's take this one step at a time, though. Caterina, we would like to hear your account of the events that led to Shaw's capture, to see if they agree with Jameson's."

"It was a fluke!" she cried. "An accident! Martin—Commander Shaw was traveling to a cell meeting on Manhattan, under an alias he'd used more than once. It was a good cover, traveling on a commercial liner with his features totally altered and equipped with a jammer to give any scanning device a false signature reading; retinal pattern, body chemistry, everything. It was the latest from Aeaea, foolproof."

"So how did they recognize him?" Eberhard asked.

"When they went into quarantine at Manhattan, one of the Earth officers who boarded got suspicious. He'd seen the Commander back on Luna a few times before the war. Maybe something about the way he moved jogged his memory. Anyway, during the customs check he found fingerprints in the Commander's room. *Fingerprints*, for God's sake! Who would think of fingerprints in this day and age?"

"Accident, hell," said Hjalmar Taggart. "That was damn smart security work by a man who knows his job. So they had Shaw's fingerprints on file, probably from when he was in trouble with the authorities in Singapore. They're probably still backward enough there to retain fingerprinting. Paper and ink are still cheaper than electronics. Well, good riddance, I say." There were shouts of agreement from many members but not, Thor noted, from all.

"And how did you get caught, Caterina?" Tomás asked.

"We found when he was being transferred from Manhattan to their lockup asteroid. One of our people in Manhattan planted a beacon on the transfer ship and—"

"You mounted a daring rescue mission and they were waiting for you," Sousa finished for her.

Caterina's usual arrogance was replaced by dejection. "Naturally. Martin warned us repeatedly that, should he be taken, we were to forget about a rescue attempt."

General Moore, now Sálamis liaison, gave her an unsympathetic glare. "It's easy to see that when they captured Shaw, they got the brains of your outfit. I take it he wasn't on the ship."

"No. At least, I don't think so. As we closed on them, they hit us with a new weapon. It was a small missile, no more than a meter long, maybe ten centimeters in diameter and very dense, probably made of depleted uranium. I got that from our screen after it had already hit us. They launched it when we were less than a half-kilometer away. Absolutely no time for evasive reaction or retaliation. It penetrated our armor and went off in the center of the ship. Not explosive but some kind of knockout gas. We all had respirators on, of course. We always do when going into action. This stuff is new. It went right through our clothes, penetrated breathing hoses, everything. Only the men in assault suits stayed conscious and they were killed within minutes when we were boarded. I woke up in A-261. They didn't have him there. He's going to their maximum security lockup at Elba."

Moore turned to his aide. "Send out a message to all units, flash priority. Inform them of this new gas missile. Henceforth, all personnel to be fully suited during assaults." The aide left. Under the flexible Sálamid system, any officer could institute an instantaneous change in procedure by invoking flash priority. It bypassed the ponderous military bureaucracy, but his career would be on the line when the inevitable board of inquiry convened to investigate the act.

"He'll be sent to Earth, of course," Sousa said. "There will have to be a show trial. It will be their first really powerful propaganda coup of the war and they will play it to the hilt. I fear it will be hard on Martin." The battered old man looked saddened. "He'll have to make up for all the victories they haven't been winning."

"Serves him right!" said someone.

"The question now," said Eberhard, "is just what are we going to do about this."

"We've never recognized Shaw before," said a representative from Melos. "Why should we now?" There were similar comments from a score of sources.

"The majority of us seem to be of the opinion that Shaw is reaping what he has sown and has no call upon our aid. Still, it has to be put to a vote. All in favor of letting Shaw stew in his own juice—"

"Wait!" Thor said. Caterina's despairing face turned to him with a faint hope. "Before you vote, let me address this body. It's important."

After some hesitation, Eberhard put down his gavel. "Very well. You have no official standing, Thor, but God knows you've earned our attention with your services these past years. Go ahead."

Thor silently thanked whatever deities watched over the Belt that he had just turned in a cheap victory. Month-old heroics never impressed anybody. "Ever since this war started, we've made the pretence of not recognizing Martin Shaw or his party. There were sound political reasons for that, and they still apply when it comes to official, *political* recognition. Still, who among us can deny that Martin Shaw is a great patriot and one of the founders of our independence?"

"He's a terrorist!" shouted someone.

"Exactly! And while we've piously shaken our heads over his deplorable methods, who has profited most from them? We have!"

There was outraged muttering from the Althing, but he had their attention. All of them looked puzzled except Tomás Sousa.

"Explain, Thor," said Sousa.

"We've determined to fight this war by the rules—a defensive war, striking only military targets and with no atrocities against enemy prisoners or noncombatants. Fine. Very virtuous. But Shaw was always our hole card. He's been willing from the start to use Tunguska bombs and they knew it. We knew it, too, and we've taken advantage of it. Why have the Earthies been reluctant to use nukes since the first days of the war?"

"Because," said Moore, "every time they tried it, we'd drop a little rock bomb, a very small one, on one of their Earth-based military facilities. We never missed and they never even came close to stopping one."

"Exactly," Thor said. "You'll notice that they never admitted to the public the nature of those missiles. They didn't dare let it be known that they were virtually helpless against mere chunks of rock. They claimed that it was sabotage and used it as an excuse for more repressive measures. But do you really think that they were beaten by the loss of some bases? They could have moved most of their operations into space and been fairly safe. They were worried about Martin because they knew he wouldn't hesitate to hit civilian targets. Theoretically, with enough rock, he could wipe out all life on Earth and damned little they could do about it. God knows there's enough rock out here in the belt."

"Martin would never do a thing like that!" Caterina protested.

"Probably," Thor said, "but they've built him into such an arch-villain that they have to take the threat seriously. After all, they know what they'd do when *they* got desperate. There have been times when they've had a chance to destroy or at least seriously cripple EOS, but they've held back. Why? Because they knew that that would leave them facing Shaw and we wouldn't be there to ride herd on him and curb his most serious excesses.

"It's an old trick in politics. Dictators have used it for ages. Have a henchman who's known to be ruthless and your enemies will be reluctant to take the ultimate step of killing you. The Earthies hate us all, but better EOS than Shaw. In effect, we've been partners with Shaw since the beginning of the war. Now we're planning to let the Earthies have him without a fight. We claim to have clean hands in this war, but it's been Martin who has kept them clean because he was willing to bloody his.

"When the histories of this conflict are written, probably long after we're all dead, we'll be remembered as the founders of the Confederacy, should we win. But our party, EOS, may go down in history as the cowards who stood by and allowed one of our brothers to be taken by the enemy because he was an embarrassment to us."

An uproar shook the chamber. Some were loudly denouncing Thor and Shaw impartially, others claiming he had a point. With a sinking heart, Thor saw that the latter were in the minority. He felt a touch on his arm and saw Cat looking at him with something less than hostility for the first time in years.

"It was a good try, Thor. But you're talking to the wrong people."

He shrugged. "I'll go after Martin myself if I have to, but I'd rather see it done right."

"Are the members ready to vote?" Eberhard asked when the tumult subsided. "All in favor of action to rescue—" He was interrupted by a peremptory beep and flashing light on his desk console. His expression grew mystified as he read his display. "It seems," he said, "that Secretary General Jameson has another communication for us."

"Two in the same day," Sousa said. "I find this most odd. The Earth government doesn't recognize us, so there can be no official communication between us, just broadcast threats. Now the Secretary General himself wants to speak to us. In the first message he gloated over the capture of Shaw. Now that we've had an opportunity to discuss the implications of the event, he wants to talk again. I believe we'll find that this message will be an offer. They're getting desperate down there. They want to make terms."

There was stunned silence. Could the Earthies actually be offering peace? But at what price?

"Only one way to find out," Eberhard said. He hit the display control, and a wall of the chamber became a view of the podium at one end of the Assembly Hall of the U.N. It was in the palatial new U.N. complex deep under Berne and supposedly proof against any attack. Beneath a gigantic U.N. seal, Secretary General Jameson sat in a huge chair at the top of a short staircase.

"I'll be damned," said the representative of a Rockbusters, Inc. community. "The son of a bitch got hisself a throne!" Derisive laughter filled the chamber.

"Imperial trappings, no less," said Hjalmar Taggart disgustedly. "He's tarted up like a banana republic general."

"Things down on Earth must be even worse than I thought," Sousa said. "This is grotesque. Well, we might as well listen to what he has to say."

The point of view zoomed in until the image of

Jameson loomed twenty feet high. The impression was intended to be majestic, but it did little more than expose that the hands that gripped the arms of the throne bore close-bitten nails. Above the collar of his purple cloak, Jameson's handsome features were composed in an actor's mask of serene majesty. Those in the *Althing* chamber who were not laughing winced.

"There are few sights more degrading," said a professor from a college asteroid, "than the spectacle of the leader of a supposed republic trying to pose as an emperor."

Jameson raised a hand in a gesture of papal benediction. "Brothers and sisters of the outerworlds," he began, "by now you have confirmed the facts of my earlier message in which I revealed our capture of the notorious criminal and terrorist, Martin Shaw. Now that you are free of the influence of this murderous madman, there exists at last a path by which we may end this wasteful conflict and be reunited in amity. It has always been the policy of Earth government that we have not been at war with the people of the outerworlds, but with their misguided leaders."

"That wasn't how you talked when you nuked M-255!" someone shouted.

"Order!" Eberhard called, banging his gavel. "Let's hear what the bastard has to say."

"Now that Shaw has been apprehended," Jameson went on, "he will stand trial at the United Nations for crimes against humanity. This is a time for motherworld and outerworlds to join together to make peace between us. If the Confederacy will send a delegation to attend the trial and join with us in denouncing and then punishing Shaw, then we may arrange an armistice. The delegation may not contain any members of the extended Ciano-Taggart-Kuroda clan. All others will be acceptable and may come to Earth for the trial under safe-conduct. This is our only offer. If you do not respond, the war will continue until the Confederacy is utterly destroyed. Do not force us to these extreme measures.

"You will require time to debate this offer of peace. Since the time is not yet proper to make public this communication, I cannot order a cease-fire while you are arriving at your decision. Do not delay. From now on, every life lost in this terrible war is your responsibility. I await your reply." The image faded as the *Althing* erupted in pandemonium.

After several minutes, the sergeant-at-arms managed to restore order. "There we have it," Eberhard said. "The price of a conditional peace—an armistice—is our complicity in Shaw's show-trial and inevitable execution. Likewise the exclusion from negotiations of the Ciano-Taggart-Kurodas. I think we can safely predict that one of the provisions of the armistice will be that no member of that clan may ever hold office or military commission. Well, let's hear what you all have to say."

A hundred speaker-lights flashed simultaneously and the *Althing* computer made a random choice. The first to speak was leader of the minority Liberation Party. "We all want peace," she said, "we want it desperately. But merely to attend peace talks under such circumstances would be a capitulation and a sellout. Nothing doing."

"They askin for peace talks," said the man from Rockbusters, "that means they hurtin. Let's bust Shaw out first, *then* say we ready to talk, only we send the delegates *we* pick, they don't got no say over that. I'm bettin they'll take it. Ain't nobody back on Earth gonna hear what Jameson just said to us, so he don't lose no face." This was greeted with uproar, the bulk of it favorable.

Thor held his peace while the debate raged. As a Taggart, he had a personal stake in the acceptance of Jameson's terms and self-interest would color any comments, however valid, he might make. This could take a while. He was tired and anxious and in bad need of relaxation. Fortuitously, the planners of the *Althing* chamber had included a bar and restaurant opening off the main room so that the sergeant-at-arms would have no difficulty collaring delegates for a vote.

"Let's get a drink," he said to Caterina. They were joined by Hjalmar and General Moore. These two had no vote in the *Althing* and served only in an advisory capacity. Between the *Althing* floor and the bar they were joined by a small woman with short, blond hair. Thor had no idea where she had come from or when she had joined them.

Hjalmar did a quick double-take as they entered the bar. "Who the hell are you and how did you get in?" He pointed to the shoulder of her coverall, which was entirely bare of the required i.d. badge. Thor thought she looked about sixteen.

"I usually get into places I want to get into," she said. "I'm Sieglinde Kornfeld. Let's grab a table. I've come a long way and I need a drink." She ignored Hjalmar as he ran a belt-scanner over her and muttered code words into his comm unit. Thor revised his estimate of her age. Maybe she was closer to twenty.

The bar was nearly deserted, due to the historic debate out in the chamber. They keyed their orders. "Sieglinde," Caterina said, "you don't look old enough to drink."

"I'm twenty-five," she said. "I age slowly. Good genes."

Hjalmar drew a pistol and leveled it at the girl. "Nobody with her readout has entered Avalon and none has been registered on any ship that's come here since the start of the war. I know you weren't grown in one of our culture vats, young woman. Now, who are you and how did you get here past all my security?"

"Oh, put that thing away, Hjalmar," Thor said. "We're all competent to protect ourselves against Sieglinde."

"Don't be so sure," said the lady in question. "And call me Linde. How I got here is a professional secret. As to why—" She unclipped a tiny pearl from an earlobe and set it on the table. It shimmered for a moment, then metamorphosed into a foot-high homunculus dressed as a magistrate from the classical Chinese opera. It was Chih' Chin Fu. The holography was of a process none of them had ever seen and its fidelity was little less than miraculous.

"Ta-Daaa!" said Fu, arms spread wide. "Pretty good trick, huh? By now, you've met Linde. Thor, I hope that's you I'm talking to. I'd hate to think you were dead. I've sent Linde out there because I think you're going to need her talents. She invented this holographic process. She's also the reason I've been operating un-caught all these years. Take care of her. She's the Ugo Ciano of this generation. I've got to run, now. Literally. They're closing in on me. 'Bye." The holo winked out and became a pearl again.

Hjalmar reholstered his pistol, grumbling. "Where are you from?" he asked.

"Mars. Tarkovskygrad. Don't bother checking, you won't find any record of me there or anywhere else. Family was from Leipzig, in old East Germany, before the reunification. I've been on my own since I was twelve."

"What is it you do?" Caterina asked. "Fu wasn't very specific. Are you a holographic engineer?"

"I'm a genius," she said.

"That's not very specific either," Thor pointed out.

She shrugged. "When you're a genius, you can do pretty much what you want. Society works with people, systems and computers. When you can outsmart all of them, there's really no limit to what you can accomplish. I make my own credit crystals and all record of my purchases is automatically purged after an interval." She looked at Hjalmar. "You just took a quick scan of my i.d. characteristics. Now try to find the record." As Hjalmar worked over his belt-comm, she sipped at her drink.

"If you're the greatest genius of the age," Caterina said, "why didn't you come out here sooner? We could have used a genius or two."

"I was too busy winning the war for you back on Luna," she said. "Fu and I gave the antiwar movement on Earth the only real fuel it had. Between us, we kept that movement not only alive, but strong and growing. I set up the holo broadcast apparatus and the network of comm lines that the activist cells used to communicate. The government was never able to tap in."

"Damn it!" Hjalmar said, punching his belt unit frantically. "It's got to be there! I just keyed it in!"

"Relax, Hjalmar," Moore said. "You're out of your league. We all are. Young lady," he said to Linde, "how would you like a Sálamid commission? Would full colonel do for starters?"

She shook her head. "I like to operate on my own. I don't need official standing. I came out here to offer my services, but it's on my own terms and on projects of my choosing. Would you like to know why Jameson is making his offer now?"

She could no longer surprise them. "The security council should hear it," Thor said, "but everyone's busy just now. Give it to us briefly."

"Things have gone from bad to worse for Earth First," she said. "They whipped up war frenzy with great efficiency, but they weren't able to follow it up with a successful war. Lack of imagination, mostly. Even the more experienced and educated just couldn't visualize the vastness of the asteroid belt. They thought it would be like taking and pacifying some penny-ante Third World republic back on Earth.

"Most Earthies have imaginations conditioned by the simplified images they see in the holos. They see the Belt as a little chain of spheres out there somewhere, maybe a little past the Moon. They can't conceive that Avalon is closer to Earth than it is to some of the other Island Worlds. Also, they went into it with the same delusion most people have; if they just opened fire and killed a few people, the rest would be terrified and would capitulate. Nobody envisioned a long, drawn-out, costly war."

"Home by Christmas," Moore commented.

"What's that?" Hjalmar asked.

"An old expression," Moore explained, "used by civilians going to war for the first time."

"At first the war was popular," Linde went on. "It was a shot in the arm for sick economies. Full employment for a while, that made people happy in the industrialized nations. But it was false prosperity. You can't sustain an economy by selling yourself weapons and then throwing them away. Pretty soon people saw that they were paying for the most expensive war in history and nothing was coming back except a mounting body count.

"Not that the casualty figures were all that great. After all, even if every uniformed Earthie who shipped out was killed, it wouldn't put a dent in Earth's population. If the whole economy were geared to building ships and sending people offworld, it wouldn't amount to a tenth of the yearly birth rate.

"No, it's year after dragging year of *no results* that wears down people's enthusiasm. That, and our endless holographic barrage. This war's been fought more with propaganda than with weapons. When you have complete control of the information that reaches people, you can do just about anything you want with them. That's what Earth First thought they had when they started the war. They were wrong. We were able to counter their propaganda with our own. They could never jam us for long. We demonstrated that nearly everything they said was a lie.

"It didn't take long for the peace movement to get started. Of course, not many people were incensed about the government killing outerworlders. What enraged them was all that money being spent on the war instead of on them. The demonstrations were noisy at first. Then they got bloody. There was one in New Delhi a few months ago in which more than six thousand demonstrators were killed by government troops. It's getting to be like that all over Earth. The war in space is bankrupting the member governments of the U.N. They have to build up their military forces to keep the population in line and that costs too."

Thor smiled thinly. "Back when I left Earth, I deposited a big chunk of my inheritance with a man named Swenson. He wanted to save rare birds from extinction. Last I heard from him was just after Bob Ciano's death.

He was going underground and putting the foundation to work combating the anti-spacer movement. I may have been bankrolling a lot of that anti-war agitation."

"Any idea how their stockpiles are holding out?" Moore asked. This was a question that deeply concerned the Confederacy; Earth's "stockpiles," stores of strategic materials, mostly minerals, for which the motherworld had depended upon the outerworlds. It was widely believed that the war effort could not long survive the exhaustion of those stockpiles.

"There's a tight lid on that information," she said. "And that says a lot. When the war started, Earth First touted the advantages of reducing Earth's dependency on space resources. They said they were becoming 'space junkies,' and that it would be a good thing to return to self-sufficiency. It was like telling people to go back to doing their laundry by hand, or digging ditches with a pick and shovel, after machines have been doing the work for generations. Even in the poorer parts of the world the development and labor costs were too high, and resources are played out everywhere."

"That concurs with what we've been able to learn," Moore said.

"So they're feeling the pinch," Thor said, "but how bad?"

"Bad enough for Jameson to be making peace overtures," Linde said. "It's not capitulation, but it's close. You're now at the point of maximum opportunity and maximum danger. How you handle the peace talks will determine whether the outerworlds have won or lost."

"It sounds to me as if we have them beaten," Caterina said. "How can we lose at this point?"

"Easily," Moore said. "We're ahead on the military end of the war. You could even say we've won, as nearly as anyone can win a war like this one. But many wars have been won on the battlefield and lost at the peace talks. Winning a war used to mean conquering. You defeated your enemy, then you looted his territory, enslaved his population, divided up the land and went looking for somebody else to conquer. Things have changed since those simple times. Now you talk around conference tables. Each side tries to bully the other into seeing things its own way. When they just can't agree, they fight for a while, then they go back to the table. The ones who negotiate usually have nothing to do with the fighting and sometimes they don't mind conceding an advantage that a lot of people died winning for them."

"Makes you wonder, doesn't it?" Linde mused. "Why do people bother fighting when it doesn't get them what they wanted, even if they win?"

"In our case," Thor said, "because it was fight or be enslaved. Earth First fought for a different reason. They hoped that they could forge unity by creating an external enemy. That's been tried before, too. Never very successfully." He glanced at a holo display, saw that the debate was still going full blast. "With them arguing like that, there won't be many voices for capitulation. I want to be on the negotiation team. I started out in this government in the diplomatic branch, such as it was. Since Jameson's demanded that no Taggarts, Kurodas, Cianos and such are to be on the team, we *have* to include a few. I'll resign my commission as soon as I can twist some arms to get in on the negotiations."

"Don't resign just yet," Moore cautioned. "There's still the matter of breaking Shaw out of durance vile. You've become a bit of a specialist in that sort of operation."

"I was hoping somebody else would get the job," Thor admitted. "I know it was me in there demanding that we get Shaw out, but I have to confess that I have no idea how to do it. You can bet that they'll have him under the tightest security possible."

"I'll get you in," Linde said. She sipped her drink and made a face, as if it disagreed with her.

"How?" Thor asked.

She shrugged. "Don't know. Haven't studied the problem yet. But I'm good at solving things. Get me the available data, I'll supply the plan." She seemed bored. Probably has her mind on bigger things, Thor thought.

Figuring a way to circumvent entropy and the heat-death of the universe, more than likely.

"I think this kid's crazy as a solo rock miner," Hjalmar said. "Might as well go along with her, though. If she can get around my security system, she may be able to do what she says."

FOURTEEN

Scenes From the War

Gunnery Sergeant Helen Jackson shifted uncomfortably inside her armored battle harness, trying to ease a maddening itch between her shoulder blades. She had been armored up for four hours and was dying to unshell and hit the showers. She checked her chronometer, saw that it was almost time to let her platoon stand down. She gave the CP screens a last look, then went out to make a final check of her guard posts before their relief arrived.

Despite the bulk of her harness, she moved easily in the one-third, Mars standard gravity. Her broad, black face was sheened with sweat. The suit's heat-exchange system was malfunctioning again. She counted herself lucky that nothing else was wrong with it yet. Three of her platoon's marauder suits were deadlined for lack of replacement parts. As the Earth forces spread ever more thinly through the rebel worlds, the supply system was breaking down. They hadn't reached crisis status yet, but she knew it wouldn't be long.

The long stone corridor ended at a platform overlooking a vast mine gallery. Miners looked up sullenly as she entered, then set back to their work. Such work as they were willing to perform, in any case. They operated with insolent slowness, and they had long since learned how to keep down to a pace that was just active enough to avoid punishment. She kept a wary eye on them, as always. The shortbeam laser cutters could be used as weapons should the colonials ever try a rebellion. There had been incidents on other asteroid worlds. The authorities tried to keep it quiet, but the rumors were coming thick through the Marine grapevine.

Ramirez and Pettijohn were manning their post, standing too close together. Bullshitting as usual, she thought. The gray paint on their armor was scratched and dingy, the drab brown of the hardened ceramic showing through the scratches.

"I trust you two ain't engaging in any unnatural sexual practices," she said. "That's forbidden by Article Two, Section J."

The two whirled, the blue globe of the U.N. flashing on their bulky shoulders. "Jesus, Gunny," Pettijohn said, "why'nt you make some noise when you come this way?" His finger released the trigger of his M42.

"You think the Rebs gonna broadcast their presence before they unzip you with one of them lasers?" She looked out over the mining operation. "How they actin'?"

"Same as always," Ramirez said, shrugging. The movement was barely perceptible in his armor. "They just crummy rockeaters. I seen more spirit in a plate of day-old macaroni."

Pettijohn fished a pack of cigarettes from a belt pouch. "Okay if I light one up, Sarge?"

"Not on guard mount, you know better than that. Put 'em away. Damn things'll kill you, anyway."

"I ain't worrying about that," Pettijohn said. "Way I hear it, we don't got a whole big chance of living through this hitch as it is. It true what we heard, that there was two whole companies wiped out on Catalina?"

"Can't believe everything you hear. Rumors is unauthorized information. You only supposed to believe what you get in the daily briefing."

The two laughed cynically. "Tell us another one,

Gunny," Ramirez said. "I 'specially like the one about the tooth fairy."

"Santa Claus was always my favorite," Pettijohn said.

"You two watch your mouths," she cautioned. "Ain't everyone in this corps as tolerant as me."

They heard shuffling feet coming down the corridor and their hands tightened around weapon butts. Two men in marauder suits stepped onto the platform. "First relief," one said.

Jackson studied the code numbers on their chests. "What company you two with?"

"Delta," said the one with lance corporal stripes.

"I thought Bravo was supposed to relieve us," she said, not releasing her grip on the pistol in her thigh-holster. "Who's the sergeant of your relief?"

"Sanders," said the taller of the two, holding his helmet by his side, dangling by its chin strap. Both had their weapons slung. "If I know him, he's in the CP soaking up coffee. Do we look like rebels?"

"Do you think *they* do?" she said. "Cover 'em."

Ramirez and Pettijohn held their weapons on the two while Jackson punched the communicator on her forearm. A battered face appeared in the set's miniature screen. "Sanders here." A tiny gold skull winked from his left earlobe.

"I'm Gunnery Sergeant Jackson, commander of the third relief. Who the hell're you and how come Bravo Company ain't relieving us?"

"I just told you who I am. Bravo's been pulled out along with Charlie and Golf. Just Alpha, Delta and Echo left on this rock, now."

A prickle replaced the itch between her shoulder-blades. Just three companies to guard the whole rock. The manpower situation was more desperate than she had thought. "Well next time, dipshit, you bring your grunts around to their guardposts and place 'em yourself."

"Up yours, bitch," Sanders said as he switched off.

"Yeah, that's a Marine, all right," Jackson said. "I must be getting jittery in my old age. Come on, you two." The taller of the two relieving marines threw her a mocking salute as she passed. He, too, wore a gold skull in his earlobe.

She rounded up the rest of her platoon in the master corridor and had to endure their bitching and grousing as they headed back to the barracks. At least she could understand them all. In the early days of the war, the U.N. had tried to integrate all nationalities as a gesture of unity. The results had been catastrophic and the experiment had died a quick death. All of the Fifth Regiment, of which her platoon was a part, was made up of English-speaking North Americans. Predictably, their chatter was all about the new pullout.

"I'm telling you, man, we're being deserted!" The speaker was Delibes, a small, thin woman from Toronto who was as cool in action as she was excitable out of it.

"Can it," Jackson said tiredly. "A pullout ain't a bugout. They'll be back. Just some little police action, most likely." She hoped her tone was as confident as her words.

"Then why didn't they tell us?" Delibes demanded.

"When do they tell you anything?" Jackson demanded. "You think it's important for you to know things? What's important is you keep your mouth shut and do as you're ordered." This kind of thing was happening more and more, lately. So many little colonies. You could take them by assault, but then you had to leave a garrison behind to keep the population peaceful. The manning of these outposts was stretching the manpower situation suicidally thin.

"Hey, Sarge," Ramirez said, "you know those two guys who relieved me'n Pettijohn?"

"Sure."

"Well, that taller one, he was wearing a little gold skull in his left ear."

"So was their platoon sergeant. Means they made ten combat assaults. I got one just like it. So what?"

"Well, I got to thinking. He was wearing it in his left ear. I heard that in Delta, they always wear 'em in their right ear, on account of their CO got his left ear shot off in—"

"Shit!" Jackson yanked out her pistol. "Lock and load, troops, we got company! Toler, take your squad and—" The first detonation cut her off. A heap of rubble dropped from the roof of the tunnel and sealed it off. Two side corridors went up simultaneously. Six of the marines went down, struck by hurtling chunks of rock.

"Pick up the wounded!" Jackson bawled. "Let's go!" Helmets on and visors down, they headed up the tunnel. She knew they were being herded, but there was nothing to do but go.

A dozen armored men swarmed out of the tunnel ahead. The marines opened fire. Ramirez went down with blood spraying from a long rent in his armor. Jackson got off six shots from her pistol before she saw what the men ahead were wheeling out.

"Cease fire!" Jackson yelled.

"Jesus," said somebody. "That's a heavy mining cutter. Chop us all down in a heartbeat." They stopped shooting, but nobody laid down any weapons.

A man in black armor came forward, pulling off his helmet. Jackson recognized the battered face. Next to him was a man she had seen not twenty minutes before, sullenly working a shortbeam cutter. He didn't look like a whipped dog now. She kept her pistol trained on "Sanders."

"Hey, man," she said. "You use that thing, you'll cut a hole clean through this rock. Let all the air out. You don't want that, do you?"

The man grinned. "These miners deal with wall breaches all the time. They'll patch it in a minute. Not soon enough to do you any good, though. Lay down your arms and you can sit out the war in a comfortable prison rock. You have ten seconds."

"Just one question," she said, not letting the pistol waver an inch. "You EOS, or Shaw's people?"

"EOS. You think Shaw's bunch would've given you a chance to surrender?"

Slowly, deliberately, she laid the pistol on the floor. "Drop 'em, people, they got us dead to rights." Muttering and cursing, the platoon laid down their arms and began stripping off their armor.

"I know you don't owe me any explanations," Jackson asked, "but how did you get in?"

Sanders jerked his head toward a group of miners who were gathering up weapons. "They cut us an airlock. You couldn't watch every bit of the surface all the time. We came in in little stealth ships, two or three at a time. We've been setting up this takeover for months."

"Hey, Reb," Pettijohn said, "how many of these have you guys pulled?"

"This makes twenty-six for my team," Sanders said. "It's getting easy now you're stretched so thin."

"Twenty-six! Damn!" Pettijohn mopped at his forehead, where a chunk of rock had gouged the skin. "And they told us we was winning!"

"Yeah," Jackson said, wearily, "so they did. But you never believed all that stuff about Santa Claus either, did you?"

Thor jerked fully awake when the alarm beeped. He had drifted into a half-sleep as he studied the readouts for Elba. There wasn't much and most of it was out of date. The Earthies had been making extensive revisions in the interior layout.

"What is it?"

"Rendezvous, Commander," said the comm officer.

"I'm on my way." He released himself from the bunk harness and pulled himself out of his quarters and into the ship's main corridor. Caterina and Linde were already there. In the course of the voyage, the two had developed a relationship that was neither friendship nor hostility, but somewhere between. Thor was stumped for a name to fit it. But he knew that somehow, deep down, Caterina was afraid of Linde. It made no sense, but he was sure of it.

"They're here," Caterina said excitedly.

"Don't be too optimistic," Thor cautioned. "This may not work out. If it doesn't, you're free to rejoin them."

"I'd love to. But I'll stay with the mission."

"Thor," Linde said. "I've been going over the Ciano holos and printouts, and—"

"Later," he said peremptorily. "We're meeting with some hard people and I don't have any attention to spare."

"That's nothing unusual," Caterina said to Linde. "He doesn't have much at the best of times."

That's all I need, he thought. The two of them ganging up on me. His team leaders were already at the dock. "Ole, Huang, no shooting unless they display hostility."

"That mean one of 'em looks crosseyed, I can shoot 'em?" Ole asked.

"Use your own judgement, but don't waste any time on deep thought. I think they'll play this straight, but some of them are pretty crazy."

"They won't make any trouble," Caterina insisted. "You're being paranoid."

"If there's trouble," Thor said, "don't shoot her, but you can dent her a little."

"Lock cycling," said a disembodied voice. They dropped their banter and faced the lock. Ole and Huang kept their hands away from their weapons, but they were the fastest men in his team. That was why they had been chosen to back him at this meeting.

"Lock cycled," said the voice. The gate before them swung open.

The first man through had a familiar face below a shock of red hair. He grinned at Thor. "Hey, kid. Been a lot of years." He stuck out a hand. He had lost the other one somewhere and wore a prosthesis in its place.

"Good to see you, Mike," Thor said.

"Jesus, kid, your face is about as marked as mine now. You must've been keeping bad company." He caught sight of Caterina and his smile faded fractionally. "Hello, Cat. How come you're still alive?"

Her face flushed crimson. "Did you expect me to commit *hara-kiri* because I got captured? Where were you when we put that job together?"

"I was on a raid into Sector Six," he said, holding up the prosthesis. "Lost this."

"Mike, if you and your people would come with me, we'll—"

"What are you implying, you red-haired bastard?" Caterina demanded.

"Just that you were dumb and you cost us seven good people on your half-assed rescue mission."

Caterina used the nearest wall to launch herself at his throat. The impact carried them both well back into the lock, meshed in a tangle of real and artificial limbs.

Ole and Huang reached for their guns, but Thor waved them back. "Are they likely to do any damage?" he asked the knot of people still in the lock, now drawing back from the combatants.

An amazingly voluptuous woman drifted forward. "It's an even match, Mr. Taggart. They won't do anything that can't be repaired. I'm Natalie Tomalis, skipper of *Juarez*. There isn't much that would make us join forces with you Eos people, but if you say you can spring Martin, we're willing to listen."

"It's good to know you have so much trust in us," Thor said.

"We don't," Tomalis retorted. "But Martin told us that you were the one person in the Eos camp we could trust absolutely."

For a moment, Thor was too startled to speak. He had no idea that Martin had harbored so high an opinion of him. "I'm flattered. If those two will separate, we can have a conference on how this is to be carried out."

The two combatants were pried apart and towed along by escorts. Apparently, such impromptu settlings of grudges were no rarity among Shaw's hair-triggered followers. Mike had a few new slashes on his face, but that seemed to be the worst of it.

"Hey, Thor," Mike said, "I'd never know you for the college boy I picked up on Luna. You've aged well." The blood, unable to trickle down in zero-g, gathered into blobs on his face.

"A quality I share with fine wine. This operation is going to be tricky, but we have—"

Mike leaned close. "Thor, that little blonde, I saw her with Chih' Chin Fu back on Luna a couple of years ago. She's spooky, even if she has a nice body."

"Nothing wrong with my ears, either," Linde said.

"It's all right if she's spooky," Thor said. "We have spooky work for her to do." It never failed to amaze him how people allowed personalities to intrude where only professionalism and the mission counted. That was the true advantage Eos had over Shaw's forces. Eos had institutional discipline which didn't require a charismatic cult-figure to keep the troops in line. In Shaw's brief absence, his organization was already beginning to disintegrate.

The newcomers climbed out of their pressure suits, causing the Eos personnel to wrinkle their noses. Conditions in Shaw's ships were even more Spartan than in the Eos vessels. How was he going to get them to cooperate with Eos when they couldn't even get along with one another?

The conference chamber was merely an emptied hold. Furniture was irrelevant in zero-gee so the chamber contained only some holographic and communications equipment. The participants oriented themselves so that all could communicate without craning their necks to face one another. It was a skill they exercised without conscious thought.

"First," Thor said, "I need to know how many people you represent."

"Forget it," Mike informed him. "That's classified information."

It confirmed a suspicion Thor had long held. Defiance had been losing personnel from the start of hostilities. Battle casualties accounted for a lot of it, but many more had deserted to Eos. They were down to a hard core of no more than a few thousand. Perhaps they only numbered in the hundreds. If they had been more numerous, they would have bragged of it. "Let it pass," Thor said, as if making a concession. "Still, I need to know if you represent *all* of Defiance. For instance, where's Thierry Ruiz?"

"That bastard," Mike said disgustedly. "I tried to warn the boss about him. He tried to take over as soon as Martin was gone and we—"

"You talk too much, Mike," Natalie said. "Forget about Ruiz. He's no longer a factor in Defiance. And stop trying to pump us for information. We're here to discuss this rescue you claim you can pull off."

"The operation is two-stage," Thor said. "First, we infiltrate Elba with our own people."

"Hold it," Mike protested. "You just float in there and infiltrate? Elba's a max-security lockup."

"As such," Thor continued, "it doesn't produce anything except corpses. It has no agricultural capability and only the most rudimentary air-producing facilities. It has to be continuously resupplied from outside. We've captured one of their supply ships and replaced its crew with our own. They'll go in on a regular supply run and be there during turnaround time when our phase-two team arrives."

"How are you going to get your supply-ship team in undetected?" Natalie asked. "They'll undergo a complete bodyscan on arrival. Imposters can't escape detection. We know. We've tried."

"Meet our secret weapon," Thor said, nodding toward Linde. "She can do anything she wants with electronic instrumentation. The people we send in will give their instruments the same readouts as the crew we captured. None of the personnel in Elba were there the last time the supply ship made that run, so there shouldn't be any embarrassing encounters with old acquaintants. All of our people have been given appropriate cosmetic treatment."

"What's phase two?" Mike asked.

"That's when we go in and get Martin. A frigate has been sent out from Luna orbit to pick him up. None of the local admirals would detach a major war vessel to send him back and the Earth authorities are too nervous to transport him in anything less powerful. We're going to destroy their frigate and replace it with one of our own. They're going to hand Martin to us. By the time we get there, the phase one team will have thoroughly undermined their defenses and their morale."

"So that's why you want us in on it," Natalie said. "We have the frigate."

"Exactly," said Thor. "You captured *Mars Ultor* last year. You're keeping her near here, which is why we chose this site for our meeting. We need that ship."

"Why should we just hand her over to you?" said Mike.

"Do you want Martin back or don't you?"

"Of course we do," Natalie said. "But we want in on the operation. You want the ship, fine. We'll take a chance on your plan. But you have to take some of us along."

"I expected such a request," Thor said.

"Not request," she corrected, "demand."

"Don't be offended, Thor," Mike said, "but we don't really figure you people can pull off an operation like this on your own."

"Don't give me that crap," Thor said affably. "I know damn well you don't want your boss to get rescued by EOS while the rest of you fight over what's left of your organization." It was a relief not to have to mince words for a change. "Now give me your decision. We don't have much time. Now that I've outlined our plan, you'll understand that I can't turn you loose until the operation's over, should you opt out."

Mike grinned. "Wouldn't miss it for the world."

"I'm in," Natalie said. She looked at an intense, blond young man who looked familiar to Thor. With a shock, he realized that it was Heimdal Roalstad, Sean's youngest son. He hadn't seen the boy since the beginning of the war and this hard-bitten skipper little resembled the shy youth he had known. But then, he thought, he didn't much resemble the Thor Taggart of a few years back, either.

"Heimdal, you're skipper of the *Tell*," Natalie said. "What do you say?" She turned back to Thor. "We renamed *Mars Ultor* as *Wilhelm Tell* when she became a Defiance ship."

"*Tell*'s a fighting ship," said Roalstad. "I don't like the idea of using her as a decoy."

"The war's not over yet," Thor told him. "You may still get your chance to cover yourself with glory in a ship-to-ship shootout. Right now, we need a frigate to get Martin out. The plan won't work without it."

Roalstad let out a long breath. "Hell. Martin always said a war's no place for sentimentality. I'm in. Since this could be a suicide mission I'll have to let my crew opt on an individual basis. They've never turned down anything so far, though."

"That's fair," Thor said. "But if any want out after they've heard the plan, they're to be held in isolation until the operation is over."

Natalie looked around at her cohorts. There were minute nods or other gestures of assent. "We're all in," she reported. "Let's do it."

"I noticed that you managed to avoid telling them that the plan was mine," Linde said.

"They wouldn't trust you," Thor said. "They think you're spooky. Hell, they only trust me because Martin told them to. Don't worry, I'll see to it that you get all the credit in the history books." He felt like needling her. There was a real woman down beneath the paranoid armoring she had built around herself and he wanted to see what she was like.

They were in her quarters, a sparsely furnished cubicle in the crew section of the Sálamid vessel. Almost everything in the cubicle that was not obviously scientific apparatus was really scientific apparatus disguised as something else.

"You know what you can do with your historical credit, don't you? Do you think I've made myself into an unperson for the sake of undying fame?"

Thor congratulated himself. He actually seemed to have gotten under her skin. She was beginning to show flashes of emotion.

"Tell me something," she went on. "Why are you so determined to spring Shaw? I mean really, not just the reasons you gave the *Althing*. You're political enemies. He's everything you think is loathesome in his paramilitary tactics. What's more, any idiot can see you've been in love with Caterina for years and she's utterly under Shaw's spell. She can't even think of another man. So why don't you want to leave him where he is?"

His ears burned at her easy analysis of his relationship, or rather non-relationship, with Cat. But it was encouraging that Linde was showing curiosity about him.

"When I first left Earth," Thor said, "I had to cut ties with my entire past. My family, my career, my standing in the society in which I'd been raised. I found myself wandering around on Luna with my past amputated and my future, which had once been so carefully planned, a complete unknown. Martin was my first real friend, and I still think of him that way." He thought in silence for a moment. "Also, I know that if it was me in that prison, he'd come get me out."

"That clarifies a few things. You're a withdrawn and calculating man, Thor. I suppose that's what makes you so successful as a diplomat and as a planner, but it makes you a little difficult to read. Your forlorn passion for Caterina has been the only fully human quality I've found in you. Now I know about your friendship and loyalty to Shaw. Who knows what storehouses of humanity are down inside you?"

"*I'm* withdrawn? *I'm* calculating?" Thor demanded, truly shocked. "You're a goddamned human data crystal. The only enthusiasm you've ever shown is a passion for secrecy. You don't even seem to exist except when you're right in front of somebody."

"Do you think I can live any other way?" she demanded. "I wasn't yet ten years old when I realized I was a freak. Worse than that, I was probably the most valuable freak in history! Picture yourself at the age of eight, taking advanced mathematics and n-dimensional physics in a university on Mars. Being a child prodigy isn't so bad, as long as people are tolerant and condescending. After all, I knew that I had absolutely nothing in common with my own age group. My teachers seemed dumb and slow, but there were always the computers to make up for their deficiencies.

"As a child, even a brilliant child, you have very little knowledge of the world and what a nasty place it can be. My mother insisted that I take some time from the sciences and study history, languages, social sciences, things like that. I resented the time it took, but I plunged into the subjects and came out with a knowledge of how damned *valuable* I was. A child prodigy is treated with amused condescension—there's that cute little girl again, talking just like a grownup. But a full-fledged, adult genius is a high-priced commodity.

"It didn't take me long to figure out what I was in for. Sooner or later, after I'd started publishing my independent research papers, some college administrator was going to realize that he had the next Newton or Einstein or Ugo Ciano on his hands. Do you know what that's worth in the modern world. It meant I'd be working for the government, for one thing. I'd spend my life on Mars or Luna, but most likely on Earth. I'd have a beautiful lab, I'd probably live in a lavish mansion, and I'd be under guard every minute of my life. Every bit of my research would become government property and most of it would be put in secret banks because not one scientist in hundreds could understand it and it would only have value if it meant immediate commercial or military advantage."

She stuck her hands into the front pockets of her coveralls. "From the moment I made that discovery, I began to make it my policy to hide how good I really was. I learned everything I could about security and information systems and I devised ways to get around them. When my parents died in the Barsoom City riots, I began obliterating my records wherever they were kept. I continued my studies but turned in the work of a mid-level prodigy, one of those early bloomers who mature into scientists of no extraordinary capability. I designed my own crystals to hold my real research. When the war broke out, I contacted Fu on the clandestine computer network. I faked my ticket and travel permits and joined his organization on Luna. I've lived like a hunted animal ever since but I'm free."

Thor had not dreamed that she was capable of such a lengthy speech. She usually pared sentences down to the bare bones and a paragraph of three sentences was a major effort for her. She smiled. My god! he thought, she actually smiles!

"Besides," she added, "Mike says I have a nice body."

"A little on the hefty side by spaceborn standards," he said, "but you'll do."

"I'm glad we've had this little heart-to-heart," she said. "Now, are you ready for some bad news?"

"Not the jailbreak plan!" he said. "Is there something wrong with it?"

"No, it's what I was trying to tell you earlier. It's the Ciano material, the stuff you've had Aeaea working on. It's not going to work."

A great, hollow space opened up somewhere beneath his stomach. "That last report said they'd succeeded!" The Aeaean report had said that the original Ciano drive had failed because the Ciano field generator had been far too bulky to install in a ship. Massive strides in miniaturization had been made since Ciano's day, however. The Aeaeans were ready to begin production on the new drive units.

Linde slapped the stack of readouts against the padded wall. "Whatever you paid for these calculations, it was too much. I'd have done it for a keg of good Franconian, and taken one-tenth the time."

"We didn't have access to you at the time," he muttered.

"These figures are correct as far as they go, but it still won't work. Not the way you want it to."

"Why not?" he demanded. "The anti-matter drive would give us a virtually unlimited source of condensed energy. We can use it to move entire asteroids. I'm no great physicist, but I've done some figuring myself. For interstellar travel, you could use the anti-matter drive to accelerate an asteroid to a velocity where a Bussard-type ramjet can cut in. The supply of interstellar hydrogen is unlimited and with the relativistic time-dilation effect, we could reach a number of planetary systems in the vicinity within one generation." A devastating thought came to him. "You're not going to tell me that we've been wrong about the frequency of planetary systems in the solar neighborhood, are you?"

"Uh-uh. If anything, we've been underestimating the likely number of systems within a few tens of light years from here. It was about the only really practical spinoff from the old SETI program. Whole bunches of Jupiter-sized planets have been found by spaceborne apodized telescopes. All current cosmogony says that, where you find a giant planet, you'll probably find smaller planets as well. I agree with that theory, which is a pretty good indication that it's correct."

"I'd never doubt it," Thor said.

"Now for the bad part. The interstellar ramjet was an interesting idea when Bussard first proposed it. That was in 1960, in *Astronautica Acta*. That was also before ultraviolet astronomy came of age in the 1970s. By the 1980s it was established, at least among those specialists working on the problems of the local interstellar medium, that the solar system was imbedded near the edge of a partially ionized gas cloud, which was some twenty light years across and whose mean density was about one atom for every ten cubic centimeters. That's a much harder vacuum than anything duplicated in a laboratory, if you're a little sketchy on this stuff. Outside this cloud, the gas temperature was higher and the density lower by more than one order of magnitude, extending for over a hundred light years. Am I beginning to sound like old Ciano?"

"Actually," Thor said uncomfortably, "he was pretty entertaining when he explained things. Alarming, but fun to watch. You've been perfectly lucid so far, but where's the problem?

She began to gesture with long-fingered, elegant hands.

"The upshot of all this, as far as the ramjet is concerned, is that under these conditions, even if you had a magnetic scoop with an effective collecting area of 100 kilometers by 100 kilometers and traveling at a velocity of a third of the speed of light," she paused for a few seconds to perform the arithmetic somewhere in the back of her mind, "then you collect scarcely a gram per second, which is way too little for the ramjet. That's quite aside from the practical problems of getting your asteroid to that velocity in the first place."

"Hold it,' Thor said. "What about the anti-matter drive itself? What about using it all the way to the destination?"

She shook her head. "As with the ramjet, so with anti-matter. People get enthusiastic about a new sort of energy and they want it to solve all their problems. They want it so bad that they ignore the hard physics of the problem. Look, I'll try to keep it simple." She held out a hand against Thor's automatic protest. "I'm not being patronizing, but the calculations are pretty complicated. I'll just sketch in the basic factors of the problem."

She held up a finger. "First, we create anti-matter from energy. The only sources of energy we now have that are suitable for such a purpose are solar power and nuclear fusion. Even if we assume an unrealistic one hundred percent conversion efficiency for the solar power cell with a light collecting area of ten thousand square kilometers, the energy available at the average distance of the asteroids from the sun is equivalent to some half a ton of anti-matter per year. In reality, you will get a lot less. The energy production rate of a usual nuclear fusion plant is at about the same level."

She held up a second finger. "The energy available from a ton of anti-matter could get a *space ship*, massing a few hundred tons, to a velocity of some one-tenth of the speed of light, if we had a one-hundred-percent efficient photon-drive available to us, which we don't. In practice, we'd be lucky to get that hundred-ton space ship to one *hundredth* the speed of light, what with the usual heat loss omnipresent in any engineering. What's more, the mass of a typical asteroid world is *not* a few hundred tons but is in the range of billions of tons. Even the small ones are millions of tons."

This was not Thor's field, but he was no ignoramus. Her analysis carried conviction. "I think I need a drink," he said, shakily. She drifted to a wall dispenser and drew a beer for him and a Steinhäger and limejuice concoction for herself. They sipped in silence for a while.

"Now that you're a little fortified," she said, "are you ready for the ballistics report?"

"You've ruined my day," he said. "Possibly my life. I might as well hear the worst."

"Even these low speeds involve considerable risk, if the ship is to carry humans. At a velocity of one-hundredth the speed of light, an interstellar grain a few tens of microns across would have an impact greater than that of a bullet from a high-powered rifle. And we can expect *much* bigger particles out there. With the available astrophysical data, we can't estimate the frequency of such impacts, but once is too many. We'd have to devise a new way to protect the ship. The presently practicable protective measures against particle impacts for interplanetary travel, which is at the velocity of less than one-thousandth the speed of light, would be inadequate at relativistic velocities."

"But we're talking about moving whole asteroids!" Thor protested. "We can leave meters of rock on the leading surface. Hundreds of meters, if necessary."

Again she shook her head. "Sorry. It's the same problem you have with any kind of armor; more mass, more energy required to accelerate it. If that wasn't a factor, you could just put a big uninhabited hunk of solid rock out in front of the occupied asteroid-ship to absorb the particles and forget about collisions. As it is, you're going to have to hollow out your asteroid completely just to get it to any kind of acceleration at all."

If he had had any gravity to assist the gesture, Thor would have slumped and buried his face in his hands.

As it was, he could only look stricken. "For all this time, since the war started, it's been my only real hope. I thought Ugo had given us a way to emigrate to new solar systems. There's just no need for us to be penned up here in this little solar system, snarling and chewing on one another, when there's so damn many places to go! Hundreds of billions of stars in this galaxy alone. Lots of those, maybe even the majority, probably have planets. And the outerworlders by definition are the kind of people who aren't too timid to pull up stakes and jump into the unknown. Hell, they'd leap at the chance. And now you're telling me that not only can we not win, we can't even get away?" For the first time since the news of Bob Ciano's death, he felt tears gathering around his eyelids.

Linde held out her plastic bulb and stuck the straw into his mouth. "Try some of this. It'll make you feel better."

Automatically, he sucked in some of the odd concoction. "God, that tastes awful."

"It grows on you. I know you want to head out. It's what I want, too. There may still be a way."

He was taking another sip of her drink and choked on it. "What! You've been puncturing all my hopes and you had the answer all the time?" He had gone in an instant from despair to utter fury.

"Take it easy! Maybe I have, but it's going to take time. First, I had to show you that the course you and the Aeaeans had been pursuing was a dead end. Or at least a very slow end. But there's another way and it's what Ciano was really working on while he was perfecting his Ciano Field for his anti-matter experiments.

"I've only read what's been published about Ciano's work on the indeterminate n-dimensional field. Even with that limited information, I can see how Ciano might have gone about developing the applied theories of the Ciano field, but even I might need a few years to figure out its practical aspects on my own. Have you kept a copy of the unpublished notes that you gave to the Aeaens?"

"I have the original. I gave them the copies. I also have access to Ugo's old lab."

"Wonderful!" She went into an animated spin. "I won't promise anything just yet, but with those notes and that lab, I might be able to figure out how to get around the luminal limitations on communication in the four-dimensional world. With that, maybe even the limits on transportation."

He grabbed her hand to stop her spinning and held onto it because he wanted to. "You lost me. Reduce that to English."

"If I had Ciano's lab notes, given time, I might be able to figure out a way to get around the speed of light limitation in sending a message from one point in four-dimensional space to another. I *might*, just might, be able to invent a way, eventually, to transport matter from one point to another without going through normal four-dimensional space, which is governed by the speed of light restriction. I can't promise you anything now. It could take years of hard work, even for me. You're going to have to buy us time at those peace talks, Thor. Buy us all the time you can."

Thor tried to say something but managed only a strangled sound. Never in his life had he been subjected to such extremes of elation and despair in so brief a time. He had entered this room thinking that, soon, he could lead humanity on the first interstellar voyage, equipped with a technology that would allow humans to visit several solar systems within a single lifetime. Then he had been told that the technology in which he had placed such faith would require many generations for even the shortest possible interstellar voyage. Now, if he understood her correctly, she might have a way to cross space instantaneously, so maybe there was no limit to the possibilities of human interstellar exploration.

He found that he was still holding her hand. He pulled her to him and kissed her. When he broke the clinch, he said, "Linde, you can't go on this mission.

It's too risky and now we can't take the chance of losing you."

"Do that again," she demanded. He did.

This time, she broke the clinch. "Now you can go to hell. I'm going. I'm the only one who can pull the communications deception and it's essential to the operation. Anyway, there isn't that much risk. I've always been able to get out of *anything* in one piece. You just don't want to have to worry about me. Well, forget it. I'll take care of myself. You worry about your end of it." She took another swig of her Steinhäger and limejuice. "Now, let's try that again. This time, try not to breathe through your nose so much."

Thor could tell that she was going to be difficult.

FIFTEEN

It always annoyed Colonel Hughes when the Party "advisers" came calling. He wished they would drop the pretense and call themselves commissars or thought police or something else that really described their function. They were the Party's loyalty watchdogs and they didn't advise anybody. They gave orders and they reported on everyone, including, it was rumored, each other.

The two that had been wished on him and who now sat in chairs before his desk were typical of the breed. Their faces were anonymous and unmemorable, in keeping with the Party's insistence on the utter equality of all mankind. Earth-dwelling mankind, anyway. Their tan coveralls were drab and they wore no insignia of rank, only their gold-on-black armbands with the $\oplus 1$ sigil.

"The Shaw interrogation hasn't been making satisfactory progress," said the one on the right. "We've given your team instructions to raise the question-intensity quotient one level.

"Such an order requires my authority," Hughes protested, knowing already that it was futile. There was no more authority anymore except Party authority. Although that might not be for long, judging by the latest messages from Earth.

"We had no doubt that you would authorize the intensification," said the one on the left with casual contempt. "We saw no need to bother you with the details."

"The Party wants Shaw alive," he reminded them. "I cannot guarantee his future viability if his interrogation intensity is raised beyond level five." The numbered level system was an obfuscation he used readily. Like most civilized men, he did not like to use the word "torture."

"We shall be responsible for getting him back to the real world alive, Colonel," said one of them, he was not sure which. They and all the others were so much alike he suspected they were stamped out by a cookie-cutter somewhere on Earth. "The Party," one of them continued, "is growing impatient for answers from Shaw."

"From what we hear lately," said Hughes with relish, "the Party may have more serious matters to worry about."

The two bristled and sat up straighter. "Are you speaking disloyalty, Colonel?" said the one on the left.

"Is it disloyal to take seriously the latest broadcasts from Earth?" Hughes said, ingenuously. "After all, the Party controls all such media communication. Or is supposed to, at any rate. Now that I think of it," he glanced at his wall chrono, "it's about time for the latest update. Shall we watch?"

Without waiting for an answer, he switched on the holo. The wall dissolved into a huge great seal of the U.N. There were a few bars of the world anthem, then the familiar face of Patrick O'Halloran, "the most trusted man on Earth," at least according to his network. The signs of stress in the famous holo-journalist's voice and face could not be covered by the best efforts of the holographic enhancers.

"Greetings, people of Earth, loyal citizens in the outerworlds, and all those serving in the space forces." He rushed through the ritual introduction without his customary serenity and launched immediately into his lead story. "The whereabouts of Secretary General Jameson remain a mystery at this hour, and government information sources deny that his unavailability has anything to do with the mysterious explosion earlier this week at the general convocation of the Earth First Party in Nairobi. There are unconfirmed reports that the Honorable Anthony Carstairs, seldom-seen chairman of the Earth First Party, was killed in the bombing."

Hughes saw the two advisers stiffen at that news. If the report confirmed what he suspected, these two were in for a surprise.

"Grand Marshal Gulmen, U.N. Chief of Staff," O'Halloran went on, "has assumed temporary leadership until the situation is resolved, but General Gabriel Edwards, Chief of the North American Department, announced this morning that North American forces will not acknowledge the leadership of a military government directed from Berne. Apparently, the U.N. charter does not clearly define—"

"Treason!" gasped one of the advisers.

"It will take a trial or two to prove that," Hughes said. He turned to the two and smiled slightly. "And I need hardly remind you that this station is administered by the North American Department. A good many things require clarification, gentlemen."

"Whatever the situation at the U.N.," blustered the one on the right, "Earth First is still the majority North American party." The tone was good but the stuffing was beginning to run out of him.

Hughes' comm unit buzzed. "Sir, the Earth Frigate has docked and the authorized party is now entering the facility."

"Inform them that I'll be with them in a few minutes," he said. Then, to the advisers: "It looks as if your interrogation is over, gentlemen. The ship is here to take Shaw back to Earth. Too bad you won't have a full confession to brighten your dossiers but, never fear. It looks as if Party leadership is in a bit of a shakeup stage just now."

"Under the circumstances," said one, sweat in his

voice, "might it not be better to, ah, dispose of the terrorist right now?"

"You mean," Hughes said, "just in case the new leadership goes all humanitarian on us and decides to dispose of the foul torturers employed by the former regime?"

"That is treasonous talk, Colonel!" protested one.

"Can it, mister," said Hughes, out of all patience. "From here on in, you're going to cover your own ass and I'm going to cover mine. My orders are to put Shaw on that ship and they'll have plenty of time to pretty him up on the trip back. Good day to you, gentlemen. If you wish, you may join me when I surrender Shaw to the frigate commander. If I were you, I'd talk that commander into a couple of berths back to Earth." The two left without so much as a sneer.

His comm buzzed again. "Colonel, two officers of the supply ship ask to see you. They say it's a matter of security."

Security? Hughes thought. What had the supply ship people to do with security? Well, in these unsettled times it made sense to cover all bases. "Send them in."

The first to come in was the supply ship's skipper, a scar-faced redhead who looked villainous enough to be one of Shaw's people. The records made it clear that he was reliable, though, and had made seven previous supply runs to Elba. With him was his communications officer, a striking little shorthaired blonde. She had a vacuous, stupid expression but was likewise vouched for by the records. A previous commandant had appended a personal note that her expertise at zero-gee sex was little short of miraculous. Hughes had been too busy to try her out himself, and maybe he'd have a little more leisure when Shaw was off his hands.

"What is it?" he asked. "I have to meet some people in a few minutes."

"Won't take up much of your time, chief," said the redhead. "I'm Matt Schuyler, skipper of the *Tarkovsky-grad*. This is my comm officer, Melinda Graves."

"I know who you are," he said impatiently. "What's so important that you have to talk to me?"

"Well," the redhead said, "everybody's been nervous, what with the situation back on the dear old motherworld goin' to hell in a handbasket, as my dear old mother used to say. My people are gettin' spooked, and so are yours."

"Please get to the point," Hughes said, tightly.

"Well, sir, some of your people are gettin' so spooked they've asked to stow on my ship when we leave here."

A cold chill touched Hughes's spine. Desertion! Maybe mutiny as well. But where could they desert *to*? No matter. People didn't behave rationally when they began to panic.

"Give me their names," he said, quietly. "I'll have them put under arrest at once."

The blonde spoke up for the first time. "I was, ah, you might say entertaining Captain Murieta in my quarters last watch," she said. Murieta was the chief of his security force. "He asked if he could stow in my locker when we left. Swore he'd rig the security check so he wouldn't be discovered. Said some of his men wanted to come along."

For a moment he was unable to think. Then his orderly mind got back into gear and began sorting possibilities. He didn't dare have Murieta arrested, until he knew who the disloyal security personnel were. He had to think fast. Then the solution appeared.

"Thank you," he said to the two officers. "Your loyalty will be amply rewarded. For now, return to your quarters and say nothing to anybody. In a few hours, I'll be needing a full report, with the names of all who approached you for passage off Elba."

"Just doin' our bit for the motherworld, Colonel," said the skipper.

And probably hoping I'd reward you with more cash than they offered, Hughes thought. When they were gone, he keyed the security HQ. The broad face of Captain Proski appeared. "Yes, sir?"

"Captain, I've just received an urgent bulletin from the Chief of Ordnance. Sabotage has been detected at the government arsenal at Herschel, on Mars. For several months, faulty power packs for small arms have been going out from there, some of them rigged to explode after a random number of charges have been fired. That's the arsenal our last lot of power packs came from." Actually, he had no idea where their power packs were from. For that matter, he wasn't sure whether the Martian arsenal was at Herschel or somewhere else. He was with the Provost Marshal's office, not Ordnance. "Turn all weapons in to the armorer for examination and replacement of power packs. That's to include officer's sidearms, Proski. See to it immediately."

"Yes, sir!" said Proski. He drew his own pistol and slid out its power pack. "Sabotage, by God!" he said, indignantly.

Hughes switched channels. "Has the commander of the frigate left his ship yet?" he asked his comm officer.

There was a pause. "No, sir, he's still on the bridge."

"Put me through to him, under confidential seal."

"Yes, sir." The bridge of the frigate materialized on the holographic wall. A man of about thirty, blond and with a scarred face, appeared. He looked familiar, somehow. Probably some young hero, lionized in the holos for a few days before a new hero came along.

"U.N.S.S. *Fearless* here," said the blond man. "I am Captain Jefferson. Is there any problem, Colonel?"

"Captain, I realize that this is irregular, but an emergency has come up here. Have you a full complement of Marines aboard?"

"Yes, sir. Two companies, all veterans."

"When you come into Elba to pick up the prisoner, please bring a platoon, fully armed. I have a serious disloyalty problem here, and I'm having all my security personnel disarmed. I'll have to arrest some people and I need trustworthy people to back me up."

"You can count on us, Colonel," said Jefferson. "There've been incidents like this in a lot of the garrisons. Never a mutiny in the regular Navy, though, or in the Marines."

"Thank you, Captain," Hughes said. "I knew I could rely on you. Out." Pompous ass, he thought as he

switched off. He poured himself a brandy and sipped it
as he waited for a few minutes. He wasn't worried. In
fact, he felt satisfied with the resourceful way he had
dealt with the situation. Maybe he'd talk to Jefferson
about a transfer into the space Navy. A less political
position looked desirable just now. With a few well-
placed bribes, he might be able to get his tenure in
command of Elba expunged from his records.

He finished the brandy and keyed the armory. "Are
all the small arms turned in yet?"

"All in," the armorer said.

"Is Captain Murieta's pistol among the weapons?"

"Well, yessir. Captain Proski brought it in with the
others. I'll start checking 'em right away, but I'm not
really sure what to look for. It can be dangerous, prying
open power packs, even if they ain't sabotaged. Don't
have the right equipment for it."

"Don't bother, just keep the arms locked up. I'll tell
you when to reissue them shortly."

"Reissue? Well, yes, sir."

That was odd, Hughes thought as he walked toward
the entrance hall serving the dock. He would have
expected Murieta to try to hold back his personal sidearm. But then, he reflected, a man contemplating desertion would be very careful to avoid the slightest
appearance of disloyalty.

He arrived at the hall just as the frigate's people were
filing through. Jefferson came in, followed by a knot of
his people and a tough-looking unit of armed Marines.
Jefferson saluted smartly. Behind him was a stunning,
dark-haired woman, built like a—my God! Hughes
thought, can those be real? An equally beautiful but
less well-endowed woman with slightly Asiatic features
stepped forward. She wore medical corps insignia.

"Colonel," said the medical officer, "is the prisoner
going to require special medical consideration?"

"Rather extensively, I'm afraid," Hughes told her.
"We've, that is to say, the Party advisers have been
conducting an over-rigorous interrogation, if you ask
me." He felt a bristling tension at the words, and it

struck him that these might all be staunch Party members. Young officers often were. "Not that the terrorist bastard doesn't deserve it," he added, to cover his gaffe.

Attendants wheeled out the gurney with its terribly disfigured burden. Hughes heard several sharp gasps from the frigate's personnel. Used to long-distance mayhem, he thought. Do 'em some good to see what it looks like close up.

"Oh, my God!" said one of the women, he couldn't tell which. "Martin!" What's this?

Behind the gurney came the two Party advisers. One of them stared at Jefferson with an expression of growing disbelief.

"That's right," Jefferson said. "I look a little different in the Party-doctored holos, don't I?"

"Jesus!" one cried in a strangled voice. "It's Thor Taggart!" Hughes couldn't tell how many of the frigate's people shot the Party advisers, but they all seemed to draw and fire at once.

Hughes broke and ran. To his great surprise, he made it to the external corridor and managed to hit the emergency close control just as a few projectiles lanced through. If he moved fast enough, he might make the evacuation dock. Then, in front of him, he saw the red-haired skipper of the supply ship. There was an expression of indescribable rage on the man's face, and— was that a *flamethrower* he was holding? The last thing Hughes saw was the fireball that engulfed him.

Thor let out a long-pent breath when he saw Linde. "All the automated defense systems are taken care of," she reported. "They're helpless now." She glanced at the gurney, gasped and turned pale. "Is that Shaw?" she said. I thought they wanted him alive! How could they do that to anybody?"

Thor put an arm around her as he reholstered his pistol. "They wanted answers and he wouldn't talk. Stubborn bastard. He's alive, after a fashion."

"Alive, hell," said a croaking voice. "I'm even conscious."

"Martin," Thor said. His voice was steady but tears streamed down his cheeks. "I'm sorry, Martin. I'm sorry we couldn't get here sooner. It was a complicated operation."

"They didn't destroy anything but my body," Shaw said. "All the essential things still work."

"The situation is changed, Martin," Thor said. "They want peace. There are crucial decisions to be made, and damn little time."

Shaw couldn't move his head, but his eyes flickered to Natalie and Caterina. "No sedation on the trip back," he said. "I have to keep my wits about me."

"You need weeks of sedation," Caterina said.

"No." The single syllable was final. The best day of my life, Thor thought, I couldn't put that much authority in a whole speech. How can he even be sane after such treatment?

"Natalie," Thor said, "take him back to the frigate. You heard his orders. No sedation." She shot him a poisonous look, but she obeyed.

Mike came in, covered with soot. "Got Hughes," he reported. "Bastard suffered all too little."

"I have no argument with that," Thor said. He nodded toward the corpses of the Party advisers. "I put some slugs into those two myself. But no more killing. They can't fight back and there's no excuse for it."

"For the garrison, all right," Mike said. "But the interrogation team is ours."

"No," Thor said, "I won't—"

"Thor," Mike said, his voice as adamant as Martin's had been, "don't make me kill you, too. I'd hate to explain it to Martin and I wouldn't like it much myself."

"He means it, Thor," Linde said. "They're not worth it."

What the hell, he thought. He was tired of playing by the rules, anyway. "All right, but only the torturers. And I want a full holographic record of this place, and reports from all the freed prisoners. Someday there'll be trials."

"We wouldn't leave anybody to try," Mike said.

Thor looked at him bleakly. "We may need this for our own defense," he said.

"The roughest part," Linde said, "was getting O'Halloran's face to look anxious. It wasn't just putting in the stress lines, it was making it look like they'd been holographically eradicated, but unsuccessfully, so that an experienced observer would still see what they were trying to cover up. That in turn would convey a subliminal sense that the whole production had been put together in a panic, increasing the viewer's anxiety and loss of confidence in the status quo. Compared to achieving that effect, circumventing the internal and external defense systems was a cinch."

Shaw managed a pained chuckle. "A cinch. Subverting the most sophisticated computers in existence was a cinch, she says. Linde, you're a treasure." He was regaining some use of his neck and he turned his head slightly to face Thor. "I need a complete briefing on your Ciano field discoveries. I'm up to hearing about it now. Thor, you needn't hang around while I'm absorbing all this, but we'll need to discuss it afterwards. If it's what I think, we're now at one of the major turning points of history. The future of all mankind will depend upon what we decide and accomplish over the next few years."

Only Martin, Thor thought as he left, could make such a statement sound like simple fact instead of pompous speechifying. They were on the return cruise, EOS and Defiance ships together, on this leg of the journey. Thor was headed for a rendezvous with the ships that would bear the peace delegation to the talks on Mars. As for the Defiance people—he wasn't really sure. Much would depend upon what Martin decided in the next few days. Thor did not regard Shaw as his prisoner.

He found Caterina alone in the galley. "I was hungry," he said. "Thought I'd hunt up a snack."

She waved to the keyboard of the food synthesizer. "Help yourself. I'm amazed you have any appetite, after being in with Martin. And after that, after seeing what they've done to him, you still plan to talk peace with the Earthies!"

He keyed some shrimp tempura and a bulb of coffee. He was beginning to see something that should have been plain to him long ago, a fact to which he had been blinded by emotional infatuation: Caterina was really pretty silly and immature.

"Spare me your indignation, Cat. He's a grown man and he knew what he was in for if he ever got caught."

"How can you be so cold-blooded? And I saw the tears on your face when you knew what had been done to him! Now you act as if the Earthies were in the right!"

"I was saddened at what had been done to an old friend. But what do you think would happen if you dropped one of your rock bombs on a civilian target? It's not like a fight in space where almost everybody dies cleanly or comes out unhurt. Thousands of people would be just like him or worse, whole hospitals full of them, maimed and crippled for life. They wouldn't all be grown people, either, or hardened fighters. Children, old people, mothers and noncombatants of every sort, and they'd stay in those hospitals for years after the war is over and forgotten by everybody else."

"But they began this!" she insisted. "They're forcing these measures on us!"

"It's always the other side's fault. And it's always cleaner when you do it from a distance. Do you think it makes any difference to a maimed victim whether his injuries were inflicted deliberately by a torturer or by some idealistic idiot who set the coordinates for a piece of rock from a hundred million kilometers away?"

"It's different," she insisted.

"No it isn't. Ask Martin. He'll tell you so."

She shoved herself out of the galley in a rage. His tempura appeared and he dipped it in the glutinous soy sauce that had been developed for zero-gee. It was excellent, but he found himself craving a good steak. It

was a shock to realize how many years it had been since
he'd eaten a steak.

"A shame," Martin said, "that the anti-matter drive
won't do all you'd hoped. It has one practical applica-
tion, though."

"Of course," Thor said. "And I knew it would occur
to you immediately. The anti-matter bomb. Forget it,
Martin."

"Thor, shame on you. A weapon like that has far
more applications than merely blowing things up. This
is now a part of your diplomacy. Armed might is as
much a part of the diplomatic process as clever talk and
double-dealing. The fact is, we don't need the armed
might, but they do. At least, they need the appearance
of that might."

"What?" Caterina said.

"Got no idea what you're talking about, Boss," Mike
agreed. But Thor grasped the point instantly. For the
first time in days, he smiled.

"But enough of that," Martin went on. "We now
have our opportunity to buy time. We need time for
Linde to fully develop the star drive."

"Don't go on unwarranted assumptions," Linde cautioned. "As it looks now, I should be able to develop the
drive, but nothing is one hundred percent certain. A
glitch could turn up and the whole thing might be
impracticable."

"That has to be taken into account," Shaw agreed.
"All we can do at the peace talks is forestall the next war.
But another war will come, believe me. Since there is
the possibility that the next war will wipe out all life on
Earth and in the outerworlds, we should start sending
out expeditions as soon as possible."

"Using the antimatter drive," Linde said, "even going
to the Alpha Centauri system would take a hundred
generations."

"Before the war," Shaw said, "there would have been
no takers. Not now. Many of the outerworlders have
suffered enough. And who better to undertake such a

voyage than asteroid colonists? They'll be living in the same environment most of them have known all their lives. The planets are as remote to them as asteroids are to Earthies. For most, there will be little change in their lives, assuming the asteroid colony undertaking the journey is provided for self-sufficiency. The only significant change will be in the view outside, and that will be very gradual."

"But to be cut off from communication and contact with other asteroids," Natalie said. "That would be hard."

"We can maintain communication with them by maser beam. It's slow, but the best we have at the moment. I'll probably crack the problem of superluminal communication first, at which time communication with the generation expeditions will become instantaneous. Should I perfect superluminal matter transmission, we can send them the technological data to make their own. Better yet, we could send them engineers and hardware so that they could continue their voyages without all the wait."

"And there's no need for them to go alone," Thor poined out. "A number could take off together, headed for the same destination. They could maintain contact throughout the voyage. That would provide backup in case of emergencies, as well."

"No doubt about it," Shaw said, "after this war, there'll be a great many people looking for a better place to live."

SIXTEEN

A hand was shaking his shoulder. Slowly, reluctantly, Secretary-General Jameson began to wake up.

"You're being buzzed by General Gulmen's office," Teresa said.

"What's he want at this hour?" Jameson asked rhetorically. He rolled over and hit the audio-only plate. His staff knew all about Teresa, but no sense giving them any more fuel than necessary. Even his wife knew about her, not that she'd dare say anything.

General Gulmen appeared in the screen, his face unshaven and his uniform rumpled. Whatever it was, Jameson thought, it had hauled his chief of staff out of bed as well.

"I'm sorry to bother you at this hour, sir," the Turk said, "but the news is urgent. Rebels have raided our maximum-security facility at Elba and seized Martin Shaw from custody."

Jameson sat straight up. "What?" he shrieked. "Why wasn't the raid repelled? How could they have gotten inside without the failsafes killing all the prisoners?"

"We don't know yet, sir," said Gulmen. "It looks as if the rebels are in possession of some new form of technology, one that can circumvent our best computer systems."

"Or," Jameson said, "it might be that there are trai-

tors among us." Jameson knew that there were traitors
all around him. He had had several executed recently.
Nobody could be trusted totally.

"I am sure that that is not the case here, sir," said
Gulmen, his beard-shadow beginning to gleam with
sweat.

"It had better not be, General," Jameson said. "I
want a full report in the morning." He snapped off the
communicator.

What now? He sat on the edge of the bed and ran a
hand through his thinning hair. Teresa knelt behind
him and began massaging his shoulders. She was a fine
secretary and a much better mistress, but right now he
needed expert advice. "Honey, give me some wake-up
and then get me Carstairs."

She passed him a thin, blue disk with a damp pad on
one side. "You should take it easy with this stuff," she
warned. "You've been using two or three doses a week,
and that's too much."

He pressed the pad against the inside of his elbow
and the drug shot through his skin and into his blood-
stream. Within seconds, he felt the weariness drop
away. "I need to be on my toes. I have enemies all
around me and I can't afford to be caught napping." He
rolled the depleted disk between thumb and forefinger
and flipped it into a waste disposal. It winked like a
firefly and disappeared.

Carstairs appeared on the screen. He was clean-shaven,
seated at his desk, and his clothes immaculate. What
time-zone was he in, Jameson wondered. Then he realized that it was the same one he was in. Didn't the man
ever sleep?"

"Yes, Mr. Secretary-General?" Carstairs had made
no effort to spruce up for his boss. His sleeves were
rolled above the elbows and there was an orderly litter
of papers and printouts on his desk. Obviously, he was
too busy for inessentials.

"Tony, something serious has happened." Hastily, he
sketched out what he knew about Shaw's escape.

"Bloody hell," Carstairs said, disgustedly. "A quid to

a bob it was Thor Taggart sprung the barstid." At times like this, Carstairs' Liverpool origins came through.

"Shall we cancel the peace talks?" Jameson asked.

"No!" Carstairs held up a palm. "You'll do no such thing. We *must* have this armistice. The rebels are telling us that they know it, too. Cheeky barstids are going to rub our noses in the fact. No matter. Let 'em get cocky. All we need is time. Once we have things under control here, we'll be after 'em again. Next time, we'll be prepared and we won't be listening to a pack of admirals who've spent the last thirty years with their arses parked in armchairs and agreeing with each other at cocktail parties. Revenge is a dish best eaten cold, Mr. Secretary-General. No, we go on with the peace talks as planned and we make no mention of Shaw. From here on, he doesn't exist."

"And the ban on delegates from the Ciano-Kuroda-Taggart-Sousa clan?"

"Forget it. Let 'em send who they want. They'd just do it anyway and we'd lose face when they defied us. We'll just refuse to recognize anyone from the Defiance party. No mention of Shaw. As far as we're concerned, he's dead. Might well be, at that. Even if he's alive, he won't be causing anybody any trouble for a long time. Our inquisitors weren't gentle with him."

"That's how we'll play it, then," Jameson said. "Good night, Tony." He switched the set off. It always made him feel better, talking with Carstairs. The man never panicked, always landed on his feet, always had the right answers. Jameson lay back on the bed, reassured and at peace. Now that he was wide awake, what was there to do? He reached for Teresa.

A few hundred kilometers to the north, the Honorable Anthony Carstairs sat back in his chair. For the ten thousandth time, he cursed the fate that had forced him to use an incompetent boob like Jameson as figurehead for the Party. Well, that might not be necessary much longer. Elective politics were almost a thing of the past, so who cared if the boss had a toothpaste-ad smile. Soon it would be time to dump Jameson and take that seat himself. Or maybe not. How could he run things if he had to shake hands and cut ribbons all the time? But Jameson! Why couldn't he have someone like young Taggart to run the public end while he took care of business?

He reached into his desk and took out a flat bottle of Glenfiddich. He poured a gill and knocked it back. There was a lot to be said for keeping a low profile. He smiled to himself as he remembered how he had bagged the cartel headed by Murdo McNaughton. Old Murdo had looked very surprised when Party police had arrested him and hauled him away. The cartel had been useful in the early days and Carstairs hadn't minded letting them think that they were using *him*.

But he hadn't forged a world government to turn it over to a pack of bloated plutocrats to milk for their own sordid profits. They had sought guarantees of protection, freedom from competition, monopolies. What they had received had been confiscation, nationalization and prison terms or execution. He despised them even more than he despised the old free-market capitalists. The old breed, that still flourished in the outerworlds, at least had guts and weren't afraid of risk and competition. Murdo's kind had pretty much done what the old Marxists had never been able to do—destroy the centuries-old system of free enterprise. They loved the labels and poses of the capitalist entrepreneurs, but they were so terrified of actually risking their money and dealing with competitors that they had been willing to establish a world government and foment a war just to protect themselves.

Well, Anthony Carstairs wanted that government and that war, too, but for different reasons. He knew that Earth was headed for a reign of utter barbarism within two generations if something didn't pull the increasingly fragmented population together and give it a common direction. The world state and the war was the only answer, and the Party was the only mechanism capable of bringing about salvation. It was tough on the outerworld colonies, but they were only a tiny minority of mankind. In any case, as far as he was concerned, anyone who abandoned the motherworld to her problems and went off to seek safety in space had no call on the sympathy of those left behind.

Enough of these ruminations. He was wasting time. "Marley!" he bellowed to the outer office. "Make up printouts on all the EOS leadership, an executive summary on the history of the war to date, and find a copy of Silverstein's *Treaties and Armistice Negotiations*. Set up a lunch appointment with General Gulmen in London and have the printed material in my briefcase by evening. I'm heading for Mars for a few days and I need the material to study up on during the trip."

"Right away, sir." The exhausted second-shift secretary began to key the required documents, looking forward fervently to his boss's departure for Mars. Didn't the man ever sleep?

The conference hall beneath Ares City was not large by Earth U.N. standards, but it was a huge indoor area for Mars. It had once been a subterranean oxygen tank for the surface settlements. Though long obsolete, it had been by turns a gymnasium, a barracks, and now a conference hall. The morning session was over and the delegates were breaking for lunch.

"The advantage of a near-dictatorship," Carstairs was saying to Thor, "is that you can tell the diplomatic corps to shift their bleedin' arses and show some results or take their ease in prison. Left to themselves, they'd still be arguing over the shape of the conference table and we'd have bugger-all accomplished."

"The negotiations have to be a little protracted," Thor said, "or the folks back home won't believe we're serious." The two sat in spindly Martian chairs near the open bar-restaurant adjoining the conference area. It was part of the public relations established for the peace talks that prominent members of the negotiation teams were to be seen publicly socializing every day, to give the illusion that the entire process was open and that there were no secret meetings or deals. Nothing could have been farther from the truth, but the pose had to be maintained. The fiction served the useful function of allowing the delegates to feel each other out and get acquainted.

The informal chat between Carstairs and Thor, minus sound, was being holographed by a team from World Network and another from Fu's pirate outfit. Jameson had protested the presence of Fu's network at the conference, but Eos had threatened to broadcast their holos of the torture facilities at Elba, and the Secretary-General had backed down. The Earthies were by no means humanitarian in their attitudes toward the outerworlds, but they lacked the stomach to face the uglier realities of the war.

The opening talks had been mere establishments of relative position. The U.N. maintained that there was no war, merely the suppression of some insurrections by malcontents calling themselves the Confederacy. The U.N. had magnanimously agreed to listen to grievances from the representatives in order to bring about a cessation of hostilities.

The Confederate party held it equally self-evident that they were the duly appointed representatives of a sovereign state, the Confederacy of Island Worlds, and that they were there to hammer out a peace treaty between two nations, including territorial borders and orbital zones of sovereignty.

The U.N. delegation began to protest the presence of national flags on the table before the Confederate delegation, and the playing of the Confederate national anthem at the opening of each session. For them to countenance such trappings, they argued, would be a *de facto* recognition of Confederate sovereignty. Carstairs passed the head of the U.N. delegation a note telling him to shut up and get on with business. Meekly, the delegation complied.

The two parties spent the first five days making their rhetorical announcements of political and ideological position. This was for consumption at home. Far more valuable had been the informal meetings at which the delegates had become acquainted well enough to be able to negotiate confidently when the time came. Both governments wanted a peace agreement and no messing around.

For the Earth First Party, the crucial question was face. Even powerful governments could fall if they lost face and were humiliated publicly. The Earth First world hegemony was rickety, indeed. The capture of Shaw was to have been its face-saving coup, but the Confederates had not cooperated.

"By the way," Thor said, "Yuri Pereira is hosting a dinner this evening at his villa. I know that Secretary-General Jameson has been invited, along with Miss Kornfeld and me. We'd be delighted if you could attend as well."

"I'd be honored," Carstairs said. Progress at last! As he returned to his quarters, Carstairs wondered again just who the intriguing Miss Kornfeld was. She was pretty, but it wasn't like Taggart to drag a mistress along to the talks. She was witty and charming, but sometimes she seemed to blank out in the middle of a conversation and just *wasn't there* any more. He would have suspected drugs, but when she snapped back she was fully lucid.

In his apartment he was about to call Jameson, then called his intelligence chief instead. Colonel Tagliotti, in civilian clothes, appeared on the screen. "Yes, Mr. Carstairs?"

"Giuseppe, what have you found out about this Kornfeld bint? I'll give you odds she's no secretary."

"Most disturbing person, sir. Every test we have identifies her body language as that of a native-born Martian colonist. Chemical testing of skin samples we've been able to take bears this out. But there are no records of her ever having lived here."

"Ridiculous," Carstairs said. "There have been complete records of every colonist here since the founding of the settlement."

"The mere lack of records is the least of it. There was a couple named Kornfeld who died in the Barsoom riots. They seem to have had a child, but no record of its birth or schooling exists. We questioned several university teachers who remembered her as an exceptionally brilliant student, a prodigy. When they tried to find their records of her, they found nothing. We suspect that she may be Chih' Chin Fu's mysterious assistant who was active on Luna."

Things clicked into place and Carstairs smiled ruefully. "And some genius subverted the impregnable computers controlling Elba. Thank you, Colonel." He clicked the set off. Why did the outerworlds have all this talent? It was part of the Earth's major problem. If people with brains like that had stayed home, the motherworld might not be in such dismal shape. He keyed Jameson's villa.

"Hello, Tony," Jameson said, heartily. "I take it you're calling about the big do at Pereira's tonight. I didn't like the idea of accepting an invitation from a pack of outerworld upstarts, but the Chief of Protocol says its politic to accept."

Carstairs held his exasperation in check. God give me patience, he thought. "Sir, I think this is where they're going to make their serious proposal. The preliminaries are over with and now we can sit down with the important members of their delegation and work out the real peace agreement."

"Exactly," Jameson said, as if that was what he had been thinking all along. Shameless bugger probably thinks it *was* his idea by now, Carstairs thought. He switched off and began to outline what he was going to say to the Confederates.

As head of the Confederate delegation, Yuri Pereira had been given a villa equal in size to the one occupied by Jameson. It had been built by a director of the old Mars Settlement Corporation, a subsidiary of Ciano-McNaughton, and it was lavish by Martian standards. The terrace overlooked a valley, under a colossal translucent dome, that had been transformed from desert to lush agricultural land, growing plants gene-engineered for Martian conditions. The fortified air was thin but quite breathable, although Earth-dwellers found themselves yawning frequently.

"I am so glad you could come, Mr. Carstairs," Pereira said when Carstairs stepped onto the terrace.

"Wouldn't have missed it," Carstairs assured him. "This is a beautiful setting."

"Isn't it? Although I am a citizen of the Confederacy, Mars is very dear to me. My grandparents, all four of them, were among the original pioneers of Tarkovsky-grad. They are buried not far from here."

Carstairs made polite noises and wended his way into the large parlor that opened off the terrace. Its walls were decorated with murals of Mars; not the true planet around them, but the mythical Mars of Burroughs, Bradbury and Weinbaum.

"Mr. Carstairs." He turned to see Thor approaching with the graceful low-grav glide he would never master. More interestingly, he was accompanied by the young lady of mystery. "Have you met Sieglinde Kornfeld?"

"I've not had the pleasure," Carstairs said, taking her hand. "So you're the young lady who beat our best computers and busted Martin Shaw right out of our clutches!" Jackpot! Taggart jerked as if he'd been hit by a cattle prod. Sieglinde didn't twitch so much as an eyelash. Christ, he thought, this is one I'm going to have to watch out for.

"The praise of peers is always welcome," she said.

"I've met many people of little significance, Miss Kornfeld," he said, "but you're the first I've encountered who doesn't seem to exist at all. Now they're ringing the dinner bell and I find myself without companionship. Would you do me the honor?" He offered his arm and she took it.

"Delighted," she said.

"I'll be looking forward to speaking with you later, Mr. Taggart," Carstairs said as he turned toward the dining room.

Thor stood nonplussed and he heard Pereira chuckle

behind him. "You said he was a formidable man, Thor. Quite a different proposition from Jameson, isn't he?"

"Jameson," Thor said, almost, but not quite spitting. "How can one man come across so well on the holos and be so boring in person?"

"Fu could probably explain it," Pereira said. "It's not my field. However, you'll be happy to know that he hasn't robbed you of female company. We've seated you with Mrs. Jameson."

Thor rolled his eyeballs toward the painted ceiling. "There are some things you shouldn't ask a man to do for his country."

The dinner was a great success and Thor found Kathy Jameson to be far more entertaining than he had feared. Condemned to a life of gazing worshipfully at her husband in public, she had a waspish wit which she exercised at that gentleman's expense. Thor deduced that all was not tranquil in the Jameson household.

Carstairs found himself even better entertained. Linde did not go into any of the semi-trances that he had observed when she had been speaking with the other members of her party during the first days of the conference. He noticed that she was giving minute directions to the waiters and seemed to have choreographed the entire dinner.

The evening passed pleasantly if inconsequentially, and after coffee and brandy had been served Mrs. Pereira invited some of the guests to tour the formal gardens, which were extraordinary for the many varieties of genetically-engineered luminous fungi developed there. This effectively removed all the nonessential people from the room.

Pereira brought out a bottle of Armagnac and Thor produced two sets of documents. "If you gentlemen are ready to do business," he said to Jameson and Carstairs, "here are our draft proposals for the armistice. Why don't you look them over while you enjoy your Armagnac."

Jameson sensed that he was being herded and took the offensive. "We'll take them home with us this evening. In a few days, perhaps, we can let you know what alterations we'll need."

"It has to be here and now, I'm afraid," Thor told him. "You'll see why in a few minutes."

"Won't hurt to look them over," Carstairs cut in smoothly. He began to scan the pages. It was an impressive document. Without forcing the U.N. to acknowledge the sovereignty of the Confederacy, it granted the Island Worlds most of the privileges of an independent nation. There were several paragraphs that were obvious throwaways. An appearance of give-and-take was always necessary to any such negotiation, even when an agreement was immediately attainable.

"Excellent proposals, for the most part," Jameson said, after he had gone over his pages. "Of course, there will have to be some changes made. Paragraph L, for instance, and that whole string of clauses under subheading 5 of paragraph P. There are a few others."

Carstairs nodded silently. At least Jameson had picked up on the throwaways.

"I'm sure something can be worked out," Pereira said. "Publicly. After all, we don't want people to think this was all settled in a smoke-filled room."

"Gentlemen," Carstairs said. "This is a fine document, and there's very little I can find fault with. Essentially, it's a return to the *status quo ante bellum*, with a few slight changes that won't bother the public at large. But I fear we still have a problem."

"I know," Thor said. "We were about to come to that. First, let me introduce the unofficial member of our delegation."

A door in one of the walls slid open and a motorized chair rolled in. The man in it was an almost shapeless mass beneath a blanket, but the battered face above the blanket had enormous power. Shaw smiled slightly at the two Earthmen. "Evening, gents. I'm glad to make your acquaintance at last. Forgive me if I don't stand and shake hands."

Jameson shot to his feet, forgetting the gravity and nearly bashing his head on the ceiling. "Shaw! I'll have you arrested and shot! Guards!" He had been startled into an automatic reflex reaction; of course there were no guards.

Carstairs stood more cautiously, but for one of the very few times in his life he was deeply shaken. "Forget it, Taggart. We won't negotiate with him. We won't negotiate with him *present*. He's the biggest criminal in history."

"Oh, sit down, you scheming bastard," Shaw said. "I'm no diplomat, so I don't have to be polite." He looked at Jameson. "You too, you pathetic moron. Sit down!" The order snapped out so savagely that the Secretary-General of the U.N., virtual dictator of Earth, dropped into his chair like a disciplined schoolboy.

"I'm here," Shaw went on, more gently, "to demonstrate that everything Thor proposes in these documents is agreed to by me. As long as you abide by the accords agreed to here, you and EOS will have no trouble from Defiance. If you break the accords, though, if you attack us while pretending friendship, or if you try to imprison or assassinate Thor, or Yuri, or me for that matter," he bent his battered lips into a smile, "I'll rock-bomb your ass into oblivion."

"You can't threaten us, Shaw!" Jameson blustered.

Carstairs recovered more swiftly. "This is neither here nor there, gentlemen. Earth First still has a problem."

"We're about to come to that," said Thor.

"Against my better judgement," Shaw said, lying through his teeth, "Thor insisted on granting you one of history's biggest concessions."

"If you'll all accompany me out onto the terrace," Pereira said.

Mystified, the two Earthmen followed. Carstairs had been wondering all evening what form this was going to take. Apparently, it was to be spectacular. The terrace was breathtaking at this hour, with its brilliant starscape above and the glowing, formal gardens below. Linde handed him a pair of goggles and he examined them curiously. They were as black as welder's goggles.

"At this moment," Pereira said, "my wife is distributing these to the other guests. Warnings are now being sent out to all settlers and visitors on the night side of Mars and in nearby orbit."

"What is this?" Carstairs demanded.

"You're about to see," said Pereira, donning his goggles. "Please put on your goggles or you'll be blind for a week." Hastily, the others complied.

"Five," Thor said, "three, two—."

There was a flash so bright, so intensely white, that Carstairs turned away from it and covered his eyes with his forearm. Even with his back to the source, he could see the flash. Through the goggles, through his sleeve and the flesh of his arm, he could see the pink outlines of his radius and ulna, as if with an x-ray. Gradually, the light faded. Carstairs had never dreamed that light could be so bright. He took the goggles off. "Now what the bloody hell was that?"

"Ugo Ciano's final invention," Thor said. "The anti-matter bomb."

"Is this your threat?" Jameson said. "Are you saying you can destroy us with this weapon?"

God, he's slow. Carstairs thought. "They can already destroy us, Mr. Secretary-General. With rock bombs."

"Exactly," Thor said. "This is *your* new weapon, demonstrated for the first time. We are properly impressed."

Jameson still didn't get it. "You mean you're *giving* this thing to us?"

Shaw laughed abruptly. "Not a chance! What we're giving you is one more lie to tell your people. Even though you are graciously determined to make peace, you've demonstrated your new weapon, the ultimate hell-bomb, just to show that you're negotiating from a position of tremendous strength."

For the first time, Carstairs spoke as head of the Earth team and let Jameson fade into the background he rated. "Deal! Now, will you guarantee that that goddamn Chih' Chin Fu will get the hell off our airwaves and refrain from buggering up what we've agreed to here?"

"Fu's his own boss," said Thor, "but I think he'll go along with my instructions."

"Right," Carstairs said. "I'll bet you five quid the barstid's been 'graphing this whole meeting." Thor, Shaw, Pereira and Linde just smiled.

As the Earth party was taking its leave, everybody chattering about the remarkable fireworks display, Carstairs took Thor aside. "This has been not only productive, but educational. I'm glad we've had this chance to meet again after all these years." He took Thor's hand and shook it firmly. "Until next time, Mr. Taggart."

The three asteroids were moderate-sized, rich in minerals for future exploitation and with plenty of room for expansion in future years. The inhabitants were a mixed bag; the curious who wanted to try something new, the religious who sought peace and serenity, scientists who sought a new environment for their experiments. The bulk, though, were families whose homes had been shattered by the war, who knew now that there was no safety even in the outerworlds. All were lifelong asteroid-dwellers, many of them second- or third-generation.

"I wouldn't want to try it," Brunhilde said. "The sun isn't much this far out, but I'd hate to have no sun at all." They were in her private yacht, a hollowed-out rock fifty meters long and furnished inside as a luxury villa, with embroidered padding on the walls and free-fall mobile decoration. Most of one wall of the main salon was an oval window of armorglass, ten centimeters thick.

"Pure sentimentality," said Linde. She floated cross-legged in the center of the salon, rotating slowly about her own center of mass. She claimed to think better when she was rotating, and her mass had increased noticeably of late. Propped atop her pregnant belly was a calculator of her own design, which looked like a rectangle of clear, thin plastic across which multicolored figures danced with dazzling speed. "Most people out here never visit any of the planets. Asteroids are all they know, so they'll never miss this solar system."

"Doesn't it make you wonder, though?" Brunhilde said. "After all those generations in interstellar space, what use are they going to have for a solar system when they find one? They won't even be physically capable of going down to an Earth-type planet if they find one. The gravity would kill them and the conditions would seem hellish."

"I suspect they'll do what people have always done," Thor said. "They'll explore. They'll raid the new system's asteroids for resources. Eventually, they'll move on. Maybe some will decide to stay behind and readapt to planetary life. It's rather pointless to make predictions. They'll be a different breed by then, fully adapted to space travel. They'll have lives we can't even imagine."

He sipped at a bulb of prized champagne, broken out by Brunhilde for the occasion. "Do you think," he went on, "that some Eighteenth Century emigrant, climbing aboard a ship at Bristol to break with the old country and go to the new world was thinking, 'My descendants are going to be computer builders and airline pilots in California'? And yet the time frame that separated him from those descendents was a hell of a lot shorter than that separating those pioneers from their arrival in the Alpha Centauri system. We've given them a shot at a new type of life for humanity. What they do with it is up to them.

"If they develop a sense of nostalgia for the old system and wish we hadn't sent them away from the overpopulation and diminishing resources and wars and hell-weapons, it'll just be because romantic foolishness hasn't died out from the human mind."

"If I'm successful," said Linde Kornfeld-Taggart, "it won't come to that anyway." She ran through a set of figures, erased, and tried it again. "So far I see nothing to stop me from developing instantaneous superluminal communication. Once I have that, matter transportation should follow. That'll take a few more years, though."

"Don't take too long," Thor pleaded. "Things are getting much, *much* worse on Earth. We're projecting a new war within twenty years. Aeaea reports a long buying list for the anti-matter engines. Forty asteroids this year alone."

"For interstellar travel?" Brunhilde asked.

He shook his head. "Most just want to move to a trans-Neptune orbit. They may be safe out there, but they'll be useless to us if it comes to war again."

"Of course," Linde said, "if my work is successful, it may affect in the most fundamental way the traditional concept of causality."

"Zero-gee agriculture was my field," Brunhilde said. "Are you saying that, if you're right, we've always been wrong about reality?" She smoothed the folds of her diaphanous gown, which she insisted on wearing no matter what the gravity.

"There shouldn't be any irreconcilable dilemma. Every few years, some discovery comes along that forces us to adjust our picture of reality. They aren't all crucial like the Copernican theory or special relativity. Usually, only specialists take notice. The universe is always self-consistent, it's only our *perceptions* of reality that prove faulty. Most often, the readjustment is a matter of degree, not something that calls for a complete overhaul of every system."

"If the war comes before the drive is perfected," Thor said, "we'll move you and Ugo's lab out past Neptune."

"You couldn't have a better scientist working on the problem," Brunhilde said.

"I know," said Thor, smiling proudly at his wife.

"I meant," Brunhilde said, "that she knows that the war will come, if your projections are correct, just about the time her children reach military age. I can't imagine a better motivation for devising a way to get the hell out of here."

"You'd better believe I've taken that into account, too," Linde said. She made some minute notations on the calculator, using the tiny stylus built into the nail of her right forefinger.

"I fear," Brunhilde said, sadly, "that you two will be seeing very little of each other for the next few years."

"We'll get reacquainted on the way out to Altair or wherever. There's no reason why we can't live for at least another hundred years. Hell, old Roseberry's still going strong and he's already talking about interstellar real estate." He stuck his bulb into the complicated decanter and refilled it. "Enough of this gloomy talk. They should be starting soon." He floated to the window and looked out at the pioneer asteroids. The speeches had all been made and the voyagers were too busy with countdown phase to socialize with those they were leaving behind, perhaps forever.

"I wish Martin was here," he said.

"He's disappeared again," Brunhilde said, "along with Caterina and most of his old gang. Running another illegal immigrant racket, I hear. But if I know him, he's around here someplace. He wouldn't miss an event like this, he has too strong a sense of drama."

Linde stopped her spinning and drifted to the window. "Is it set to opaque instantly? We don't want to be blinded and even at full opacity it'll be pretty bright in here."

"All set," Brunhilde reported. They crowded together, waiting for the big event.

"What was it old Ugo used to say," Thor asked, putting an arm around Linde's expanding waist, "when he sent out another record-breaking expedition?"

Brunhilde smiled. "Hey out there," he used to say. "Here we come!"

The thrusters of the orientation rockets glowed as, slowly and majestically, the first expedition set forth to make humanity an interstellar species. Warning flashers began to blink along the anti-matter engines as they neared the finish of their ignition sequence.

Then the blinding, supernova brilliance of pure, glorious white light was all they could see.

Here is an excerpt from IRON MASTER by Patrick Tilley, to be published in July 1987 by Baen Books. It is the third book in the "Amtrak Series," which also includes CLOUD WARRIOR and THE FIRST FAMILY.

PATRICK TILLEY
IRON MASTER

The five sleek craft, under the control of their newly-trained samurai pilots, lifted off the grass and thundered skywards, trailing thin blue ribbons of smoke from their solid-fuel rocket tubes. Levelling off at a thousand feet, they circled the field in a tight arrowhead formation, then dived and pulled up into a loop, rolling upright as they came down off the top to go into a second—the maneuver once known as the Immelmann turn.

There was a gasp from the crowd as the lines of blue smoke were suddenly severed from the diving aircraft. A tense, eerie silence descended. The first rocket boosters had reached the end of their brief lives. Time for the second burn. The machines continued their downward plunge—then, with a reassuring explosion of sound, a stabbing white-hot finger of flame appeared beneath the cockpit pod of the lead aircraft. Two, three, four—five!

The watching crowd of Iron Masters responded with a deep-throated roar of approval. Cadillac, who was positioned in front of the stand immediately below his patrons, Yama-Shita and Min-Ota, swelled with pride. These were the kind of people he could identify with. Harsh, forbidding, and cruel, with unbelieveably rigid social mores, they nevertheless appreciated and placed great value on beautiful objects, whether they be works of nature or some article fashioned by their craft-masters. Cadillac knew his flying machines appealed to the Iron Masters' aesthetic sensibilities. Like the proud horses of the domain lords, they were lithe and graceful, and the echoing thunder that marked their passage through the sky conveyed the same feeling of irresistible power as the hoofbeats of their galloping steeds. Here, in the Land of the Rising Sun, he had been taken seriously, had been given the opportunity to demonstrate his true capabilities, and had been accorded the praise and esteem Mr. Snow had always denied him. And his work here was only just beginning!

As the five aircraft nosed over the top of the second loop, leaving a blue curve of smoke behind them, their booster rockets exploded in rapid succession. Booooomm! Ba-ba-boom-boomm. Booom!

Cadillac, along with everyone else in the stand behind him, watched in speechless horror as each one was engulfed by a ball of flame. The slender silk-covered spruce wings were ripped to pieces and consumed. On the ground below, confusion reigned as the shower of burning debris spiralled down towards the packed review stand, preceded by the rag-doll bodies of the pilots.

Steve Brickman, gliding high above the lake some three miles to the south of the Heron Pool, saw the fireballs blossom and fall. It had worked. The rocket burn had ignited the explosive charge he, Jodi, and Kelso had packed with loving care into the second of the three canisters each aircraft carried beneath its belly. Now there could be no turning back. Steve caught himself invoking the name of Mo-Town— praying that everything would go according to plan.

General To-Shiba, seated on his left, was quite unaware of the disaster. Fascinated by the bird's-eye view of his large estate, the military governor's eyes were fixed on the small island in the middle of the lake two thousand feet below. It was here, in the summer house surrounded by trees and a beautiful rock garden, that Clearwater was held prisoner. The beautiful creature who was now his body-slave and who possessed that rarest of gifts—lustrous, sweet-smelling body hair. The thought of his next visit filled him with pleasurable anticipation. As a samurai, To-Shiba had no fear of death but, at that moment, he had no inkling his demise was now only minutes away. . . .

July 1987 • 416 pp. • 65338-5 • $3.95

To order any Baen Book, send the cover price plus 75¢ for first-class postage and handling to: Baen Books, Dept. BB, 260 Fifth Avenue, New York, N.Y. 10001.